About the author

Scott Sigler is the world's most successful podcasting author, with a rabidly loyal following of more than 30,000 subscribers per book. His books have held the number one audiobook position on all the podcast aggregators, including iTunes, and his remarkable triumph has made him the subject of profiles and coverage in the *New York Times*, *Washington Post*, *Business Week* and elsewhere. He lives in San Francisco with his wife and their two dogs.

You can find Scott Sigler online at www.scottsigler.com.

Also by Scott Sigler

EarthCore
Ancestor

INFECTED
SCOTT SIGLER

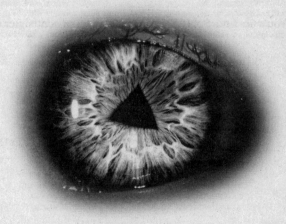

HODDER

First published in Great Britain in 2008 by Hodder & Stoughton
An Hachette Livre UK company

First published in paperback in 2008

1

Published by arrangement with Crown Publishing Group,
a division of Random House, Inc.

Originally released in slightly different form as a podcast in 2006

A CIP catalogue record for this title is available from the British Library

ISBN 978 0 340 96353 1

Typeset in Plantin Light by Hewer Text UK Ltd, Edinburgh

Printed and bound in the UK by CPI Mackays, Chatham ME5 8TD

Hodder & Stoughton policy is to use papers that
are natural, renewable and recyclable products and made
from wood grown in sustainable forests. The logging and
manufacturing processes are expected to conform to the
environmental regulations of the country of origin.

Hodder & Stoughton Ltd
338 Euston Road
London NW1 3BH

www.hodder.co.uk

Grateful acknowledgement is made to Alfred Publishing Co., Inc.
for permission to reprint an excerpt from 'I've Got You Under My Skin',
words and music by Cole Porter, copyright © 1936 by Cole Porter,
copyright renewed and assigned to Robert H. Montgomery, trustee of the
Cole Porter Musical & Literary Property Trusts Chappell & Co., owner
of publication and allied rights throughout the World. All Rights
Reserved. Reprinted by permission of Alfred Publishing Co., Inc.

To my mom and dad, the best people I have ever known.
To my wife, for the endless patience.
To my O.J.'s — you know who you are.

I've got you under my skin,
I've got you deep in the heart of me,
So deep in my heart, you're really a part of me,
I've got you under my skin.

I tried so not to give in,
I said to myself, 'This affair never will go so well.'
But why should I try to resist, when,
darling, I know so well
I've got you under my skin.

I'd sacrifice anything come what might,
For the sake of having you near,
In spite of a warning voice that comes in the night,
And repeats and repeats in my ear,

'Don't you know, little fool, you never can win,
Use your mentality,
Wake up to reality.'
But each time I do, just the thought of you
Makes me stop, before I begin,
'Cause I've got you under my skin.

Cole Porter, 'I've Got You Under My Skin'

Let the skies turn black
Let the infection burn
This is a new beginning

Killswitch Engage, 'World Ablaze'

Prologue

THIS IS THE PLACE . . .

Alida Garcia stumbled through the dense winter woods, blood marking her long path, a bright red comet trail against the blazing white snow.

Her hands shook violently. She could barely make a fist out of her talonlike fingers, nearly numb, wet from the big clumps of snow that fell thick and fast all around her, melting almost as soon as they hit her skin. When the time came, could she even pull the trigger on Luis's old revolver?

A searing pain in her stomach brought her thoughts back to the mission, the divine mission.

Something was wrong. Well, fuck, it was *all wrong*, and had been from the first moment she started scratching at her belly and her elbow. But something was even more wrong, something *inside*. It wasn't supposed to be like this . . . somehow, she knew that.

She looked behind her, along the bloody path through the snow, eyes searching for pursuit. She saw nothing. She'd spent years in fear of the INS, but it was different now. They didn't want to deport her—now they wanted her dead.

Her hands and legs oozed blood drawn by scratching branches. Her left foot bled thanks to the shoe she'd lost some time ago; the snow's thin, jagged crust made every step a cutting *crunch*. She didn't know why her nose bled, it just did, but all those things were trivial compared to the blood she vomited every few minutes.

She had to go on, *had to go on*, find the place . . . the place where it would all begin.

Alida saw two massive oak trees, reaching out to each other like centuries-old lovers, a freeze-frame of perpetually denied longing. She thought of her husband, Luis, again, and thought of the baby. Then she pushed those thoughts away. She could think about that no more than she could think of the nasty thing on her belly.

She'd done what she had to do.

Three bullets for Luis.

One for the baby.

One for the man with the car.

That left one bullet.

She stumbled, then tripped. She reached out to try and stop her fall, but her bloody hands punched through the knee-deep snow. Her frigid hand hit an unseen rock, bringing more flaring, cold-numb pain, and she dropped headfirst through the white crust. She came up, wet snow and ice sticking to her exhausted face. Then she threw up—again—blood gushing from her mouth to splash bright red against the white snow.

Blood, and a few wet chunks of something black.

Inside, it *hurt*. It hurt *so bad*.

She started to get up, then stopped and stared at the twin oak trees. They dominated a natural clearing, bare branches a sprawling, skeletal canopy at least fifty meters across. A few stubborn, dead leaves clung to the branches, fluttering slightly in the winter wind. She hadn't known what she'd been looking for, just that she had to walk into the woods, *deep* into the woods, where people didn't go.

This was it, this was the place.

Such a long journey to wind up here. She'd taken the man's car back in Jackson. The man had said he wasn't *la migra*, wasn't the immigration police, but those people had chased her all her life and she knew better. He had stared at the gun, said he wasn't *la migra*, said he was just looking for a liquor store. Alida knew he was lying. She had seen it in his eyes. She had left him there, taken his car and driven through the night, then abandoned the car in Saginaw. There she hopped a freight train and just started watching for big woods. As long as she kept moving mostly north, it didn't matter.

Moving north, really, was the story of her life. The farther north you went, the fewer questions people asked. Childhood in Monclova, Mexico. Teenage years in Piedras Negras, then at nineteen she snuck across the border and started moving through Texas and beyond. Seven years of working, hiding, lying, always moving north. She'd met Luis in Chickasha, Oklahoma, then together they worked their way through America: St. Louis, Chicago, joining her mother in Grand Rapids, Michigan. A brief change, heading east when Luis found regular construction work in Jackson.

Then the itching started. And not long after, the urge to move north again. No, not just an *urge*, as it had been before.

The itching made it a *mission*.

But finally, after twenty-seven years of life, she could stop moving. She stared at the oak trees, the way they reached out to each other. Like lovers. Like husband and wife. She couldn't stop thinking of him anymore, couldn't stop thinking of her Luis. But it was okay now, because she could join him.

She looked back one more time. The thick, falling snow

was already covering the comet path, turning the red to a fuzzy pink, soon to be all white again. *La migra* was looking for her, they wanted to kill her . . . but unless they were only fifteen or twenty minutes behind, her trail would soon be gone forever.

Alida turned again to stare at the trees one more time, the image a glorious sculpture in her brain.

This is the place.

She pulled the old .38 revolver out of her pocket and pressed the barrel against her temple.

When she pulled the trigger, her cold fingers worked just fine.

1
CAPTAIN JINKY

'FM 92.5 morning call-in line, what's on your mind?'

'I killed them all.'

Marsha Stubbins groaned. Another 'I'm so funny' asshole trying to take the weird route to get on the air.

'Did you now? That's nice, sir.'

'I have to get on with Captain Jinky. The world has to know.'

Marsha nodded. It was 6:15 A.M., just about time for the loonies and the jerks to roll out of bed, hear Captain Jinky & the Morning Zoolanders goofing off on the air, and feel they had to be part of the show. This happened every morning. Every . . . single . . . morning.

'Captain Jinky has to know what, sir?'

'Has to know about the Triangles.' The voice was soft. The words came between big breaths, like someone trying to talk just after an intense workout.

'Right, the triangles. Sounds more like a personal problem, sir.'

'*Don't patronize me, you stupid cunt!*'

'Hey, you don't get to scream at me like that just because I'm a phone screener, okay?'

'It's the Triangles! We have to *do something*. Put me on with Jinky or I'll come down there and stick a fucking knife in your eye!'

'Uh-huh,' Marsha said. 'A knife in my eye. Right.'

'I just killed my whole family, don't you get it? I have their blood all over me! I had to! Because *they told me to*!'

'This isn't funny, you idiot, and by the way, you're the third mass murderer that's called here this morning. If you call back, I'm calling the cops.'

The man hung up. She sensed he was getting ready to say something, to scream at her again, right until she said the word *cops*. Then he hung up and hung up fast.

Marsha rubbed her face. She'd wanted this internship, and who didn't? Captain Jinky had one of Ohio's highest-rated morning shows. But man, this phone-screening gig, with the crazy calls day after day . . . so many retards out there who thought they were funny.

She rolled her shoulders and looked at the phone. All the lines were lit up. Seemed everyone in the city wanted to get on the air. Marsha sighed and punched line two.

In Cleveland, Ohio, there is a room on the seventeenth floor of the AT&T Huron Road Building, formerly known as the Ohio Bell Building.

This room does not exist.

At least, what's *in* the room does not exist. On maps, building records, and to most people who work on the seventeenth floor, Room 1712-B is just a file-storage room.

A file-storage room that is always locked. People are busy, no one asks, no one cares—it's like millions of other locked rooms in office buildings all over the United States.

But, of course, it's not a file-storage room.

Room 1712-B doesn't exist, because it's a 'Black Room.' And 'Black Rooms' don't exist—the government tells us so.

To get inside this Black Room, you have to run a gamut of security screens. First, talk to the seventeenth-floor guard.

His desk happens to be just fifteen feet from 1712-B. He's got security clearance from the NSA, by the way, and is perfectly willing to cap your ass. Second, slide your key card through the slot next to the door. The card has a built-in code that changes every ten seconds, matching an algorithm based on the time of day—this one makes sure only the right people can enter at the right times. Third, type your personal code into the keypad. Fourth, press your thumbprint onto a small gray plate just above the door handle so a fancy little device can check your thumbprint *and* your pulse. Truth be told, the fingerprint scanner isn't worth a crap and it can be easily fooled, but the pulse check is handy—just in case you're a tad overly excited because someone has a gun to your head, a gun that was probably used to kill the aforementioned security guard.

If you successfully navigate these challenges, 1712-B opens to reveal the Black Room—and the things *inside* that also do not exist.

Among those goodies is a NarusInsight STA 7800, a supercomputer designed to perform mass surveillance on a mind-boggling scale. The NarusInsight is fed by fiber-optic lines from beam splitters, which are installed in fiber-optic trunks carrying telephone calls and Internet data into and out of Ohio. This technojargon means that those lines carry all digital communication in Ohio, including just about every phone call made in and out of the Midwest. Oh, you're not from the Midwest? Don't worry, there are fifteen Black Rooms spread around America. Plenty for everyone.

This machine monitors key phrases, like *nuclear bomb, cocaine shipment,* or the ever-popular *kill the president.* The system automatically records every call, tens of thousands at a time, using voice-recognition software to turn each conversation into a text file. The system then scans the text file for those potentially naughty terms. If none are found, the system dumps the audio. If they *are* found, however, the audio file (and the voice-to-text transcript) is instantly sent to the person tasked with monitoring communication containing those terms.

So yeah, every call is monitored. Every. Single. Call. For terrorism words, drug words, corruption words, all the stuff you'd expect. But due to some rather violent cases that had popped up in recent weeks, a secret presidential order added a new word to the national-security watch list.

And in this case 'secret' wasn't some document that people discussed in hushed tones with Beltway reporters. This time, 'secret' meant that nothing was written down, no record of any kind, anywhere.

What was that new word?

Triangles.

The system listened for the word *triangles* in association with words like *murder, killing,* and *burn.* Two of those words happened to be used in a certain call to a certain guest line for Captain Jinky & the Morning Zoolander's radio show.

The system translated that call to text, and in analyzing that text found the words *triangles* and *killed* in close proximity. 'Stick a fucking knife in your eye' didn't hurt, either. The system marked the call, encrypted it, and shipped it off to its preassigned analyst location.

That location happened to be yet another secret room, this one located at the CIA headquarters in Langley, Virginia. When a room at the CIA headquarters is secret, a secret from people who spend their lives creating and breaking secrets, that's some pretty serious black-ops shit.

The preassigned analyst listened to the call three times. She knew after the first listening this was the real deal, but she listened twice more anyway, just to be sure. Then she placed a call of her own, to Murray Longworth, deputy director of the CIA.

She didn't know, exactly, what it meant to have *murder* and *triangles* in close proximity, but she knew how to spot a bogus call, and this one seemed authentic.

The call's origin? The home of one Martin Brewbaker, of Toledo, Ohio.

It wasn't the kind of music you'd expect to hear at that volume.

Heavy metal, sure, or some angry kid pissing off the neighborhood with raw punk rock. Or that rap stuff, which Dew Phillips just didn't get.

But not Sinatra.

You didn't crank Sinatra so loud it rattled the windows.

I've got you . . . under my skin.

Dew Phillips and Malcolm Johnson sat in an unmarked black Buick, watching the house that produced the obscenely loud music. The house's windows literally shook, the glass vibrating in time with the slow bass beat and shuddering each time Sinatra's resonant voice hit a long, clean note.

'I'm not a psychologist,' Malcolm said, 'but I'm going to throw out an educated guess that there's one crazy Caucasian in that house.'

Dew nodded, then pulled out his Colt .45 and checked the magazine. It was full, of course, it was always full, but he checked it anyway—forty years of habit died hard. Malcolm did the same with his Beretta. Even though Malcolm was just under half Dew's age, that habit had been instilled in both men courtesy of the same behavioral factory: service in the U.S. Army, reinforced by CIA training. Malcolm was a good kid, a *sharp* kid, and he knew how to listen, unlike most of the brat agents these days.

'Crazy, sure, but at least he's alive.' Dew slid the .45 into his shoulder holster.

'*Hopefully* he's alive, you mean,' Malcolm said. 'He made that call about four hours ago. He could be gone already.'

'I'm crossing my fingers,' Dew said. 'If I have to look at one more moldy corpse, I'm going to puke.'

Malcolm laughed. 'You, puke? That'll be the day. Say, you going to bang that CDC chick? Montana?'

'Montoya.'

'Right, Montoya,' Mal said. 'The way this case is going, we're going to see a lot of her. She's pretty hot for an older chick.'

'I'm fifteen years older than her, at least, so if she's "old," that means I'm ancient.'

'You *are* ancient.'

'Thanks for pointing that out,' Dew said. 'Besides, Montoya is one of those educated women—far too smart for a grunt like me. Afraid she's not my type.'

'I don't know who is your type. You don't get out that much, man. I hope *I'm* not your type.'

'You're not.'

'Because if I am, you know, that's going to make my wife nervous. Not that there's anything wrong with that, of course.'

'Knock it off, Mal,' Dew said. 'We can wallow in your rapier wit later. Let's get on point. It's party time.'

Dew's earpiece hung around his neck. He fitted it into his ear and tested the signal.

'Control, this is Phillips, do you copy?'

'Copy, Phillips,' came the tinny voice through the earpiece. 'All teams in position.'

'Control, this is Johnson, do you copy?' Malcolm said.

Dew heard the same tinny voice acknowledge Malcolm's call.

Malcolm reached into his jacket pocket and pulled out a small leather business-card holder. Inside were two pictures, one of his wife, Shamika, and one of his six-year-old son, Jerome.

Dew waited. Malcolm usually did that before they talked to any suspect. Malcolm liked to remember why he did this job, and why he had to always stay sharp and cautious. Dew had a picture of his daughter, Sharon, in his wallet, but he wasn't about to pull it out and look at it. He knew what she looked like. Besides, he didn't *want* to think about her before he went on a mission. He wanted to insulate her against the kinds of things he had to do, the kinds of things his country *needed* him to do.

Malcolm snapped the card holder shut and tucked it away. 'How'd we get this choice gig again, Dew?'

'Because good ol' Murray loves me. You're just along for the ride.'

Both men stepped out of the Buick and walked toward Martin Brewbaker's small, one-story ranch house. An even two inches of snow covered the lawn and the sidewalk. Brewbaker's place was near the corner of Curtis and Miller, just off the tracks in Toledo, Ohio. It wasn't rural by any stretch, but it wasn't packed in, either. The four lanes of busy Western Avenue kicked up plenty of noise—not enough to drown out Screamin' Frank Sinatra, but close.

In case things got crazy, they had three vans, each filled

with four special-ops guys in biowarfare suits. One van at the end of Curtis where it ran into Western Avenue, one at Curtis and Mozart, and one at Dix and Miller. That cut off any escape by car, and Brewbaker didn't have any motorcycles registered on his insurance or DMV record. If he ran north, across the freezing Swan Creek, the boys in van number four parked on Whittier Street would grab him. Martin Brewbaker wasn't going anywhere.

Did Dew and Malcolm get biowarfare suits? Hell no. This had to be kept quiet, discreet, or the whole fucking neighborhood would freak out, and then the news trucks would come a-courtin'. Two goons in yellow Racal suits knocking on the door of Mr. Good Citizen had a tendency to shoot discretion right in the ass. Not that Dew would have worn the friggin' thing anyway—with the shit he'd been through, he knew that when it was time to check out, you were checking out. And if things went according to plan, they'd isolate Brewbaker, bring in gray van number one real discreet-like, toss his ass in and haul him off to Toledo Hospital where they had a quarantine setup ready and waiting.

'Approaching the front door,' Dew said. He spoke to no one in particular, but the microphone on his earpiece picked up everything and transmitted it to Control.

'Copy that, Phillips.'

This was their chance, finally, to catch a live one.

And maybe figure out just what the fuck was going on.

'Remember the orders, Mal,' Dew said. 'If it goes bad, no shots to the head.'

'No head shots, right.'

Dew hoped it wouldn't come down to pulling the trigger, but somehow he had a feeling it would. After weeks of chasing after infected victims, arriving to find only murdered bodies, moldering corpses, and/or charred remains, they had a live one.

Martin Brewbaker, Caucasian, age thirty-two, married to Annie Brewbaker, Caucasian, twenty-eight. One child, Betsy Brewbaker, age six.

Dew had heard Martin's call to Captain Jinky. But even with that crazy recording, they weren't *sure* yet. This guy might be normal, no problems, just liked to blast his Sinatra on eleven.

I tried so . . . not to give in,
I said to myself, 'This affair never will go so well.'

'Dew, do you smell gasoline?'

Dew wasn't even halfway through the first sniff when he knew that Malcolm was right. Gasoline. From inside the house. Shit.

Dew looked at his partner. Gas or no gas, it was time to go in. He wanted to whisper to Mal, but with Sinatra so fucking loud he had to shout to be heard.

'Okay, Mal, let's go in fast. This asshole probably wants to light the place on fire like some of the others. We have to take him down before he does that, got it?'

Malcolm nodded. Dew stepped away from the door. He could still kick a door in if he had to, but Mal was younger and stronger, and young guys got off on that shit. Let the lad have his fun.

Malcolm reared back and gave one solid kick—the door slammed open, the deadbolt spinning off inside somewhere, trailing a few splinters of wood. Mal went in first, Dew right behind.

Inside the house, Sinatra roared at a new level, so loud it made Dew wince.

In spite of a warning voice that comes in the night,

And repeats, repeats in my ear,

A small living room that led into a small dining room, then a kitchen.

In that kitchen, a corpse. A woman. Pool of blood. Wide-eyed. Throat slit. A brow-wrinkled expression of surprise, not terror . . . surprise, or confusion, like she'd passed on while looking at a *Wheel of Fortune* puzzle that really had her stumped.

Mal showed no sign of emotion, and that made Dew proud. Nothing they could do for the woman now anyway.

Don't you know, little fool, you never can win,
Use your mentality, wake up to reality.

A hallway that led deeper into the house.

Dew's feet squishing on the brown shag carpet. Squishing because of the thick trail of gasoline that made the carpet an even darker brown.

Mal and Dew moved in.

First door on the right. Mal opened it.

A child's bedroom, and another corpse. This one a little girl. Six years old, Dew knew, because he'd read the file. No look of surprise on that face. No expression at all, really. Just glassy-eyed blankness. Slightly open mouth. Blood all over her tiny face. All over her little Cleveland Browns T-shirt.

This time Mal stopped. The girl was the same age as his Jerome. Dew knew, right then and there, that Mal would probably kill Brewbaker when they found him. Dew wouldn't stop him, either.

But this wasn't the time for sightseeing. He tapped Mal on the shoulder. Mal shut the girl's door behind him. Two more doors: one on the right, one at the end of the hall. The music still blared, offensive, overpowering.

But each time that I do, just the thought of you
Makes me stop, before I begin,

Mal opened the door to the right. Master bedroom, no one there.

One door left. Dew took a deep breath, nose filling with gasoline fumes. Mal opened the door.

And there was Martin Brewbaker.

Mal's theory back in the car turned out to be prophetic—there *was* one crazy Caucasian in that house.

Wide-eyed and smiling, Martin Brewbaker sat on the bathroom floor, legs straight out in front of him. He wore a gas-soaked Cleveland Browns hoodie, jeans, and was barefoot. He'd cinched belts around both legs, just above the knee. In one hand, he held an orange lighter. In the other hand, a nicked-up red hatchet. Behind him sat a red and silver gas can, lying on its side, its contents making a glistening wet puddle against the black and white linoleum floor.

'Cause I've got you . . . under my skin.

'You're too late, pigs,' Brewbaker said. 'They told me you'd come. But you know what? I'm not going, I'm not taking them. They can fucking walk there themselves.'

He raised the hatchet and whipped it down hard. The thick blade slid through skin and denim just below his knee, crunched through his bone, and *chonked* into the linoleum floor, severing his leg. Blood sprayed all across the floor, mixing with the pool of gas. His severed leg and foot sort of flopped on its side.

Brewbaker screamed, an agonizing scream that drowned out Sinatra's jamming orchestra. His voice screamed, but his eyes didn't—they kept staring at Dew.

That happened in one second. In the next second, the hatchet came up again and went down again, severing the other leg, also just below the knee. Brewbaker tipped backward, the now-missing weight throwing off his equilibrium just a bit. As he rolled back, his stubby legs sprayed blood into the air, onto the bathroom counter, onto the ceiling. Dew and Malcolm both instinctively raised an arm to block the blood from hitting them in the face.

Brewbaker flicked the lighter and touched it to the floor. The gas flamed up instantly, igniting the puddle, shooting down the wet path into the hallway and beyond. Brewbaker's gas-soaked hoodie snapped into full flame.

In a blur of athletic motion, Mal holstered his weapon, whipped off his coat and rushed forward.

Dew started to shout a warning, but it was already too late.

Mal threw his coat on Brewbaker, trying to smother the flames. The hatchet shot forward again—burying itself deep in Mal's stomach. Even over the Sinatra, Dew heard a muffled *chlunk* and knew, instantly, that the hatchet blade had chipped the inside of Mal's spine.

Dew took two steps into the flaming bathroom.

Brewbaker looked up, eyes even wider, smile even wider. He started to say something, but didn't get the chance.

Dew Phillips fired three .45 rounds from a distance of two feet. The bullets punched into Brewbaker's chest, sliding him backward on the blood- and gas-slick floor. His back slammed into the toilet, but he was already dead.

'Converge, converge! All units move in, man down, man down!'

Dew holstered his weapon, knelt, and threw Mal over his shoulder. He stood with strength he didn't know he still possessed. Brewbaker burned, but the flames hadn't spread to his right arm. Dew grabbed Brewbaker's right hand, then stumbled down the flaming hall, carrying one man and dragging another.

2

THE RAW AND THE COOKED

Dew staggered out of the burning house. Winter air cooled his red face, while inferno heat singed his back through his suit.

'Hold on, Mal,' he said to the bleeding man on his right shoulder. 'Hold on, ace, help's on the way.'

Dew slipped on the unshoveled sidewalk and almost pitched into the snow-covered lawn, but he recovered his balance and made it to the curb. He crossed the street, stumbling like a drunk, then slid Brewbaker's body into a shallow snowbank, where it hissed briefly like a match dropped into a stale drink. Dew knelt on one knee and eased Malcolm onto the ground.

Mal's once-white shirt was a sheet of red around his stomach. The hatchet had gone in deep, deep enough to cut through intestines. Dew had seen wounds like that before, and he didn't have much hope.

'Hang on, Mal,' Dew whispered. 'You just remember Shamika and Jerome, and you hang on. You can't leave your family alone.' He held Malcolm's hand, which felt hot and wet and was covered with puffy burn blisters. The screech of tires split the air as several nondescript gray Chevy work vans slid to a stop. The van doors opened; a dozen men dressed in bulky chemical-weapons gear leaped onto the slush-wet pavement. They brandished compact FN-P90 submachine guns and moved with practiced precision, rushing to set up a perimeter around Dew and Malcolm, around the burning house. Some of the men rushed to Malcolm's side.

'See, buddy?' Dew said. His mouth was inches from Malcolm's ear. 'See? The cavalry is here, you'll be at the hospital before you know it. You just hang on, brother.'

Malcolm let out a groan. His voice sounded whispery, like windblown paper scraping against dirty concrete.

'That . . . asshole . . . dead?' Malcolm's lips, or what was left of them, barely moved when he spoke.

'Fuckin'-A right he is,' Dew said. 'Three in the ticker, point-blank.'

Malcolm coughed once, sending a wad of thick, dark blood shooting out onto the snow. The men in chemical-warfare suits hurried him to one of the waiting vans.

Dew watched as the soldiers loaded Brewbaker's smoldering corpse into another van. The remaining soldiers moved Dew to the last van, half helping him, half pushing him. He got in, heard the door shut, then heard a small hiss as the sealed van became negatively pressurized. Any surprise leaks would let air in, not out, in case Dew was contaminated with the unknown spore. He wondered if they'd have him in the airlock again, watching him for days on end, waiting to see if he showed the few known symptoms or—even better, kiddies—developed new ones. He didn't care, as long as they could help Malcolm. If Malcolm died, Dew didn't think he could forgive himself. Less than twenty seconds after the vans had screeched to a halt, they tore down the street, leaving the burning house behind.

3
ONE SMALL STEP . . .

After a journey of unknown distance, unknown time, the next batch of seeds dropped from the atmosphere like microscopic snow, scattering wildly at the tiniest breath of wind. Wave after wave washed through the air. The most recent waves had been close to success, the closest yet, but still hadn't caused the critical mass needed to accomplish the task. Changes were made, new seeds released. It was only a matter of time until things were right.

Most of the seeds survived the feathery fall, but the real test was yet to come. Billions died at the touch of water or the kiss of cold temperatures. Others survived the landing, but found conditions unsuitable for growth. A scant few landed in the right place, but wind, or the brush of a hand, or perhaps even fate, swept them away.

A minuscule percentage, however, found conditions perfect for germination.

Smaller than specks of dust, the seeds tentatively held their place. Rigid microfilaments ending in Velcro-like hooks helped each seed stay fast to the surface. With the fortuitous landing began a race against time. The seeds faced a nigh-impossible task of attaining self-sufficiency, a battle for survival that started with a minuscule arachnid.

A simple mite.

Demodex folliculorum, to be precise. While microscopic, a *Demodex* is larger than the dead skin upon which it feasts. So much larger, in fact, that it can ingest a tiny flake in a single bite. The mites hide in hair follicles, mostly, but sometimes at night they slide out and crawl around on the hosts' skin. They are not some parasite found only in dirty Third World countries where hygiene is a luxury, but on every human body in the world.

Including the host.

The host's mites lived their entire, brief, skin-gobbling lives without ever leaving his body. In their incessant feeding frenzy, some of the mites came across the seeds—which looked suspiciously similar to flakes of human skin. The mites gobbled up the minute seeds; just another mouthful in an endless and bountiful banquet of dead flesh.

The mite's digestive system hammered at the seed's outer coat. Protein-digesting enzymes, called proteases, ate away at the membrane, breaking it down, weakening it. The membrane ruptured in several places but did not dissolve completely. Still intact, the seed passed through the mite's digestive tract.

And that's where it all began, really—in a microscopic pile of bug shit.

The temperature hovered around seventy degrees much of the time and often reached eighty degrees or more with suitable cover. The seed needed such temperatures. It also needed certain measures of salinity and humidity, which the host's skin unwittingly provided. These conditions triggered receptor cells, turning the seeds 'on,' so to speak, and preparing it for growth. But there were other conditions that had to be right before germination could occur.

Oxygen was the main ingredient in this recipe for

growth. During its long fall, the airtight seed coat prevented any gases from reaching the contents contained within, contents that—were it biological—might have been called an embryo. The *Demodex* mite's digestive system, however, ravaged the seed's protective outer shell, allowing oxygen to penetrate.

Unthinking, automated receptor cells measured the conditions, reacting in an exquisitely intricate biochemical dance that read like a preflight checklist;

Oxygen? Check.
Correct salinity? Check.
Appropriate humidity? Check.
Suitable temperature? Check.

Billions of microscopic seeds made the long journey. Millions survived the initial fall, and thousands lasted long enough to reach a suitable environment. Hundreds landed on this particular host. Only a few dozen reached bare skin, and some of those expired before ending up in bug feces. In all, only nine germinated.

A rapid-fire growth phase ensued. Cells split via mitosis, doubling their number every few minutes, drawing energy and building blocks from the food stored within the seeds. The seedlings' survival depended on speed—they had to sink roots and grow protection in a soon-to-be-hostile environment. The seeds did not need leaves, only a main root, which in plant embryos is called a *radicle*. These radicles were the seeds' lifeline, the means by which they would tap into the new environment.

The radicle's main task was penetrating the skin. The skin's outermost layer—composed of cells filled with tough, fibrous keratin—formed the first obstacle. The microscopic roots grew downward, slowly but incessantly pushing through this barrier and into the softer tissues beneath. One seed couldn't break that outer layer. Its growth sputtered out, and it died.

That left eight.

Once past that obstacle, the roots quickly dug deeper, slipping beyond the epidermis, into the dermis, then through the fatty cells of the subcutaneous layer. Receptor cells measured changes in chemical content and density. Underneath the subcutaneous layer, just before the firmness of muscle, the roots began a phase change. Each of the eight roots became the center for a new organism.

The second stage ensued.

This rapid growth had depleted the seeds' food stores. Now nothing more than used delivery vehicles, the little husks fell away. Under the skin, second-stage roots spread out. They weren't like roots of a tree or any other plant, but more akin to little tentacles, branching out from the center, drawing oxygen, proteins, amino acids and sugars from the new environment. Like biological conveyor belts, the roots pulled these building blocks back to the new organism, fueling an explosion of cell growth. One of the seedlings ended up on the host's face, just above the left eyebrow. This one couldn't draw quite enough material to fuel the second-stage growth process. It simply ran out of energy. A few of the seedling's parts kept growing, assembling, automatically drawing nutrients from the host and creating raw materials that would never be used—but for all intents and purposes this seedling ceased to be.

That left seven.

The surviving seedlings started building things. The first construct was a microscopic, free-moving thing that, if you had an electron microscope handy, looked like a hair-covered ball with two saw-toothed jaws on one side. These jaws sliced into cell after cell, tearing open the membrane, finding the nucleus, and sucking it inside the ball. The balls read raw DNA, the blueprint of our bodies, identifying the code for biological processes, for building muscle and bone, for all creation and maintenance. That's all the DNA was to the balls, really; just blueprints. Once read, the balls returned this information to the seedlings.

With that data the seven knew what needed to be built in order to grow. Not at a conscious level, but at a raw, data-in and data-out machinelike state. Sentience didn't matter—the organisms read the blueprints, and knew what to do next.

The seedlings drew sugars from the bloodstream, then fused them, a fast and simple chemical weld that created a durable, flexible building material. As the building blocks accumulated, the organisms created their next autonomous, free-moving structures. Where the balls had *gathered*, these new microstructures *built*. Using the growing stores of the building material, the new structures started weaving the shell. Without fast shell growth, the new organism might not live five more days.

It needed that long to reach stage three.

4

A CASE OF THE MONDAYS

Perry Dawsey threw back the heavy bedspread and mismatched covering blankets, exposing himself to the sudden grip of winter-morning chill. He shivered. The part of his brain that always beckoned him to sleep, to set the alarm for another fifteen minutes, tugged at him. A mild hangover didn't help his resolve.

See? the voice seemed to say. *It's cold as hell this morning. Crawl back under the covers where it's nice and warm. You deserve a day off.*

It was his morning ritual; the voice always called, and he always ignored it. He stood and shuffled the four steps from his bedroom to the tiny bathroom. The linoleum greeted his feet with unwelcome cold. He shut the door behind him, started up the shower, and let the bathroom fill with deliciously warm steam. As he stepped into the nearly scalding water, the nagging morning voice faded away, just as it always did. He hadn't missed a day of work—or even been late—in three years. He sure as hell wasn't going to start now.

Scrubbing himself roughly, he came fully awake. His left forearm flared up with a tiny itch; he absently scratched it with his thick fingernails. Perry shut off the shower, stepped out, grabbed a rumpled towel that hung over the shower-curtain rod and dried himself. The steam hung like a wafting cloud that bent and drifted with his every movement.

The bathroom was little more than a closet with plumbing. Just inside and to the right of the door sat the small Formica counter that held the sink, its once-white porcelain stained with rusty orange from a combination of hard water and an ever-dripping spout. The countertop had about enough room for a toothbrush, a can of shaving cream and a shrunken, cracked bar of soap. All the other necessities resided in the medicine cabinet behind the mirror mounted above the sink.

Just past the countertop was the toilet, the other side of which almost bumped up against the tub. The bathroom was so small that Perry could sit on the toilet and touch the far wall without leaning forward. Used towels of various unmatched colors hung from the towel rack, the shower curtain and both sides of the doorknob, creating a rainbow terry-cloth contrast to the lime-green walls and scratched tan linoleum floor.

A small digital scale, dented and pockmarked with rust, was the only decoration. With a sigh of resignation, he stood on it. The bottom LED of the 'ones' digit never lit up. It made the last digit look like an *A* rather than an *8*, but it didn't hide his weight: 268.

He stepped off the scale. Another itch—this one on his left thigh—hit quickly, like the bite of a mosquito. Perry twitched with the sudden discomfort and gave the area a solid scratch.

He finished toweling off his hair, then stopped suddenly, jerking his hand away. Something hurt above his left eyebrow—that angry-dull pain of accidentally hitting a big zit.

With his towel he wiped steam from the mirror. A

shadow of bristly red beard covered his face. Bright red beard and straight blond hair, the strange distinctive mark of Dawsey men for as far back as Perry knew. He wore his hair shoulder length, not for style, but rather because it helped hide the striking facial resemblance he shared with his father. The older he got, the more the face in the mirror looked like the one face he wanted most to forget.

'Fucking desk job. Making me a fat boy.'

He focused his attention on the eyebrow zit. It looked *sort* of like a zit but also looked . . . strange. Small, gnarled red bump. It felt odd, like a teeny bug was biting or stinging him.

What the hell is that?

He leaned forward, skin almost touching the mirror as his fingers prodded the painful spot. Firm, solid skin, with something really small sticking out of it. The something was . . . black, maybe? A tiny speck. He dug at it for a second with his fingernails, but the spot hurt. Probably an ingrown hair or something like that. He'd try to leave it alone, let it firm up and deal with it later.

Perry reached for the shaving cream. He always took a good look at himself before shaving and brushing his teeth, not out of vanity but rather to see just how much further along his body was toward Old Fogey-Ville.

Back in college his body had been hard, chiseled, six-foot-five, 240 pounds of muscle befitting his All–Big Ten linebacker status. In the seven years following the knee injury that ended his career, however, his body changed, gradually adding fat while depleting unused muscle. He wasn't overweight by anyone else's standards, and his body still drew plenty of looks from women, but Perry could see the difference.

He shaved, slapped some mousse in his hair and

brushed his teeth to complete his repetitive morning preparation. Perry dashed out of the bathroom into the cold apartment. He dressed quickly in jeans, an old AC/DC concert T-shirt and a warm San Francisco 49ers sweatshirt. Finally protected against the cold, he headed to the kitchen nook (he could never think of it as a 'kitchen,' he'd been in houses with a 'kitchen,' this six-by-eight-foot alcove stuffed with a stove, cabinets and a fridge was and would always qualify as nothing more than a 'nook').

He reached for the cupboard containing the Pop-Tarts, then arched his back in sudden surprise as another itch, this one burning and almost painful, erupted on his spine just below the shoulder blades. Perry reached a hand up over his shoulder and under his shirts to dig at the spot.

He scratched the itch into submission, wondering if he had contracted a rash or possibly suffered from dry skin caused by the arid winter air. Perry pulled down the box of Pop-Tarts and pulled out one of the two-tart silver foil packets. The stove's digital clock read 8:36. Cramming a cherry Pop-Tart into his mouth, Perry walked the two steps to his computer desk and started stuffing papers into his beat-up, duct-tape-patched briefcase. He'd meant to get some work done over the weekend, but the Chiefs and Raiders had played on Saturday, and then he'd spent all day Sunday watching the games and *SportsCenter*. He finished up Sunday night with a trip to the bar to watch the Lions get their asses kicked, as usual. He snapped the case shut, threw on his coat, grabbed his keys and headed out of the apartment.

Three flights of stairs later, he exited the building and entered the knife-slash cold sting of December in Michigan. It felt like a thousand tiny pinpricks on his face and hands. His breath billowed wispy-white.

Jamming the second Pop-Tart into his mouth, he walked toward his twelve-year-old, rust-shot Ford, praying to the Great Gods of Piece-of-Shit Cars that the old girl would start.

He slid behind the wheel (he never bothered to lock the car, who the hell would want the thing?) and closed the door. The frost-covered windows filtered the morning sun in icy-white opaqueness.

'Come on, sister,' Perry mumbled, his breath curling up and around his head. He gave a small grunt of victory as the old car coughed to life on the first try. Perry grabbed the ice scraper and stepped out of the car, only to have yet another itch stab at his right ass cheek like a sandpaper needle. He reflexively grabbed at it, which made him lose his balance and landed him butt-first on the parking lot. Digging his fingers through the jeans and roughly scratching the spot, Perry felt the seat of his pants dampen with melting snow.

'Yep,' Perry said as he stood and brushed himself off. 'It's definitely a Monday.'

5

ARCHITECTURE

The shells grew in size and durability. Still too small to see with the naked eye, it wouldn't be long before they could not be missed. The same tiny, cell-like devices that built the shells used the available material to start making what went *under* the shells—a framework that would comprise a new organism, a larger organism.

A *growing* organism.

The seedlings built their third and final free-moving microstructure. Where there had been 'readers' to gather the DNA blueprints, and 'builders' to make the shell and the framework, now came the 'herders.'

The herders washed out into the host's body, seeking very specific kinds of cells—stem cells. The DNA blueprints showed that these were what the seedlings needed. The herders found these stem cells, then cut them free and dragged them back to the growing framework. First the herders cemented the stem cells to the framework with simple chemical bonds, then the reader-balls moved in.

The saw-toothed jaws sliced into the stem cell, but gently this time. Microfilaments bare nanometers across slid into the stem cell DNA. Slid in, and started making changes.

Because the 'readers' weren't there just to *read* . . .

They were also there to *write*.

The stem cells were not conscious. They had no idea they had just been enslaved. They did what they always do: grow new cells. The new cells they produced were only slightly different from those they had been originally designed to build. Those new cells spread out through the growing framework, adding muscle and other, more specialized tissues.

What arrived as a microscopic seed had hijacked the host's body and used the built-in biological processes to create something foreign, in a way far more insidious than even a virus.

And while the seedlings had no concept of time, their mission would be complete in just a few short days.

6

THE DAILY GRIND

Perry walked into American Computer Solutions (ACS to those in the industry) at seven minutes to nine. He jogged through the building, catching and throwing *hellos* as he headed for his cubicle. Sliding into his chair, he tossed his briefcase on the gray desktop and started his computer. It chimed, seemingly in happiness at escaping the purgatory of 'off,' and started through its RAM checks and warm-up cycles. Perry glanced at the wall clock, which was placed high enough that all could see it from their cubicles. It read 8:55. He'd already be working away when the clock struck 9:00.

'Thought I was going to get you today,' said a woman's voice behind his back. He didn't bother to turn around as he opened the briefcase and pulled out the unorganized wad of paper.

'Close but no cigar, boss,' Perry said, smiling a little at the daily joke. 'Maybe next time.'

'Samir Cansil from Pullman called,' the woman said. 'They're having network trouble again. Call them first thing.'

'Yes ma'am,' Perry said.

Sandy Rodriguez left Perry to his work. Most of ACS's customer-support staff arrived a few minutes late, but Perry was always on time. Sandy rarely addressed the staff's tardiness problem. Everyone knew she didn't really care if people were a little late, as long as they didn't abuse that privilege and got their work done. She didn't care, and yet Perry was always on time.

She'd given him a chance when he had no job, no references and an assault conviction on his record. No, not *just* an assault—an assault conviction on his *former boss.* After that incident he was sure nobody would ever hire him for white-collar work again. But his college roomie Bill Miller had put in a good word at ACS, and Sandy had given Perry a shot.

When she hired him, he swore to himself that he'd never let her down in any way. That included being early every day. As his father used to say, there's no substitute for hard work. He pushed the sudden and unwelcome thought of his father from his mind—he didn't want to start the day in a bad mood.

A full twenty-five minutes later, Perry heard the distinctive sounds of Bill Miller sliding into the adjoining cubicle. Bill was late as usual, and, also as usual, he didn't give a damn.

'Morning, sissy-girl,' Bill said, his ever-present monotone drifting over the five-foot cubicle walls. 'Didums sleep well?'

'You know, Bill, I'm a little bit past the "I drank more than you" stage. I'd like to think you'll grow up one of these days.'

'Yeah, you're probably right,' Bill said. 'Although I did drink more than you, girlie-man.'

Perry started to reply, but a stabbing itch on his right collarbone stole his voice and replaced it with a slight gasp of surprise. He dug his fingers through the sweatshirt, scratching at the skin underneath. Maybe he was allergic to something. Maybe a spider had crawled into his bed last night and tried to bite its way out.

He scratched harder, intent on blasting the itch into compliance. The irritation on his forearm acted up again, and he switched his focus to that spot.

'Fleas?' Bill's voice came from above, unhampered by the divider walls. Perry looked up. Bill's upper body leaned over the fabric-panel wall that separated the cubicles, his head just inches from the ceiling. He attained this height by a frequent practice of standing on his desk. Bill, as always, looked immaculate despite the fact he'd left the bar the same time as Perry—which meant he couldn't have had more than four hours' sleep. With his bright blue eyes, perfectly trimmed brown hair, and a clean-shaven baby face free of even the tiniest blemish, Bill looked like a model for teenage zit cream.

'Just a little bug bite is all,' Perry said.

Bill retreated back behind the divider wall.

Perry stopped scratching, although the skin still itched, and called up the Pullman file on his computer. As he did, he launched his instant-messenger program—even though people were only a few cubes away, instant messaging often proved to be the preferred method of communication within the office. Especially for communication with Bill, in the next cube, who usually had plenty to say that he didn't want others in the office to overhear. The IMs let them share sophomoric humor that helped to pass the day.

He started off the daily ritual with a message to Bill's instant-message handle, 'StickyFingazWhitey.'

Bleedmaize_n_blue: Hey. R we doing Monday Night Football tonight?

StickyFingazWhitey: Does the Pope wear women's underwear?

> **Bleedmaize_n_blue:** I thought the phrase was, 'does the Pope wear a funny hat' ???
>
> **StickyFingazWhitey:** He already wears a big dress, although my sources say he doesn't deserve to wear white, if ya know what I mean. ☺

Perry snorted back a laugh. He knew he looked like an idiot when he did that, big shoulders bouncing, head down, hand over his mouth to hide laughter.

> **Bleedmaize_n_blue:** lol. Cut it out, I just got here, I don't want Sandy to think I'm watching YouTube clips again.
>
> **StickyFingazWhitey:** How about you watch Popes Gone Wild™ on your own time, mister, you sick, sick man.

Perry laughed, out loud this time. He'd known Bill for . . . God, was it almost ten years already? Perry's freshman year in college had been a tough one, a time when his violent tendencies ran roughshod and unchecked. He'd landed at the University of Michigan courtesy of a full-ride football scholarship. At first they'd roomed him with other football players, but Perry always viewed them as competition even if they didn't play the same position. A fight inevitably ensued. After his third altercation, the coaches were ready to yank his scholarship.

That crap may float at other schools, like Ohio State, they told him, *but not at the University of Michigan.*

The last thing they wanted, however, was to lose him—they hadn't recruited him and given him a full ride for nothing. The coaching staff wanted his ferocity on the field. When Bill heard of the situation, he volunteered to room with Perry. Bill was the nephew of one of the assistant coaches. He and Perry met during freshmen orientation, and the two had hit it off quite well. Perry remembered that the only times he smiled during those first few months were when he was around Bill's irrepressible humor.

Everyone thought Bill was crazy. Why would a five-foot-eight, 150-pound English major volunteer to room with a six-foot-five, 240-pound linebacker who benched 480 and had already beaten the holy hell out of three roommates, all of whom were Division I football players? But to everyone's surprise, it worked out perfectly. Bill seemed to have a talent for laughter, laughter that soothed the savage beast. Bill saved not only Perry's athletic career but his collegiate one as well. Perry had never forgotten that.

Ten years he'd known Bill, and in all that time he'd never heard the man give a straight answer about anything that wasn't related to work.

Music drifted over from Bill's cube. Ancient Sonny & Cher ditty, to which Bill cleverly sang 'I got scabies, babe' instead of the original lyrics. The IM alert chimed again:

StickyFingazWhitey: You think Green Bay is going to give the Niners a good game tonight?

Perry didn't type in an answer, didn't really even see the question. His face scrunched into a mask of intense concentration that one might mistake for pain. He fought against the urge to scratch yet again, except this time it was far worse than before, and in a far worse place.

He kept his hands frozen on the keyboard, using all his athletic discipline not to scratch furiously at his left testicle.

7

THE BIG SNAFU

Dew Phillips slumped into the plastic chair next to the pay phone. After this ordeal even a young man would have felt like a week-old dog turd, and at fifty-six, Dew's youth was far behind him. His wrinkled suit stank of sweat and smoke. Thick smoke, black smoke, the kind that only comes from a house fire. The odor seemed alien in the clean, dirt-free confines of the hospital. Somewhere in his head, he knew he should feel grateful that he was in the waiting room at the Toledo Hospital and not in the airtight quarantine chamber at the CDC in Cincinnati, but he just couldn't find the energy to count his blessings.

Greasy soot streaked the left side of his weathered, heavily lined face. His bald head also showed streaks, as if flames had danced precariously near his mottled scalp. The small patch of red hair, which ran from ear to ear around the back of his head, had escaped the smoke stain. He looked weak and exhausted, as if he might teeter off the chair at any second.

Dew always carried two cell phones. One was thin and normal. He used that for most communication. The other was bulky and metallic, painted in a flat black finish. It was loaded with the latest encrypting equipment, none of which Dew understood or gave a rat's ass about. He pulled out the big cell phone and called Murray's number.

'Good afternoon,' said a cheery but businesslike woman.

'Get Murray.'

The phone clicked once; he was on hold. The Rolling Stones played 'Satisfaction' through the tinny connection. *Jesus,* Dew thought, *even super-secret, secure lines have fucking Muzak.* Murray Longworth's authoritative voice came on the line, cutting off Mick in mid-breath.

'What's the situation, Dew?'

'It's a big SNAFU, sir,' Dew said. The military-parlance acronym stood for *Situation Normal, All Fucked Up.* He leaned his forehead on the pastel blue wall. Looking down, he noticed for the first time that the soles of his shoes had melted, then cooled all misshapen and embedded with bits of gravel and broken glass. 'Johnson's hurt.'

'How bad?'

'The docs say it's touch and go.'

'Shit.'

'Yes,' Dew said quietly. 'It doesn't look good.'

Murray waited, perhaps only long enough to give the illusion that Malcolm's life was more important than the mission, then continued. 'Did you catch him?'

'No,' Dew said. 'There was a fire.'

'Remains?'

'Here at the hospital, waiting for your girl.'

'Condition?'

'Somewhere between medium and well-done. I think she's got something to work with, if that's what you mean.'

Murray paused a moment. His silence seemed weighted and heavy. 'You want to stay with him, or should I have some boys watch over him?'

'You couldn't drag me away with a team full of mules tied to my balls, sir.'

'I figured as much,' Murray said. 'I assume the area was checked and sterilized?'

'As in three-alarm sterilized.'

'Good. Margaret is on the way. Give her whatever help she needs. I'll get there when I can. You can give me a full report then.'

'Yes sir.' Dew hung up and flopped back into the chair.

Malcolm Johnson, his partner of seven years, was in critical condition. Third-degree burns covered much of Mal's body. The hatchet wound in his gut wasn't helping things. Dew had ample experience with horribly wounded men; he wouldn't take two-to-one odds for Malcolm's survival.

Dew had seen some crazy shit in his day, more than most, first in 'Nam and then with almost three decades of service to the Agency, but he'd never seen anything like Martin Brewbaker. Those eyes, eyes that swam with madness, *drowned* in it. Martin Brewbaker, legless, covered in fire like some Hollywood stuntman, swinging that hatchet at Malcolm.

Dew let his head fall into his hands. If only he'd reacted faster; if only he'd been just *one second* faster and stopped Mal from trying to put out the fire on Brewbaker. Dew should have known what was coming: Blaine Tanarive, Charlotte Wilson, Gary Leeland—all those cases had ended in violence, in murder. Why had he thought Brewbaker would be any different? But who would have expected the crazy fuck to set his *whole house* on fire?

Dew had one more call to make—Malcolm's wife. He wondered if Malcolm would still be alive by the time Shamika flew in from D.C.

He doubted it. He doubted it very much.

8

WOULD YOU LOOK AT THAT?

At lunchtime Perry sat in the bathroom stall, pants around his ankles, 49ers sweatshirt in a pile on the tile floor. On top of his left forearm, atop his left thigh, and on his right shin were small red rashes about the size of a No. 2 pencil eraser. Three other spots itched just as maddeningly; his fingers told him that similar rashes perched on his right collarbone, on his spine just below his shoulder blades and on his right ass cheek. He also had one on his left testicle—that one he tried not to think about.

Their itching came and went, sometimes fading in and out like a slowly turned volume knob, other times arriving with full-bore force like hitting the 'power' button of a maxed-out stereo. Definitely spider bites, he figured. Maybe a centipede; he'd heard they had nasty venom. What amazed him was how he'd slept through such an attack. Whatever it was that had bitten him, it must have hit just before he awoke. That would explain why he saw no marks when he prepared for work—the poison had just entered his system, and his body was slow to react.

They itched and were a touch disconcerting, but all in all it was no big deal. Just a few bug bites. He'd simply have to discipline himself not to scratch, and sooner or later they'd go away. If he left them alone, they'd probably disappear. Trouble was, he had an awful time of leaving skin blemishes alone, whether they be scabs, zits, blisters or anything else, but his bad habit of picking at such blemishes wouldn't help matters. He'd simply have to focus, have to 'play through the pain,' as his high-school football coach used to say.

Perry stood, buttoned his pants and put his sweatshirt back on. He took a deep breath and tried to clear his mind. *It's just a test of will,* Perry thought. *A test of discipline, that's all. You've got to have discipline.*

He left the bathroom and headed back to his desk, ready to work hard and earn his pay.

9

PAYIN' THE COST TO BE THE BOSS

Murray Longworth looked over the list of personnel who had enough security clearance to join Project Tangram. It was a short list. Malcolm Johnson was down for the count. That made Dew a solo operative, which is what Murray had wanted in the first place. But Dew had insisted on bringing in Johnson. Murray shook his head—that decision would fuck with Dew, probably for the rest of his life.

Casualties, unfortunately, were the cost of doing business. You sent flowers to the funeral, you moved on. Murray understood that. Dew, he never did. Dew Phillips made shit personal. That was why Murray was the number-two man in the CIA and Dew Phillips was still a shit-stomping grunt. A grunt in a nice suit, sure, but a grunt nonetheless.

That was also why five presidents had called on Murray to get things done. Secret things. Unsavory things. Things that would never make the history books, but had to get done anyway. And this time the President of the United States of America had asked Murray to find out what the hell was turning normal Americans into crazed murderers. Murray, *from the CIA*, mind you, and *not* the FBI, who should have handled a domestic issue. It was, in fact, illegal for the CIA to run this op on U.S. soil, but the president wanted Murray to handle it—if it was terrorism, it might require some creative tactics. Tactics that just might be just a *smidgen* outside the law.

Five victims to date in a plague that would throw the country into an unparalleled panic, and he had precious little information. So far he'd done a masterful job of keeping the lid on things—he had more than a hundred people at his immediate disposal, yet fewer than ten knew what was actually going on. Not even the Joint Chiefs had the whole story.

When Margaret Montoya had contacted the CIA with that first strange report, the call eventually landed with Murray. She wasn't just some crank caller or some science-type doom-and-gloomer preaching about yet another pending global-warming catastrophe. She was from the CDC, and she suspected she might have stumbled onto a terrorist bioweapon. Her credentials and her urgency convinced enough people to push her through the phone maze, each level passing the call upward, until it reached Murray.

Margaret said she hadn't gone through the proper channels in the CDC because she feared leaks. Murray knew that was only partially true—the rest of the story was that Margaret wanted to be the one tracking this bizarre killer. If she went through normal channels, she feared some supervisor would take the case away from her and grab all the recognition while Margaret was pushed to the wayside of anonymity.

He'd met with her, and it took only one look at her case files—and those pictures of Charlotte Wilson and Gary Leeland—to convince him that she was right; there was a new threat in town.

The best part of it all was her relative obscurity. She

wasn't some world authority on disease or some Nobel Prize-winner or anyone of note. She was a very competent epidemiologist who worked out of the Cincinnati CDC office; she wasn't even high-ranking enough to be at the main CDC center in Atlanta. Murray knew he could monopolize her time—draft her, if you will—and only a handful of people would notice her absence.

He'd put people to work searching for references to 'triangles' or anything else that might reveal additional cases. That search turned up Blaine Tanarive, who a week earlier had contacted Toledo TV station WNWO, claiming a 'triangle conspiracy.' WNWO notes described Mr. Tanarive as 'paranoid' and 'irrational.'

Two days later, neighbors discovered the bodies of Tanarive and his family in their house. Tanarive was reported as being in a 'highly advanced state of decom- position.' His wife and two daughters were also found dead, although their level of decomposition was not as advanced. Forensics showed that each of the women had been stabbed at least twenty times with a pair of scissors. WNWO then did a follow-up story on Mr. Tanarive's phone call and the message of the 'triangle conspiracy.'

A murder/suicide. Tanarive had no record of violence. Neither he nor his family had any history of mental illness. All the physical evidence pointed to Tanarive. Investigators wrote off the case as a sudden, tragic, inexplicable onset of mental illness. The case had been closed until Murray's search for information related to 'triangles.'

Margaret's information, combined with the Tanarive case file, was all Murray needed to see. He'd taken the info to the director of the CIA, then called an emergency meeting with the president. Not a meeting with the pres- ident's chief of staff, not with the secretary of defense, but a quiet little sit-down with the head honcho himself. Murray brought Montoya along for good measure.

Her report proved quite convincing. The pictures really captured the president's attention: pictures of Gary Leeland's blue triangle growths; pictures of similar, rotting growths on Charlotte Wilson's corpse; pictures of Blaine Tanarive's oozing, pitted, skeletal body, covered with that eerie green fuzz.

The president gave Murray carte blanche, anything he wanted.

Murray had the power to draft whomever he needed, but he didn't want a big team, not yet. He had to keep things quiet, controllable. When the news of this hit the streets the panic would be legendary. More than likely the country would basically shut down; people wouldn't leave their homes for fear of catching the disease, and those who did leave would flood the hospitals with everything from diaper rashes to flea bites. And Murray knew that sooner or later the news *would* get out. He had to gather as much information as he could before the panic hit, because when it did, things were going to get very complicated.

Five cases to date—two more discovered after the presidential meeting. First, Judy Washington, age sixty-two, found one day after Gary Leeland had died, but obviously infected earlier. Dew and his partner found her pitted skeleton in a field outside the retirement community where both she and Leeland lived. Her infection had already run its course. And now the disaster that was Martin Brewbaker. Five cases in sixteen days, and he knew there were more the CIA had yet to uncover.

He suspected things were only going to get worse.

10

HALF AN AUTOPSY
IS BETTER THAN NONE

She hated herself for feeling this way, but she was thrilled at the chance to examine a fresh body. She was a doctor first, a healer; that had been her training, if not her true calling, and she held the sanctity of life in the highest regard. She knew she should feel upset over the new death, but excitement had washed over her the second that Murray ordered her to Toledo.

Margaret wasn't exactly *happy* at another death, of course not, but she had yet to see a body that wasn't ravaged by days of highly accelerated decomposition. Here she was, seemingly the sole defender against this bizarre affliction, and she'd had almost nothing to study, nothing to work with. To Margaret this wasn't just another body— the fifth so far—it was a chance to gain headway against a disease with the potential to make Ebola and AIDS look as insignificant as the common cold.

So much could change in such a short time. Sixteen days earlier she'd been an examiner for the Coordinating Center for Infectious Diseases' Cincinnati office. The CCID was a division of the Centers for Disease Control, or CDC. She was good at her job, she knew, but things hadn't been stellar career-wise. She wanted to move up the ladder, to gain prestige, but at the end of the day she had to admit to herself she just didn't like conflict brought on by office politics—she simply didn't have the balls.

Then she got the call to examine a body in Royal Oak, Michigan, a body suspected of containing an unknown infectious agent. When she saw the body, or what was left of it, she knew it was a chance to make a name for herself. Only seven days after examining that body, she had sat down at a meeting with CIA Deputy Director of Intelligence Murray Longworth, and—believe it or not, children—the president himself. She, Margaret Montoya, sitting down with the president to help decide policy.

And now, less than twenty-four hours after a second secretive meeting in the Oval Office, a CIA agent escorted her as if she were some head of state. She absently chewed on a Paper Mate pen, gazing out the passenger-side window as the black Lexus pulled in to the entrance of the Toledo Hospital.

Four remote television vans dotted the parking lot, all close to the front and emergency entrances.

'Dammit,' Margaret said. She felt her stomach do flip-flops. She didn't want to deal with the press.

The driver stopped the car, then turned to look at her. 'You want me to take you in the back way?' He was a stunningly handsome African-American youngster named Clarence Otto, assigned to her on a semipermanent basis. Murray Longworth had ordered Clarence to accompany her everywhere. Mostly to 'grease the wheels,' as Murray put it. Clarence took care of all the little things so Margaret could concentrate on her work.

It struck her as funny that Clarence Otto was a full-blown, gun-toting CIA agent, and yet he really didn't know what this was all about, while she, a midlevel epidemiologist for the CDC, was knee-deep in what might be the greatest threat ever to face the United States of America.

His looks distracted her, so she usually spoke to him while gazing in another direction. 'Yes, please . . . avoid the press and get me to the staging area as soon as possible. Every second counts.'

That was an understatement. In her twenty-year career, she'd examined more bodies for more diseases than she cared to remember. Once a body died the corpse conveniently waited for examination. Put it on ice and it will keep until you're ready to take a peek. But not with this crap—oh no not at all. Of the three bodies they'd actually recovered, two were already so decomposed as to be of little or no use. The other, which was the first body discovered, had literally dissolved before her eyes.

That was the first hint that something truly disturbing was afoot. Paramedics in Royal Oak, Michigan, had brought in the corpse of Charlotte Wilson, age seventy. Wilson had just murdered her fifty-one-year-old son with a butcher knife. She then attacked two cops on sight with said knife, screaming how she wouldn't let 'a bunch of Matlocks' take her alive. The police really had no choice, and killed her with a single shot. The paramedics reported strange growths on the woman's body, the likes of which they'd never observed or heard of. They had pronounced her dead on the scene, then called for the morgue to come pick up the body.

Ten hours later, during the autopsy, the strange growths prompted county health officials to call the CDC's Cincinnati office, which sent Margaret and a team. By the time she arrived six hours after that—sixteen hours after the woman had been shot and killed—the body was already in bad shape. In the course of the next twenty hours, the body disintegrated into a pile of pitted bones, thick mats of an unidentified gossamer green mold, and a puddle of black slime. Refrigerating didn't slow the decomposition. Neither did flat-out freezing. The factor that attacked the body was unknown and new, an efficient chemical reaction that seemed unstoppable. Margaret still didn't know how it worked.

Shortly after Wilson's disintegration, Margaret hit the computer databases scanning for the words *triangular growth*. She found the record of Gary Leeland, a fifty-seven-year-old man who went to the hospital complaining of triangular growths. Less than half a day after being admitted, Leeland killed himself by setting his hospital bed on fire. The pictures of Wilson, combined with the initial pictures doctors had taken of Leeland, were the reasons that Margaret was here.

Otto skirted the news vans and the bored-looking camera crews. The unmarked Lexus drew casual glances and nothing more. It pulled up near a back door, but a rogue reporter and a cameraman were waiting there as well.

'What has the press been told?' Margaret asked.

'SARS,' Otto said. 'It's the same story as with Judy Washington.'

Dew Phillips and Malcolm Johnson had found Judy Washington's decomposed body four days earlier in an abandoned lot near the Detroit retirement home where she lived. Her corpse had been the worst yet—nothing more than a pockmarked skeleton and an oily black stain on the ground. There wasn't a single shred of flesh left.

'Second case in eight days,' Margaret said. 'The press will think it's a full-blown SARS epidemic.'

SARS, or severe acute respiratory syndrome, had been

tagged by the media several times over as the next 'nightmare plague.' While the disease was potentially fatal, and had racked up a significant body count in China, it wasn't a major threat to a country with an efficient medical system like the United States. SARS was, however, a contagious, airborne disease, which explained the Racal suits and the quarantine. The bottom line on SARS? Enough of a danger to make people pay attention, but it really threatened only the elderly and Third World countries—and in America, that was never enough to create a panic.

She got out of the car. As a unit, the reporter and the cameraman pounced like a trapdoor spider, a spotlight flicking on and hitting her in the eyes as the microphone reached for her face. She flinched away, trying to figure out what to say, already almost ready to vomit. But as fast as they were, Clarence Otto was faster, covering the camera lens with one hand, grabbing the microphone with the other and using his body to shield Margaret long enough for her to reach the door. He moved with the fluid grace of a dancer and the speed of a striking snake.

'I'm sorry,' Otto said with his charming smile. 'No questions at this time.'

Margaret let the door slip shut behind her, cutting off the reporter's vehement protests. Clarence Otto could handle the media. He could probably handle a lot of things, some of which she didn't want to know about, and some of which she thought about each night she spent alone in a hotel bed. She suspected she could easily seduce him; even at forty-two, she knew her long, glossy-black hair and dark eyes were part of a look that attracted many men. She thought herself an attractive Hispanic woman— men who wanted her told her she was 'exotic.' Which was funny to her, because she was born in Cleveland. Sure, she had some extra baggage around the hips (and who the hell didn't at forty-two?), and the wrinkles were becoming a bit more prominent, but she knew damn well she could have just about any man she wanted. And she wanted Clarence.

She quickly shook her head, trying to clear her thoughts. When she got stressed, she got horny, as if her body knew the one surefire way to relieve mental tension. She was going to examine a corpse, for God's sake, and she needed to keep her hormones in check. Margaret breathed deeply, trying to control her stress level, which seemed to soar higher with each case.

Almost as soon as she entered the hospital, another CIA agent, this one a middle-aged man she'd never seen before, fell in at her side and escorted her through the empty halls. She figured this guy, like Clarence, knew little of the whole story. Murray wanted it that way—the fewer people who knew, the fewer places from which information could leak.

She entered the morgue, which housed the recently erected portable decontamination chambers. Amos Braun, her only help in this hunt for answers to a biological nightmare, was waiting for her.

'Good morning, Margaret.'

She always thought his voice made him sound like a frog. Or maybe a toad. A drunk toad, slow and growly and maybe with only half his lips working correctly. The beyond-skinny Amos was somewhat effeminate and always the snappy dresser, though about ten years out of style. Most people initially assumed he was gay. His wife and two children, however, provided some evidence to the contrary. He always looked to be an hour or two behind on his sleep, even though his energy never faded.

Amos had been with her in Royal Oak when they'd examined Charlotte Wilson, and every step of the way since. He was one of the best in the business, granted, but he was all she had. She'd asked Murray for more staff, told him she *needed* more staff, but he'd refused—he wanted to control the flow of information, limit the number of those in the know.

'I'm surprised you beat me here, Amos.'

'Some of us aren't off gallivanting around with the president, my dear. Becoming quite the celebrity, aren't you?'

'Oh shut up and let's get ready. We don't have a lot of time if this body is like the others.'

They stepped into two small dressing areas concealed by plastic dividers. Inside each area hung an orange Racal suit, designed to protect the wearer against all types of hostile agents. The suits always reminded her of hell, of burned human skin hanging like some satanic trophy.

First she removed her clothes and donned surgical scrubs. She slid into the Racal suit, which was made of flexible Tyvek synthetic fabric, impermeable to air, chemicals or virus particles. The ankles, wrists and neck had intricate metallic rings. With the suit on, she stepped into special boots that had a metallic ring matching the ones on the suit legs. She snapped the rings together with a satisfying springy click, signifying an airtight seal. She then wrapped the seam with brown sticky tape, further sealing off her feet against possible contamination. She did the same with the thick Tyvek gloves, taping herself off at the wrist. Tape was overkill, particularly with the state-of-the-art Racal suit, but after seeing what this mysterious condition did to victims, she wanted all the precautions she could get. Margaret loosely wrapped several layers of tape around her arm; if she accidentally cut the suit, she could plug the leak as fast as possible.

They didn't understand how the infection spread. Other than shared symptoms, there seemed to be no connection between the five known victims. It might be spread by contact via some unidentified human carrier; via airborne transmission (although that seemed very unlikely based on the fact that no one exposed to the victims contracted the infection); via common vehicle transmission, which applied to contaminated items such as food, water or any medication; or via vectorborne transmission, the name given to transmission from mosquitoes, flies, rats or any other vermin. Her current theory was far more disturbing: that it was being intentionally spread to specific targets. Any way she sliced it, however, until she knew the transmission mode for certain, she wasn't taking any chances.

When Margaret came out from behind the curtain, Amos was already waiting for her. In the bulky suit with no helmet, he looked particularly odd—the suit's helmet ring made his thin neck look positively anorexic.

She'd had to argue with Murray Longworth to keep Amos. Murray actually thought she could figure out a completely unknown biological phenomenon all by herself. She needed a full team of experts, but Murray wouldn't hear of it.

She needed Amos's expertise in biochemistry and parasitology. She knew the former discipline was vital for analyzing the victims' bizarre behavioral changes, and she had a nagging feeling the latter would be increasingly significant. He was a smart-ass, but he was also brilliant, insightful and seemed to require little or no sleep. She was desperately grateful to have him.

Amos helped her with the bulky helmet, locking the

ring to create the seal around her neck. The faceplate instantly fogged up. He wrapped her neck seal with the sticky tape, then started the air filter/compressor attached to the suit's waist. She felt a hiss of fresh air; the Racal suit billowed up slightly. The positive pressure meant that in case of a leak, air would flow out of the suit, not in, theoretically keeping any transmission vectors away from her body.

She helped Amos with his helmet.

'Can you hear me?' she asked. Her voice sounded oddly confined inside her helmet, but a built-in microphone transmitted the sound to a small speaker mounted on the helmet's chin. External microphones picked up ambient sound and transmitted it to tiny built-in speakers, giving the suit's wearer relatively normal hearing.

'Sounds fine,' Amos said. His froggish voice came through somewhat tinny and artificial, but she understood his words clearly.

The hospital didn't have an airtight room. Murray had provided a portable one, a top-secret Biohazard Safety Level 4 lab. Margaret hadn't even known such a thing existed until Murray acquired it from the U.S. Army Medical Research Institute for Infectious Diseases, or USAMRIID. USAMRIID probably should have been the ones studying Brewbaker and the others, but since Margaret already knew, she got to run with the ball. Biohazard safety levels ran from one through four, with BSL-4 being as bad as it got.

The portable BSL-4 lab was small, designed to fit inside existing structures. Its flexible walls were set up within those of the morgue, almost as if kids had set up a large white, plastic tent in their parents' basement. She knew exactly what she'd see in the small space, as she'd left very specific instructions for Murray. She'd find a stainless-steel morgue table with a full drainage system to capture Brewbaker's liquefying body, a computer for sending and receiving information on a completely closed network, and a prep table with all the equipment she'd need, including a stack of BSL-4 sample containers that could be completely immersed in decontaminant solvent in the airlock, then shipped off to other BSL-4 labs for analysis.

Margaret and Amos entered the airtight room through the flexible airlock.

Inside, Dew Phillips was waiting—and he wasn't wearing a biosuit. He stood next to the charred body laid out on the steel table. It was horribly burned, especially around what was left of the legs.

Margaret felt anger wash over her; this man could be contaminating her lab, impeding any work she might accomplish now that she had an actual body and not a disintegrating pile of rotting black flesh. 'Agent Phillips, what are you doing in here without a biosuit?'

He just stared at her. He pulled a Tootsie Roll from his pocket, unwrapped it slowly, popped the candy into his mouth, and then dropped the wrapper on the floor. 'Nice to see you, too, Doc.'

Dew's deep green eyes resembled the color of dark emeralds. His skin was pale, his face stubbled and haggard, his suit wrinkled beyond all repair. His mottled scalp shone under the harsh lab lights. Age hadn't affected his body, not much—it looked rock solid under the wrecked suit.

'Answer my question,' Margaret demanded, her voice mechanized by the suit's small speaker. She hadn't liked him from the start, hadn't liked his cold demeanor, and this incident wasn't helping change her opinion at all.

Dew chewed for a moment, cold eyes staring into

Margaret's. 'I got up close and personal with this guy. If he's contagious, I've got it, so what's the point in putting on a human condom?'

She walked up to the table and examined the body. The fire had briefly touched the head, burning away all hair and leaving a scalp dotted with small blisters. A twisted expression of wide-eyed rage etched the corpse's face. Margaret suppressed a shiver, first at the very picture of lunacy on the table before her, then at Dew Phillips, who had looked straight into this horrid expression and pulled the trigger three times.

The arms and legs were the worst, burned to blackened cinders in places. Where the skin remained, it was the leathery greenish black of third-degree burns. The left hand was nothing more than a skeletal talon covered with chunks of cindered flesh. The right hand was in better shape, almost free of burns, an oddly white area at the end of a shriveled, carbonized arm. Both legs were gone below the knee.

The corpse's genitals were badly burned. Second-degree burns covered the abdomen and lower torso. Three large bullet wounds marked the chest, two within inches of the heart and one directly over it. Smears of blood were now bone dry, flaking away, leaving whiter spots on the scorched skin.

'What happened to his legs?'

'He cut them off,' Dew said. 'With a hatchet.'

'What do you mean, he cut them off? He cut off his own legs?'

'Right before he set himself on fire. With gasoline. My partner tried to put him out, and got a hatchet in the belly for his troubles.'

'Jesus,' Amos said. 'He chopped off his own legs and burned himself?'

'That's right,' Dew said. 'But those nice bullet holes in his chest, those are mine.'

Margaret stared at the corpse, then back up at Dew. 'So . . . does he have any?'

Dew reached down and turned the corpse over. For some reason it surprised her to see he wore surgical gloves. He flipped the body over with minimal effort—Martin Brewbaker hadn't been a big man, and much of his weight had been consumed by fire.

The wounds were much worse on Brewbaker's back, fist-size holes ripped open by the .45-caliber bullets, but that wasn't what caught Margaret's attention. She unconsciously held her breath—there, just left of the spine and just below the scapula, sat a triangular growth. It was the first growth she'd seen live, and not as a picture, since her examination of Charlotte Wilson. One of the bullet wounds had ripped free a small chunk of the growth. Flames had caused even more damage, but at least it was something to work with.

Amos leaned forward. 'Are there any more?'

'I thought I saw some on his forearms, but I'm not sure,' Dew said.

'Not sure?' Margaret stood. 'How can you not be sure? I mean, either you saw them or you didn't.' She noticed Amos wince behind his faceplate, but it was too late.

Dew stared at her, anger visibly whirling behind his dead eyes. 'Sorry, Doc, I was busy looking at the *fucking hatchet* the bastard was burying in my *partner's* stomach.' His voice was slow, cold and threatening. 'I know I've only been doing this shit for *thirty years,* but next time I'll pay better attention.'

She suddenly felt very small—one look at the body and she'd forgotten all about Dew's partner laid up in critical condition. *Jesus, Margaret,* she thought, *were you born an insufferable bitch or did you have to work at it?*

'Dew . . . I'm sorry about . . . about . . .' The name of Dew's partner escaped her.

'Malcolm Johnson,' Dew said. 'Agent, husband, father.'

Margaret nodded. 'Right, of course, Agent Johnson. Well . . . I'm sorry.'

'Save it for the medical journals, Doc. I realize I'm supposed to answer your questions, but you know, all of a sudden I don't feel so swell. Something about the smell in here is making me sick.'

Dew turned and headed for the door.

'But Dew, I need to hear how it went down! I need all the information I can get.'

'Read my report,' Dew said over his shoulder.

'Please, wait—'

He slipped out through the airlock and was gone.

Amos went to the prep table. Among other instruments, the prep team had left them with a digital camera. Amos picked it up and started circling the body, taking picture after picture.

'Margaret, why do you let him walk all over you like that?'

She turned on Amos, her face flushing with anger. 'I sure didn't see you standing up to him.'

'That's because I'm a pussy,' Amos said. He snapped another picture. 'I'm also not in charge of this shebang—you are.'

'Shut up, Amos.' In truth, she was happy to see Dew leave. The man had an aura about him, a sense that he was not only a death dealer, but one waiting impatiently for his own demise as well. Dew Phillips gave her the willies.

She turned back to the body and gently, ever so gently, poked the triangular growth. It felt squishy underneath the burned skin. A tiny jet of black ooze bubbled up from one of the triangle's points.

Margaret sighed. 'Let's get rocking. Excise samples of the growth, and let's send them out for analysis right away—the body has already started rotting, and we don't have a lot of time.'

She picked up Dew's Tootsie Roll wrapper, dropped it in a medical waste bin, cracked her knuckles through the large gloves, then got to work.

11

RUMBLIN', STUMBLIN', BUMBLIN'

'That was a bullshit call!' Perry's booming voice joined the fused protests of the other bar patrons. 'There's no way that's interference!'

While hooting and hollering football fans packed the bar, there was a noticeable space around Perry and Bill's table. The narrow-eyed scowl etched on Perry's face was the same one he had unconsciously worn on the football field. The other patrons cast frequent, discreet glances his way, keeping an eye on his huge, tense form as if he were some predator that might snap at any moment.

The ten-foot projection TV screens of Scorekeeper's Bar & Grill blazed San Francisco's crimson jerseys and gold helmets along with Green Bay's tradition-rich green and yellow. The slow-motion replay showed a perfect spiral descending toward a Packers receiver, then the 49ers defensive back reaching up and swatting the ball away.

Perry screamed at the TV. 'You see that?' He turned to stare in disbelieving anger at Bill, who sat calmly sipping from a Budweiser bottle. 'You see that?'

'Seemed like a good call to me,' Bill said. 'No bout-a-doubt-it. It was practically rape when you look at it.'

Perry howled in protest, beer spilling from his mug as his hands moved in accordance with his speech. 'Oh, you're crazy! The defender has a right to go for the ball. Now the Packers have a first-and-ten on the friggin' fifteen-yard line.'

'Try to keep some of that beer in the mug, will you?' Bill said, taking another sip from his bottle.

Perry wiped up the spilled beer with a napkin. 'Sorry. I just get pissed when the refs decide who's supposed to win and don't just let them play.'

'It is a cruel and unjust existence, my friend,' Bill said. 'We cannot escape the inequities of life, even in the sporting world.'

Perry set his mug on the table, his eyes focused on the screen, his right hand casually scratching his left forearm. A corner blitz swept around the left offensive end, crushing the Green Bay quarterback for a seven-yard loss.

Perry shook his clenched fist at the screen. 'Take *that*, baby. Man, I love to see that. I hate quarterbacks. Friggin' nancy-boys. It's good to see someone put a snot-bubbler on the QB.'

Bill looked away and put up a hand as if to say, 'Enough.' Perry smiled and drained the rest of his beer in one long pull, then scratched at his thigh.

'Beer make you break out in hives or something?' Bill said.

'What?'

'Your fleas again. You're on your fifth beer, and with each one you scratch a little more.'

'Oh,' Perry said. 'It's no big deal. It's just a bug bite.'

'I'm starting to wonder if we should be sitting in the same booth—I wouldn't want to catch lice.'

'You're a regular comedian.' Perry signaled to the waitress. 'You want another?'

'No thanks,' Bill said. 'I'm driving home after this.

You better slow down, cowboy—you're getting a little excitable.'

'Aw, Bill, I'm fine.'

'Good, and we're going to keep it that way. You know how you get if you've had too much to drink. You're done for the night.'

Annoyance flared at the command, and Perry's eyes narrowed. Who the hell was Bill to tell him what to do?

'Excuse me?' Perry said. Without thinking, he leaned toward Bill, lip curling into a small sneer.

Bill's face showed no change. 'You know when you scowl like that you look just like your father?'

Perry flinched as if he'd been slapped. He sat back, then hung his head. He felt his face flush all hot and red with embarrassment. He pushed the beer mug away.

'I'm sorry,' Perry said. He looked up with pleading eyes. 'Bill, I'm really sorry.'

Bill smiled reassuringly. 'Don't sweat it, buddy. You're under control. It's okay.'

'No, it's not okay. I can't talk to people like that—you especially.'

Bill leaned forward, his tone soft and supportive. 'Give yourself a break, Perry. You haven't had an incident in years.'

Perry stared off into space. 'I still worry. I might slip up, you know? Not be paying attention, smack the shit out of someone before I realize what I'm doing. Something like that.'

'But you *haven't* smacked anyone. Not for a long time, man. Just relax. Your sob story is bringing tears to my manly eyes.' Bill's smile showed his understanding.

Perry thanked the powers that be, and not for the first time, that he had a friend in Bill Miller. Without Bill, Perry knew he'd probably be in jail somewhere.

Bill put his hand on Perry's arm. 'Perry, you gotta give yourself some credit. You're *nothing* like your father. You've left all that behind. You just have to be careful, that's all— your temper is fucked up, man, just stay on point. Now can we stop with all this sissy-boy simpering and watch some football? The time-out is over. What do you think the Pack will do here?'

Perry looked up at the screen. He let go of the small incident, let go of memories of his father's endless violence. It was always easy to lose himself in football.

'I'll bet they go off-tackle on this one. They'll try to catch the 'Niners sleeping, but they haven't been able to block the inside linebacker all day. He's creeping up right on the snap—he better watch his ass or they'll go play-action and throw behind him when he comes barreling in.'

Bill's reassuring touch had started Perry's arm itching again. He dug at it absently as he watched the Packers running back go off-tackle for two yards before the inside linebacker drilled him.

Bill took a swig of beer and stared at Perry's arm. 'You know, I understand that your protruding brow is indicative of a certain caveman mentality, but maybe you should set aside your negative feelings toward the medical profession and see a doctor.'

'Doctors are a rip-off. It's all a big racket.'

'Yes, and I'll bet you saw Elvis last night and there's some great alien hookers at the trailer park down the road. You've got a college degree, for God's sake, and you still think doctors are medicine men who bleed you with razors and use leeches to suck away the bad spirits.'

'I don't like doctors,' Perry said. 'I don't like them, and I don't trust them.'

On the screen, the Packers QB took the snap and faked

a handoff. The inside linebacker took a step forward, and as soon as he did, Perry saw the opening in the middle. The QB saw it too—he stood tall in the pocket, the picture of poise, and rifled the ball into the end zone just a few yards behind the linebacker. The receiver hauled it in with a diving catch, giving the Packers a 22–20 lead with only fourteen seconds left in the game.

'Fuck,' Perry said. 'I fucking hate quarterbacks.' He felt that gnawing jealousy inside, the one that always came when he watched someone blow a play he himself would have easily made. It was so hard to watch the weekly NFL battles, knowing damn well that's where he belonged, knowing damn well he wouldn't have just been competitive, but dominant. He silently cursed the injury that had ended his career.

'First the Lions, now the 'Niners, and you still haven't figured out the problem in Pullman,' Bill said. 'Looks like this just isn't your week.'

'Yeah,' Perry said as he scratched his forearm. His voice sounded resigned. 'You can say that again.'

12
CLUES

Margaret arched her back and took a deep breath, trying to calm her nerves, the Racal suit encumbering her every movement. Her hands shook, only slightly, but it was enough to disturb her control of the laparoscope.

The laparoscope, a surgical tool used for operations in the abdominal cavity, consisted of a sensitive fiber-optic camera and an attachment for various probes, scalpels, drills and other devices. The camera, complete with its own light, was barely larger than a piece of thread. The rig included a big monitor on a video tower. Surgeons utilized the equipment to perform delicate operations without cutting into the patient via traditional means.

Few people used such equipment for autopsies, but Margaret wanted to examine the area surrounding the growth while disturbing it as little as possible. Her strategy seemed to have paid off.

Just as in her examination of Charlotte Wilson's corpse, the growths had already rotted into a liquefied black pulp. There was nothing in the growth itself she could examine. The surrounding tissues were decomposing at a frighteningly fast pace, but this time she was ready. Using the laparoscope, she'd probed the area in and around the growth. Deep inside, almost to the bone and in the midst of rotting black flesh, she'd found a piece of matter that clearly didn't belong to the victim.

She cracked her knuckles one at a time. The bones popped silently, muffled by the Racal suit. She drew another breath, then took the camera's control with her left hand. The monitor showed the growth's blackened, decaying interior. She knew the rot would soon spread to other parts of the body, dissolving it into a useless pile of putrefaction in a few scant hours. Every second counted.

Her hands grew steady; they had to be for such delicate work. The piece of material, barely a quarter inch across, looked to be part of the growth. It was black, the same color as the decomposed gore around it, but reflected the light almost like plastic. That reflective quality was the only reason she'd spotted it.

Her left hand maneuvered the camera, pushing it closer to the black piece. Her right hand controlled a trocar, a hollow tube through which specialized surgical instruments could access a patient's body cavities without cutting him or her open. Her trocar carried a tiny pair of pincers. Like a kid with a hundred-thousand-dollar video game, she moved the pincers closer to the black plastic fleck. Her finger rested on a trigger that, when pressed, would close the pincers.

Margaret tweaked the camera controls. The image, slightly distorted from high magnification, focused in on the mysterious shiny fleck. The pincers looked like metallic monster claws about to pluck a lone swimmer from a sea of black.

She gently squeezed the trigger. The pincers gripped firmly on the strange material, squishing out thick bubbles of rancid goo as they closed.

'Nice job,' Amos said. 'First try. Give the lady a cee-gar.'

She smiled and pulled back on the pincers. The material resisted the pull. She looked closely at the monitor, then gently moved the pincers from side to side, wiggling the clamped object. The reason for the resistance became clear—the object appeared to be embedded in a rib. She pulled back gently, slowly increasing the pressure. The object bent slightly, then popped free. They heard a wet squelch as the tiny pincers—smeared with black slime—pulled free from the wound.

Amos held a petri dish under the pincers. Margaret released the trigger, but the little fleck clung to the goop on the bottom pincer. He grabbed a scalpel, then gently used the point to push the object into the petri dish.

She took the dish and held it close to her faceplate. The fleck had a shape to it, and she could see why it had stayed so firmly planted in the bone. It looked just like a black rose thorn.

She felt a rush of satisfaction. They were still a hundred miles from figuring out the key to this horrific puzzle, but thanks to Charlotte Wilson she knew better what to look for and how much time she had to work with. The black fleck was something new, and it brought them one step closer to an answer.

'Hey,' Amos said, 'what do you make of this?' He stood next to Brewbaker's hip, one of the places least damaged from the flames. His finger rested beside a small lesion, sort of like a gnarled zit.

A gnarled zit with a tiny blue fiber sticking out of it.

'So he had some acne,' Margaret said. 'Do you think it's significant?'

'I think everything is significant. Should we excise it and send it out?'

She thought for a moment. 'Not yet. It doesn't look

like there's any decomposition on that spot, and I want to examine it for myself. Let's focus on the areas that are rotting, as we know we won't have much longer to work with those, then come back to it, okay?'

'Sounds good,' Amos said. He grabbed the camera from the prep table. He leaned in close to the zit, snapped a picture, then put the camera back on the prep table. 'Right, we'll come back to it.'

'How much longer until we get the results from the tissue analysis of the growth?'

'We'll have info tomorrow. I'm sure they're working through the night. DNA analysis, protein sequencing and anything else that might pop up.'

She checked her watch—10:07 P.M. She and Amos would also be up all night and well into the next day. Had to be. They knew from hard-earned experience that they had only a few days before Brewbaker's body rotted away.

13

TWO-FER TUESDAY

'Good God, Perry,' Bill said. 'Two days in a row. I've seen flea-ridden dogs scratch like that, but never a human.' Bill, half hung over the cubicle wall, looked down at a madly scratching Perry.

'Of course, I'm *assuming* you're human,' Bill added. 'Scientists still debate that one.'

Perry ignored the mild gibe, concentrating instead on his left forearm. He'd pushed the sleeve of his ratty Detroit Lions sweatshirt up past his elbow. His right hand looked a blur as he raked the hairy forearm with his fingernails.

'I hear scabies is nasty this time of year,' Bill said.

'Damn thing itches like all get-out.' Perry stopped for a moment to stare at the welt. Its texture resembled a small strawberry—if strawberries were yellow and oozed tiny drops of clear fluid. The yellowish welt felt solid, as if a piece of cartilage had broken free from somewhere in his body and lodged in his arm. His arm, and six other places.

The digging nails left long, angry-red scratches. The scratches surrounded the welt like egg white around an overcooked yolk.

'Gee, that looks healthy,' Bill said, then slipped back into his cube.

'It's no big deal.' Perry turned his attention to his screen, which displayed a computer network diagram. He absently reached up and brushed a lock of straight, heavy blond hair out of his eyes.

StickyFingazWhitey: Dude, seriously . . . nasty.
Bleedmaize_n_blue: It's no big deal, mind yer own.
StickyFingazWhitey: God forbid you just go buy some— oh, dare I speak the word that should never be spoken— MEDICINE?

Perry tried to ignore Bill's sarcasm. As if the wonderful rashes weren't enough of a distraction. Perry had been working on the Pullman problem, the same one he hadn't solved the day before, for more than an hour. At least he *tried* to work. The rashes made it difficult to concentrate on customer support.

'Quit being such a macho stud-boy and go buy some Cortaid.' Bill hung over the gray cubicle wall like a puppy trying to decipher a new and unusual sound. 'You don't have to go to Mr. Evil Witchdoctor, for God's sake, just buy something to help that itch. A disinfectant wouldn't hurt either, by the looks of things. I'll never understand why you like to sit in pain rather than partake in the wonders of a modern society.'

'Your doctors couldn't do anything for my right knee, now could they?'

'I was at the game, Perry, remember? I saw your knee when I visited you at the hospital. Jesus H. Christ couldn't have brought that knee back from the dead.'

'Maybe I'm just a Cro-Magnon, that's all.' Perry fought the urge to scratch again. The rash on his right ass cheek demanded attention. 'We still hitting the bar tonight?'

'I don't think so, contagion-boy. I prefer the company

of at least semi-healthy people. You know, those with rubella or smallpox? Perhaps a bit of the Black Death? I'd rather associate with them than deal with scabies.'

'It's just a rash, asshole.' Perry felt anger slowly swell up in his chest. He immediately fought it down. Bill Miller seemingly lived to irritate people, and once he got rolling he didn't quit. It would be 'scabies this' and 'scabies that' for the rest of the week—and it was only Tuesday. But they were just words, and good-natured words at that. Perry calmed himself. He'd already let his temper slip once this week—he'd be damned if he'd insult Bill like that again.

Perry moved his mouse and clicked, magnifying a section of the network schematic. 'Leave me alone, will ya? Sandy wants this thing fixed right away. The Pullman people are going apeshit.'

Bill slid back into his cube. Perry stared at the screen, trying to solve a problem taking place more than a thousand miles away in the state of Washington. Analyzing computer glitches over the phone wasn't an easy job, especially with network difficulties where the problem could be a wire in the ceiling, a bad port, or a single defective component on any of 112 workstations. Many times in customer support, he faced problems that would have chewed up Agatha Christie, Columbo and Sherlock Holmes in one big swallow. This was one such problem.

The answer danced at the edges of his mind, but he couldn't focus. He leaned back into his chair, which set the itch on his spine afire with maddening intensity. It was like a thousand mosquito bites all rolled into one.

Perry's train of thought dissolved completely as he ground his back into the office chair, letting the rough cloth dig through his sweatshirt. He grimaced as the welts on his leg flared up with itching so sudden and so bad that he might as well have been stung by a wasp. He attacked the leg welts, clawing his nails through blue-jean denim. It was like trying to fight a Hydra—each time he stopped one biting head, two more flared up to take its place.

From the next cube, he heard Bill's poor impression of a Shakespearean actor.

'To scabies, or not to scabies,' Bill said, his voice only slightly muffled by the divider. 'That is the infection.'

Perry gritted his teeth and bit back an angry reply. The welts were driving him nuts, making him easily irritated by little things. Still, although Bill was his friend, sometimes the guy didn't know when to quit.

14

DIRTY FINGERNAILS

Margaret stared into the microscope's eyepiece, trying to focus on the magnified image. Her eyes were red from lack of sleep. She couldn't rub them, thanks to the plastic faceplate and the cumbersome biosuit. She blinked a few times to clear her vision. How long had she been working on Brewbaker? Twenty-four hours and counting, and no end in sight. She bent and stared into the microscope.

'Hmm, what have we here?' The sample's meaning seemed rather obvious, but her fatigue and the horrid condition of the victim's skin made her unsure. 'Amos, come over here and look at this.'

He put down his chemical samples and moved toward the microscope. Like Margaret, he hadn't slept in more than a day. Even with the lack of sleep and the awkward Racal suit, however, he moved with a smooth grace that made him look as if he floated rather than walked. He bent into the eyepiece without touching anything.

After a moment he asked, 'What am I looking for?'

'I was hoping you'd see it right away.'

'I see a lot of things, Margaret,' Amos said. 'Perhaps you could be a little more specific. Where is this skin sample from?'

'The area just outside the growth. See anything that

would indicate moderate skin trauma?' Amos half rose to answer, but Margaret cut him off. 'And don't give me one of your smart-ass answers, please. I know damn well the whole body is ripped to shreds.'

Amos bent back to the eyepiece. He stared for a few seconds, silence filling the sterile morgue. 'Yes, I see it. I see some scabbing and some damage down past the subcutaneous layer. It looks like a long groove—like a claw wound, perhaps.'

Margaret nodded. 'I think I'll take another look at those skin samples we got from under the victim's fingernails.'

Amos stood straight and looked at her. 'You don't think he did this to himself, do you? This tear is all the way to the muscle, and it looks like repetitive damage. Do you know how much that would hurt?'

'I can take a guess.' Margaret stretched her arms high, bent to the left, then to the right. She was sick of the lab and sick of the limited sleep. She wanted a real bed, not a cot, and a real bottle of wine to go with it. As long as she was dreaming, she might as well throw in Agent Clarence Otto in a pair of silk boxers.

She sighed. Agent Otto would have to wait for another day. Right now she had other things to worry about, like what could make a man use his fingernails like claws to tear into his own body?

The computer terminal let out a long beep: information had arrived. Amos shuffled over and sat down.

'This is odd,' he said. 'Most odd indeed.'

'Give me the Cliffs Notes version.'

'Results on the excised growth, for starters. They said their sample had almost completely liquefied by the time they got it. They did what they could, though. The tissue was cancerous.'

'What do they mean, it was cancerous? We saw it. It wasn't a mass of uncontrolled cells—it had structure.'

'I agree, but look at these results—cancerous tissue. That, plus massive amounts of cellulase and trace amounts of cellulose.'

Margaret thought on that for a moment. Cellulose was the primary material in plant cells, the most abundant form of biomass on the planet. But the key word there was *plants* —animals didn't make cellulose.

'The cellulose didn't last, either,' Amos said. 'Within hours of reception of material, cellulose decomposed into cellulase. They did everything they could to stop it, including attempts to freeze the material, but it didn't freeze.'

'Just like the enzyme that's decomposing the flesh. It's like a . . . self-destruct mechanism.'

'Suicidal cancer? That's a bit of a reach, Margaret.'

It *was* a reach. A big one. And yet maybe she needed to reach; reach for something that was beyond accepted science.

15

ONE MAN'S HOME . . .

Coming home to apartment B-203 always generated mixed feelings. The place wasn't much, one meaningless apartment in a massive cluster of identical buildings. Windywood was the kind of complex where even flawless directions would have people guessing; there were enough buildings to necessitate a little network of roads with smarmy names like Evergreen Drive, Shady Lane and Poplar Street. After one or two wrong turns, the plain-looking, three-story, twelve-unit complexes were all you could see.

His building was only two down from the complex entrance, right across the street from the Washtenaw Party Store. Made things quite convenient. Meijer's grocery store was only a couple of miles away; he hit that for the big grocery runs. For everything else the party store did the trick. It was a low-rent part of town, and the party store wasn't exactly a high-class operation—there was always some welfare reject on the pay phone just outside the door, working a 'deal' or having a far-too-loud argument with a significant other.

Perry didn't have jack squat to eat at home. The party store had a great little deli, so he stopped for a ham sandwich with Texas mustard, and grabbed a six-pack of Newcastle beer. Sure enough, some chick was screaming into the phone. She held the receiver in one hand, a well-bundled baby in the other. Perry tried to ignore her as he walked in and tried to ignore her again as he walked out, but the girl was *loud*. He didn't feel any sympathy for her—if he could rise above his background and upbringing, anyone could. People who lived that way *wanted* to live that way.

He pulled into the apartment complex and into his carport, which was less than an eighth of a mile from the entrance. The girl bothered him—if he'd made it to the NFL, he'd live in a big house somewhere, far from the rabble of Ypsilanti. He couldn't shake the feeling that he was a failure. He should have more than this. The apartment was nice in its way, and he hated to feel ungrateful for the things that he had, but there was no denying the place was low-rent.

Seven years ago no one thought he'd wind up in anything less than a mansion. 'Scary' Perry Dawsey, then a sophomore at the University of Michigan, had been named All–Big Ten linebacker along with senior Cory Crypewicz of Ohio State. Crypewicz went in the first round to Chicago. He pulled down $2.1 million a year, not counting the $12 million signing bonus. It was a far cry from Perry's meager tech-support salary.

But Crypewicz hadn't been as good as Perry, and all the country knew it. Perry had been a monster, the kind of defensive player who could dominate a game with his sheer ferocity. The press had tagged him with several nicknames, 'Beast,' 'Cro-Mag' and 'Fang' among them. Of course, ESPN's Chris Berman always seemed to have the last word on nicknames, and the first time he used the 'Scary' tag, it stuck.

My, but how a cheap-ass cut block could change things.

The knee injury had been awful, a complete blowout damaging the ACL, the medial collateral, every frigging ligament in the area. It even caused bone damage, fracturing the fibula and chipping his patella. A year's worth of reconstructive surgeries and rehabilitation didn't bring him back to full speed. The fact was, he just couldn't cut it anymore. Where he'd once raged across the football field, inflicting his savage authority on anyone foolish enough to cross his path, now he could do little better than hobble along, chasing running backs he could never catch, taking hits from blockers he could never avoid.

Without the release provided by football's physical play, Perry's violent streak threatened to eat him up from the inside. Thank God for Bill, who'd helped him adjust. Bill had been there for the next two years, acting as Perry's conscience, making him aware of his ever-present temper.

Perry yanked up the Ford's parking brake and hopped out. He was Michigan born and bred, and he loved the cold months, but winter made the complex look desolate, barren and hopeless. Everything seemed pale-gray and lifeless, as if some fairy-tale force had sucked the color from the landscape.

He put his hand in his pocket. The crinkly white Walgreens bag was still there. The itching was just too intense. He'd stopped at a drugstore just a few blocks from his apartment complex and bought a tube of Cortaid. It was silly to feel like he'd given in, like he was weak just for buying a tube of anti-itch medicine, but he felt that way regardless.

He wondered what priceless piece of wisdom his father would have regarding the medicine. Probably something along the lines of, *You can't tough it out from a rash? Jee-zus, boy, you piss me off. Somebody's going to have to teach you some discipline.* He'd have followed up that comment with the belt, or a backhand, or his fist.

Dear ol' Dad. Humanitarian and all-around great guy. Perry shook the thoughts away. Dad was long dead, the victim of well-deserved cancer. Perry didn't need to concern himself with that man anymore.

Sliding over the parking-lot snow, that thin film no shovel could seem to finish off, he reached the apartment building's dented green front door and keyed in. He grabbed his mail, mostly junk mail and coupons, then trudged up the two flights to his apartment. Walking up the steps dragged his jeans against the welts on his leg, amplifying the itching— it was as if someone had jammed a burning coal in his skin. He forced himself to ignore it, to show at least a modicum of discipline, as he unlocked the door to his apartment.

The layout was simple: facing out the door to the hall, the kitchen nook was to the left and the living room was to the right. Just past the kitchen nook was the 'dining area.' The spot was tiny to begin with; cluttered by both the computer desk that held his Macintosh and a small round table with four chairs, the place had barely enough room to maneuver.

The living room was decent-size, comfortable and sparsely furnished with his big old couch, in front of which sat a hand-me-down coffee table. An end table with a lamp tucked up against the couch. A small recliner—too small for Perry's body—was the habitual territory for Bill on football Sundays. Directly across from the couch and to the right of the door was the entertainment center with a thirty-two-inch flat-screen and a Panasonic stereo system, the only expensive items Perry owned. No need for a landline phone: work provided his cell, and cable modem provided his Internet connection.

There were no plants and few decorations. On the wall above the entertainment center, however, were Perry's numerous football accolades. A shelf held trophies for high-school MVP awards and his treasured Gator Bowl MVP trophy from his freshman year. Plaques dotted the walls: Big Ten Defensive Player of the Year, *Detroit Free Press* Mr. Football award from his senior year in high school, a dozen others.

Two items hung side by side, obviously commanding a place of honor among the awards. The first was something he'd been stunned to see, even when he knew it was coming, something that had marked a turning point in his life: his acceptance letter from the University of Michigan. The other item he both loved and hated: his snarling, sweat-streaked, helmet-clad face on the cover of *Sports Illustrated*. In the picture he was tackling Ohio State's Jervis McClatchy, who was completely wrapped up in Perry's bulging, dirt- and grass-covered arms. The cover read, 'So good it's *SCARY*: Perry Dawsey and the Wolverine D lead Michigan to the Rose Bowl.'

He loved the cover for obvious reasons—what athlete *doesn't* dream of making the cover of *SI*? He hated it because, like many football players, he was superstitious. The cover of *SI* was suspected by many to carry a curse. If you're an unbeatable team and you make the cover, you're going to lose the next game. Or, if you're the best linebacker in a decade and you make the cover, your career will soon be over. Part of him couldn't shake the stupid feeling that if he hadn't made that cover, he'd still be playing football.

The place was small and admittedly a bit ghetto, but it was a veritable luxury condo compared to his childhood home. He treasured his privacy. It was a little lonely at times, but he could also do anything he wanted anytime he wanted. No one to track his schedule, no one to care if he brought home some girl he met at the bar, no one to bitch if he left his dirty socks on the kitchen table. No one to scream at him for reasons unknown. Sure, it wasn't the mansion he should have had, it wasn't the abode of an NFL star, but it was *his*.

At least he'd found a job in Ann Arbor, home of his alma mater. He'd fallen in love with the town during college. Hailing from a small town like Cheboygan, he distrusted cities, felt uncomfortable in some sprawling metropolis like Chicago or New York. At the same time, however, he was the proverbial farm boy who'd seen the bright lights of the bigger world, and he couldn't go back to small-town life, which seemed devoid of culture and fun by comparison. Ann Arbor was a college town of 110,000 that retained a cozy, small-town warmth, giving him the best of both worlds.

He tossed his keys and cell phone onto the kitchen table, threw his briefcase and heavy coat on the beat-up old couch, pulled the Walgreens bag from his pocket and headed for the bathroom. The rashes felt like seven searing electrodes grafted to his skin and connected to a ten-thousand-watt current.

He'd deal with the rashes, but first thing first—that zit-thing above his eyebrow had to go. He set the bag down, opened the medicine cabinet and pulled out tweezers. He gave them a habitual flick, hearing them hum like a tuning fork, then leaned into the mirror. The weird zit-thing was still there, of course, and it still hurt. He'd seen Bill pop a zit once: the process took like twenty minutes. Bill was methodical and a bit of a pussy, so that was fine. Perry had a higher tolerance for pain and a lower tolerance for patience. He took one deep breath, fixed the tweezers on the small, gnarled red bump and *yanked*. The chunk tore free—the pain came hot and sweet. Blood trickled down his face. He took another deep breath as he grabbed a wad of toilet paper and pressed it to the new wound. He held up the tweezers with his free hand. Just a small dot of flesh. But in the middle there, was that a hair? It wasn't black at all, it was *blue*, a deep, dark, iridescent blue.

'Friggin' weird.' He ran the tweezers under hot water, washing away the odd zit. He grabbed the Band-Aids from the cabinet: only six left. He ripped the paper off one and put it over the small, bloody spot where the zit-thing had just been. That had been the easy part—any pansy could deal with pain. But *itching*, that was a different story.

Perry dropped his pants and plopped down on the toilet. He pulled the Cortaid from the white bag. Squirting a healthy portion into his hand, he plastered the goo on the yellowish welt atop his left thigh.

He immediately regretted it.

The direct contact made the welt rage with intense itching pain, a blowtorch burning white-hot, as if his skin had melted away in glowing, molten drips. He scooted on the seat and nearly cried out. Controlling himself after only a second or two, he took a long, slow breath and forced himself to relax.

Almost as soon as the pain started, it died down, then seemed to subside completely. Smiling at the small victory, Perry gently worked the salve into the welt and the surrounding skin.

He almost laughed with relief. Using far more caution, he worked the Cortaid into the other welts. When he finished, all seven of them fell quiet.

'The Magnificent Seven,' Perry mumbled. 'You aren't so magnificent now, are you?'

With all seven itches battled into submission, he felt giddy, he felt like howling with joy. But more than anything else, he felt tired. The maddening itches created constant stress; with that stress suddenly gone, he felt like a schooner with the wind dying out of its sails.

Perry stripped out of all but his underwear, left his clothes in the bathroom and walked to the small bedroom. His queen-size bed left little space for a single dresser and a nightstand. Less than eighteen inches separated the sides of the mattress from the wall.

He practically fell into the comfortable old bed. He pulled the loose blankets around himself, shivering as the cool cotton raised goose bumps on his skin. The blankets quickly warmed, and at 5:30 P.M. he was sound asleep, a small smile still tickling his face.

16
VEINS

Margaret walked, trying to stretch her muscles, but there wasn't much room in the claustrophobic BSL-4 tent. She wandered over to Amos, who was transfixed by a slide set under a high-powered microscope.

'What have you got on that thorn?'

'Still doing a few tests. I've found another structure that you should take a look at. And make it quick, it's decomposing as we speak.' He stood, letting her peer into the microscope. The highly magnified image looked to be a deflated capillary, a normal vein. But it wasn't *all* normal. Part of it looked damaged; from that area ran a grayish-black tubule. The tubule ended with a decomposing area showing the ubiquitous rot so common in all the victims. Amos was right, she could *see* the tissue dissolving right before her eyes. She focused her attention away from the rapid-rot spot and back onto the tubule.

'What the hell is that thing?'

'I love your subtle use of scientific terminology, Margaret. That appears to be a siphon of some sort.'

'A siphon? You mean this was tapping into Brewbaker's bloodstream, like a mosquito?'

'No, not like a mosquito, not at all. A mosquito merely inserts its proboscis into the skin and draws out blood. What you're looking at is another level entirely. That

Infected

siphon draws blood from the circulatory system, but it's *permanently* attached; there's no visible means for opening or closing the siphon. That means there are probably matching siphons that return blood to the circulatory system—otherwise the growth would fill up with blood and burst.'

'So if it returns the blood to the circulatory system, it's not feeding directly on the blood?'

'No, not directly, but it's definitely capitalizing on the host's bodily functions. The growth obviously draws oxygen and possibly nutrients from the bloodstream. That must be how it grows. It may also feed directly on the host, but I doubt that; that would entail a digestive process and a method for eliminating waste. Granted, the growths we've seen have been completely decomposed, so we can't confirm or deny the existence of a digestive tract, but from what we've got here I doubt there is one. Why would something evolve a complicated digestive system when there's no apparent need—the blood would supply the growth with all sustenance.'

'So it's not just a mass of cancerous tissue, it's a full-blown parasite.'

'Well, we don't know that it's really *living* in the usual sense,' Amos said. 'If it's a growth, it's just that, a growth, whereas a parasite is a separate organism. Remember, the lab results didn't show any tissue other than Brewbaker's—that and the huge amounts of cellulase. But it does appear to be using the host's bodily functions to stay alive, so at least for now I'd have to agree with you and define it as a parasite.'

Margaret noticed a touch of astonishment in his voice. He was really beginning to admire the strange parasite. She stood.

Amos bent back to the microscope. 'This is a revolutionary development, Margaret, don't you see that? Think of the lowly tapeworm. It doesn't have a digestive system. It doesn't need one, because it lives in the host's intestine. The host digests food, so the tapeworm doesn't have to—it merely absorbs the nutrients surrounding it. Where do those nutrients go if the tapeworm doesn't get them? They go into the bloodstream. Blood carries those nutrients, along with oxygen, to the body's various tissues and then takes out waste materials and gases.'

'And by tapping into the bloodstream, the triangle parasites get food and oxygen. They don't need to eat or breathe.'

'That's how it appears. Quite astonishing, isn't it?'

'You're the parasitologist,' Margaret said. 'If this keeps up, you'll be in charge and I'll be the lackey.'

Amos laughed. Margaret hated him at that moment— over thirty-six hours into their marathon session, with little more than twenty-minute catnaps to pace them, and he still didn't seem tired.

'Are you kidding me?' Amos said. 'I'm a total chicken-shit, and you know it. First sign of danger—physical or emotional—I run for the hills. My wife actually has my balls in a jar back at the house. She's taller than me, she puts the jar up on a shelf where I can't reach it.'

Margaret laughed. Amos was famously open about who ran his household.

'I'm fine where I'm at,' Amos said. 'I rather like being the lackey if being in charge means having to deal with Dew Phillips and Murray Longworth. But if I do wind up calling the shots, just remember I like my coffee black.'

They sat in silence for a moment, tired brains processing the strange information that seemed to provide no answers.

'This can't stay a secret forever,' Amos said. 'Off the top of my head, I can name three experts who should be here right now. Murray's secrecy policy is asinine.'

'But he's got a point, you have to admit,' Margaret said. 'We can't have this story out, not yet. We'll have anyone with a rash, bug bite or even dry skin flooding the hospitals. It's going to make it very difficult to find someone who's actually infected, especially as we have no idea what the early stages of this infection look like. If the story got out now, we'd have to look at *millions* of people. Hopefully we can at least come up with some kind of screening process or test for infection before this story breaks.'

'I understand the precarious nature of the situation,' Amos said. 'I just think that Murray is taking this too far. It's one thing to keep a lid on something—it's quite another to be completely understaffed. What the hell happens if a hundred Martin Brewbakers suddenly pop up, and no one is prepared for it, let alone warned it could happen? You think a bomb is a terror weapon? It's nothing compared to hundreds of Americans going psycho on each other. What happens if we keep this a secret until it's too late to do anything about it?'

He walked back to his station, leaving Margaret to stare at the half body. The constant decomposition had partially relaxed Brewbaker's talon hand—where it had once stood straight up, it now hung at forty-five degrees, halfway to the tabletop. His blackening, liquefying body didn't have much time left.

Margaret wondered about Amos's comment; if there was some rogue lab with the technology to genetically engineer a parasite that could alter human behavior, wasn't it *already* too late?

17

CAT SCRATCH FEVER

Perry awoke with a scream. His collarbone raged with pain, like he'd dragged a razor blade across the thin skin atop the bone, peeling back flesh like a cheese grater rubbed across some Cheddar. The fingers of his right hand felt cold, wet and sticky. A sunrise beam of light pierced his half-drawn curtains, lighting up the window frost crystallized on the pane. His room filled with the hazy glow of a winter morning. In the dim light, Perry stared at his hands; they looked to be covered with chocolate syrup, thick and tacky-brown. He fumbled with the lamp on his nightstand. The bulb's glow lit up the room and his hands. It wasn't chocolate syrup.

It was blood.

Eyes widening in horror, Perry looked at his bed. Thin streaks of blood dotted the white sheets. Still blinking sleep-crust from his eyes, he ran to the bathroom and stared in the mirror.

Trickles of dried blood and finger-smears of the same streaked his left pectoral, clotting in his thin blond chest hair. He'd torn the skin during the night, digging into the flesh with his fingernails, which were caked with blood and bits of dried skin. Perry looked down at his body. Blood smudges, some wet, some tacky and some completely dry, covered his left thigh.

With a sudden start of horror, he saw bomb-run droplets of blood on his underwear. Pulling the waistband out, he looked down. A sigh of relief—no blood on his testicles.

He'd torn into himself during the night, ripping away at the itches with an abandon that didn't exist during waking hours. How had he not woken up? 'Sleeping like the dead' was an understatement. And despite more than thirteen hours of sleep, he still felt tired. Tired and hungry.

Perry stared at himself in the mirror. Pale skin, nearly white, smeared with streaks of his own blood dried to a reddish black, as if he were the canvas for a child's finger painting, or perhaps some ancient shaman bedecked for a tribal ritual.

The rashes had grown in the night. Each was now the size of a silver-dollar pancake, and had taken on a coppery color. Perry craned his neck, trying to use the mirror to see the blemishes on his back and ass. They looked okay, which was to say he hadn't scratched them raw during the night. In truth, they looked anything *but* okay.

Not knowing what else to do, Perry took a quick shower to wash off the dried blood. The situation was fucked up, obviously, but there was little he could do about it now. Besides, he had to be at work in a few hours. Maybe after work he'd actually break down and make a doctor's appointment.

Perry scrubbed up, then applied the rest of the Cortaid, being very careful with the raw wounds on his leg and collarbone. He applied Band-Aids to both areas, then dressed and made himself a whopping breakfast. His stomach groaned with a ravenous hunger, more intense than his normal morning cravings. He made five scrambled eggs, eight pieces of toast, and washed everything down with two big glasses of milk.

Overall, the rashes *felt* fine, although they looked worse than ever. If they didn't itch anymore, they couldn't be that big of a deal. Perry felt certain the rashes would subside by day's end, or at least be on their way out. Confident his body could handle the problem, he gathered up his battered briefcase and headed to work.

18

NERVES

Margaret looked at the readout with disbelief.

'Amos,' she called through the biosuit's tinny microphone. 'Come here and take a look at this.' Amos glided over, as unaffected by fatigue as ever, and stood next to her.

'What have you got?'

'I finished the analysis on samples taken from all over the body and found massive quantities of neurotransmitters, particularly in the brain.'

Amos leaned forward to read the screen. 'Excessively high levels of dopamine, norepinephrine, serotonin . . . my God, his system was out of control. What do you think did this to him?'

'That's not my specialty, I'll have to check into it. But from what I do know, excessive levels of neurotransmitters can cause paranoid disorders and even some psychopathic behaviors. And I'm not sure there has *ever* been a case documented with levels this high.'

'The growth is controlling the victims with natural drugs. I wish we could get our hands on a live victim so we could see the insides of those damn growths. This is twice now we've had victims to examine, but both times the growths have been completely rotted out. It's almost as if the person who created these things intentionally added the rotting aspect, so it would be harder to examine the little buggers.'

Margaret rolled the concept around in her brain, but it didn't take hold. She was already suspicious of the growths' incredible complexity—another theory began to take shape.

Amos pointed to the screen. 'The growth either produces or causes to be produced excess neurotransmitters, which create reproducible results. Brilliant. Absolutely brilliant.'

'There are other variances as well,' Margaret said. 'There was *seventy-five* times the normal level of enkephalins in the tissue surrounding the growth. Enkephalin is a natural painkiller.'

Amos thought for a moment. 'That makes sense. It's hard to tell with all the rot, but it looks like the growth causes a lot of damage to the surrounding tissue. Whoever engineered the growth doesn't want the host to feel that damage. The level of complexity is astronomical.'

'Amos, you don't have to *root* for the little buggers,' Margaret said, a dressing-down tone in her voice. 'We're here to stop these things, remember?'

He smiled. 'It's hard not to be astounded. Come here and take a look at what I've got under the ultraviolet microscope.'

Margaret shuffled to the device, where Amos had been working for the last thirty minutes. Her Racal suit *zip-zipped* with each step as if she wore children's footed pajamas.

She peered into the microscope. The sample looked like a normal nerve cell. Amos had done a perfect job of isolating and preparing the tissue: fingerlike dendrites, stained and glowing electric-blue under the ultraviolet light, reached out and over the thicker axons. It was the same connection that provides signal communication for every animal on the planet.

'It's an isolated cluster of nerve cells,' she said. 'Where is this from?'

'I found it near the eighth cranial nerve. The rot is working its way through there, but I was able to find a few relatively clean areas.'

Inside the awkward biosuit, Margaret frowned. The eighth cranial nerve, or the vestibulocochlear nerve, was where signals from the ear entered the brain.

'It's heavily damaged, shows signs of decomposition, but still obviously nerve tissue,' Margaret said.

Amos remained quiet. Margaret looked up from the microscope.

Amos leaned forward. 'You're sure?'

Margaret wasn't in the mood for games, but she took another look anyway. She could see nothing unusual.

'Amos, if you've got a point to make, please make it.'

'The cells don't belong to Martin Brewbaker.'

Margaret stared blankly, not understanding the statement. 'Not Brewbaker's? Why are you looking at other samples? If they're not Brewbaker's nerve cells, then whose . . .' Her voice trailed off as the significance hit home.

'Amos, are you telling me these belong to the growth?'

'I performed protein sequencing on the black thorn and the vein siphon. The results turned up some unknown proteins, definitely not human. So I took some samples from around the body and ran the same sequence. I found high concentrations in the brain—that's how I discovered the cluster on the cranial nerve. I found the protein in other places, but no more nerves, only remnants of that peculiar rot. There were high concentrations in the cerebral cortex, thalamus, amygdala, caudate nucleus, hypothalamus and septum.'

Margaret felt overwhelmed. Much of the brain's higher functions remained a mystery, even in this day of rapidly ascending scientific knowledge. The sections of Brewbaker's brain infected with the rot composed part of the limbic system, which was thought to control memory storage and emotional response, among other functions.

What the hell was the growth doing in Brewbaker's brain? It already had him controlled with the neurotransmitter overdose, didn't it?

Amos continued. 'What you're looking at here is the only sample I've found that wasn't completely decomposed. I've never seen proteins like this, so I assume they're synthetic, man-made. If they're natural, they're nothing I've encountered. I've searched all the academic and biotech databases and found nothing similar. That means if the proteins *are* synthetic, someone is keeping their research well guarded, which doesn't surprise me considering the vastly advanced technology we're dealing with.'

She was awed. It was unthinkable that the organism's creator had engineered a new parasite that could grow from a very small embryo, possibly even a single cell, and latch on to a human host. It was even more unthinkable that this creature produced neurotransmitters like some kind of factory, dumping them into the bloodstream. But it was numbing—yes, *numbing*—to comprehend the genius that had bioengineered artificial nerves so accurately that they could interact with human nerves.

'I follow the vein siphon, that makes sense,' she said. 'But the siphon is just a physical attachment to draw nutrients. What good does it do the parasite to grow mimic nerves?'

'You've got me. But one must draw the logical conclusion that the growths tapped in to the nervous system, just as they tapped in to the circulatory system.'

'But *why*?' She spoke more to herself than to Amos. 'The neurotransmitter overdose produces somewhat predictable, *reproducible* results. If the goal is to make people crazy, then why would they go through the trouble of tapping in to the nervous system? And what's the purpose for doing so?'

Amos shrugged. He rolled his shoulders and twisted at the waist, trying to loosen up. He walked around the table, doing mini laps, trying to shake off the fatigue.

Margaret shuffled to her station, her mind spinning with possibilities and a new level of fearful respect for the mystery organism.

It had seemed so obvious—unbelievable and awe-inspiring, but still obvious—that this was an organism bioengineered to make people violent and unpredictable. Now, however, she wasn't so sure. There was something else to the mystery, something that a theory of high-tech terrorists didn't explain.

'Hey, Margaret, bring me the camera.' She looked back—Amos stood next to Brewbaker's hip. All parts of him were being consumed by the black rot, but some spots weren't quite as advanced. The hip was one such spot. She grabbed the camera from the prep table and handed it to Amos.

He pointed to the hip, to the little lesion they'd seen earlier.

'Margaret, look at this.' He knelt down and took a picture.

'I see it. You already showed me.'

'Yes, but do you see anything different?'

Margaret sighed. 'Amos, no more drama, please. If you've got something to say, say it.'

He said nothing. Instead he stood, fiddled with the camera, then stood shoulder to shoulder with her so they could both see the camera's small screen. The screen showed a close-up of the lesion, a tiny blue fiber sticking out of it.

'So?' Margaret said. 'We've got shit to do before his body is goo, Amos.'

'That's the picture we took when we first saw it,' he said, then hit the advance button on the camera. The picture changed. 'And *that* is the picture I took just now.'

Margaret stared. The two pictures looked exactly the same, except for one thing—the second picture showed not one fiber, but three, a small red one, a small blue one, and the original blue one, which was three times as long as it had been before.

Even though Martin Brewbaker was dead, the fibers were still growing.

19

HUMP DAY

By noon the damnable things started itching again, and Perry had to wonder if he should see a doctor. But it was just a little rash, for crying out loud. What kind of a wuss goes to see a doctor for a little rash? If you don't have self-discipline, what do you have?

He'd always been a very healthy person. He hadn't vomited from a non-alcohol-related incident since the sixth grade. While others succumbed to the flu, Perry would suffer only a runny nose and a slightly queasy stomach. While others called in sick at the drop of a hat, Perry hadn't missed a day of work in three years. He'd inherited his resilience, as he had his size, from his father.

Perry had been twenty-five when Captain Cancer finally claimed Jacob Dawsey, the toughest sonofabitch this side of Brian Urlacher. Prior to that last trip to the hospital, from which Jacob Dawsey never returned, he had missed only one day of work in his entire life. That day came when Perry broke his father's jaw.

Perry had returned home from late-season football practice to find his father beating his mother. Snow had been falling on and off for a week, enough to cover the sparse grass with patchy white, but not enough to accumulate on the dirt road that led up to the house—the road glistened with cold wetness.

His father had thrown his mother off the front porch, into a slushy puddle, and was in the process of whipping her with his belt. The scene was nothing new, and to this day Perry had no idea why he snapped, why—for the first time in his life—he fought against his father's incessant rage.

'Gonna show you who's in charge, woman,' Jacob Dawsey said as he brought the belt down with a *crack*. 'Give you women an inch and you take a mile! Who the hell do you think you are?' Even though his father had spent all his life in northern Michigan, he had the faintest trace of a drawl. It colored his words, making *hell* sound like *hail*.

At the time Perry was a high-school sophomore, six-foot-two, 200 pounds and growing like a weed. He was no match for his father's six-foot-five, 265 pounds of solid muscle. But Perry rushed him anyway, hit his father with a flying tackle that carried them both into the tattered front porch. Rotten lattice shattered around them.

Perry got up first, screaming, snarling, and hit his father with a heavy left hook. That blow broke his father's jaw, but Perry only found that out later. Jacob Dawsey tossed his son away like so much rubbish. Perry jumped up to press the attack. His father grabbed a shovel and proceeded to give Perry the worst beating he'd ever suffered.

Perry fought like he'd never fought before, because he was sure he was going to die that day. He landed two more shots on his father's jaw, but Jacob Dawsey barely flinched as he brought the flat of the shovel down again and again.

The next day the pain was too much for even the mighty Jacob Dawsey. He went to the hospital, where the doctors wired his mouth shut. When his father returned home, he called his son to the kitchen table. Black-and-blue, cut in a dozen places, Perry could hardly walk after the shovel-beating, but he sat at the table as his father scrawled out childish writing on a piece of paper. Jacob Dawsey was only semiliterate, but Perry could make out the message.

Can't talk, broke jaw, said the scribbled writing. *You fought like a man. Proud of you. It a shit world, you got to learn to survive. Someday you understand, thank me.*

What had been fucked up—like, *really* fucked up beyond belief—wasn't the beating itself. It was the look in his father's eyes. The look of sorrow, of love and the look of *pride*. The look that said, 'This hurt me more than it hurt you,' and not because of the broken jaw. His dad saw the shovel-beating in the same light a sane father might see a spanking—something unsavory that had to be done as a parenting responsibility. Jacob Dawsey didn't think he'd done anything wrong—in fact, he thought he'd done the right thing, the responsible thing, and although he hated hurting his only begotten son, he'd do what had to be done to be a *good father.*

Yeah, thanks Dad, Perry thought. *Thanks a bunch. You're the best.*

But as much as he hated the man, Perry couldn't deny that his father had made him who he was. Jacob Dawsey had set out to make his son tough, and he had succeeded. Perry's toughness helped him excel on the football field, which earned him a scholarship and a college degree. As crazy as Jacob Dawsey was, he'd also instilled a die-hard work ethic that Perry very much considered a key part of his personality. He *liked* working hard. He *liked* being the one people relied on to get the job done.

And rash or no rash, Perry was at work and doing his

job. But being at work and being effective were two different things. He just couldn't concentrate. He continuously pursued the same avenues, the same possible solutions over and over again in his mind. His brain felt *fuzzy*, as if it couldn't grip the task at hand.

'Perry, can I speak to you for a moment?'

He turned to see Sandy standing just inside his cube. She didn't look happy.

'Sure,' he said.

'I just got a call from Samir at Pullman. Their network has been dropping out for three days now.'

'I'm working on it. I thought I had it fixed yesterday. I'm sorry it's taking so long.'

'I know you're working on it, but I'm not sure you're paying attention. According to Samir, you had him reboot the network routers yesterday. Twice. And even though it didn't work either time, you had him do it again this morning.'

Perry's brain searched for an answer, but found none.

'They're losing money, Perry.' Sandy sounded more than a little angry. 'I don't mind if my people can't solve a problem, but I don't want you bullshitting your way through something if you don't know how to solve it.'

Perry felt his own anger rise. He was working as hard as he could, dammit! He was the best one in the department. Maybe there were problems that just couldn't be solved.

'So can you tell me what's wrong with their system?' Sandy asked. Perry noticed for the first time that her eyes grew very wide and her nostrils flared when she was angry. The look seemed childish, petulant, like some spoiled little girl who thinks people should jump at her orders.

'I don't know,' Perry said.

Her eyes widened further and her hands went to her hips. Perry felt another stab of anger at her haughty posture.

'How the hell can you not know?' Sandy said. 'You've been on this for three days. You haven't known for three days and you haven't asked for help?'

'I said I'm working on it!' Even to himself his voice sounded strange—full of anger and impatience. Sandy's eyes flashed with trepidation as she looked down. Her gaze returned to his face, the petulant look gone, replaced by a questioning, slightly fearful expression. Perry looked down himself to see what she'd stared at. His hands were balled into fists, squeezed so tight the knuckles glowed white against his reddish skin. He realized his whole body was coiled with aggressive tension, the same posture he used to have before the snap of the ball—or before a fight. The office suddenly seemed very quiet. He pictured how frightening the scene must be to her; his big angry body hovering predatorily over her smallish, weak frame. He must have looked like a rabid bear about to pounce on a wounded fawn.

He willed his hands to open. His face flushed with embarrassment and shame. He'd made Sandy afraid of him, made her afraid that he'd lash out and hit her (*just like the last job*, his conscience teased, *just like the last boss*).

'I'm sorry,' Perry said quietly. The fear left Sandy's eyes, replaced by concern, but despite the change, she backed another step out of the cube.

'You seem to be under some stress lately,' Sandy said quietly. 'Why don't you take the rest of the day off and relax.'

Perry blanched at the thought of leaving work early. 'I'm okay. Really, I can fix the problem in Pullman.'

'I don't care about that,' Sandy said. 'I'll get someone else to fix it. Go home. Now.' She turned and walked away.

Perry stared at the ground, feeling like a failure, feeling he'd betrayed her loyalty. He'd been moments away from hitting the one person who'd given him a chance, who'd let him straighten out his life. She'd done everything for him by giving him that chance. This was how he thanked her. In unison, the seven itches flared all over his body, adding to his frustration. Like a huge child, he packed his duct-tape-patched briefcase and sluffed into his coat.

His IM alert dinged:

StickyFingazWhitey: Hey man, you okay? Can I help?

Perry stared at the message for a second. He didn't deserve help, he didn't deserve sympathy. Without sitting down, he typed in a reply:

Bleedmaize_n_blue: Don't worry about me. I'm tip-top.

StickyFingazWhitey: Like hell you are. Just be cool, go home, I'll patch this up for you.

Bleedmaize_n_blue: No, stay out of it.

StickyFingazWhitey: Fine, I promise I won't say a word to Sandy. Of course, I lie a lot. I also 'promise' I won't fix Pullman for you.

StickyFingazWhitey: Go watch your Pope Porn™, I've got this. No bout-a-doubt-it.

Bill had his back. Somehow that made Perry feel even worse. Even if he insisted Bill leave it alone, his friend would just do the work anyway.

He walked out of the office, feeling the eyes of everyone on his back. Red-faced and frustrated, Perry walked to his car and headed home.

20

SHORTHANDED

It was hard to believe it had only been seven days since Murray had sent for him. Seven days ago, when he'd never heard of triangles, Margaret Montoya or Martin Brewbaker. Seven days ago, when his partner wasn't in a hospital bed, a bed that for all intents and purposes, Dew had put him in.

Seven days ago Murray had called for Dew. They'd fought side by side back in the day, but after 'Nam they didn't exactly keep in touch. When Murray called, it meant only one thing—he wanted something done. Something . . . unappealing. Something that required getting a little dirt under the fingernails, something that Murray—with his tailored suits and his manicures—wasn't willing to do. But they'd been through hell together, and even though Murray had advanced in the CIA ranks and done his damnedest to rise above the shit-stomping lieutenant he'd been in 'Nam, when Murray called, Dew always answered.

It was only seven days ago that Dew had stood in Murray's waiting room, eyeing the twenty-something, red-haired secretary, wondering if Murray was fucking her.

She looked up with her sparkling green eyes and a genuine smile. 'Can I help you, sir?'

Irish accent, Dew thought. *If he's not banging her, or at least trying, he must be impotent.*

'I'm Agent Dew Phillips. Murray is expecting me.'

'Of course, Agent Phillips, go right in.' The redhead added in a confidential tone, 'You're a few minutes late, and *Mister Longworth* hates tardiness.'

'Does he? Ain't that a bite in the ass. I'll have to get on some kind of schedule.'

Dew walked into Murray's sprawling, spartan office. A bullet-ridden American flag decorated one wall. On the opposite wall hung a row of pictures showing Murray with each of the last five presidents. The pictures were like a stop-action movie of Murray's aging process, from hard-bodied young man to more-than-slightly-overweight, cold-eyed piece of gristle.

Dew noticed the absence of any pictures showing Murray in his army uniform, either dress or fatigues. Murray wanted to forget that time, forget who he'd been back then, forget the things he'd done. Dew couldn't forget—and he didn't want to anymore. It was a part of his life, and he'd moved on. Mostly, anyway.

He certainly remembered the flag on Murray's wall, remembered the firebase where he and Murray and six other men had been the only survivors of an entire company, remembered fighting for his life with all the savagery of a rabid animal. It had been like something from World War I at the end, just before the choppers arrived, fighting hand to hand in wet, sandbagged trenches, the 2:00 A.M. stars hidden by clouds that poured rain and turned the firebase into a slick sea of mud.

Murray Longworth sat behind a large oak desk devoid of decoration, unless you counted the computer. The desk's empty top gleamed with layers of polish.

'Heya, L.T.,' Dew said.

'You know, Dew, I'd appreciate it if you didn't use that nickname. We've had this talk before.'

'Sure thing,' Dew said. 'I guess I forgot all about that.'
'Have a seat.'

'Nice place you've got here. You've had this office something like four years now? Glad I finally get to see it.'

Murray said nothing.

'It's been, what, three years since we talked, L.T.? Seven years since you needed something from me? Your career in trouble again, is that it? You need Good Ol' Dew to come in and pull your ass out of the fire? Make you look good, is that it?'

'It's not like that this time.'

'Sure, L.T., sure. You know, I'm not as young as I used to be. My old body may not be up to your dirty work.'

Dew stood in front of the flag. A grimy-brown color stained the top left corner; *just delta mud,* Murray told anyone that asked. But it wasn't mud, and Dew knew that better than anyone. The flag had once been attached to a flagpole that Dew used to kill a VC, driving the brass point into the enemy's gut like some primitive tribal spearman. The bottom right corner held a similar stain, where Dew had tried in vain to stop the blood pouring from Quint Wallman's throat after an AK-47 round had all but decapitated the eighteen-year-old corporal.

They hadn't used the flag for motivation, because at the time none of them had been particularly patriotic. The flag just happened to be where they made their last stand, where they held off the attack until the choppers came and bailed them out. Murray was the last one to board, making sure the other men—all wounded, including Dew—were on before he worried about himself. He grabbed the flag, the bloodstained, burned and bullet-ridden flag, on the way out. No one knew why at the time, probably not even Murray. When they realized it was all over, that they had escaped death, left the corpses of both friends and enemies behind, the flag somehow took on more meaning.

Dew stared at the tattered fabric, the memories pouring back, and it was a second before he realized that Murray was softly calling his name.

'Dew? Dew?'

Dew turned and blinked, quickly returning to reality, to the present. Murray gestured to the chair in front of his desk. Dew thought about antagonizing Murray some more, then walked to the chair and sat down.

Dew pulled a Tootsie Roll from his jacket pocket, unwrapped it, popped the brown candy into his mouth then dropped the wrapper on the floor. He chewed for a moment, staring at Murray, then asked, 'Did ya hear about Jimmy Tillamok?'

Murray shook his head.

'Ate a bullet. Used an old .45—wasn't much left of his face.'

Murray's head sank, and a long sigh hissed from his body. 'My God, I hadn't heard.'

'Imagine that,' Dew said. 'He's only been in rehab a half dozen times in the last four years. He crashed hard, Murray. He crashed hard and he needed his friends.'

'Why didn't you call me?'

'Would you have come?'

Murray's silence answered the question. He looked up from the floor to return Dew's stone-eyed stare. 'So we're the last ones, then.'

'Yep,' Dew said. 'Just the two of us. Golly gee, it's a good thing we stayed so close all these years. Now we've got each other to rely on. Let's get to the fucking point, L.T. What do you want?'

Murray pulled out a manila folder and passed it to Dew. It was labeled PROJECT TANGRAM. 'We've got what could be a major problem.'

'Murray, if this is just some bullshit where I get shot at so your career can advance, I'm not doing it.'

'I told you it's not like that this time, Dew. This is serious.'

'Yeah? Batting cleanup again, Murray? Who gave you their dirty laundry this time?'

'I can't tell you.'

Dew stared hard at Murray. L.T. didn't mind dropping names, that was for damn sure. It all clicked at once: Murray couldn't say who, and he'd called the one man who would do whatever it took to get the job done.

'Holy shit,' Dew said. 'This is from the big man, isn't it? This is some secret presidential action, am I right?'

Murray cleared his throat. 'Dew, I said I can't tell you.'

The classic nondenial denial. Murray's way of confirming Dew's theory without actually saying the words.

Dew opened the folder and started browsing the contents. There were only four files: three case reports and an overview. Dew read the overview twice before he looked up, his expression ashen and disbelieving. He looked back to the report and started quoting some of the more fantastical phrases.

'"Biological behavior manipulation"? "Bioengineered organism"? "Infectious terrorist weapon"? Murray, are you yankin' my crank with this stuff?'

Murray shook his head.

'This is bullshit,' Dew said. 'You think that some terrorist created a . . . let's see here . . . "bioengineered organism" to make people psychotic?'

'That's not exactly what it says, Dew. We've got three

cases so far where normal people have contracted some kind of growth, and shortly afterward they became psychotic. We don't know for certain that this is a terrorist activity, but I think you appreciate that we have to act like it is. We can't be caught sitting on our hands.'

Dew read. Charlotte Wilson's report had a picture attached, a Polaroid that showed a bluish triangular mark on her shoulder. The picture attached to Gary Leeland's file showed a scowling old man. A hateful, suspicious expression marred his wrinkled, stubbly face. The lumpy, bluish triangle on his neck accentuated the unpleasant expression.

'So this thing turns people into killers?'

'It made Charlotte Wilson, a seventy-year-old grandmother, kill her own son with a butcher knife. It made Blaine Tanarive kill his wife and two young daughters with a pair of scissors. It made Gary Leeland, a fifty-seven-year-old man, set his own hospital bed on fire, killing himself and three other patients.

'Could this be coincidence? Did we check the background of these people? Any mental conditions?'

'I've checked it out, Dew. I wouldn't have called you in if I hadn't. In all these cases, the victims had no history of violence, no medical conditions, no psychological problems. All their friends and neighbors said they were good people. The only thing they have in common, in fact, is the sudden onset of acute paranoid behavior and those triangular growths.'

'What about foreign occurrences? Anyone else dealing with something similar?'

Murray again shook his head, a solemn look on his face. 'Nothing. And we've looked, Dew, we've looked *hard*. As far as we know, we're the only country with cases like this.'

Dew nodded slowly, now understanding why Murray chose to see a conspiracy amid the carnage. 'But how could terrorists come up with something like this?'

'I don't think terrorists invented it,' Murray said. 'But terrorists didn't invent nuclear warheads, sarin gas or passenger jets. *Someone* created this, and that's all that matters.'

Dew reread the report. If it was a terrorist weapon, it was a doozy. It made car bombs and random plane hijackings look worthless by comparison: imagine a country where you never know if your friends or neighbors or coworkers are suddenly going to snap and try to kill everyone in sight. People wouldn't go to work, wouldn't leave their houses without a gun. You would suspect that *everyone* was a possible killer. Hell, if parents murdered their own children, no one was safe. Such a weapon would cripple America.

Dew reached for another Tootsie Roll. 'Murray, this couldn't be one of *our* weapons, could it? Something that maybe accidentally-on-purpose got a bit out of control?'

Murray was shaking his head before Dew finished the sentence. 'No, no way. I checked everything, and I mean *everything*. This isn't ours, Dew, I give you my word.'

Dew unwrapped the candy and again dropped the wrapper on Murray's immaculate carpeting. 'So how's it work?'

'We don't know for sure. The logical theory is that the growths produce drugs, which are dumped right into the bloodstream. Kind of like a living hypodermic needle pumping out bad shit.'

'How many people know about this?'

'A few people know bits and pieces, but as far as those that know the whole enchilada, there's myself, the director, the president and the two CDC doctors listed in the reports.'

Dew stared at the photos. They gave him an uneasy feeling, down deep, at an instinctual level.

'I need you on this one, Top,' Murray said. The name chafed Dew as badly as L.T. chafed Murray. *Top*—short for *Top Sergeant*, the rank he'd held when he'd served under Murray back in 'Nam. For years that had been his only name, a name that commanded respect. Once upon a time, everyone he knew had called him Top— now the only one left who even knew the name was Murray, the guy who wanted to pretend that Vietnam had never happened. Somehow Dew didn't find humor in the irony.

'And I don't care how old you are, Top. As far as I'm concerned you're still the best agent in the field. We need someone who will do whatever it takes to get the job done. And even if you only believe half of what's in that report, you *know* we have to find out what's going on and damn fast.'

Dew studied Murray's face. He'd known that face for over thirty years. Even after all this time, he could tell when Murray was lying. Murray had asked for help before, and on each of those occasions Dew knew damn well it was to benefit Murray's career. But all those times Dew had done it anyway, because it was Murray, because it was L.T., because he'd fought side by side with the man during the most nightmarish period of their lives. But now it was different—L.T. wasn't doing this for personal gain. He was *scared*. Scared shitless.

'Okay, I'm in. I've got to bring my partner in on this.'

'Absolutely not. I'll get you someone else, someone I know. Malcolm doesn't have your clearance.'

Dew was taken aback for a moment, shocked that Murray knew his partner's name. 'What's clearance got to do with it, L.T.? You just want someone who'll pull the trigger whenever you need it pulled, and as much as it pains me to admit it, that's who I am. But I've been with Malcolm for seven years, and I'm not going after this crazy-ass hullabaloo without him. Trust me, he's reliable.'

Murray Longworth was a man used to getting his way, used to having his orders followed, but Dew knew he was also a politician. Sometimes politicians had to give a little to get what they wanted—that was the nature of the game that Dew could never grasp, the game that Murray played so well.

'Fine,' Murray said. 'I trust your judgment.'

Dew shrugged his shoulders. 'So what do we do next?'

Murray turned his gaze to the window.

'We wait, Top. We wait for the next victim.'

He'd waited then, and he was waiting now. Seven days ago he'd been waiting for something to happen, for a chance to see if this crazy Project Tangram crap was for real, a hoax or something whipped up to earn Murray another promotion. Now, however, he was waiting for his best friend to die.

A death that would have never occurred if Dew hadn't insisted—*insisted*, God dammit—on getting Mal involved.

Rested but still weary, fueled more by anger than sleep, Dew sat alone in his hotel room, the big cell phone pinched between his shoulder and ear.

'Your partner still in critical?' Murray asked.

'Yeah, still touch and go. He's fighting his ass off.' On the table in front of Dew lay a yellow cloth, on top of which sat a disassembled military-issue Colt .45 automatic. The dull, smooth metal winked blue-gray under the hotel room's glaring lights.

'The docs are working on him?' Murray asked.

'Day and night,' Dew said. 'That CDC bitch came in to take a look at him, too. Can't she at least wait until the body is cold, Murray?'

'I sent her in, Dew, you know that. She needs all the information she can get. We're grasping at straws here.'

'So what information does she have?'

'I'm flying in tomorrow. I'll get a firsthand report and then I'll fill you in. You just sit tight until then.'

'What's the national picture? We have any new clients?' Dew finished oiling and assembling the gun. He set it aside and pulled out two boxes, one full of empty magazines, the other full of .45-caliber cartridges.

'Not that we know of,' Murray said. 'All's quiet on the western front, it seems. And if we do have any other clients, you don't need to worry about them. You need a break. I'm working on bringing some more people in.'

With mechanical, habitual speed, Dew loaded the first magazine. He set it aside and started on the second. Dew sighed, as if his next words would seal his friend's fate. But duty came first . . .

'Mal ain't gonna make it, Murray. It may suck to say that but it's the truth.'

'I've got someone lined up for you. I'm going to brief him shortly.'

'No more partners.'

'Fuck you, Dew,' Murray said, his calm tone suddenly turning angry. Murray hid his emotions well, always had, but now his frustration rang through. 'Don't you start flaking out on me. I know I wanted you solo on this, but it's getting too big. I want someone with you. You need some help.'

'I said no more partners, Murray.'

'You'll follow orders.'

'Send me a partner and I'll shoot him in the knee,' Dew said. 'You know I'll do it.'

Murray said nothing.

Dew continued, his voice halting only slightly, colored by a tiny sliver of emotion.

'Malcolm was my partner, but he's as good as dead. The shit I saw was crazy, Murray. People infected with this crap aren't human anymore. I saw that for myself, so I know what we're up against. I know that Margaret needs something to work with, and she needs it fast. I can get that on my own. If I have to get used to someone else I can't move like I need to. I fly solo from here on out, Murray.'

'Dew, you can't make this personal. This is no time for stupid thoughts to cloud your judgment.'

Dew finished the second mag. He held it in his left hand, staring at it, staring at the glossy tip of the single exposed bullet.

'This isn't revenge, Murray,' Dew said. 'Don't be a dumb-ass. The asshole that got Malcolm is already dead, so what can I take revenge against? I'll just work better *sans* partner.'

Murray fell silent for a moment. Dew didn't really care if Murray agreed or not—he was working alone and that was that.

'All right, Dew,' Murray said quietly. 'Just remember we need a live victim more than we need another corpse.'

'Call me when you get into town.' Dew hung up. He'd lied, of course. It *was* personal. If you thought about it enough, everything was personal in one way or another. Sooner or later he'd find out who was making these little triangular buggers. Malcolm was gone, and somebody was going to pay.

He popped a magazine into the .45, chambered a round, then walked to the bathroom. Holding the gun in his right hand, finger on the trigger, Dew carefully examined himself in the mirror. He wasn't going out like that, not like Brewbaker. His skin looked fine, but small red spots seemed to fade in and out, catching the corner of his vision and then disappearing when he stared. His imagination, fucking with his head. If he contracted the infection, would he be sane long enough to know the symptoms? He didn't need to hold on to his sanity for long—just long enough to pull the trigger.

Dew walked to the bed. He set the loose magazine on the nightstand, slid the .45 under his pillow, lay down and immediately fell into a light sleep.

He dreamed of burning houses, rotten corpses and Frank Sinatra singing 'I've got you under my skin.'

21
THE FIZZLE

It felt so good to be out of the Racal suit. She couldn't wait to take a shower, because she smelled riper than a rotten egg. She had to clean up—Murray was on his way to the hospital for an official update. At the moment, however, the shower had to wait. She read the report on the analysis of the strange fiber growing out of Martin Brewbaker.

'After a few hours, the fiber dissolved,' Amos said. 'They still can't figure out why. It seemed rot-free when we cut it out, but something triggered the effect.'

'But this report came before that, right? This is from the fiber itself, not from the rot?'

Amos nodded. He was also thrilled to finally be free of the suit. He looked as relieved as a teenage boy who's just lost his virginity.

'That's right, they were able to analyze it before the effect kicked in. Pure cellulose.'

'The same material that made up that triangular growth.'

'Exactly. Well, almost. The growth's cellulose seemed to be a structure—shell, skeleton, elements responsible for form. Most of the growth was the cancerous cells.'

They were out of the suits because there was no more point in examining a body that was nothing but black, lique-fying tissue and a strange green mold that covered half the table. They'd done all they could, as fast as they could. They hadn't really found any answers, just more questions. One such question bothered her to no end—the cellulose.

'So the blue fiber, same material as the triangle structure, both sources composed of cellulose, a material not produced by the human body,' Margaret said. 'And we think this is some kind of parasite. You have any theories on the blue fiber?'

'I think it's a fizzle,' Amos said.

'A fizzle?'

'I think the blue fiber is part of a parasite that didn't quite make it to the larval stage.'

'We know the stages now?'

Amos shrugged. 'For lack of a better term, let's call the triangle in the body the larval stage. Obviously, there's a prelarval stage. The triangle is mostly cellulose, the fiber is cellulose, you do the math.'

It made sense in a way. Some cellular automata producing raw materials that were never quite used, or perhaps a mutation of the parasite that just produced cellulose and never moved to the 'larval' phase, as Amos suggested.

And that word bothered her as well.

'So if there's a larval stage,' she said, 'I suppose it turns into something else in the *adult* phase.'

Amos clucked his tongue at her. 'Don't ask stupid questions, Margaret. Of course it does. And no, I don't know what that is. Right now I don't care—I want a shower before I have to face Murray Longworth.'

Maybe Amos could turn off his curiosity, but Margaret could not. Perhaps more accurately, she couldn't turn off her fear.

If this *was* a larval stage, just what the hell awaited them in the *adult* form?

22

DON'T WAIT, EXFOLIATE

Perry sat slumped on his couch, a Newcastle Brown Ale in one hand and the remote control in the other. He flipped through the channels without really seeing the programs.

He'd known the blue and green plaid couch since he'd been a kid, when his dad brought it home from the Salvation Army as a surprise for his mom. At the time the couch was in pretty good shape for a hand-me-down, but that was some fifteen years ago. After his mother died, the couch—and the dishes and silverware, none of which matched—was all he'd taken from the old house. As far as he knew, the house was still sitting on that dirt road in Cheboygan, crumbling into nothingness. During Perry's childhood, Dad's repetitive handyman-special repairs were the only thing that kept the place standing. Perry knew that no one else would ever want the ramshackle house; it was either rotting away or already bulldozed under.

He'd had the couch for several years, first at college, then in his apartment. After that long it fit the contours of his big body as if it were custom-made for him. But even the couch, a beer and the remote control couldn't remove the blackness that had followed him home from work. He'd been sent home early. *Sent home,* for crying out loud, like some undisciplined, lazy worker. That alone would have been enough to crush his spirit, but the Magnificent Seven simply refused to subside.

And they didn't just itch anymore. They *hurt*.

It wasn't just the thick, crusty scabs that throbbed incessantly. There was something else, something that ran *deep*. Something in his body told him that things were spiraling out of hand.

Perry had always wondered if cancer patients *knew* something was horribly wrong. Sure, people always acted surprised when the doctor gave them that 'x-amount-of-time-to-live' shit, and some of them probably *were* a little surprised, but a lot of people suffer pain that they *know* isn't natural. Like his dad.

His dad had known. Although he never said a word to anyone, he grew even quieter, even more serious and even more angry. Yeah, although Perry didn't put the pieces together until his father entered the hospital, the old man had *known*.

And now Perry *knew*. He had a weird feeling in his stomach. Not an instinct or intuition or anything like that but a feathery, queasy feeling. For the first time since the rashes had flared up on Monday morning, Perry wondered if it might be something . . . fatal.

He stood and walked to the bathroom. Removing his shirt, he stared at his once-buff body. Obviously, the lack of sleep caused by his condition (it was a 'condition' now, because of the feeling that something was really wrong) was getting to him. He looked pathetic. He always rubbed his head when he became nervous, and his hair stuck up wildly in all directions. His skin appeared paler than normal, even for a German boy trudging through a Michigan winter. The darkness under his eyes was pronouncedly unattractive.

He looked . . . sick.

Another detail caught his eye, although he wondered if it was his imagination. His muscles seemed slightly more defined. He slowly rotated his arm, watching the deltoid flutter beneath his fatty skin. Was he more cut than before?

Perry unbuttoned his pants and kicked them into the corner. He opened the medicine cabinet and grabbed the tweezers, then sat on the toilet. The cold seat made goose bumps run up and down his flesh.

He gave the tweezers a flick with his finger. They vibrated with a soft tuning-fork hum.

The rash on his left thigh was the easiest one to get at. He'd done a lot of damage to it, both from intentional scratching and his unconscious attack during the previous night. Scabs, both crusty-old and newly red, caked the three-inch-diameter rash. Seemed like as good a spot as any to get rolling.

He pinched the area around the scab-encrusted rash with his right forefinger and thumb, making it bulge out a little. Part of the scab's edge had begun to peel naturally. He started picking with the tweezers, pinched them down on a flake of scab and gently pulled. The scab lifted, but stayed firmly affixed to the skin.

Perry leaned forward, eyes narrowing with determination and intensity. It would hurt like the proverbial bitch, but he was getting that thing off his body. He squeezed the tweezers harder and yanked. The thick scab finally gave, accompanied by a flash of pain; it came free with the tiniest of tearing sounds.

He set the tweezers down on the counter, then pulled off a strip of toilet paper. He dabbed at the bleeding, open sore. After a few seconds, the bleeding stopped. The exposed skin underneath didn't look right. It should have had that wet look, that shiny look, like skin-in-progress or something. This looked different.

Too different.

The flesh looked like an orange peel, not only in color but in texture as well. It smelled faintly of wet leaves. Tiny tears oozed watery blood.

A chill of stabbing panic knifed through his body. If this had happened to his leg, had it also happened to . . . ?

He reached down to his testicles and slowly lifted them to get a good look, hoping to God they would look normal.

In effect, God told Perry to piss off.

It was the scariest thing he'd ever seen. Pale orange skin covered the left side of his scrotum. The area was mostly bald; only a few curly pubic hairs remained.

He'd been nervous up till now, even heading into the wonderful world of pure dread, but these were his balls. His *balls,* for crying out loud! He sat, frozen, the toilet seat refusing to warm up, the drip under the sink suddenly so loud he wondered in amazement how he'd ever managed to sleep in the tiny apartment.

His mouth felt paper dry. He heard himself breathing. Everything seemed so quiet. Perry fought to control the panic dancing back and forth through his mind; he tried to rationalize the situation.

It was just a strange rash, that's all. He'd go to the doctor and get it cleared up. Might take a shot or two, but it probably wouldn't be worse than the gonorrhea and syphilis tests he'd had in college.

Gathering his courage, he let his fingers explore the area. It felt firm and unnatural. This wasn't something a shot of penicillin could clear up, because it wasn't just on the surface. He felt something *inside* his scrotum, something that had never been there before, something just under the thick orange skin.

A coppery chill hit Perry as he realized, suddenly and with perfect clarity, that he was going to die. Whatever this shit was, it was going to kill him, slowly, as it grew into his sac and up into his dick. A terror sat inside him now, growing just as surely as the Magnificent Seven grew, creating a dark, cold, shaky vibration in his soul.

Breathe, he told himself. *Just breathe. Control yourself. Discipline.* He forced himself to let go of the nasty, growing, firm lump and the thick orange skin. That peculiar mental fuzziness overtook him again, and he stared at the wall with a blank expression.

Without conscious thought, he clutched the tweezers and viciously jabbed them into the side of his thigh. The needlelike points slid effortlessly into the skin and poked out through the top of the scab-wound. Perry screamed in pain; his mind cleared—he realized both what he was doing and what he had to do.

He ripped the tweezers free. Bright red blood streaks flew in all directions, landing on his linoleum floor like tiny threads, as did thin wet strands of a much darker red, so dark it looked . . . purple.

Blood (and purple) trickled down his leg. He set the tweezers on the counter and yanked free a rolling wad of toilet paper, which he pressed firmly into the wound. The paper turned bright red. The bleeding quickly subsided.

Perry gently lifted the wad of bloody paper. The stabbing tweezers had ripped through the orangish skin, leaving a thick, torn piece sticking up from the center.

This thing had to go, and it had to go right motherfucking now.

Play through the pain.

He fastened the tweezers around the flap of orange skin, squeezed tightly, and yanked as hard as he could. Ripping, clawing pain shot through his leg, but he smiled with satisfaction as the orange flesh tore free. More blood spilled to the floor.

He held the piece of flesh up to the light. It was *thick*, thick like the skin on one of those fat Sunkists, the kind that are as large as grapefruit. Thin white tendrils stuck out from the sides like a thousand minute jellyfish arms. The fleshy thing was ripped and torn in a dozen places, but had come off in one solid piece.

He set it aside and dabbed at the wound with fresh toilet paper. Despite the pain, he felt surprisingly good, like he'd finally taken control of the situation. The newly exposed flesh seemed incredibly sensitive, and even the slightest touch hurt. Tiny rivulets of blood slowly ran from the wound's edges.

But something wasn't right. He stared at his bloody thigh, and his in-control feeling faded away—this wasn't over, not yet. A discolored, pale whitish patch the size of a quarter sat in the wound's center.

It seemed perfectly round, but bits of normal flesh swelled up around it and covered the edges of the white patch. Perry used the pointy tweezers to poke at the white growth—it seemed firm, yet flexible.

As the cold feeling of panic grabbed hold of his brain, he realized that he didn't actually *feel* the poking tweezers. He didn't feel them, because the whitish patch *wasn't him*.

When he pinched at it, the normal flesh around the edges easily peeled up and away from the white spot. The white spot was a separate . . . *thing* . . . from his own skin. It was as if a rounded plastic button had spontaneously grown within the muscles of his thigh.

He pushed the loose flesh from the edges of the white

growth. The thing's shiny coating made it look like a piece of bone china.

Did cancer look like this? Maybe, but he was pretty sure that cancerous flesh didn't make perfect circles and didn't just spring up in a matter of days.

Cancer or no cancer, the sight of the milky white growth stirred a primal fear in his soul, as if a rusty bear trap had clamped down on his heart, pinching it shut, preventing it from pumping. He tried to master his breathing, tried to calm himself.

He carefully slid the tweezers under the whitish growth. The points scraped against his raw muscle, but he ignored the pain. He lifted the tweezers from the underside—the hard growth tilted within his flesh, but it stayed anchored into his leg. Blood pooled each time he moved it.

He carefully used his fingers to pull his flesh back as far as it would go, probing underneath with the tweezers. Like putting your hands in your pocket and being able to 'see' what's there, Perry felt a stem—a stem that extended farther into his thigh, anchoring the white thing in place.

Doctor time.

Definitely doctor time.

But first, he wanted this *thing* out of his leg, and he wanted it out now. He *had* to remove it; he couldn't stand to leave this fucking thing in his flesh for even one more second.

With the tweezers centered on the unseen stem, Perry pulled up gently. As he lifted the growth, he *felt* the stem's length via a strange combination of sensations from his thigh muscles and resistance against the tweezers. The whitish mass pulled free of his flesh with a *pop* of inrushing air. Thin blood trails arced from the open wound, splashing against his leg and adding to the red and purple streaks on the worn tile floor, but the stem stayed firmly anchored deep in his thigh. Agonizing pain crept up his leg, but he ignored it, kept it distant from his consciousness.

He had to do this. It was time to turn the Magnificent Seven into the Big Six.

Keeping the tweezers firmly gripped on the strange stem, he yanked up as hard as he could, yanked with the strength of a condemned man fighting for his life.

The tough, resilient stem stretched and stretched and stretched, until the tweezers-gripped head was a good two feet above his thigh. It stretched thin like taffy, bits of blood and clear slime masking the milky white color.

The stretching slowed, then stopped.

With a snarl, Perry pulled harder.

The unseen anchor ripped free; the stem shot out of his leg like a rubber band and wetly slapped against his wrist.

He looked at his thigh. A narrow opening, smaller than a pencil and already closing, sank down into his raw flesh like a tiny black hole. A rivulet of blood poured out, pushed up the tube like squeezed toothpaste as the thigh muscles expanded and closed the hole.

A smile broke across Perry's face. A feeling of primitive success coursed through him, as did a limited blast of hope. He turned his attention to the strange white growth, the rounded head pinched firmly between the tweezers, the stem—or tail, or whatever the hell it was—wrapped wetly about his wrist, held to his skin by bloody slime.

He moved his hand toward the light to get a better look at the growth. As he rotated his wrist, marveling at the strange thing, he felt a brief tickling sensation, almost imperceptible, like the smallest mosquito trying to land.

Perry's eyes shot wide open with revulsion. He felt his stomach churn and his adrenaline surge . . .

The white thing's tail squirmed like a snake trapped in a predator's grip. With a shout of fear, Perry threw the tweezers into the bathtub where they clanked against the white porcelain and clattered near the drain. The squirming, wet, wiggling, white thing remained wrapped about his wrist, the tail tickling his skin as the heavy, round, plastic-button head hung limp and free, swinging wildly with Perry's every movement.

Perry screamed, both in disgust and in panic, and violently snapped his wrist as if he were flinging mud from his fingers. The white thing hit the mirror with a little *splat*. It looked like a moving piece of cooked spaghetti hanging loosely from the glass. Still writhing, its desperate motions smearing wet slime across the mirror, it slowly started to slide down.

That thing was inside *me! That thing was* alive*! It's* STILL *alive!*

Perry instinctively slapped hard against the mirror, his huge hand rattling the glass with a loud bang. The squirming growth erupted as if he'd slammed a soft-boiled egg. Thin gouts of thickish purple gel spewed across the mirror. Perry yanked his hand away. Bits of white flesh, now limp and saggy, covered his palm, as did globs of the purple goo. Curling his lip in revulsion, he quickly turned to grab the towel that hung from the shower curtain rod—too quickly. His sudden move tangled him in the pants still hanging about his ankles. His balance gone, he fell forward.

He reached his hands out to brace his fall, but there was nothing to grab before his forehead smacked against the toilet seat. A sharp *crack* reverberated off the narrow bathroom's walls, but Perry was out before he even heard the sound.

23

PARASITOLOGY

Martin Brewbaker was no more. Wednesday, less than three full days since he'd been shot to death, and all that remained was a pitted black skeleton missing the legs from the knees down. That and delicate gossamer mold that now grew in little patches not only on the skeleton and on the table, but in spots all over the BSL-4 tent. Even Brewbaker's talon-hand had finally relaxed. It lay on the table, finger bones crumbling into a jumbled pile. Cameras inside the tent provided pictures—both live and still—that let Margaret watch the corpse's final degenerative state.

She hadn't felt such a black sense of foreboding since her childhood, during the ever-so-deadly pissing contests between the United States and the Soviet Union. Mutually assured destruction, the promise that any conflict could rapidly escalate into full-blown nuclear war. Bang. Dead. Done.

She'd only been a young girl, but more than smart enough to grasp the potential disaster. It was funny, really, that back then her parents had thought she understood because of her high intelligence, as if only a gifted child could comprehend the imminent threat of nuclear war. But, as they had in years before and had in years since, probably always would, adults mistake children's innocence for ignorance.

Margaret knew exactly what was going on, and so did most of her classmates. They knew the Communists were something to fear, something more tangible than the Thing Under the Bed. They knew that Manhattan, their home, would be among the first places destroyed.

Why do people think the end of the world is such a difficult concept for a child to understand? Much of childhood is spent in fear of the unknown, in fear of creeping shadows and lurking monsters and things that promise a long, ugly, and painful death. A nuclear war was just one more boogeyman that threatened to take them all away. Only this boogeyman also scared her parents and all the other grown-ups, and the children tuned in to that frequency of fear as surely as they tuned in to Bugs Bunny.

You could run from a monster, you could dodge the boogeyman, but the nuclear war was out there and out of their hands. It might come at any moment. Maybe when she was on the playground at recess. Maybe when she sat down to dinner. Maybe after she went to bed.

Now I lay me down to sleep, I pray the Lord my soul to keep. If I should die before I wake, I pray the Lord my soul to take.

That hadn't just been an abstract prayer in those days. It had been a possibility as real as the sunset. She remembered living in constant fear of that unknown. Sure she played, went to school, laughed and carried on with her friends, but the threat was always there. Each thready white contrail in the sky was a potential first finger of doom.

And the game would be played out, win or lose, without her able to do anything about it.

She tried to tell herself that this wasn't the same thing. She was on the forefront of this potential holocaust, after all; she was the front line of defense. This wasn't out of her control but rather—quite literally—resting squarely in her hands. For some reason, however, that rational, adult knowledge couldn't banish the little girl's fear that there was nothing she could do to affect this game's outcome.

She wondered how Amos could ignore that feeling, or if he even felt it at all. He hummed the theme song to *Hawaii Five-O* for the millionth time, yet Margaret was too tired to complain. She sipped at her coffee. She'd downed pots of the stuff, hoping it would stimulate her, yet nothing seemed to cut through her lethargy. It felt good to breathe normal air, air not filtered by the biosuit. She wanted to sleep, or at least stretch out and relax, but there really wasn't time. They needed to finish up the work, incinerate the decomposed remains, and get the hell out of that hospital.

Amos turned to her. His hair was askew, his clothes wrinkled, yet his eyes were alive with excitement.

'This is really quite amazing, Margaret,' he said. 'Think about it. This is a human parasite of unparalleled complexity. There's no question in my mind that this creature is perfectly suited to its human host.'

Margaret stared at the wall, her words quiet, barely audible. 'I hate to paraphrase a tired old cliché, but it's almost too perfect.'

'What do you mean?'

'Like you said, the creature is ideally suited. It's like a hand in a glove. But think about it, Amos, think of current technology levels—this creature is miles above that. It would be like the Russians suddenly landing on the moon while the Wright brothers were still struggling at Kitty Hawk.'

'It's amazing, sure, but we can't ignore the fact that it's

right here in front of us. This is no time for sensitive American egos. There's some genius out there that's so far beyond us we can't even comprehend it.'

'What if there is no genius?' Margaret asked, her voice still small.

'What are you talking about? Of course there's a genius—how else could this thing have been created?'

She turned to look at him, her skin almost gray, fatigue covering her face like a caul. 'What if it's not created? What if it's natural?'

'Oh *come on,* Margaret! I know you're tired, but you're not thinking straight. If this is natural, how could we have never seen it before? A human parasite of such size and virulence, and there isn't one documented case before this year? That doesn't make sense. For this thing to be so closely matched to human hosts would constitute *millions* of years of coevolution, yet we've never seen anything like this in *any* mammal, let alone primates or humans.'

'I'm sure there's many, many things we haven't seen,' Margaret said. 'But I just can't accept that someone *created* this thing. It's just too complex, too advanced. Regardless of what the scare-tactic media like to spout, American science is state-of-the-art. Who's more advanced? The Chinese? Japan? Singapore? Sure, maybe some countries are starting to get an edge on us, but an *edge* is one thing, and an *exponential shift* is another. If we can't create something that's even close to this, I find it hard to believe anyone else could. That's not ego, that's just the facts.'

Amos seemed annoyed by her persistence. 'It's highly improbable that this affliction has existed but has never been documented. Sure, there are species as yet undiscovered, I grant you that, but there's a difference between some unknown microscopic creature and this. There's *nothing* like this. I can't even think of a tribal myth or folk-tale that resembles this. So if this is natural, where in the blue blazes did it come from?'

Margaret shrugged. 'You've got me. Maybe some kind of dormancy. This may have been a known quantity in prehistoric times, and something caused it to die out. But it didn't die out all the way. Somehow it stayed dormant for thousands of years until something caused this outbreak. There are orchid seeds that can stay dormant for twenty-five hundred years, for example.'

'Your theory sounds about as far-fetched as the Loch Ness Monster,' Amos said.

'Well what about the coelacanth? People thought it was extinct for seventy million years until a fisherman caught one in 1938. Just because someone hasn't seen it doesn't mean it isn't there, Amos.'

'Right,' Amos said. 'And this thing happened to remain dormant for hundreds of years in areas of extreme population density? It would be one thing to find this deep in the Congo jungle, but quite another to find it in Detroit. This isn't AIDS, where people just *die*—these are defined, triangular growths. In the communication age, something like this doesn't go unreported. Pardon my brusqueness, but you'll have to find another theory.'

Margaret nodded absently. Amos was right. The concept of a dormant human parasite didn't wash. Whatever these things were, they were new.

Amos changed the subject. 'Have Murray's men found any connection among the victims?'

'Nothing yet. They've traced the travel of all victims and anyone the victims came in contact with. There's no connection. Most of the victims hadn't traveled anywhere. The only link is that Judy Washington and Gary Leeland, the two Detroit cases, happened within a week of each other and happened at the same retirement home. They checked that place out with a fine-tooth comb. No one else shows any signs of infection. They've run tests on the water, the food, the air—nothing out of the ordinary, although we're still not sure what to look for so that doesn't rule anything out.

'The two Toledo cases were weeks apart, but within a few blocks of each other physically. There seems to be some proximity effect. The transmission vector is unknown, but Murray still thinks there's a terrorist out there deliberately infecting random people.'

'That fits with our observations,' Amos said. 'I'm more and more convinced that Brewbaker and the others may have been contaminated but weren't contagious. We've found nothing on him indicative of eggs, an embryonic form, or anything else that could be responsible for new parasites. Besides, Dew hasn't shown any symptoms, nor has anyone who came in contact with Brewbaker's body.'

Margaret rubbed her eyes. God, she needed a nap. Shit, what she *needed* was a week in Bora-Bora with a sleek cabana boy named Marco catering to her every need. But she didn't have Bora-Bora, she had Toledo, Ohio. And she didn't have a cabana boy named Marco—she had a gossamer-mold-covered, pitted black skeleton formerly known as Martin Brewbaker.

24

THE BATHROOM FLOOR

The genetic blueprint recognized when the shells reached the proper thickness; energies then turned to the body's growth. Cells split again and again and again, a nonstop engine of creation. Internal organs began to take shape, but they wouldn't fully develop until later. Because the host still provided all food and warmth, most of the internal organs could wait—right now the most important needs were the tendrils, the tails and the brain.

The brain developed rapidly but remained a long way from forming anything that resembled an intelligent thought. The tendrils, however, were of a relatively simple design. They grew like wildfire, branching out in all directions, spreading into the host. The tendrils sought out the host's nerve cells, intertwining with the dendrites like fingered hands clasping tightly together.

Starting slowly, almost tentatively, the organisms released complex chemical compounds called neurotransmitters into the synaptic cleft, the space between the tendrils and the dendrites. Each neurotransmitter was part of a signal, a message—they slid into the axons' receptor sites, just like a key into a lock, causing that nerve cell to generate its own neurotransmitters with its own specific message. As in the host's normal sensory process, the action produced an electrochemical chain reaction: the messages repeated through the nervous system until they reached the host's brain. The process—from the time the message fires until it finally reaches the brain—takes less than one-thousandth of a second.

Although they had yet to achieve conscious thought, at a primitive level the organisms inside Perry knew they had been attacked. They instinctively triggered an immediate growth process. The tail began a phase change of its own. Specialized cells grew, ensuring the organisms would remain anchored in their environment long enough to fully develop.

The six remaining organisms grew, rapidly and unimpeded, as the host lay passed out on his bathroom floor.

The linoleum felt nice and cool on Perry's face. He didn't really want to try to sit up. As long as he lay still, the pain was only mildly intolerable.

When was the last time he'd been knocked out? Eight years ago? No, it was nine, when his dad had hit him in the back of the head with a full bottle of Wild Turkey whiskey. He'd wound up with nine stitches in his scalp.

Had it hurt this bad after Dad hit him with the bottle? That was so long ago, and it seemed like nothing compared to the dull waves of pain that now washed through his head. He tried to sit up, which only made it worse. It was like a tequila hangover times ten.

He felt sick to his stomach. Every little move toward an upright position shot more thick blasts of pain through his skull. He felt a puke coming on, working its way around his lukewarm, queasy stomach.

He reached up and gingerly touched his abused forehead. At least he wasn't bleeding. He felt a pronounced bump, a half golf ball embedded in his skull.

He realized his pants were around his ankles, which added to the difficulty of sitting up. This was going to be a wonderful story to tell at parties —just as soon as he remembered what that story was. He slowly rolled to his back and pulled up his jeans. The room looked fuzzy and out of focus.

Perry grabbed the toilet seat. It wobbled weirdly as he used it to pull himself up. The seat was cracked in two at the oval's front edge. Must have done that with his head.

His stomach churned once, twice, then rebelled. Perry leaned forward and vomited into the toilet, spilling a large quantity of bile into the water, a guttural grunt echoing in the ceramic bowl. His clenched stomach relaxed its grip, allowing him to breathe, but the air froze in his throat as shearing pain cut through his head.

His eyes shut tight. He groaned weakly against the rhythmic pounding of his skull. The pain immobilized him as assuredly as a straitjacket. He couldn't even get to his feet to find a dozen or so Excedrin.

Somewhere in his head he remembered hearing that people puke when they get a concussion. He wondered how boxers or pro quarterbacks put up with it. This feeling wasn't worth any amount of money.

Another wave of nausea slammed into his stomach, pushing more bile into the cloudy bowl. The acrid odor of vomit filled the bathroom. The smell made him even more nauseous, which made his head hurt more, which made him feel like puking yet again. It was one of those vicious circles that make even nonreligious people ask God what they had done to deserve such trauma.

'Must have been a child molester in a previous life,' he muttered to himself. 'That or Genghis Khan.'

A third wave of nausea hit him. There was nothing left

to vomit, but his stomach didn't care. It clenched with explosion-violent fury that doubled him over, pushing his head almost into the toilet bowl.

His face scrunched as tight as his clamped diaphragm. His stomach refused to relax for a full five seconds, preventing him from drawing a breath. When it finally relaxed and air filled his lungs, he opened his watering eyes just in time for the pain to slam into his head like a seventy-mile-per-hour semi truck squashing a baby raccoon. He saw a few black spots, then his face slid back onto the cool linoleum.

25

'DELUSIONAL PARASITOSIS'

Morgellons disease.

Margaret stared in disbelief at the CDC report. The disease that wasn't a disease at all, but believed by the majority of the health-care community to be 'delusional parasitosis.'

'Delusional,' Margaret said. 'Get a load of that.'

'Seems the vast majority of the cases are,' Amos said. 'Symptoms range from feelings of biting or stinging to things crawling under the skin. Some cases have the strange fibers, and most involve some form of mental condition: depression, acute onset of ADHD, bipolar disorder and . . . take a guess at the last three.'

'Paranoia, psychosis and psychopathy?'

'You're just racking up the cee-gars these days, Margo.'

Margaret, Amos and Clarence Otto waited in the hospital director's office, a plaque-lined room with warm wood paneling and four well-groomed potted ficus trees. The director had been asked to leave by the persuasive Agent Otto, who apologized for the intrusion while at the same time leaving no possible way for the director to say no. Margaret thought Otto was a born salesman—a guy who could make you do whatever he wanted while making you think it was your idea the whole time. Margaret and Amos sat on a leather couch, both looking at pages of a report spread out on a coffee table. Otto had taken the director's chair, behind the ornate wooden desk. He spun the chair in slow circles and seemed to relish the implied authority of the spot—smiling like a little kid playing grown-up boss.

Murray was on his way. They would give him their report face-to-face.

'I know I'm the dummy of the bunch,' Otto said. 'So pardon me for asking—but you have a CDC report. What you're saying is the stuff you guys have been studying for the past few days, that turns out to be a known factor?'

Amos shook his head. 'No, not even close. This Morgellons thing, people don't know if it's real or a kind of group delusion. It took years of pressure from victims' groups to force the CDC to at least pretend to take it seriously. The CDC created a task force, but so far they don't even have a clear case definition of what Morgellons is. Most of the cases actually do turn out to be delusional parasitosis. People *think* they're infected with something, organisms that can only be observed by the patient. In fact, the term Morgellons has been around for just a few years, and since it started to get publicity, more and more people report the symptoms.'

'Which means it's spreading,' Margaret said.

'Not necessarily. It could mean that, or it could mean that once unstable people hear about the disease, their minds decide that's what they have. They invent the symptoms in their own brain—hence the "delusional" part.'

Otto spun in the director's chair, three full circles as he spoke. 'So the more people that claim to have this disease, the more publicity it gets, then more people hear about it, and then more people think they have it.'

'Full circle of nuttiness,' Amos said.

'Goddamn Murray,' Margaret said. 'He's right about

keeping this quiet. This is exactly what he said would happen if word got out. And that's just for this itchy thing, the bugs-under-the-skin thing. Just imagine what the response is going to be like if people see pictures of the triangles.'

'Or get wind of grannies slicing up their kids, then playing all Scarface with the cops,' Otto said. 'Psycho grandmamas would definitely upset Mister and Missus Average American.'

Amos nodded. 'Murray does have a point, I suppose. There were a dozen Morgellons cases five years ago, now there are over fifteen hundred, reported in all fifty states and in Europe.'

'So why haven't we heard more about the triangles?' Margaret asked. 'We *know* this isn't delusional. We've seen the little buggers, and we've seen the chemical imbalances in Brewbaker's brain. This is *real*, Amos.'

'Because *most* of the cases are delusional, but not *all*. It's the fibers, Margaret. There are documented cases with blue, red, black and white fibers that are made up of cellulose. There have been three instances where doctors had the fibers analyzed over the past four years, and guess what—they had the *exact* chemical composition as Brewbaker's. *Exact*, as in down to the molecules.'

'Your fizzles.'

Amos smiled. 'Yes, the fizzles. We have the triangle cases we've seen in the past few weeks. Let's assume those are cases where the organism made it to the larval stage. However, this Morgellons research indicated there have been multiple cases, over several years, where we see the fibers, where we see fizzles. It's possible there were full-blown larval infections *before* the last few weeks, sure, but if they existed, no one has heard about them.'

Agent Otto whipped himself in circles. He seemed to be trying to see how many spins he could get off of one push. 'So the fibers have been around for a while, but only now are reaching this larval stage? Does that mean they're evolving?'

Margaret started to speak, a kind of automatic reaction to correct a layman's guess at science, but stopped. Otto oversimplified it, but his concept was right on the money.

'Amos,' Margaret said, 'has this task force been mapping the occurrences of the actual fibers?'

Amos shrugged. 'I would imagine so, but I'm not sure. We'd have to talk to them.'

Margaret flipped through the pages. 'Doctor Frank Cheng. He's the project lead. I need to talk to this man. I don't know if Murray will let me call him.'

'Margaret, may I say something?' Otto asked.

'Sure.'

He spun once in his chair, then gripped the desk with both hands, smiling the whole time. 'You seem to let people push you around. You ever notice that?'

She felt her face turning red. Just because she had a problem, and everyone knew she had a problem, didn't mean Otto had to actually *talk* about it.

'That's none of your business,' she said.

'Because it seems to me you're a lot stronger than you think. We're dealing with some pretty crazy stuff here, am I right?'

She nodded.

'So if you've got something you feel we need to do, maybe you should stop being such a pussy.'

'Excuse me?'

Amos slapped the coffee table. 'Preach on, Brother Otto!'

'I said, Margaret, stop being such a pussy.'

'I *heard* what you said.'

'So stop letting Murray tell you what to do.'

Margaret's jaw dropped. 'Are you completely deranged? He's the deputy director of the CIA, man! How can I *not* let him tell me what to do?'

'So he's the deputy director. Do you know what *you* are?'

'Tell her!' Amos screamed. He stood and raised his hands to the sky. 'Tell the good sister what she is!'

'Yes, Agent Otto, please tell me what I am.'

Otto spun twice, then spoke. '*You* are the lead epidemiologist studying a new, unknown disease with horrific implications.'

'Horrific!' Amos echoed.

'You are short-staffed, and you can't get the experts you should have.'

'It's a *sin*!' Amos said.

'Amos,' Margaret said, 'just knock it the fuck off.'

Amos smiled, then picked up a magazine off the coffee table and sat down, pretending to read.

'Margaret, he put you in charge of this. What will happen if you insist on talking to this Cheng guy? Do you think Murray is going to bring in someone else to replace you?'

She started to speak, then stopped. No. Murray wouldn't do that. Not because she was the end-all be-all, but because he wanted to keep this tight as a drum. Murray *needed her*.

'So,' Otto said as he gave one strong push. He started spinning, speaking one syllable on each revolution, almost as if he'd read her mind. 'Use . . . what . . . you . . . have.'

Her anger faded.

Agent Clarence Otto was right.

26

THE POISON PILL

The seedlings continuously monitored development, fed by data from the roaming readers. At a certain point, the seedlings' checklists determined that the readers' jobs were completed. A chemical signal rolled through the host. The readers went through a phase change. With a simple adjustment, the sawlike jaws dropped off and the balls sealed up tight.

Inside the balls, death started to brew.

They inflated, filling themselves with a new chemical compound. Herders moved the chemical balls throughout the framework, wedging them here, wedging them there.

Where the jaws had been, a crusty cap appeared. The deadly compound ate away at the inside of the cap, but the seedlings flooded the structure with another chemical that added thickness to the cap from the outside. It was a delicate balance, but as long as the seedlings remained 'alive,' kept making the chemical, the poison balls would remain sealed.

If the seedlings ceased to function, however, the caps would disintegrate and the vile catalyst inside would spread through the framework, dissolving it, the modified stem cells and all the cells they had created. Cells would blacken, die, then dissolve, the resulting waste material moving on to poison other cells. The ensuing chain reaction would dissolve every soft tissue it reached—framework, muscle, skin, organs . . . everything.

To stop this from happening, the seedlings had to survive.

But this host had no way of knowing that.

27

GOOD-BYE

'I'm sorry, Mister Phillips,' the doctor said. 'He just slipped away. We thought we had him out of the woods, and then he was just gone.'

Dew stared at the doctor, who looked tired and bedraggled. It wasn't the doctor's fault; the man had done everything possible. Dew still couldn't stop the wave of fury that swept over him, that had him wondering how easy it would be to snap the little doctor's skinny neck.

'What killed him?'

'It wasn't one particular thing. I think the whole incident was just too much for his body to handle. To be blunt, he should have died back on Monday, but he was strong enough to fight another sixty hours. Because of that, we thought we might be able to save him, but there was just too much damage. I'm very sorry. Now if you'll excuse me, I have to go talk to his wife.'

'No,' Dew snapped. Then, quietly, 'No, I'll do it. I was his partner.'

'As you like, Mister Phillips,' the doctor said. 'I'll be nearby if you need me.'

The doctor strode away. Dew stared at the floor, gathering his courage. It wasn't the first time he'd lost a partner, and it wasn't the first time he'd had to break the news to a new widow. It never got easier. It was funny how you could get used to *killing*, but not to *death*.

He wearily looked down the hall. Shamika stared at him, her son, Jerome, asleep in her lap. Her eyes filled with tears of denial. She knew. Dew still had to tell her, though; the words had to be said.

He walked toward her. Dew remembered another hospital, a day six years earlier, the day Jerome was born. He remembered sitting in the waiting room with Malcolm, who'd been so nervous he'd thrown up twice. He remembered talking to Shamika just hours after the delivery.

He kept walking toward her. She started shaking her head side to side, clutching Jerome tighter. She mumbled warbling words that couldn't be understood, yet their meaning rang clear. Dew wished he were anywhere else, anywhere but facing this crying woman, the wife of his friend, his partner . . . the man he'd failed to protect.

He fought back tears of his own, an empty sorrow rolling in his chest alongside the burning hatred and rage. The only thing that kept him strong was the knowledge he'd find out who was responsible. And when he did, oh daddy, daddy-o, the fun he would have.

28

THE BATHROOM FLOOR—AGAIN

For a moment, Perry slipped back in time. He was seventeen. His mother crying, as usual, shaking him gently. Perry slowly opening his eyes, feeling the pain roaring through his brain, fingers touching the back of his head, coming away with blood. His dad sitting at the kitchen table, drinking steadily from the bottle of Wild Turkey that he'd used as a weapon against his only child.

The bottle wore a small streak of tacky blood, half on the label, half beaded up on the glass.

Jacob Dawsey stared at his son, his cold eyes fixed in their permanently angry stare. 'How you feelin', boy?'

Perry slowly sat up, his head throbbing so bad he could barely see.

'Someday, Daddy,' Perry mumbled, 'someday I'm going to kill you.'

Jacob Dawsey took another swig, his eyes never leaving his son. He set the blood-streaked bottle on the table, then wiped his mouth with the back of his dirty hand. 'You just remember that it's a violent world, son, and only the strong survive. I'm preparing you is all—someday you'll thank me. Someday, you'll understand.'

Perry shook his head, trying to clear his thoughts, and found himself lying on his own bathroom floor. It wasn't nine years ago. He wasn't in Cheboygan. Daddy was dead.

That chapter of his life was over, but that didn't make his head feel any better.

His face felt crusty and squishy on the linoleum. The scent of bile filled his nose. Didn't take him long to figure out why. His rebellious stomach had apparently found something else to cough up while he was passed out.

A little shiver tickled his soul. It was a good thing he'd been lying facedown, or he could have choked on his own vomit, just like Bon Scott—the original lead singer from the band AC/DC. Bon had passed out in the back of a black Cadillac, so the story went, bombed out of his skull on whiskey and perhaps a few other controlled substances, so blasted he couldn't wake up; he drowned in his own puke.

Perry wiped his hand across his face, scraping away vomit slime. He had some in his hair as well. His stomach felt tired but otherwise fine; the regurgitation festival was apparently over. Most of the awful smell emanated from the toilet bowl. Perry laboriously sat up and flushed.

How the hell had this happened? Vague, out-of-focus pieces flitted back and forth across his brain like moths circling a streetlight. His left leg ached with a cold-iron throbbing.

Using the counter to pull himself to his feet, he slowly stood. His whole body felt very weak, which made him wonder how long he'd been unconscious. In the bathroom with the door half shut, there was no way of telling time; sunlight could not reach down the hall.

Resting his weight against the sink, he looked at himself in the mirror. 'Look like shit' couldn't describe it. A green-yellow film of vomit caked the right side of his face, matting down his hair. A black-and-blue bump on his forehead stuck out like a unicorn's starter kit. The dark circles under his eyes were so pronounced they were almost comical, as if he were wearing overdone movie makeup meant for an extra in *Night of the Living Dead*.

What really caught his eye wasn't his face, but the dried-up crap all over his mirror. Rivulets of some odd liquid had dribbled down the glass, then dried in black streaks. Papery chunks of grayish matter clumped on the mirror like old paste, or perhaps a smashed insect.

Only it wasn't an insect, and Perry knew that. Memories of the mess on the mirror jostled his fuzzed-out, pain-fogged brain. He didn't know what it was, but he knew it was evil. The thing was death, something to be very afraid of. At least it had *been* something to be afraid of.

He needed some Tylenol and he needed to wash this filth from his body. Even reaching down to turn on the shower made his head pound. He couldn't remember the last time he'd hurt like this, or if he'd *ever* hurt like this.

'Doctor time,' he mumbled to himself. 'Fucking doctor time.'

Perry headed to the kitchen for some Tylenol. He moved slowly and carefully, holding his head as if he might stop his hammering brain from falling onto the floor. He looked at the stove's digital clock: 12:15.

It took his thudding head a minute to get the picture, and he actually asked himself how the sun could be out at a quarter past midnight, then realized his stupidity with a small sigh. It was 12:15 P.M.—a quarter past noon. He'd slept through work. There was no way he could go in, at least not until his head felt better. He told himself he'd call in and try to explain things, but only after a shower.

The Tylenol bottle sat on the microwave, right next to the wooden cutlery block that held the knives. His eyes rested on the chicken scissors. Only their brown plastic handles showed, but hidden inside the block of wood were the scissors' thick, stubby blades that could easily cut through raw meat as if it were paper and chicken bone as if it were a dry twig. They held his fascination for a moment, then he reached for the Tylenol bottle.

He tossed four pills into his mouth, made a bowl out of his hands and gulped tap water to swallow them down. That done, he shambled back toward the bathroom, stripping off clothes as he went. He stepped into the steaming shower and basked in the spray, tilting his head to let the water wash the slime from his hair and face. The stinging-hot water revived his flaccid muscles. The fog in his brain lifted a touch. He hoped the Tylenol would kick in soon—his head hurt so bad he could barely see.

29

MOTIVATION

Dew refused to cry. Just wasn't going to happen. It wanted to come out, and he had trouble fighting it back, but no way in hell. He wasn't in this business to make friends. It hurt, sure it did, but Malcolm Johnson wasn't his first friend to die in the line of duty.

How much of this did he have to deal with? How much could he take? How many more people did he have to see die?

How many more people . . . did he have to kill?

He sniffled and wiped his nose with the back of his hand. He needed to reconnect.

Dew picked up his small cell phone, the normal one, and dialed. It rang three times before she answered.

'Hello?'

'Hi, Cynthia, it's Dew.'

'Oh, hi, how are you?' Her words carried history, decades of back story, if you will. Dew and Cynthia had hated each other once, hated each other with a passion that went even beyond what he felt for the enemy during a battle. That hatred was born out of love, deep, all-encompassing love for the same person.

That person was Sharon, Dew's only child.

'To tell you the truth, I've been a lot better, a lot of times,' Dew said. 'But don't tell Sharon that, okay?'

'Sure thing. You want me to put her on?'

'Please.'

'Hold on one sec.'

They would never, ever be friends, he and Cynthia, but at least they had respect for each other. They had to, because Sharon loved them both, and when Dew and Cynthia fought, it tore Sharon apart.

It had been hard to hear that his little girl thought she was a lesbian. But that was nothing compared to the pain and anger he felt seven years later when he heard Sharon and Cynthia were more than 'partners''—they had performed some union ceremony or what have you, and they were basically married. Wife and wife. He'd raged, screamed at them both, called them names he wished he hadn't. Cynthia, of course, had screamed back. She wanted to protect Sharon, Dew understood that now. Cynthia also happened to despise men in general, especially gruff, bossy, unemotional military men—which happened to sum up Dew Phillips in a nutshell. But Cynthia's constant attacks on Dew, both when he was there and when he wasn't, took their toll on Sharon. Dew hated. Cynthia hated. Sharon just wasn't wired that way. Sharon loved, pure and simple.

It took another two years after the 'union' bullshit, but Dew finally understood that this was the real deal for his daughter. This wasn't a passing fancy — she was going to be with Cynthia for the rest of her life. Once he came to that realization, he did what any good soldier would do—he sucked it up and he got the job done. He'd met Cynthia at what they both called the SDMZ, or the 'Starbucks Demilitarized Zone,' and they agreed on an uneasy détente. They could hate each other all they wanted, and nothing could change that, but they agreed to be civil and to treat each other with respect. And over the years, in the process of being civil, he came to understand that Cynthia was a good kid—as far as bull dykes go, that is.

'Hi, Daddy!' Sharon's voice, unchanged from the time she was five. Well, that was bullshit, and Dew knew it, but that's exactly what his ears heard every time she talked.

'Hi, sugar. How are you?'

'I'm doing great. I'm so glad you called. How are you?'

'Tip-top. Couldn't be better. Work is going well.'

'You're still doing the desk job?' He heard the worry in her voice. 'They're not making you go out in the field anymore, right?'

'Of course not, at my age? That would be crazy.'

'It most certainly would.'

'Listen, sugar, I only have a minute. I just wanted to call and hear your voice.'

'Well here it is. When are you coming to Boston again? I want to see you. We can go out, just you and me.'

Dew swallowed. If a gutted Malcolm Johnson wasn't going to make him cry, he sure as shit wouldn't let the waterworks go over a phone call with his daughter.

'Come on, sugar, you know I'm okay with Cynthia now. We'll all go out, spend some time together.'

Dew almost laughed when he heard Sharon sniffle. Whereas he could hold back tears seemingly forever, she cried if the wind blew funny. 'Yeah, I know, Daddy. And you have no idea what that means to me. What it means to us.'

'Stop with the crying already. I got to go. I'll talk to you soon. Bye now.'

'Bye-bye, Daddy. And be careful. You might get a splinter from that desk.'

Dew hung up. He took one deep breath, and then the

emotions faded away, pushed back to their normal hiding place. That was what he'd needed, to reconnect with the *why* of what he did. It was for her. It was for a country in which his daughter could live as she pleased, even if that meant living with another woman, even if her father hated it, and hated her mate, with all his heart. There were many places in the world where Sharon would have been killed—or worse—for doing what came naturally to her.

Was that cliché? To keep on fighting, and killing when need be, because America was the greatest nation on earth? Probably, but Dew didn't care if the reasons were good, logical or even cliché. They were his reasons.

And that was enough.

30

MR. CONGENIALITY

Margaret, Amos and Clarence Otto stood as Murray Longworth entered the commandeered office. Murray shook everyone's hands, then all three sat. Murray, of course, sat behind the big desk.

'What have you got for me? We got you a relatively fresh one this time. I trust that an unrotted body gave us some clues as to what the hell these things are?'

Margaret led the charge. 'It didn't stay "unrotted" for long. All the tissue is gone. Only his skeleton is left—it looks the same as the remains of Judy Washington and Charlotte Wilson. We have the liquefied remains, but I think we've learned all we can from that material. Before Brewbaker fully decomposed, however, we were able to gather some valuable and disturbing information. First of all, we believe the growth isn't a modification of tissue, but rather it's a parasitical organism.'

Murray's face wrinkled in mild disgust. 'It's a parasite? What makes you think that?'

'Just as with Charlotte Wilson's case, the growth itself was already decomposed. We could get nothing from it, but we found structures in the surrounding tissue that made us classify it as a parasite. The growths are tapped into the host's circulatory system, drawing oxygen and possibly nutrients from the blood.'

Murray stared at her, like a limestone statue just beginning to show the effects of wind, rain and erosion. 'What you're telling me is that these triangular things are alive, that they're not part of the victim but rather a separate, living creature?'

'Exactly.'

'So why are the "hosts," as you call them, going nuts?'

'We found excessive neurotransmitter levels in the brain,' Margaret said. 'Neurotransmitters are the substances that pass signals from nerve cell to nerve cell, allowing the body to communicate with the brain and vice versa, as well as allowing the brain to function. Dopamine and serotonin, in particular, were at extremely high levels. Excess dopamine is implicated in severe schizophrenia, and excess serotonin can cause psychotic behavior and paranoia. We also found extremely high levels of epinephrine and norepinephrine throughout the brain. These two hormones are vital to the fight-or-flight response, key in reaction to emergencies and perceived threats. They also cause some of the physiological expressions of fear and anxiety. When the hormones exceed normal levels, anxiety disorders are very common.'

Murray nodded with understanding. 'So these *parasites* make people go crazy by increasing neurotransmitters?'

'Right,' Amos said. 'But there's more. The parasite grows structures that mimic human nerves. We found such structures in the area surrounding the growth, but we found traces in the brain as well, particularly in the cerebral cortex and the limbic region.'

'What's the limbic region?'

Margaret answered. 'It's a cluster of areas including the thalamus, the hippocampus and the amygdala, among others, that is thought to control emotion and comprise the basic structures for memory storage and recall. The growths in that area may have been some kind of endocrine system for secreting the excess neurotransmitters. Based on case studies of excess dopamine in the limbic region, hosts may develop extremely acute paranoia. That's consistent with the behavior observed in Brewbaker, Blaine Tanarive, Gary Leeland and Charlotte Wilson. But if the growth was actually artificial nerves, it may have had another purpose—it's possible the parasite was somehow wired into the brain.'

Anger flashed in Murray's eyes. 'Oh come on. I agree with your "drug delivery" theory, that makes sense, but wired into the brain? What are you saying, that this isn't just some chemical overdose, that the parasite is somehow *controlling* the host?'

'It is a possibility,' she said.

'Why don't you just tell me the hosts are possessed by evil demons, Doctor Montoya? I'm beginning to suspect I made a serious mistake by putting you in charge of this. How the hell can you expect me to believe a parasite can *control* people, make them do all those horrible things?'

'We didn't say the parasite used people like some kind of robot,' Amos said. 'However, there are parallels found in nature where parasites modify the host's behavior. For example, there is a trematode that parasitizes a species of mud snail. To complete its life cycle, the trematode must pass from a snail to a sand flea. The trematode larva somehow forces snails to high ground, out of the water, where the snails will die. It *makes* them commit suicide, if you will. At that point the trematode exits the snail and enters a flea. Think also of the thorny-headed worm, which starts in a cockroach and moves on to a rat. To facilitate the change, the worm actually makes the cockroach less aware of danger, so it is more likely to be eaten by a rat. Then there is the—'

Murray held up his hand, cutting off Amos's next example. 'I get the point, Doc. That's riveting stuff, really it is, but snails and fucking roaches are a hell of a ways away from human intelligence.'

'Behavior is merely a chemical reaction, Mister Longworth,' Amos said. 'Human behavior involves more complicated reactions, but they are reactions nonetheless, and if a snail or—as you so eloquently put it, an *effing roach*—can be manipulated, then so, too, can a human.'

Murray rubbed the bridge of his nose, as if some monster headache pounded the inside of his skull. 'You know, I came here hoping for some good news, but this just gets worse every second. Okay, so someone out there has created a parasite that can manipulate human behavior. When the hell are you two going to give me something I can use?'

'Mister Longworth, this is something incredibly advanced,' Margaret said. Her voice grew cold and angry. This man wanted simple answers, yet there were none to give. 'We're talking a high degree of technological superiority. If this is an engineered organism, someone out there is so far ahead of us it's difficult to conceive. To put it another way, *if* this parasite is engineered, we're in a lot of trouble.'

Murray scowled—it was clear that additional complications were not welcome. 'What do you mean "if"?'

'I suspect, and I should note that Amos disagrees with me, that this psychopathic behavior may not be intended, but is actually a side effect. The possibility remains that this is some kind of natural parasite, or if not natural, then it was not *specifically* designed to make people crazy.'

Murray shook his head, then stared at the plaques on the wall. 'It's a weapon, Doctor Montoya, and a damn good one at that. Don't make this so complicated you can't see what's blatantly obvious. You handle the chemicals and such, and leave the strategic analysis to me. Now, I need ideas from you on how to fight this thing. Do you have any suggestions?'

Actually, Margaret had several suggestions, most of which involved a sledgehammer and Murray Longworth's ass, but those she kept to herself. 'There are a couple of things we need to do. First, we need to expand the staff. We need some psychiatrists on board.'

'Why?'

'All the hosts have shown severe behavioral disorders. If we're going to learn how this thing works, we need a living host. We need a bigger staff and we need it quick, particularly a neurobiologist and neuropharmacologist. A psychologist might help us figure out how to handle deranged victims. And in the long run, we need to learn how to combat the parasite's effects, possibly with drugs that modify behavior by countering the neurotransmitter overdose.'

'I don't think adding staff is a good idea, Margaret.'

'We need these people, and we need them *now*. We could lose control of this any second. Information control is one thing. Letting a plague break out on our watch is another.'

Murray's fingers drummed the desktop. 'Fine. I'll start looking for people. I don't need to tell you again just how secret this whole operation is, so I'm not going to have someone for you tomorrow or the next day. What have you got that I can use *now*?'

'Brewbaker had a small growth with colored fibers

growing out of it,' Margaret said. 'This symptom is consistent with a condition called Morgellons disease. We think that the fibers are a parasite that died, but parts of it keep working. The fibers are made of cellulose, a material common in plants but not produced in any way in humans.'

'Are the fibers conclusively connected with the triangles?'

'They are,' Amos said. 'The structure of the triangles is the same material as the fibers—cellulose. There is no way it's a coincidence.'

'And if you have the fibers,' Murray asked, 'then you have the triangles? You're going to go psycho?'

Margaret leaned forward. 'No, that's not the case. It seems people can have the fibers and *not* develop the full-fledged parasite.'

'And we haven't seen the triangle growths before, not before the last few days? The CDC doesn't have anything on it?'

'Not that we know of,' Margaret said. 'That doesn't mean there haven't been, or aren't currently, more cases. They may have existed. We just didn't find them.'

'So the fiber thingies have been around for a few years, but the triangles are new,' Murray said. 'Sounds like whoever is making the weapon is getting better at it.'

Margaret swallowed. If she was going to get her way, now was the time. 'The CDC may have information on Morgellons, including potential time lines of the condition and maps of people claiming to have this disease. We need to talk to Doctor Frank Cheng, who's leading the investigation.'

Murray leaned back in the director's chair and looked up at the ceiling.

'We can't get the CDC involved, Margaret. That's why I lifted you out of that organization.'

'We *have* to talk to this man,' Margaret said. 'It's possible they have a database on this. If we're lucky, they are tracking symptoms, dates of infection and other data that could potentially lead us to other parasite victims.'

'I can't allow it.'

'You *will* allow it, Murray!' Margaret said. Murray's gaze lowered until his cold eyes locked with hers. She couldn't stop now, she had to see it through. 'I've played this how you want it so far, but I *will* talk to this man, with or without your permission.'

She expected a huge fight, a battle of wills, but Murray just sighed. 'Okay, you can talk to him. But you cannot, and I repeat it just to be perfectly clear, *cannot* tell him about the triangles. Deal?'

'Deal.'

'Find out what they've got. And I'm giving you executive-order clearance on this. Otto, make a call to the CDC director. Doctor Cheng will cooperate with Doctor Montoya, and he doesn't need to know why.'

'Yes, sir,' Otto said. He smiled at Margaret. It was a small smile, but she couldn't miss it.

'Okay, Montoya, you get your little chat,' Murray said. 'But if that doesn't turn up anything, we need alternatives. Give me something to work with.'

'The excess neurotransmitters create a biochemical disorder,' Margaret said. 'Based on what we've seen of living hosts, they suffer symptoms of paranoid schizophrenia, possibly complete with intense hallucinations. Based on reported behavior, the hosts' paranoia is quite acute, with elaborate threats and conspiracies, but I'm sure that doesn't just happen overnight. There's probably a buildup process, an amplification of paranoia. These hosts may be looking for help in the early stages, but according to what we've seen in the five known cases, they are very suspicious and tend to stay away from institutions like hospitals and doctors. We have to make ourselves available to these calls for help.'

'How do we do that?' Murray asked.

'We could run ads in the paper. Vague ads, things that might appeal to the host's paranoid nature, but wouldn't attract attention from anyone else. Perhaps businesses with the name Triangle or something like that, something the hosts would see and instantly associate with. Paranoids construct elaborate fantasies about the world around them. If we play into likely fantasies, we might draw them in.'

Murray nodded. 'Newspaper ads are good. It will take a little time to create a fake business and we have to avoid anything unusual that might draw the press, but we'll get it going. What other ideas do you have?'

Otto cleared his throat. 'Excuse me for interrupting, sir, but most people don't get their news from papers anymore, they get it from the Internet. You can set up a web page and have it indexed so the major search engines will find it. The Net is anonymous, so a host might surf it for information on the growths. They can contact you right from the web page.'

Murray's nod picked up speed. 'Yes, yes I see your point. I'll get people on it right now. We'll come up with some different ways to attract the hosts. What else have you got, Doctor?'

'That's about it,' Margaret said. 'The triangles decompose so fast we haven't been able to get a good, clean look at one. We either need a live host or one that's only been dead for an hour at the most—and I stress, Murray, the need to see a *live* host above all other possibilities. That's the only way we're going to learn more.'

31

WASH THAT THING
RIGHT OUT OF YOUR HAIR

Perry stepped out of the shower into the steam-filled bathroom, toweling off lightly and feeling oddly peaceful now
that all his senses (and his wayward memory) had returned.
It might well have been the longest shower of his life, and
it was worth every second. His head pain had faded to a
mere whisper of its former screaming strength. He was
hungry. Really hungry. Cleaning up the bathroom would
have to wait until he'd hit the fridge. Some Pop-Tarts
would hit the spot, for starters.

The strange thing was how he didn't itch anymore. In
fact, now that he thought about it, he hadn't itched a bit
since waking up on the floor, except for a scratchy growth
of bright red beard that itched plenty.

Trying to keep his newly clean feet from stepping in
the gunk on the floor, he moved over to the steam-covered
mirror. He used his hand to clear a patch. The water-
beaded reflection showed beard growth, looked like two
days' worth.

Jesus . . . just how long had he been out?

Wrapping a towel around his waist, he walked into the
living room and turned on the TV. Channel 23, the Preview

Channel, always listed the time and date in the bottom left-hand corner of the screen.

It was 12:40 P.M. But it wasn't Thursday, December 13. It was December 14.

Friday.

He'd been unconscious since returning home from work on Wednesday. Somewhere in the vicinity of forty-eight hours. Almost *two full days*.

That wasn't passing out, that was a fucking coma. Two days? He'd lain in a pool of his own vomit for two days? No wonder he was so hungry.

Perry grabbed his cell phone. Sixteen messages waited for him. Most of them probably from Sandy, wondering if he planned on showing up for work.

Work. Counting when he'd been sent home, he'd missed *two full days* of work. He was probably fired by now. There was no way he could stroll in at 1:00 P.M. on a Friday. What a great story this would be: '*Sorry, boss, but I tripped in my own bathroom, clunked my head on the toilet seat and slipped into a coma while lying in a puddle of my own sick.*'

Perry sat down on the couch and sorted through the messages. Sure enough, two were from Sandy, seven were from Bill, the rest hang-ups from telemarketers. Four of the work messages were from Thursday. Bill sounded concerned. On the final message from Friday, Bill said he was coming over to see if Perry was all right.

Perry erased the messages. He turned off the phone's ringer; the last thing he wanted to do was talk to anyone, even Bill. Perry moved to the front door. Sure enough, tacked to the outside was a note.

DEAR BLEEDMAIZE-N-BLUE,

KNOCKED, RING DOORBELL,
URINATED ON YOUR DOOR,
STILL NO ANSWER. NOTE,
EVERYTHING IS COOL. GIVE ME A
CALL WHEN YOU GET BACK.
SANDY ISN'T THAT PISSED.
YOU DON'T HAVE TO CALL HER, BUT
SHE WOULD LIKE TO KNOW
IF YOU'RE OKAY. SO WOULD
I, BUDDY. I SAW YOUR OLD
BEATER IN THE PARKING LOT,
SO EITHER YOU'RE HIDING OUT
OR YOU WENT SOMEWHERE WITH
SOMEONE. CALL ME
                    —STICKYFINGAZWHITEY—

Two days. He'd missed two days of work. What the hell would Dear Ol' Dad have said about that? Nothing good, Perry knew that for certain. He'd make it up to Sandy. If he had to work double shifts and weekends for the next three months with no overtime, he'd make it up. Concussion or no concussion, there was no excuse for missing that much work. He couldn't just call her. That would be cowardly. He'd drive in right away and take his medicine face-to-face. After, of course, he got his ass to the hospital.

His stomach growled. He had to get some food first.

In minutes his last two eggs were frying up in a butter-coated pan. The smell drew loud grumbles from his stomach and made his mouth water. He dropped two pieces of bread into the toaster, then crammed a third piece in his mouth and chewed ravenously.

Before the eggs finished cooking, he reached into the cupboard, pulled out the last of the Pop-Tarts and wolfed them down. The toast popped up as he slid the eggs onto a plate. He jammed a piece of toast into the first yolk, and took a big, satisfying bite. His stomach rumbled again—happily, this time—as he finished off the first egg and raised his toast to puncture the second yolk.

Then he froze, half-chewed food hanging in his mouth.

The round, yellow-orange yolk glistened, surrounded by a bed of white. Orange. Orange that at one time had been a baby chicken, growing in a shell.

Growing. Growing. Growing.

Grown.

The toast dropped to the floor. It landed butter side down.

What the hell had he been thinking, eating a pile of eggs and worrying about work when he still had these fucking things inside him? He pulled back the towel's edge to examine his thigh, exposing the wound that had helped knock him out cold for two straight days. The shower had cleared away the dried blood, leaving fresh pink scar tissue with only a small, dark red scab-pebble in the middle. The wound looked healthy. Normal. The whitish growth that had caused his itching was long gone.

It was gone . . . but the others weren't.

He sat at the kitchen table and pulled his right knee to his chest, getting a good, close look at his shin.

The orange-peel skin was gone. What had taken its place didn't make him feel any better.

Where a circle of thick, pebbly, orange skin had once been, a peculiar triangle now lay. A triangle that was *under* his skin. Each of the triangle's sides was about an inch long.

The skin covering the strange triangle had a pale bluish tinge to it, the same color as the blue veins in the underside of one's wrist. But it wasn't really *his* skin. There was no break in the skin that wrapped around his leg, that covered his whole body for that matter, but somehow what covered the blue triangle just didn't seem to be his. It felt tougher than his own.

Near each of the triangle's three points was a quarter-inch slit pointing to the triangle's center. They reminded Perry of the slits in a homemade apple pie—if, of course, apple pie were triangular, made of human skin, and held a bluish tinge.

What the fuck was it?

Perry's breath came in rapid, short, shallow gasps. He had to get to a hospital.

His father had gone into a hospital. His father had never come out. The doctors didn't do a fucking thing for his father. Jacob Dawsey spent the last two months of his life slowly shriveling up on a hospital bed, good-for-nothing doctors sticking him full of needles, poking and prodding and testing. All the while his barrel-chested, 265-pound father shrunk to a six-foot-five, 150-pound living mummy, a character out of some childhood nightmare.

Perry had gone into the hospital once himself, right after that Rose Bowl injury to his knee. Damn doctors were supposed to be able to fix anything. Turned out they couldn't. Months later a second set of specialists (and there's always plenty of specialists for an All-Big Ten linebacker, thank you very much) said the first doctors had screwed things up, that Perry might have continued his career if they'd done things right.

But this wasn't a blown knee. This wasn't even cancer. Cancer was a semi-living mass of flesh. The thing he'd pulled out of his leg had been *alive,* it had moved *on its own.*

And there were six more. Six more that had grown unhindered for two days, while he'd been unconscious. It had only taken three days for the things to go from a little rash to a squirming horror, and another forty-eight hours to transform into these bizarre triangular growths. What the hell might they become in the *next* twenty-four hours? The next forty-eight?

Perry rushed to throw on the first clothes he could find, grabbed his keys and coat and headed for his car.

Hospital time.

Definitely hospital time.

32

CALLING DR. CHENG,
CALLING DR. CHENG

Margaret waited for Dr. Cheng to come to the phone. She didn't like to be made to wait, but it was hard to be upset when Agent Clarence Otto's strong hands worked her bunched-up shoulder muscles. She was still in the director's office, except now *she* was sitting in the big-girl's chair. Murray was on his way back to Washington. Amos was taking advantage of the downtime to get some sleep in one of the hospital's empty rooms.

Cheng was a bit of a bigwig at the CDC headquarters in Atlanta. She didn't know the man from Adam, but she had to admit it was fun to hear people at the main CDC office jump when she called. One phone call from Murray opened a lot of doors.

'This is Doctor Cheng.' Margaret shook her head slightly. She'd expected an Asian accent. This guy sounded like he was from Bakersfield.

'Doctor Cheng, Margaret Montoya.'

'How can I help you today, Margaret? It seems you've got something important to discuss, important enough for the director to call me and tell me to make sure you get everything you need.' He sounded annoyed, as if her call had pulled him away from something that *he* thought was very important.

'Yes, Doctor Cheng. I'm actually CDC myself.'

'Really? I wonder why I've never heard of you. Do you work in Atlanta?'

Margaret grimaced at the question. 'No, actually, CCID in Cincinnati.'

'Ah,' Cheng said. There was a lot of contempt and derision loaded in to that single syllable.

'Doctor Cheng, I need some information on your Morgellons task force,' Margaret said.

'You bothered me for *that*?'

'Afraid so. We're working on a related disease.'

'Must not be much of a relation,' Cheng said. 'Because there is no disease. Just a lot of crazy people who have convinced themselves they have bugs crawling under their skin.' He sounded about as compassionate as a guy opening up the gas valve at a Nazi death camp.

'I'm more interested in the fibers.'

Pause. 'Yes, well, there is something strange there, but it hardly merits all the attention. I'll tell you, I wasn't thrilled to be put in charge of this mass delusion. Fibers in your skin don't make you crazy, although I will say that the pain suffered by some victims seems very real. A few have genuine fibers that seem to be created by their own bodies, but for most of them these "fibers" turn out to be carpet fibers, clothing fibers, things like that. They convince themselves they have this infestation, they scratch themselves bloody, and these tiny fibers get stuck in the wounds. Hardly an epidemic.'

'But you've seen some of these "genuine" cellulose fibers growing out of the skin, yes?'

'We have found a few, yes,' Cheng said.

'I'm hoping you have a database on those claiming to be infected, particularly those who actually show the fibers.'

The question seemed to anger Cheng. 'Of *course* we have a database, Doctor Montoya. We've sent out bulletins to all medical professionals, asking them to report anything that fits in to the myriad symptoms of these Morgellons *victims*. Tell me what you're working on. If it's a Morgellons case, it falls under the purview of this task force. You should be reporting it to me.'

Margaret slunk into her chair and rubbed her eyes. This wasn't going the way she'd thought it would.

'Margaret,' Otto whispered. She opened her eyes. Now he was on the other side of the desk. He pointed to her, then held his left palm down at waist level. His right hand whipped back and forth in front of his groin, like he was spanking an imaginary person bent over in front of him. Then he pointed at the phone. 'Go on, girl, whip that ass.'

Margaret nodded. *That's right. I'm in charge now, I'm not this guy's bitch. If anything, he's mine.*

'I haven't got all day, Montoya,' Cheng said. 'What are you working on?'

'Afraid I can't tell you, Cheng,' Margaret said. 'You're not cleared to have that information. And in this instance you're reporting to me. You did hear about the executive order, didn't you?'

A pause.

'*Didn't* you?'

'Of course I did.'

'Good. I don't have time for this. Either stop being an insufferable prick or I'll just call the CDC director and let him know I can't get you to cooperate.'

A longer pause. Otto had moved on from slapping the imaginary booty, and was now 'riding the pony.' He looked ridiculous, a big grown man, CIA agent, in the black suit and the red tie, twirling in a circle with an expression of affected ecstasy on his face. Margaret couldn't help but smile.

'Fine,' Cheng finally said. 'What do you need?'

'What I need you to do, right now, is call up your most recent reports. And I'm looking for dates of first symptoms, as reported by the patient. So I'm not interested in people who said they've been suffering for ten years and just came in.'

'I understand what "date of first symptoms" means,' Cheng snapped.

She heard keys clacking as he worked his computer.

'We had a case in Detroit two weeks ago,' he said. 'A Gary Leeland. Visited his primary caregiver, reported the fibers growing out of his right arm. Multiple sores from scratching. Then . . . two cases in Ann Arbor, Michigan. These are less than a week old. Kiet Nguyen, art major at the University of Michigan. And Samantha Hester, who brought in her daughter, Missy, to the same physician, actually.'

Margaret scribbled notes furiously, even though she'd have Cheng email her all the files. 'When? When did they call in?'

'Nguyen was seven days ago, Hester was six.'

'And have you had any contact with them?'

'As a matter of fact, yes. I personally examined Missy. Girl had a tiny fiber sticking out of her right wrist. I removed it, gave her a full examination, she had no other rashes, fibers or marks of any kind.'

'How long ago was that?'

'Four days ago. Delightful little girl. I'm actually flying back there later today to examine her again.'

'No need for that, Doctor Cheng. I'll be in Ann Arbor and I'll examine her.'

'Oh really? And do you know what you're looking for?'

'Yes, Doctor,' Margaret said. 'I know exactly what I'm looking for. How about Mister Nguyen?'

'He was another story. Quite rude.'

'What did he say?'

'Well, I called him to follow up, and as soon as I told him I was from the CDC, he asked me . . . let me check my notes here . . . Yes, here it is. He said, "If you show your fucking face around here, you fucking spy piece of shit, I will cut off your fucking balls and shove them in your fucking mouth. I'll kill anyone you send. Fuck you." Then he hung up. Needless to say, he's low on the list of people to interview.'

'Any others?'

'None in the past six months.'

'Send me those case files, and do it now. Do you have addresses for Nguyen and Hester?'

'I told you, we have a database, Doctor Montoya.'

'Thank you, Doctor Cheng, you've been most helpful.' She hung up, then immediately dialed Murray.

33

DRIVIN' & DRINKIN'

Doom swirled before Perry's eyes like the tender flakes of snow gracefully kissing his windshield. He drove through town, down Washtenaw Avenue, heading for the hospital.

The University of Michigan Medical Center was supposed to be one of the best hospitals in the world. Lots of innovative research, new techniques, top-shelf doctors—if there was any help to be had, that was the place. But that was a big 'if.'

It was all over, really. What were the doctors going to tell him, anyway? Maybe they could tell him *something*. Better to go out knowing his killer than to just sit in the apartment and waste away to nothing. But more than likely, he knew, the doctors would look at him, examine him, poke him and prod him, then announce that this disease was a 'new development.' And somehow, even though they would know as much about the disease as the Pope knew about making hard-core porn, the doctors would still try to sound intelligent. Doctors were like that, always trying to come across as wise men, never for a moment losing the charade of competence.

He slowed to turn right on Observatory, but had to wait for pedestrians to cross the slushy street. He was on campus now, and U of M students were renowned for their lackadaisical attitude toward cars. They lazily strolled through crosswalks, even on busy streets, immortal in their youth and confident that cars would slow for them. They were college students, and for most of them the concept that they might face a quick and unfair death had yet to hit home.

'Your day will come,' Perry said quietly to the bundled and backpacked students as they passed in front of his car. 'Mine sure as hell has.' He finished his turn onto Observatory. Now he was only a few blocks from the medical center.

Perry realized he had yet to call work. What difference did it make if he called in, anyway? A lot of good his three years of devotion did at this point. Never late once, and would that help him survive?

'Fuck 'em all, Perry said quietly. His coworkers would hear about it soon enough on the news. He could hear the teaser now: 'Michigan man dies from new disease, which is named after his doctor, who is still very much alive and getting pretty frigging rich on the lecture circuit. Story at eleven.'

He stopped for a red light at Geddes. East Medical Center Drive was just up on the right. Cottony clumps of snow swam in the fluctuating wind, hanging weightless and spinning one second, whipping about as if on an intangible roller coaster the next. Despair filled his skull more tightly than even his own brain. All around him were cars filled with normal people. Perfectly unaware of the disease turning Perry's body inside out. Fucking normal people.

Or . . . or *were* they normal? How did he know they weren't suffering from the same condition? Maybe they sat in their cars, fighting the urge to itch, to scratch until their fingernails came back bloody. How was he to know if the people around him were normal or infected?

It hit him, suddenly and solidly, that it was highly unlikely he was the first person with this disease. And if he wasn't the first, a disturbing question reared up to confront him: *Why hadn't he heard of this before?*

A horn blast sounded behind him, jerking him back into awareness. The light was green. Heart racing, mind drowning in a sea of strange questions, he pulled through the intersection, then off to the side of the road. On his right was a snow-covered cemetery. How friggin' perfect. Traffic rolled along behind him, the people who might or might not be normal going on about their business. He gripped the steering wheel to keep his hands from shaking.

Why hadn't he heard of this before?

He had fucking *blue triangles* growing under his skin, for the love of God. The disease seemed so unusual—the media would have reported such a thing long ago, wouldn't they? Of course they would have. Unless . . . unless the people with this disease went *into* the hospital, but never came *out.*

Perry sat very still, staring out the windshield, the cold air filtering into the car and chasing away the artificial heat. What if the hospital was waiting for people like him? Maybe they wouldn't even try to help him. Maybe they would just study the triangle, lock him up like a prisoner so they could watch him die. And maybe they'd just kill him and dissect him like some lab animal.

It was the only thing that made sense, or he'd have heard of this *somewhere.* There was more to this situation, much more. It wasn't just a simple disease, after all; he was marked for death sure as if he were in a Nazi concentration camp and the triangles were Stars of David sewn onto his clothes.

But if he couldn't go to the hospital, what was he going to do? What the hell *could* he do?

Fear slowly sank its claws into his consciousness, squeezing out his breath, joining with the biting cold to make his big body shiver.

'I need a drink,' Perry whispered. 'And just a little time to figure this out.'

He did a U-turn and kept driving. He didn't stop until he reached the Washtenaw Party Store. The pay phone was not in use, for once—he didn't talk to anyone, he didn't look at anyone, he made his purchase and left.

34

TURKEY SHOOT

Perry shambled back into his apartment carrying two bottles of Wild Turkey—one full, the other already half empty. The promise of violence hung off his frame like the potential energy of a safe hanging fifteen stories over a crowded street.

Friday night, and it was party time.

Perry calmly set the bottles on the kitchen table, then strolled into the bathroom. The floor there was crusted not only with dried vomit, but with dried blood as well. He noticed a good three inches of water remained in the tub, still and dead like stagnant pond water, disturbed only by the *plunk* of occasional drops from the shower head. Chunks of the thick orange skin clogged the drain. Smaller parts floated on the water's filthy soap-scum surface. He heard a faint trickle slipping down the drain, filtering past the disgusting clog.

He hadn't even thought about it when he'd showered. The orange skin apparently came off on its own. His free hand gently touched his collarbone, fingers tracing the slightly too-firm outline of a triangle. It felt more defined, the edges slightly more discernible to the touch. The blue looked a bit more pronounced, still faint, but now clearly visible with a color like that of a faded tattoo.

He walked back to the kitchen. He grabbed a fork and

then a knife out of the butcher's block, eyes once again lingering on the thick-handled, thick-bladed chicken scissors. He was dying. So many things yet to do, to experience. He'd never see Germany, never go deep-sea fishing, never visit the Alamo or all the historical sites of colonial America. He'd never get married. Never have children.

It wasn't all bad. He'd lived a full life. He'd been the first in his family to attend college. He'd played Division I football, been on ESPN, lived his childhood dream of being a Wolverine playing in front of 112,000 screaming fans at the Big House. But above all, he'd escaped his father's life of violence. He had surpassed his environment, surpassed his heritage, fought and clawed his way into respectability.

But for what? For nothing, that's what.

He sat down at the kitchen table, set the knife on the tabletop, then took a long pull from the half-empty fifth. It tasted awful and seared his throat, but those sensations barely registered on his brain. He knocked it back as if it were water. The Wild Turkey was already roaring through his head. By the time he finished the bottle he knew he'd be three sheets to the wind. Ripped. Drunk-ass wasted.

He'd be *feeling no pain*.

Tears of despair tugged at his eyes. It wasn't fair. He refused to cry. His father hadn't cried once during that whole cancer ordeal, and if Dad hadn't, Perry wouldn't, either.

Good old 'Dirty Bird' carried a kick as severe as its taste. Perry felt light-headed and his toes tingled. His thoughts seemed thick, syrupy. He sat for a few minutes more, fighting back the tears, the Wild Turkey worming its way into his brain.

He picked up the knife.

The blade was almost ten inches long. The kitchen's fluorescent ceiling lights seemed to glint off of each and every tiny serration. When he cooked chicken or beef, he used the sharp butcher knife to cut through the

no no no no no

raw meat with little effort. Perry doubted that the knife would be any less effective on human flesh, particularly the thin skin atop his shin.

His eyes blurred a little and he shook his head. He realized he was about to cut into his own body with a butcher knife. A little Wild Turkey goes a long way. Yes, he was going to cut himself, but there was something in his body that

no no no no

didn't belong.

He was going to die, sure, so be it, but he was taking these fucking triangle things with him. It was time for the Big Six to lose a member. Perry laughed out loud—anytime you drop players from the lineup, you have to make a *cut*.

He polished off the last of the fifth, the liquid searing its way down his throat. He tossed the empty bottle aside, then used the knife to cut right through his jeans. The denim offered little resistance to the blade. In a few seconds, his pant leg hung in two long, ragged strips, exposing his tree trunk of a leg.

Perry lifted his foreleg and laid it on the kitchen table like a pot roast served at a family dinner. The wood felt cool against the back of his calf. The Wild Turkey buzz droned through his mind like a horde of lazy bumblebees. He knew if he didn't act soon, he wouldn't be able to do anything but babble, drool and pass out.

It was time to get down to

no no no no kill

business.

Perry steeled himself with a few deep breaths. He was acting crazy, he knew that, but what difference did it make to a dead man? He poked at the triangle with the fork. Nothing had changed since his earlier examination.

'You're going to kill me?' Perry said. 'No-no-no, my friend, I'm going to kill *you*.'

He pushed the fork into his skin, just firmly enough to hold the triangle in place. The three metal tines made deep indents in the bluish skin.

Small flecks of rust dotted the knife blade. He'd never noticed them before. He noticed them now. He was suddenly noticing a lot of things about the knife, things like the nicks in the wooden handle, things like the two silvery rivets that fastened the comfortable wooden handle to the blade, things like the grain of the wood, like a hundred little minnows forever trapped mid-swim in a soft, warm, brown stream.

He'd made the first cut before he really knew what he was doing. He found himself staring drunkenly at a two-inch gash. Hot, tickling blood spilled down the side of his calf, spreading across the tabletop, then falling in thick red splatters against the white linoleum floor. He heard the dripping of the blood before he felt the pain, which was severe but distant—separated, as if it were pain seen on TV while Perry was curled up on the couch under a fuzzy blanket with a cold Coke in one hand and the remote control in the other.

no kill no please
no kill

He felt as if he were on autopilot, gliding through this bizarre action like a spectator. Who knew there would be this much blood? It covered his leg, smeared against his pale skin, made it difficult to see the triangle's edge, yet he pushed down hard on the fork, put the knife blade perpendicular to his skin and made another fast cut. More blood spilled across the table and onto the floor. The pain didn't feel distant now, not at all. Perry ground his teeth in an effort to control himself, to finish the job.

The blood somehow found its way up the knife blade and onto his hands. He heard the steady stream-drip of his own blood pattering to the floor below.

'How's it feel, you little fucker?' Perry's words were slow and slurred. 'How's it feel? Do you like that? Kill me? No-no-no, I'll kill *you*. You've *got* to have discipline.'

Perry steeled himself, forcing his vision to clear once more and his mind to center on the next task. Despite his drunken state, his hands remained amazingly steady— he'd definitely missed his calling in life.

n o k i l l p l e a s e n o k i l l no

His face furrowed in confusion. Something tickled at the edge of his mind, like a dream trying to crawl in and stir up nocturnal secrets. He violently shook his head, then stared with new focus at the bloody fork and knife. The second cut had left one side of the triangle in place, like a door hinge—he slid the blade under the angular flap and flipped it back like a bloody piece of raw bacon.

c o l d n o k i l l c o l d cold

What he saw stopped him instantly. A low hiss leaked from his mouth like air from a punctured tire.

'How's that for a prize in your Cracker Jacks?'

He stared at the thing that had made him itch, made him tear into himself like a wild animal in a trap—at what was undoubtedly killing him. Blood pooled and flowed around a dark blue triangular lump. Perry wiped away the pulsating blood to get a better look.

It was deep blue, shiny, although maybe that was from the wetness of the blood rather than its true color. The triangle's surface wasn't smooth, but gnarled, twisted . . . malignant, like tree roots massed together and exposed to the soil surface, or like the texture of steel cable without the orderly lines.

Sobriety suddenly swam its way to the surface, spurred on by a horror-fueled fight-or-flight response. This was a whole 'nother ball game from the rashes, a completely different league than the thick orange blisters. His body hadn't made this thing, *couldn't* have—where the hell had it come from?

Perry snarled. The growling voice of a rabid animal escaped his throat. He not-so-gently slid the fork under the bloody blue triangle. The metal tines scraped against his own raw flesh. He'd never felt pain so

n o   f e e l   n o   k i l l   n o   kill

pure, so dense, so all-encompassing, but he ignored it completely, focusing instead on the abomination buried in his shin.

Play through the pain.

He felt the tines of the fork meet the slightly giving resistance of the triangle's stem. He gently fished around until the fork slid all the way through, its red-smeared prongs poking their little heads out from underneath the triangle's other side.

The blood-covered table felt cold and sticky under his calf. Perry raised the fork. The triangle seemed to lift easily. The stem itself, however, was another affair, far more solid and firm than before. It would take strength to pull this one out.

Sweat poured from his face as pain sheared through his leg. It was slammingly intense, but he held it in check with the promise of purging this abomination from his body. Perry yanked up hard on the

n o   k i l l   n o   k i l l

fork, but the stem held firm. Blood spilled anew from the leg, splashing into the puddle that blazed red against the white linoleum floor.

His head lolled to the right. Spots appeared before his eyes. He scrunched his eyes shut and shook his head, blinking fast as his equilibrium and vision returned. He'd almost passed out. Had he lost that much blood? His head started to spin—he didn't know if it was from the Wild Turkey or blood loss. He felt control slipping away.

p l e a s e   n o   n o   n o

n o   n o   n o   no

He jammed the fork in deeper, allowing more of the tines to poke through the other side, enough for him to get a decent hold with his free hand. He held the fork as if it were a curling bar and he was ripping off a few quick reps. His meaty biceps twitched in anticipation. He took a breath and

N O   N O   N O   N O   N O   N O
N O   N O   N O   N O

yanked.

He heard a ripping sound and felt a blast of searing nuclear fire rage through his leg. Something in the stem snapped. Perry's momentum carried him backward over his chair and spilled him onto the floor.

Blood had trickled before—now it gushed, this time from the *back* of the leg. A wave of gray washed across his eyes.

Have to stop the bleeding. I'm not gonna die on the kitchen floor . . .

He pulled off his T-shirt and leaned forward, ass and

legs spreading blood all across the linoleum. Perry wrapped the shirt around his gushing calf, tied a granny knot, then yanked it tight with all his strength. His short scream filled the small apartment.

He rolled to his back, body tightly tense with agony, the gray washing over him yet again. He fell limp.

His chest moved in regular breaths as he lay on the blood-smeared floor.

35

COMMUNICATION BREAKDOWN

The five remaining organisms conducted a 'poll' of sorts. Following deeply ingrained instructions, they measured densities of thyroxine and triiodothyronine, hormones that stimulate the metabolic rate. Both hormones are produced by the thyroid gland, which is located in the neck region of all vertebrates. By measuring the densities of these chemicals in the bloodstream, the five organisms detected which of their number was closest to the neck.

Or, more accurately, which was closest to the brain.

The triangle on the host's back, the one on the spine, just below the shoulder blades, came out the winner. This new discovery stimulated additional specialized cell development from that triangle—like a stealthy snake approaching an unknowing victim, a new tendril slowly grew along the spinal column toward the brain.

Once there, the tendril split into hundreds of long strands, each microscopically thin. The tendrils sought out the brain's convergence zones. These zones act like mental switching stations, providing access to information and linking that information to other relevant data. The tendrils sought out specific areas: the thalamus, the amygdala, the caudate nucleus, the hypothalamus, the hippocampus, the septum, and particular areas of the cerebral cortex. The tendrils' growth was very specific, very directed.

Sentience was limited but progressing—they had only just begun to think, to be aware of themselves. Words had floated about their environment, and they had picked up a few, but with the growth into the brain they would learn more and learn them quickly.

They had tried to stop the host, but their messages were weak. They simply didn't have enough information to communicate properly. That was changing; soon they would be strong enough to *make* him listen.

36

WAKE UP WE HUNGRY

wake up we hungry

Waking up on a linoleum floor was getting to be an annoying habit. His head hurt again. This time, however, he immediately identified the pain as a hangover.

The kitchen lights glared in his eyes. He saw flies behind the clear plastic that sat in front of the fluorescent lights. The bugs had flown up there, looking to do whatever it is that bugs want to do with lights, then they got cooked, burned to a crispity-crunchity finish.

His leg ached. His stomach grumbled. Loudly. First thing in his mind (besides the bugs) was the fact that he hadn't really eaten anything in three days. Depending, of course, on how long he'd been out *this* time. No sunlight filtered in from the living room, so obviously it was sometime in the evening.

Perry looked down at his leg. The bleeding had stopped. The shirt had gone from athletic gray to a sickly dried brown, a tie-dyed T-shirt suitable for Marilyn Manson.

Dried blood smears coated the linoleum floor, blackish brown against the shiny white. It looked as if a three-year-old had come in from playing in the rain, covered in puddle mud, then rolled on the floor.

His leg hurt with the dull, throbbing, pulsating pain of a recent wound struggling to heal. There was no sign of the Big Six acting up; from those areas he felt no itching, no pain. That didn't make Perry feel any better; there was no telling what the little bastards were up to now.

'Big Six?' A rather unhealthy smile tickled the corners of Perry's mouth. 'That's not quite right. I got another one. You're not the Big Six anymore—now you're the Starting Five.'

He wanted to find the fork, the one he'd used to pull the creature from his body. He wanted to see what the blue thing looked like when it wasn't latched on to his leg like a suckling kangaroo imbedded in the pouch of its mother.

His leg not only hurt like a bitch, but felt funny in a way he couldn't quite identify. What had the Triangle done on the way out?

Perry rolled to his stomach and struggled to rise without putting weight on his bad leg. He hopped up on his good leg and leaned on the counter, then scanned the floor for the fork. It had slid against the refrigerator.

He took one careful hop, leaned on the other counter, then stooped to pick up the fork.

'I hope it hurt, you fucker,' Perry said quietly as he examined his grisly trophy.

The Triangle looked like flaky, dried-up black seaweed wrapped around the fork in a permanent death embrace. He could barely make out the once-triangular shape, as it was now a lifeless hunk of crap without form or function.

But it wasn't the body that held his rapt attention or made his jaw hang open with astonishment and an additional serving of fear. It wasn't the body at all.

The creature's tail was just as dry, light and stiff as the body, but the very end was something totally unexpected. Hooked, bony protrusions stuck out of the end like little claws or teeth. Perry gingerly touched one—sharp as a knife. As sharp as the butcher's knife he'd used to cut into his own leg like some narcissistic cannibal. Some of the claws hooked inward; these showed visible breaks and cracks. They must have helped hold the tail to the shin-bones. Five of the claws, however, pointed outward or hooked wickedly upward, toward the now-dried head.

'But how would that help hold on to anything?' Perry murmured. 'What the hell is this?'

His lip curled in revulsion as their purpose became suddenly clear. The outwardly curved hooks couldn't help hold the tail in place—they could only cut and slash if the creature were pulled from its human burrow.

That's why his leg had bled all over, because he'd dragged five of the quarter-inch, razor-sharp claws through the meat of his calf and out his shin.

They were a defense mechanism. Intended to hurt Perry if he tried to remove the Triangle. Now that he knew what was buried in his body, the claws served as

a   w a r n i n g

a warning of what would happen if he tried to remove any more. He'd been lucky with the leg—if one of these wicked claws had cut through an artery, it would have killed him.

n o   t r y   i t   again

Perry wondered if he should try it again, try to get the rest of them out. But brute force obviously wasn't the way to . . . to . . .

Perry blinked a few times. His mind dry-fired, stayed blank as he tried to comprehend what had just happened.

He'd clearly heard a voice. Was he going loopy? His mind filled with vague memories of his homespun surgery and that same voice echoing through his drunken head.

Great. On top of dying, now he was developing a split personality. He was going loopy. Cuckoo for Cocoa Puffs. Insane in the membrane.

'I'm crazy. That's it. I'm apeshit crazy. That's the only answer.'

y o u   n o   c r a z y   w e   n o
t h i n k   so

That one stopped Perry cold. He managed a parched swallow and ignored an untimely rumble from his underpaid belly.

The voice had said, 'we no think so.'

We.

As in more than one.

As in . . .

As in the Starting Five.

Perry was beyond speechless—he was thoughtless.

'I'll be a sonofabitch,' Perry whispered.

s o n o f a b i t c h

the voice echoed, a voice he heard as clear as day, although his ears didn't pick up a thing. He could *hear* the voice in his head—no vocal characteristics or tone, just words.

s o n o f a b i t c h   f e e d   us

It was them. The Starting Five. They were talking in his head. Perry leaned heavily against the counter, in danger of falling to the floor as if struck by a physical blow. His rashes had turned into triangles, and now they were talking to him. Should he answer them?

Hello, Perry thought—no response. He tried concentrating, focusing. *HELLO,* he thought, as hard as he could. Still no response.

f e e d   u s   w e   hungry

'Feed you?'

A response slammed through his head like the roar of a Rose Bowl crowd on New Year's Day.

yes yes yes feed us
we hungry

They'd answered him. Perry squinted his eyes and 'thought' as loudly as he could. *Why'd you answer me that time?* He waited, but again heard no response. *Answer me!*

His stomach grumbled loudly, the sound bordering on an internal roar. Despite the shock of hearing voices in his head, he couldn't deny the gnawing feeling in his gut.

'I'm pretty hungry myself,' Perry whispered.

so are we feed us
we hungry

His head lifted with final understanding. 'Can you hear me?'

yes we hear you

'You can talk into my head, but you can't hear my thoughts?'

we send words through your
nerves your nerves no send
words back are you hungry now

What escaped Perry's mouth was somewhere between a laugh and a cry and a stutter. A sick, twisted bark of despair, a laugh that may have once echoed through Andersonville, Buchenwald or any of history's dark places where human beings give up all hope.

Perry fought back tears, tears that welled up in response to an emotion he couldn't define. His chest felt tight. His one good leg felt weak. He leaned heavily on the kitchen counter, head hanging down, eyes staring at the floor but seeing nothing.

feed us we hungry

The voice in his head grew louder, as did the grumbling

in his stomach. Sudden stabbing pains in his belly snapped
him out of his grim reverie. He hadn't eaten properly in
days. Grinding hunger combined with a slight echo of
sickly pink nausea.

s o n o f a b i t c h   f e e d
u s   w e   hungry

The voice in his head (it felt funny to use that term in
all seriousness, for it was a term reserved for comedy or
bad horror novels, but now it was simply accurate) gave
up all attempts at sentence structure and moved toward
steady chanting.

f e e d   u s   f e e d u s
feedusfeedusfeedus

Perry hobbled a bit to open the fridge and survey the
contents. Some leftover tuna fish; a mostly empty tub of
Country Crock; a mostly full jar of Hershey's chocolate
syrup; an old, slightly gamey jar of Smucker's strawberry
preserves; and—stop the presses—an unopened jar of
Ragu spaghetti sauce.

Perry removed the jar from the fridge and explored
the cupboard, looking for noodles. True to his current run
of luck, he had none, only some Rice-A-Roni and a half-
empty bag of Cost Cutter plain white rice. He also found
one can of Campbell's Pork & Beans, half a loaf of bread
and a three-pound can of butter-flavor Crisco. What a
time to realize that he'd let his shopping duties slip.

It was enough to get started, anyway—he felt so hungry
he wouldn't have turned down chocolate-covered cock-
roaches. He crammed two slices of bread into the toaster
and another into his salivating mouth. He opened the pork
and beans and took a big sniff,

y e s y e s y e s y e s y e s y e s y e s

then dumped them into a bowl and tossed them in the

microwave. He finished chewing the bread and stuffed another piece into his mouth before the toast came up. He immediately put in two more slices.

The microwave timer beeped insistently. Perry removed the scalding-hot bowl, grabbed his toast and hopped to the table. It was covered with blood. His blood. He decided to eat standing at the counter. He leaned over to the silverware drawer, grabbed a fork and dug in even though the beans were still hot enough to burn his tongue.

Aside from a piece of toast and some egg yolk, he'd gone *days* without food. His body rejoiced in the meal. The pork and beans tasted better than anything he'd ever eaten before—better than shrimp, better than steak, better than fresh lake trout.

By the time he polished off the beans and all the bread, he felt much more himself. His hunger satiated for the moment, his thoughts centered on the rather unique problem at hand. He realized that the Starting Five hadn't made a peep since he'd started eating.

'Hey,' Perry said. He doubted anything could feel as surreal as talking to Triangles embedded in his body, which apparently talked back to him via his own nervous system.

'Hey, are you there?'

y e s   w e   here

They sounded calmer, far more relaxed than when they'd complained of hunger.

'Why aren't you talking?' He wanted to hear them talk, both because he wanted to know more about these bizarre horrors and because they had been quiet for days, and when they'd been quiet, they had *grown*.

w a i t   t o   eat   f o o d
c o m e s   now

That phrase sent a shiver through his chest. He

immediately understood the situation. The Triangles were like a tapeworm or something, absorbing the food he digested. Even though he had huge triangular organisms living in his body, he found the internal vampirism even more horrifying.

These critters were anchored into his muscles, tendons and skeleton, and tapped into his bloodstream like a baby cow nursing off a mother's teat. Anger swelled up inside him, hot and tumultuous and lava-red. But as the anger brewed, so did a realization.

They couldn't eat unless he did, which meant they weren't feeding *on* him. The good news? *They're not eating you from within.* The bad news? *They're growing inside you even faster thanks to a highly nutritious pork-n-beans buffet.* He felt violated, like the victim of some horrible, biological rape.

He grew more aware of the pain in his body. His head hurt. His leg hurt. His stomach felt a little queasy. His eyes kept closing. He wanted to crawl into bed and give up, forget about the whole thing and let fate run its sadistic course.

He made it as far as the couch, hopping carefully on his one leg before easing himself onto the welcome and waiting cushions. The couch seemed to caress his body, sucking away his stress, taking it, perhaps, under the cushions with the dirt and loose change. Maybe he'd die in his sleep, but he couldn't stop sleep from coming.

37

GONNA NEED A STEAM CLEANER FOR THAT

Dew smelled it right off.

Unmistakable. Unforgettable.

The smell of death.

Faint, just a touch coming on the wind. It was still early, but he knew from hard-won experience that in a few hours that smell would grow until the neighbors caught a whiff or two.

'Control, this is Phillips. Clear odor of decomposing human body coming from Nguyen's house. I need to move in right now.'

'Understood, Phillips. Move in. Support teams are in position.'

Dew walked up the unshoveled sidewalk, feet crunching on a combination of snow and salt crystals. Ann Arbor, Michigan. Home to forty thousand college kids, many crowded into big, old, beat-up homes like this one. A single-family dwelling that in 1950 was a hallmark of middle-class success, housing Mom and Dad and a passel of kids, now held a half dozen students, usually more, packed in two to a stinky, beer-stained room.

There wasn't a sound coming from the house. The university had just let out on break, the fall semester closing only two days earlier. Still, even with the break, he could hear a basketball game blasting from the house on his left and on his right. TV blaring, drunken kids singing fight songs and screaming at the television. But the one in the middle? Nothing.

He tried the handle. Locked. He peeked in a window, but it was boarded up from the inside with plywood. A quick check showed that all the windows were boarded up.

Dew was tired of fucking around. Just plain tired of it. He stood in front of the door, drew his .45, reared back and gave it a solid kick. It took two more, but the door finally swung open.

And the smell rolled out like Satan's breath.

Dew swallowed, then stepped inside.

'Jesus,' he said. He wasn't a religious man, but he couldn't think of anything else to say.

'Phillips, Control here. Are you okay?'

'I'm pretty fucking far from okay,' Dew said quietly, his microphone picking up every sound. 'Send in all three teams, right now. Come in quiet and hot. Three civvies dead by small-arms fire, perp probably still inside. And call the body wagons, we got a big haul here.'

In the living room alone, Dew counted three bloated bodies. Despite their greenish skin, swollen stomachs and the flies swirling around them, he recognized that each had a gunshot wound to the head. All of them had their hands and feet tied. They had been executed. Probably three or four days earlier, maybe a day or two before the end of the semester—with classes over, and more than half the students heading home, the kids in this house wouldn't have been missed.

'Where are you, you little fucking gook?' Dew said. He knew it was a bad thing to think, a bad thing to say, but the kid who did this was Vietnamese, and he was right about the age of the ones Dew used to kill back in the jungle. Well this one was getting his ticket punched, and right fucking now.

Four men in Racal suits and carrying P90s entered the house behind him, silent despite the bulky material. Dew used hand signals, telling them to spread out through the first floor. He sent a second four-man team into the basement, and took the final team with him upstairs. The house remained deathly quiet. He could hear the game, faintly, from both of the houses next door. The cheer-to-roar told him the Wolverines had just thrown down a serious dunk.

Dew led the walk up the creaky stairs. Up there, somewhere, was an infected jibbering madman. Like Brewbaker, but this one had a gun.

'This is Cooper,' the voice said in Dew's earpiece. 'Downstairs, one more body.'

Yep, going to get his ticket *punched*.

Dew reached the top of the stairs. He checked in each room, ready to fire instantly if he saw a weapon. Every room was messy, the casual decor of college kids. This wasn't one of the houses for the rich kids. This one was full—correction, *had* been full—of kids that actually worked to get through school. Even so, every room had a computer. Every computer had a neat bullet hole through the screen.

The last room, of course, held the answers. And the answers were some shit Dew Phillips really didn't want to see.

A bloated body tied to a chair. A body missing both feet. Both hands. Half the head gone, a fucking hammer sticking out of the skull like a handle. Flies swarming, showing a real preference for the brains.

And on the floor, a pitted black skeleton sitting in a giant black stain on the green carpet.

Gonna need a steam cleaner for that, Dew thought, then instantly wondered if he was going just a little bit crazy.

The skeleton lay on top of a .22 rifle. The back of the skull had a neat little hole in it. Fucking gook had shot himself in the eye.

Dew quickly looked around the room. What he saw on the back wall made him shake his head in near exhaustion. These infected *victims,* if you could manage to call the murdering assholes that, were some seriously crazy fuckers.

'This is Phillips. Primary objective found, deceased. Let's get this scene locked down tight, and as soon as we do, get Doctor Montoya over here. Squad One, lose the Racal suits and take up positions at the entrances, two at the front door, two at the back. No one gets in unless I let 'em in. Squad Two, start cataloging the crime scene. Get a shitload of pictures, and bring in the photo printer. Montoya is only going to be here long enough to see the scene firsthand, then I want her out and I want pictures ready for her to take with. And get into the university's database and get me pictures of these kids when they were alive, she'll need that for comparison. Let's move, people. The locals aren't going to be happy when they hear about the body count.'

Another miss. He wondered if Otto and Margaret would fare any better with the other lead from Cheng's files. Couldn't be worse—mass-murdering art student versus a seven-year-old girl with one of those strange fiber things, which itself had been removed six days ago.

Hopefully, they could find something important.

At least they didn't have to look at a scene like this.

The SARS story wouldn't cover six bodies. People

might make a sad face when they hear about a seventy-year-old woman killing her son, or some random guy going nutso and whacking his family, but six dead college kids . . . that was another matter. A mass murder like this would be on every station in the country if Dew didn't lock this shit down tight, and right now.

Fortunately, even in a game of big swingers, Dew had the president of the United States of America hitting cleanup. And the president carried a damn big bat.

Dew knew exactly what he needed even before he pulled out his cell phone and dialed Murray Longworth.

38

COUCH-POTATO BUG

The throbbing of the leg brought him out of his dead-man sleep. It was a double-pulse thump, just a hair off time with the rhythm of his heart.

Perry wasn't medically inclined enough to know what had happened, to know the disaster that lurked in his left leg just beneath the surface of his skin. He had no way of knowing that his Achilles tendon floated in two useless pieces, torn to shreds by the sharp hooks of the Triangle's tail.

What he did know was that it hurt. Hurt like a bitch. Throbbed. Thumped. Thump-thumped. He had to take something for the pain. He groaned as he sat up on the couch and gingerly slid his legs over the edge, resting his feet on the floor. Despite the pulsating body aches, his head felt a bit better. But how much better could he feel knowing what twisted and grew and wormed about inside his body? They were killing him, of that there was no doubt—but why? What did they want?

Where had these things come from? Perry had never heard of any parasite like this, one that somehow 'talked' in his head, capable of . . . *intelligence*. No, this was definitely something new. Maybe it was some government experiment. Maybe he was a guinea pig for some sinister plot. Possibilities began to flood his mind. He wanted some answers.

'Hey,' Perry hissed. 'Hey, you fuckers.'

y e s   w e   a r e   here

'What do you want with me?' There was a pause, then a . . . scratching sound in his head. Or maybe it sounded like static. He concentrated on the sensation—it reminded him of turning a radio tuning knob very fast, so that static, music and voices all blended together into one indiscernible mass of sound.

A lumpy sound.

Perry waited for their answer, wondering what they were up to.

w h a t   d o   y o u   mean

The voice was monotone, short and to the point. No inflection, a steady stream of syllables that shot forth almost too fast to understand. It was nearly comical, like the voice of an alien in a cheap sci-fi flick—the ones who spout trite and overused lines like 'resistance is futile' and 'you humans are inferior' or other such drivel.

'You know damn well what I mean.' Perry felt more than a little frustrated. Not only were these things anchored inside his body, but they were playing dumb to boot. Another pause, more scratching, more lumpy sound.

w h a t   d o   y o u   mean

Perhaps he'd been too generous when he called them 'intelligent.' Maybe they weren't playing dumb. Maybe they were just plain stupid.

'I mean, what are you doing in my body?' He pushed himself to stand up, using the arm of the couch to support his weight. Again the pause, the lumpy sound.

w e   n o t   know

Perry leaned heavily on the couch, head hanging down so low that his blond hair dangled in front of his face.

His leg throbbed, thump-thumping off the inside of his skull and back down again.

'How the fuck can you not know?'

Pause.

Lumpy sound.

They were full of shit. That was the only answer. They had beamed into his body—or grown out of some evil mushroom or something—and they had to be there for a *reason,* didn't they?

As he waited for their answer, he tried to listen more closely to the lumpy sound. He focused, and caught occasional words, but they came so fast he couldn't recognize them. It was like trying to see individual stones on a highway shoulder while driving at sixty-five miles per hour—you could see them for a second and know what they were even if you couldn't identify them. It was as if they were scanning for the right words. Scanning their limited vocabulary, perhaps. Scanning through . . .

w e   n o t   know

. . . through . . .

w e   n o t   k n o w   w h y   w e
a r e   here

. . . through his brain.

They weren't just in his body, they were in his fucking brain, using him like a computer to call up data.

'Is that what I am to you?' Perry screamed. 'Am I some kind of library?' Spit flew from his mouth and his body shook in rage.

Pause.

Lumpy sound.

He sat in vibrating frustration, unable to do anything or help himself in any way while the Triangles searched for an answer.

He screamed so loud that vocal cords ripped and snapped, 'What are you doing *in my head*?'

we are trying to find words and things to talk with you

A rocket shot of pain raced up from his thump-thumping ankle, bringing his thoughts back to his strange leg wound. He needed some more Tylenol. He drew a deep breath, steadied himself and took an experimental hop toward the kitchen.

The good foot hit the ground firmly, but the motion jarred the bad leg. A new, fresh round of pain flashed bright and loud, seemingly generous in sharing the shock with every part of his body.

Play through the pain. It was intense, but now that he knew what to expect, he could control it. He could block it out. He could be tough. He made the eight hops to the kitchen counter, gritting his teeth so hard that his jaw muscles began to feel the burn.

He focused, took a deep breath, and looked down at his muscular leg—jeans dangling in two long denim flaps, dried blood flaking off his skin, little pieces hanging like red dandruff from his blond leg hairs. He'd fucked up the works pretty good, but what did it matter? He'd be dead soon anyway.

He grabbed the Tylenol bottle off the microwave top and shook out six pills. He gulped them down with a handful of tap water from the sink. He hopped back to the couch and gently sat down, grimacing against the pain.

It occurred to him that he still hadn't called work. What was it, Saturday? He'd lost track of the days. He didn't even have a clue how long he'd slept.

A thought struck him. Where the hell had he contracted this Triangle disease? As far as he knew, he might have *gotten* it at work. Obviously the Triangles started small. Maybe they were airborne, or maybe they were delivered via an insect bite, like malaria.

Or maybe he was right about being a guinea pig, and maybe work was in on it. Work, and perhaps even the apartment building. That sounded logical as well. Maybe everyone in the apartment building was stuck inside right now, contemplating the newfound guests growing in their bodies.

The things must have come *from* somewhere. They'd landed on him, or an insect—or even something artificial—had delivered them.

Did that mean these things were custom-built for people? They were getting along a little too well with his body for this to be some fluke of nature. His body hadn't rejected them, that was for fucking sure. No, he doubted this could be accidental. Either more people in town or in the building had the same disease, or someone had singled him out as an experimental host.

Perry's mind swam in a tar pit of possibilities. He tried to put the thoughts away, because he simply didn't want to think about it anymore, didn't want to think about how fucked he was.

The pain in his leg eased a little as the Tylenol took effect. He felt cold. He hopped to his room and threw on a white University of Michigan sweatshirt, then hopped back to the living room and sat on the couch. He wasn't sleepy, wasn't hungry—he needed a diversion to keep his thoughts away from the Triangles. He reached for the remote control and clicked on the flat-panel TV. The Preview Channel said the time was 11:23 A.M.

He flicked through the channels, not finding much. Infomercials. Scooby Doo. Basketball, Wolverines at Penn

State—if it had been football, maybe, but he couldn't focus on basketball right now. *Seinfeld* reruns. Soon the NFL pregame shows would be on for the Saturday game, and he would be riveted to the TV. That would let him forget. And after the pregame, the games. But for now, a television wasteland. He was about to give up when he hit the jackpot: a *Columbo* movie.

He'd seen this one, but it didn't matter. Columbo—with his old basset hound in tow—shuffled his way about yet another mansion, rumpled tan trench coat hanging from him like he'd just hopped off of a freight train full of hoboes. He was trying to climb down from a balcony and was stuck in the nearby tree (which the killer must have used either to get into the bedroom or to get out of it). The basset hound waited patiently at the base of the tree; Columbo awkwardly fell to the ground. As he struggled to rise, the Mandatory Rich Person walked up and accosted him with the ever-so-familiar, 'Have you taken leave of your senses, Mister Columbo?'

w h o   i s   there

Perry almost jumped out of his seat when the Triangles spoke. 'What?' he said, looking around the room, eyes darting to every corner.

w h o   i s   there

Dread filled Perry. Was someone here to finish the experiment, perhaps kill him and dissect him? Or maybe take him away? Did the Triangles know something he didn't?

'What are you talking about?' Perry said. 'I don't see anyone, there's no one here.'

n e w   V o i c e   n e w w w
v o i c e   n e w   voice

The TV droned with Columbo's nasal growl. 'Sorry to disturb you again, ma'am,' Peter Falk said to the Mandatory

Rich Person, 'but I was wondering if I could ask you just a few more questions.'

Columbo. They heard the TV. A laugh escaped Perry's lips, which surprised him. The Triangles didn't know what television was.

Or maybe . . . maybe they didn't know what *reality* was. More accurately, they didn't know the difference between fantasy and reality. They couldn't see a thing, but they could hear. They didn't know the difference between a real person talking and sound from the television.

'That's Columbo,' Perry said quietly, trying to figure out how to handle this new plot twist. He didn't know what good this information would do him. It wasn't like it could save his condemned ass, but something in the back of his head told him not to let on about the TV. Perry decided to trust his instincts and turned the set off.

who   is   columbo   who

'He's a cop, a police officer.'

Perry felt the now-familiar pause and the burst of lumpy sound, which grew so loud he almost winced. The Triangles worked his brain like a big thesaurus, hunting for meaning.

In a way, the searching was worse than the pain, worse than seeing the things under his skin, even worse than hooks wrapped around his bones or the creatures sucking nutrients from his blood. They scanned his brain, using him like wetware, like their own personal computer.

The concept hit him with force. If they could scan through his brain, through the chemical-storage processes that locked memories down, then this was some seriously advanced shit. Perhaps they didn't know what TV was, but *something* was going on here that was beyond the cutting edge of science and

no cop no cop no cop no no not
tell him we here no no no no no

The Triangles' burst of words interrupted Perry's thoughts and filled his soul with a wave of fear that ripped through him like a blast of November wind. His adrenaline surged against some perceived threat even as he realized it wasn't *his* fear, but *theirs,* the Triangles' fear. Something about the rumpled Columbo had them scared shitless.

no no no no no
coming to get us

Their fear felt corrosive, almost tangible, a jet-black snake squirming and writhing under the grip of some heartless bird of prey.

'Take it easy!' Perry winced at the bizarre feeling of alien emotions coursing through his own mind and body. 'It's okay, he's gone, I got rid of him.' He thought it might be easy to make the fear go away if he told them about TV, told them there was no police officer

coming to get us

in the apartment, but his instincts told him to keep that trump card. He might find some use for it later.

cop is gone cop is
gone no no no

'He's gone! Now take a chill pill and shut the fuck up!' Perry's hands involuntarily went to his head, trying to hold in his brains against the pounding tumult of shouts and anxiety slashing through his skull. Contagious fear. Perry felt the cold fingers of panic wrapping around his chest. 'He's fucking gone! Now relax and *stop screaming in my head*!'

coming to GET us

They sounded different, and not just because of the fear. They actually had some *tone* to their words now, something deep, and a certain slowness that he found vaguely familiar.

h e ' s   c o m i n g   t o   G E T   us

He *felt* their terror. It was nothing like the emotionless monotone he'd first heard—they'd increased their intensity, or maybe just lost their restraint.

n o   T E L L   h i m   w e   h e r e

'I won't tell, okay?' Perry lowered his voice, tried to relax himself in hopes that it would, in turn, relax them. 'It's okay, he's gone now, you just have to take it easy.'

The claustrophobic fear instantly vanished, as suddenly as if he'd been in a dark room and someone had flicked on the lights.

t h a n k s   t h a n k s   t h a n k s

'Why the hell do the police scare you so bad?'

c o m i n g   t o   G E T   u s

Why were they afraid of the police? That made no sense. Perry supposed this might mean he wasn't alone, might mean that someone knew about the Triangles and wanted to destroy them. But why hadn't he heard about it? Surely the police couldn't keep a secret like this from the press. And how could the Triangles know of hostile police in the first place? They'd grown from nothing, all the while in his apartment—they had no contact with the outside world. Could they have some preprogrammed memory of potential threats?

They didn't recognize the words *cop* or *police* right away—they'd had to scan and scan hard to find the meaning that frightened them so badly. But they found something in Perry's Unabridged Brain Dictionary, something that they knew. At least, they *thought* they knew.

'What do you mean, he's "coming to get" you? Does someone know you're here?' Perry felt the Triangles search his mind, his memories, for the right words. The more they searched, the more familiar he became with the feeling, like an eye slowly adjusting to the dim light of a dark room.

m e n   a r e   l o o k i n g   f o r
u s   K I L L   u s   y i k e s   Y i k e s
YIKES

Yikes? The word stuck in Perry's head. Yikes. They used the word *yikes*. And they had shouted it along with *kill*. Why were they suddenly talking so funny? The monotone was gone—there was actual inflection in the words. The speech had taken on a slower, dreamier quality, to the point where the Starting Five talked almost with a drawl.

But the important thing wasn't the new speech, it was their paranoid fear of cops. Was this some kind of instinctive memory? How could it be that they didn't know why they were in his body, but they knew enough to fear the police? Were they just plain lying to him? What did they have to gain by being honest about anything? But he'd *felt* their fear of the police. Or maybe . . . maybe it wasn't police at all. Maybe it was men in uniforms.

Perry realized that when he thought of cops or police, his initial mental image was that of a Michigan state trooper. Those guys were always fairly big, with immaculate uniforms, robotic politeness and a very prominent gun.

This was probably the picture the Triangles read, because it was the first thing *he* thought of when he heard the word *cop*. And his mental image of the state troopers—with their perfect uniforms and attitudes and guns—wasn't really that of a cop as much as it was that of . . .

Of . . .

A soldier.

Were the Triangles afraid of soldiers? Two possibilities

flashed through Perry's mind. Either the Triangles knew what soldiers were by experience or instinct, or they had a broader knowledge of the world around them than they let on. Somehow they knew things that Perry didn't.

A brief flicker of hope flared up in his chest. The Triangles feared soldiers. Was there some group that knew of the Triangles? If so, did it mean that Perry wasn't the only one suffering through this horror?

'Why do you think they're coming to get you?'

Pause.

Lumpy sound.

they WANT to kill us
kill Kill KILL

'How do you know that? How can you when you don't even know where you come from?'

A double pause.

talking to friends

Friends. Were there other Triangles? Were there other people infected with these things? Maybe he *wasn't* the only one—maybe this was bigger than just him.

'What do these friends say?'

Only a short pause this time.

hungry feed us

'Your friends are hungry too?'

hungry feed us feed
Feed FEED

'Oh, *you're* hungry?'

feed Feed FEED
Feed feed

'Forget about the food,' Perry said insistently. 'Tell me about your friends. Where are they?'

FEED NOW

The command sounded like a cannon exploding inside

his head. His eyes shut tight. His teeth ground in reaction to the pain.

FEED NOW

Perry let out a small, choked groan, he couldn't think straight, he couldn't grip what he needed to do to

FEED NOW NOW NOW
NOW NOW NOW NOW
NOW

'*Shut the fuck up!*' Perry shouted as loudly as he could, his voice a deep, guttural blast of pain and anger. 'We'll eat, *we'll eat!* Just stop screaming in my head!'

okay feed us now okay
feed us now now now

Like the return stroke of a bowstring after release of an arrow, his mind snapped back to normal. A single tear trailed down his cheek. Their shouting had been so intense he'd been unable to move, almost unable to speak.

now Now Now

Perry jumped up as he heard their intensity start to creep higher. He'd hopped the eight hops to the kitchen before he gave it a second thought, his body acting from fear of that pain.

He was snapping to attention like a soldier under orders, not thinking, only doing as he was told, like some good little Nazi carrying out the master plan. *Jawohl, Herr Kommandant. I'll kill the Jews and the Gypsies and the Czechs because I have no mind of my own, and it's okay because someone told me to do it.* He was a robot, a remote-controlled servant. It humiliated him, somehow dug away at his pride as a man. A man, after all, was in charge of his own destiny, not at the whim of some slave driver, some controller.

He tried to console his damaged pride by telling himself he was very hungry and would have eaten anyway—it wasn't because the Triangles had told him to. But that was bullshit. Right now he felt like a puppet on a string, doing a funky little dance each time the Starting Five tweaked at one of his nerves. Worse than a puppet—he felt like he was ten years old again, jumping with fear every time his father spoke.

Still had the Ragu. He fished it out of the fridge and pulled a box of Rice-A-Roni from the cupboard. He was almost out of food and would have to shop very soon. Wouldn't that be a hoot? The condemned man, dying of some freaky parasite, pushing a cart at Kroger's and picking out the last meal he would cook for himself. Now that's a liberal death row.

A flash of cooking inspiration came to him as he put the Rice-A-Roni back and grabbed the half-full bag of Cost Cutter rice. No noodles, but the Ragu looked just too darn good to pass up. Fishing a measuring cup out of the cupboard, he set a pot to boil.

n o w   N o w   now

The words drifted menacingly through his head.

'Just hold your horses. Dinner's going to be ready in about twenty minutes.'

n o w   n o w   now

'It's not ready yet,' Perry urged, his voice pleading. He poured the Ragu into a mismatched pot and set it to simmer. 'Like I said, you'll just have to wait a few minutes.'

The lumpy noise probed at his brain.

w h a t   i s   a   m i n u t e   sonofabitch

'A minute. You know, sixty seconds.' It seemed so obvious it was difficult to explain. It was odd the Triangles wouldn't know the concept of time. 'Do you know what a second is? What time is?'

s e c o n d   n o   t i m e   yes

That reply came back fast, with only a touch of lumpy noise. They knew what time was. He'd have to illustrate 'a second.' He looked at the clock on the stove—if they could see that, it would be easy to explain.

'You can't . . .' A chill washed over him, cutting off the question. Suddenly he wasn't sure if he wanted an answer. 'You can't . . . see . . . can you? See through my eyes?' He hadn't given much thought to exactly what these bastards could do. They could 'read' his mind, in the literal sense, so could they pick up and read optical impulses from his brain? Pick them off in midstream?

n o   w e   c a n n o t   see

The answer was a relief, but a short-lived relief, cut in half by the rest of the answer:

n o t   yet

Not yet.

They were still growing. Maybe they were simply going to take over his mind, pushing Perry's own consciousness out of the way one step at a time. Maybe they were slowly choking out his brain, just as a gangly, fibrous weed in a garden methodically robs sustenance from a rose. The rose may be beautiful, glowing and soft, but the weed . . . the weed is the survivor, the one that grows in harsh soil, rocks, bad weather, low light. The one that faces impossible conditions and not only survives, but flourishes.

Perry was suddenly quite sure he knew what was happening—the Triangles were growing *into* him, taking over his body and his mind, keeping the shell, leaving the outside world none the wiser. *Invasion of the Body Snatchers.* It was the typical Hollywood script. And why not? It made sense. Why send armies and conquer the earth when you could slowly replace the human race? More efficient, more economic. Neater. *Tidier*. No messy bodies to clean up. Better even than the infamous neutron bomb that killed all the people and left the buildings standing.

Soon they'd tap in to his eyes. What next? His nose? Hell, maybe they were already smelling the rice simmering on the stove. Or maybe his mouth—they could speak to him through his own voice. Then what? His muscles? His very motions? Just how efficient were the little bastards?

And how long were they going to be *little*? Maybe they weren't separate at all. Maybe they were just different parts with different missions. Living jigsaw-puzzle pieces all planning on connecting in the swinging-singles Triangle bar known as Perry's Place.

A warm flash of fuzzy noise interrupted his doom-and-gloom thoughts.

how long is a second
how long is a minute
how long

Perry desperately wanted to avoid that mental screaming, that insistent chain saw of Triangle demand grinding through his thoughts.

'Okay, let's figure this out.' He talked quickly, hoping to prevent any agitation. 'See, a minute is sixty seconds, and a second is a very short piece of time.' The fuzzy noise seemed stuck on a high-pitched buzz—as he talked, they searched the database to keep up with the meaning of his words. 'And a second is, like, this long . . . here, I'll count to five using seconds. Pay attention to how long each count is, and that's a second. One . . . two . . . three . . . four . . . five.' A flash of childhood memory reared to the surface, the jazzy counting song from the show *The Electric Company* (one-two-three four, five, six-seven-eight-nine-ten, eleven tweh-eh-eh-elve).

'That was five seconds, get it?' The high-pitched searching grew louder, followed only by the briefest buzz of a low pitch.

second is short
minute is sixty
seconds hour is sixty
minutes correct

All inflection left the Starting Five's voice. He could only assume that the word *correct* had been part of a question and not a statement, as there wasn't even the smallest lilt in the words that echoed through his head. Whatever the reason for their brief digression into spaced-out land, they had returned to their emotionless monotone.

'Correct.' He'd never mentioned the concept of an 'hour.' They had pulled it out of his brain, probably based on its association with the minute and the second. Their ability to scan his brain grew faster and faster.

It hit him—quite suddenly, with the shuddering force of truth and revelation—that people were just complicated machines. They were no different than computers. The brain was simply a control center and a storage device; when you needed to remember something, the brain sent some kind of signal to recall stored data, exactly like telling a program to open a file. The command was sent, and another part of the computer

twenty-four hours in
a day

looked for data with code that matched the command, found it and sent that information to the processor where it was read and displayed on the screen. The brain was *exactly* the same thing. Memories were stored in there somehow, some chemical process tied up in the cerebrum or cerebellum or what have you. With the right technology, you could read that stored data as easily as you could read the stored data in a hard drive, or the stored data on the pages of a book. They were all just mediums for keeping track of simple bits of information that

s e v e n   d a y s   i n   a   week

formed something more complex. But just like matter (compounds, then elements, then atoms, then protons and electrons), everything could be broken down into smaller and smaller parts.

It was looking more and more like the Triangles were constructed to read those little parts . . . to be able to fetch Perry's stored memories off the hard drive he'd been carrying since before his birth: his brain. The sheer

f o u r   w e e k s   i n   a   month

complexity of the Triangles' ability was daunting. And they learned quickly; their search times seemed to grow progressively faster. They were also learning not only to pick up the single memory or word he had spoken, but associated words and memories as well. So far it looked like they could only tap into his long-term memory: time concepts, vocabulary, words with images attached in order to define meanings.

These creatures

t w e l v e   m o n t h s   i n
a   year

had the ability to read his brain like a hard drive, but they had no initial concept of simple things like

t e n   y e a r s   i n   a   decade

time, or the technology of television, or that voices could be projected, not real.

Something was missing from this mystery, or perhaps something was just a bit out of place. He still didn't know what the Triangles were, where they came from or how long he had until they took over his body.

But maybe he could stop them. Maybe . . . if he got help.

The mythical Soldiers were out there, and they *knew*. They knew about the Triangles. They wanted to kill the Triangles. Fuck up the Starting Five and send them packing. The big question, Perry old boy, the big twenty-thousand-dollar question is *who are these 'soldiers'?*

This wasn't Hollywood. There were no Men in Black to save the day with a handsome smile and a witty comment. No *X-Files* agents crashing through his door to cast plaintive looks his way. No superhero from another planet with a special gun to blast the boogers right out of his body. He didn't know whom to call, where to go, but there had to be somebody out there.

t e n   d e c a d e s   i n

A sudden thought froze him. If they could scan his brain, how much longer until they could read his active thoughts? And when that happened, what would they do if they knew he wanted to contact the Soldiers? They'd scream so loud his brain would turn to puree, drip out of his ears and dribble out his nose like snot.

Maybe they were listening right now.

He had to stop thinking about it. But if he didn't think about it, how was he going to contact anybody? He couldn't even think about killing the Triangles—they'd fry him from the inside out first. Cook his brain like a microwave potato. But he couldn't stop *thinking*, could he? And if he did stop, if he did tune such thoughts of survival from his brain, then he was surely doomed.

Stress steadily built up inside him, gaining steam like a wall of bricks crashing down from an exploding building.

The buzzer on the stove loudly announced that the

rice was done. His mind grabbed on to this new distraction like a drowning man clinging to a life preserver, gripping it with all he had, focusing all his thoughts on the thrilling subject of dinner.

Perry didn't realize that it was a temporary escape. He didn't realize that his mind was already beginning to crack and fissure under the stress of the impossible-to-believe situation that unfolded around him and inside him. The floodwaters were slowly rising, inevitable, unstoppable, irresistible—and the high ground would only stay above the waterline for so long.

39

MOMMY'S LITTLE GIRL

Clarence Otto stopped the car. Cell phone pressed to her ear, Margaret looked out the window at a neat, two-story brick house on Miller Avenue. White shutters and trim. Dead-looking ivy branches covering one side of the house—in the summer that side would be a flat wall of leafy green, the very epitome of old-school collegiate housing.

Amos sat in the backseat, clearly annoyed at the whole process. While he was indefatigable in the confines of a hospital, being outdoors in the cold brought out his surly side.

'We just pulled up to the girl's house,' Margaret said into her cell phone.

'Tell Otto to stay sharp,' Dew said. 'I've got six bodies over here, it's spinning out of control. Your backup team is there?'

Margaret turned in the seat to look back, even though she knew what she'd see. Gray van, unmarked, parked right behind them.

'It's here. We'll let Otto lead, of course, but I think we're okay—the girl just had the Morgellons fibers, no triangles.'

'Fine, just stay sharp,' Dew said. 'These guys are psychos. And as soon as you're done, get over here.'

'What have you found?'

Dew paused. 'Seems our college boy was an artist. I think you'll want to see this.'

'All right, Dew. We'll be there as soon as we can.'

Dew hung up without another word.

'What did he say?' Amos asked.

'Six more bodies,' Margaret said absently. 'The other side of town. We're heading over there when we're done here.'

In the backseat Amos hung his head. This was wearing on him, Margaret knew. Behind his sunglasses, Agent Clarence Otto showed no sign of emotion, but the muscles in his jaw twinged slightly.

'Are you ready?' Otto asked. She nodded.

They approached the house, Margaret and Amos keeping two steps behind Otto. Otto knocked on the door with his left hand—his right hand hidden inside his jacket, resting on the hilt of his weapon.

There was little chance of danger. Cheng's report showed he had given the girl a careful examination, and would have certainly seen anything resembling a triangle or triangle-to-be. They still had to keep things as quiet as possible—if they kicked in the door to find a perfectly normal family, a little bit more of the secrecy would die, and Americans would be a little bit closer to discovering the nightmare blossoming in their midst.

Snow covered the ground and the leafless trees. Most of the houses on this street had white lawns, thick with undisturbed snow. Some, like this one, had lawns trampled over and over by tiny feet, the snow's beauty crushed by the tireless energy of playing children.

The door opened. In the doorway stood a little angel— blond pigtails, blue dress, sweet face. She even held a rag doll, for crying out loud.

'Hello, sweetie,' Otto said.

'Hello, sir.' She didn't look afraid at all. Nor did she look happy or excited, just matter-of-fact.

'Are you Missy Hester?'

She nodded, her curly pigtails bouncing in time.

Otto's empty right hand came out of his jacket, slowly dropping to hang at his side.

Margaret stepped to Otto's right, so the girl could see her clearly. 'Missy, we're here to see your mother. Is she home?'

'She's sleeping. Would you like to come in and sit down in the living room?'

She stood aside and gestured with her hand. A regular little hostess.

'Thank you,' Otto said. He walked inside, head turning quickly as he seemed to scan every inch of the house. Margaret and Amos followed. It was a small, simple affair. Aside from a scattered layer of brightly colored toys, the place looked immaculate.

Missy led them into the living room, where Margaret and Amos sat on a couch. Otto chose to remain standing. The living room gave a view of the stairs, the front door and another doorway that led into the dining-nook area of a kitchen.

'How about your daddy?' Margaret said. 'Is he home?'

Missy shook her head. 'He doesn't live with us anymore. He lives in Grand Rapids.'

'Well, honey, can you go wake up your mom? We need to talk to her and to you.'

The girl nodded, curls jiggling, then turned and ran up the stairs.

'She seems perfectly healthy,' Amos said. 'We'll take a

good look at her, but she doesn't seem to show any signs of infection.'

'Maybe cutting out the threads works in the new strain,' Margaret said. 'Morgellons cases have been going on for years without any triangle growths. Something had to have changed.'

'They're just being built better,' Otto said. 'No disrespect to either of you, but you think too much. Murray hit it right on the head. Sometimes the most obvious answer is just that, the answer.'

'Occam's razor does seem to apply,' Amos said.

'What's that?' Otto asked.

Amos smiled. 'Never mind. It just means you're probably right.'

All three of their heads turned as a little boy appeared in the open doorway to the kitchen. He couldn't have been more than seven, maybe eight—he wore a cowboy hat, gun holsters on his hips, chaps with fringe and a slightly crooked black mask—the full-on Lone Ranger costume. Otto tensed at the sight of the six-shooters in the boy's hands, but each had a barrel capped with bright orange plastic. Cap guns. Toys.

'Hold it right there, pardners,' the boy said. He made his little voice all gravelly, trying to sound tough, but he just sounded cute.

Otto laughed. 'Oh, we're holding it, Lone Ranger. Is there a problem?'

'Not if you keep your hands where I can see 'em, mister.'

Otto raised his hands to shoulder height, palms out. 'You'll get no trouble from me, Ranger. No trouble 'tall.'

The boy nodded, the very picture of seriousness. 'Well, let's just keep it that way, and we'll all get along *reallllll* nice like.'

Missy bounced down the stairs, making far more noise than should have been possible out of a tiny, six-year-old body.

'My sister will take real good care of y'all,' the boy said. 'I got me some business to attend ta.'

'Be safe, Ranger,' Otto said.

'Cute kid,' Amos said as the boy slid back into the kitchen and shut the door behind him. They heard him banging around, yelling at imaginary robbers.

But something about the boy gave Margaret a bad feeling. They'd rushed things, been sloppy—they hadn't even checked to see how many people were in the family. The father was gone. One brother. Was there another? Any sisters?

'Mommy won't wake up,' Missy said. 'I've been trying for a couple of days, but she won't wake up. And she smells funny.'

Margaret felt a coldness flush through her stomach.

The girl took a step forward. 'Are you from the gov-ren-ment?'

Amos slowly stood up.

Otto calmly walked between the girl and Margaret. 'Yes, honey, we're from the government. How did you know?'

'Because my brother said you would come.'

Margaret wanted out of there. Now. They had come for the girl, but it never crossed their minds that someone else in the house might be infected.

'Oh, no,' Amos said. 'Do you smell natural gas?'

Margaret did, suddenly and strong, coming from the kitchen.

'Get the girl out of here,' Otto said. His voice was quiet, calm, but totally commanding. 'Do it now.'

Margaret stood and ran the three steps to Missy, then hesitated. She didn't want to touch the little girl—what if she had those things? What if they were wrong, and she was contagious?

'Margaret,' Otto hissed. 'Get her out of here.'

She ignored her instincts and picked the girl up, her skin crawling as she did. She took one step toward the door, but before she could take another, the kitchen door opened.

The little boy walked out, holding a cap gun in each hand. The smell of gas billowed out of the kitchen.

He still wore the cowboy hat, but not the mask. He only had one eye. The other socket held a misshapen blue lump, under the skin, that had pushed out his eyelids and eyebrow to obscene proportions. The lump stretched the eyelid out and open, showing a blackish, gnarled textured skin underneath. Whatever it was, it had grown between the boy's eye and his eyelids—his eye was back there somewhere, behind that . . . *thing*.

'You've been bad,' the little boy said. 'I'm going to have to gun . . . you . . . *down.*'

He raised the cap guns.

Amos raced past Margaret, heading for the door. She turned and ran with him, still carrying the girl. Heavy footsteps told her that Agent Otto was right behind her.

Margaret ran out the door as she heard the caps firing, the boy pulling the trigger over and over again. She made it out the front porch and was down the steps when the gas finally ignited.

It wasn't a big explosion, so much as a really large *whuff*. It didn't even blow out the windows like on TV, just gave them a good rattle. She kept running and felt the heat on her back—just because it didn't explode didn't mean it wasn't hot, didn't mean the house wasn't burning, and didn't mean the little boy wasn't already engulfed in flames.

40

DINNER IS SERVED

Perry loaded up his plate and managed to hop to the couch without spilling any of the rice-Ragu concoction. He slumped into the waiting cushions, winced at the waves of pain that shot through his leg, then gripped his fork and dug into the meal, not knowing if it would be his last.

The Ragu wasn't thick enough to make the rice clump, so it was more like a heavy soup than Spanish rice. But it was still tasty, and it quelled his stomach's grumbling. He shoveled it in as if he'd never seen food before in his life. Man, wouldn't a Quarter Pounder and some supersize fries hit the spot right now? Or Hostess cupcakes. Or a Baby Ruth bar. Or a big old steak and some broccoli with a nice white-cheese sauce. No, scratch all of the above, a bajillion soft tacos from Taco Hell would be the most satisfying thing on the planet. Cram 'em down with Fire Sauce and a bottomless cup of Mountain Dew. It wasn't that his rice was bad, but the texture just didn't ring of *solid* food, and his stomach longed to be filled like a water balloon on a steamy-hot summer day.

Summer. Now that would have been a nice season to die. His timing, as usual, was terrible. He could have contracted this 'illness' in the spring, or in the summer, or at least in the fall. All three seasons were unbelievably beautiful in Michigan. Trees everywhere either bursting with new-growth greenery or exploding in the spectacular, jewel-reflection colors that heralded the coming winter. Dying in summer would have been good—Michigan is just so green once you get outside the cities and towns, out onto the innumerable country roads. The highways to northern Michigan and the Upper Peninsula are a black slash of pavement cutting through an endless sea of forest and farmland that sprawls out on either side.

Farmland, forest, swamps, water . . . the three-hour drive from Mount Pleasant to Cheboygan was interrupted by little more than roadkill and highway-stop towns like Gaylord that presented a splotch of buildings and cars before they were gone, fading away in the rearview mirror like the vestiges of a tasteless dream that dissipates into the buttery solution of delicious sleep.

Summer was warm, at least early summer. Later on in the season, the true nature of Michigan's swamps revealed themselves in sweltering humidity, clammy sweat, swarms of mosquitoes and blackflies. But even that posed little problem, as you were never more than five or ten minutes' drive from a lake. Back home, swimming in Mullet Lake, cool water leaching away the oppressive heat. Sun blasting down, turning white bodies red and leaving streamers in the eye from where it bounced off the surface like a million infinitely bright, tiny supernovas.

As perfect as summer could be, winter was equally oppressive. Sure, it was beautiful in its own right, with snow-covered trees, sprawling fields converted to expanses of white nothingness bordered by woods and dotted with farmhouses snugly nestled into the landscape. But beauty didn't hold much over substance when that substance was freeze-your-balls-off cold. Up north the winters were spectacular. Down in the southern part of the state, where population expansion never ceased, the forests and fields were only something he glimpsed on the way to work. Here, winter made life miserable. Cold. Freezing. Wet. Icy. And even the snow looked dirty, pushed to the side of the road in mangy, gravel-embedded slush piles. Sometimes the trees were bedecked with an inch of snow on every last branch and twig, but most of the time they were barren, brown dead and lifeless. That's why he'd always wanted to make sure he was cremated when he died—he couldn't imagine spending eternity in the frozen soil of a Michigan winter.

And yet his last days played out in that same Michigan winter. Even if the Soldiers could find him, what could they do for him? How far gone was this monotone cancer that shouted in his head like Sam Kinison on a bad acid trip?

He scraped the last grains of rice into his mouth.

'Pretty tasty, eh?' He tossed the plate carelessly onto the coffee table. Hey, he was dying, no point in cleaning up the mess, now was there? High-pitched fuzzy noise babbled in his head.

we don't taste just absorb

Don't. A contraction. How about that? The Starting Five's vocab was improving.

He leaned back into the couch's familiar cushions. His stomach rumbling gradually subsided, then ceased. Staring out at the blank TV screen, he was struck by a sudden question—what to do?

During this entire bizarre scenario, he'd never exactly had to worry about entertainment. He'd either been sleeping, passed out, cutting into himself like some freak from a Clive Barker movie or talking to the Starting Five. The one time he'd tried to watch a little TV, good ol' Columbo had gotten him into more trouble than he cared to remember.

But with TV out of the question, what was he going to do? He had, of course, brought computer books from work in order to study at home, but he'd be fucked if he'd spend whatever hours he had reading about managing Unix networks or integrating open-source code. He did, however, like the idea of reading something, anything that might give him even a few moments' reprieve from this awful situation.

He was about a third of the way through *The Shining* by Stephen King, but hadn't read a single page in weeks. Well, now was his opportunity. He wasn't going anywhere. And perhaps engrossing himself in the book would relieve his mind from the background battle of Not Thinking About the Soldiers (and how loud the screams would be if he *did* think about them).

But first he had to clean the spaghetti sauce off his face and hands. Dinner had been a little messy. The stains on his sweatshirt he could care less about, obviously, but that sticky, tacky feeling on his face would distract him. He slowly rose from the couch and hopped to the bathroom, contemplating another trip down Tylenol Lane while he was at it. The pain in his leg was starting to get worse again.

He let the sink run until the water reached near-scalding temperatures, then washed off his face and hands. Gazing at his wet face in the mirror, he couldn't help but again think of the George Romero classic *Night of the Living Dead*. He could have *been* one of the walking departed: skin with a sickly gray pallor, deep circles hanging under his bloodshot eyes, dry hair askew.

But it wasn't all bad. His paunch had vanished. His

muscles looked well defined for the first time in years. He could even see the beginnings of his six-pack. He'd lost at least fifteen pounds—all of it fat—in the past few days. He moved his arm and watched his deltoid flutter, muscle fibers visible and rippling.

Great fucking diet plan. I'd like to see Richard Simmons compete with this.

There was more to see than his musculature. He hadn't looked in on one of the Triangles in quite a while. He wasn't sure if he wanted to see what they looked like now. Maybe they were bigger, enlarging themselves as they continued their march on Mount Perry.

He had to look.

The one near his neck was the most convenient. Perry pulled back his sweatshirt collar, exposing the Triangle beneath. It lay just above the collarbone, near the trapezius.

That was the first muscle name he'd learned. When he was a child, his father would grab the trapezius with a paralyzing grip that made Mr. Spock's little nerve pinch pale by comparison. Man-oh-man, how that had hurt. Dad usually accompanied the pinch with a phrase like, 'It's my house, and you're going to live by my rules' or the ubiquitous, 'You've got to have *discipline*.'

Perry pushed away thoughts of his father and concentrated on the Triangle. It was bluer, now more like a new tattoo rather than a faded one, and firmer, the edges clearly defined. Just as his fluttering muscles became more obvious seemingly by the hour, the Triangle's rough texture was beginning to show through the skin. He tested the skin with a poke from his free hand. Definitely firmer. He leaned in over the sink until his face was only six inches from the mirror, allowing himself the best look he'd ever had at one of the little invaders.

He stared at the edges. At the slits. At the blueness. At the pores of his skin that still looked perfectly normal except for the thing underneath. He noticed the number of blue lines that extended out from the Triangle. Used blood. Deoxygenated. Same shade as the little veins on his wrists. That's why the Triangles appeared blue—they took in oxygen from his own blood through their tails or whatever, the blood worked its way up the tiny body and the deoxygenated blood dissipated on top just under the skin. It all made perfect sense.

The slits seemed much more developed than the last time he'd looked. They had a pucker to them, almost like thin lips, or maybe more like . . . like . . .

A snippet of their voice flashed back to him—*no we cannot see . . . not yet.*

Not yet.

'Oh my God don't let that be what I think it is.'

Once again, God wasn't listening.

Each of the three slits opened, revealing the deep, black, shiny surfaces underneath. If there was any question as to what they were, it disappeared when all three sets of lids blinked in unison.

He was looking at his collarbone, and his collarbone was looking right back at him.

'Motherfucker,' Perry said, panic once again creeping into his voice. When were these things going to stop growing? What was next? Were they going to grow out of him, grow little hands and feet or claws or tails?

His breath came in thin, shallow gasps. His eyes fuzzed out of focus, his mind seeming to go away somewhere for a quick break. Hopping had become so normal for him that he managed to get back to the couch and plunk down without breaking his trance.

His brain ran on autopilot, ran like a movie that played on and on and on while Perry sat back and watched, unable to change the channel, unable to look away from the flashing images.

He remembered a show he'd seen on The Learning Channel. There was this wasp, an evil little fucker. It attacked a specific type of caterpillar. The wasp didn't kill the caterpillar, only paralyzed it for a while—during which time the wasp laid eggs inside the caterpillar. *Inside,* thank you very fucking much. The wasp, its mission complete, then flew off. The caterpillar woke up and went on about its leaf-munching life, apparently unaware of the vile disease incubating in its guts.

It was the most horrible thing Perry had ever seen. The wasp eggs didn't just hatch and rip their way out of the caterpillar . . .

They *ate* their way out.

When the eggs hatched, the new wasp larvae fed on the caterpillar's innards. And they grew. The caterpillar struggled for life but could do nothing about the larvae eating it from the inside. The caterpillar's skin bulged, rippled, moved as the larvae inside continued to eat, methodically chewing away at its guts with the same slow, robotlike precision that the caterpillar used to dispose of a leaf. It was appalling. It was a living cancer. And to make it worse, via some horrid instinct the larvae knew what to eat; they consumed the fat and internal organs while leaving the heart and brain alone, preserving the crawling buffet for as long as possible.

So perfect was the larvae's evolution that they didn't kill the caterpillar until they finished their growth cycle— as they ripped their way out of the caterpillar's skin, glistening with the wet slime of the chewed guts, their victim kept squirming, writhing with what little energy it had left, amazingly alive even though its innards had been munched on like the Sunday breakfast bar at Big Boy.

Was that what faced Perry? Were they consuming him from the inside? But if that was the case, then why were they always screaming at him to eat? They weren't going to take over his mind. That much was obvious—if they could take over his mind, they wouldn't need eyes, now would they? Maybe this was just the first stage—if they could grow eyes, why not a mouth? Why not *teeth*?

He calmed himself, forcing himself to focus, think logically. He was, after all, an educated man. A *college boy*, as Daddy would say. All he had to do was think, and maybe he could come up with some answers on his own.

He just didn't have enough information to form any kind of hypothesis, nothing to go on. No clues. Even Columbo would have been stuck with this one. Of course, Columbo would play the blithering buffoon, countering the suave, rich attitudes of his homicidal targets. Columbo would let stupidity show, wear his weakness on his sleeve, allowing his targets' confidence to grow and grow and grow until they let something slip, something tiny, something that would normally go unnoticed. Unnoticed by normal eyes, but not Peter Falk's cross-eyed stare. That's what he had to do; play dumb, and get them talking.

'Hey fuckers.'

h e y   hello

'What is it you fellas want with me?'

w h a t   d o   y o u   m e a n   want

'Why are you in my body?'

w e   d o n ' t   know

So much for detective work. There was really nothing else to do. Just sit. Sit and wait. He was nothing more than a walking, talking buffet table. Sit and wait. Sit and listen.

You gonna let 'em push you around like that, boy?

Another voice . . . his daddy's voice. It wasn't real, it wasn't a voice in his head like the Triangles', it was a memory. No, not a memory, a phantom. His daddy's voice, as if his daddy were with him in spirit.

'No, Daddy,' Perry said, his voice a dry husk. 'I won't let them push me around.'

He hooked his index finger under his sweatshirt collar and pulled it back violently, ripping it slightly, exposing the Triangle on his collarbone. He couldn't see it, but he knew that the icy-black eyes were blinking away, taking in the view of the living room and all the knickknacks that Perry had acquired since high school.

The fork still sat on the plate, a few rivulets of spaghetti sauce clinging to the tines. Perry grabbed it with a caveman grip, clutched it like a murderous dagger. He giggled once as he remembered the punch line to an old grade-school joke.

'Fork you, buddy.'

With all the force he could muster, he jammed the fork into his trapezius. The center tine poked through one of the black eyes with a tiny, wet, crunching noise.

The tines kissed off his scapula and out the back side of his trapezius, accompanied by a double-squirt of red and purple that landed wetly on the couch's worn-thin upholstery.

He wasn't even sure if he felt it. He didn't have to scream in pain—the Triangles took care of that.

It wasn't even a scream, really, just a noise. A loud noise. A fucking hellfire and bear-the-cross loud noise, blaring like a klaxon alarm stuffed down his auditory canal to rest nicely against his eardrum. He rolled off the couch, thrashing his head in sudden and all-encompassing agony.

He rolled onto his back, reached up, grabbed the fork and twisted it, driving it up at an angle deeper into his shoulder.

Perry couldn't know that on the second thrust the fork tines punched a neat hole through the Triangle's main nervous column just below its flat head, killing it instantly. Had he known, he probably wouldn't have cared—all he knew was that he wasn't a patsy, wasn't some pushover, he was Scary Perry Dawsey and was once again whipping ass.

'You *fucks*!' Perry screamed louder than ever before, perhaps needing to hear himself over the horrid death-shriek that raged through his head. 'How do you like it? How's it feel?'

stop stop stop stop
stop stop stop stop

'The *fuck* I'll stop! How's it feel? How does it *feel*?' Tears found their way out of Perry's tightly shut eyes. Pain raged through his body, but his conscious mind felt none of it.

fucker you will pay
stop stop STOP

'Bite it, baby!' Perry fed on the pain like an alcoholic diving into that first off-the-wagon drink. 'I'm doing this one and then I'm calling the Soldiers to come get the rest!' He twisted the fork again and started to say something, but lost the words as the fork stuck deeply into a tendon. He made the major mistake of giving in to the pain, rolling in useless protest—his shoulder and the end of the fork hit the front of the couch, driving the prongs in ever deeper.

S T O P STOP STOP
STOP

Perry tried opening his eyes, but vision came only in strobelike bursts. The klaxon scream in his head was too much to bear. He'd lost again, he knew it, but he couldn't even mutter a single word. Couldn't

S T O P STOP

tell them he was so sorry

S T O P STOP

couldn't tell Daddy he would behave

S T O P STOP

couldn't beg Daddy to *please God* STOP ripping into my brain!

S T O P STOP
STOP

S T O P
S T O P

He fell to the ground, motionless, not hearing the angry, irritated stomping coming from the ceiling above.

41

HOWDY, NEIGHBOR

Al Turner pounded his heel into the floor. He'd had just about enough of this shit. He pounded again, and the yelling stopped.

He absently scratched his ample, hairy gut, then slid a hand into his boxers to scratch his sweaty ass. Frigging hemorrhoids were killing him. They could put a man on the moon, but they couldn't make your asshole stop burning. Figures.

What the hell had gotten into that kid? Screaming his head off like that. The guy had always been so quiet, Al rarely gave him a second thought. Well, not since the kid had moved in, anyway, and Al had found out that 'Scary' Perry Dawsey lived right below him. Al introduced himself, had Dawsey sign a football for his nephew and a couple of U of M shirts for himself. Dawsey had smiled, as if he were surprised that someone would want his autograph. The smile had faded when Al asked him to sign the Rose Bowl shirt. That had probably been a little crude, but then again Al didn't exactly subscribe to the Miss Manners school of thinking, right?

He'd never expected Dawsey to be so *huge*. Sure, football players all looked big on TV, but to stand next to them was another thing entirely. The kid was a fucking monster. Al had briefly entertained the thought that he and Perry could hit the bar every Saturday during football season, maybe hang out on Sundays to watch the games. Wouldn't Jerry at work be jealous of *that*, Al Turner hanging out just as casual as you please with one of—if not *the*—greatest linebacker to ever wear the maize and blue. But that had changed when he met the kid. Just standing next to Dawsey made Al feel like a seven-year-old. He didn't want to drink beers with that freak of nature. It was like those science shows on big cats—fine to watch on TV, as long as you didn't have to meet one face-to-face in the fucking jungle.

Al twitched as his asshole flared with another round of burning. Felt like a goddamn red-hot poker was jammed in there. He grimaced and scratched. This shit could piss off the Pope, and Dawsey's screaming fits weren't helping his mood.

42

THE LOCAL YOKELS

In Dew's experience, local cops rarely looked like happy campers. These particular local cops? Well, they looked downright pissed. Three Ann Arbor police cars were parked in front of Nguyen's house. They'd pulled right up on the lawn and sidewalk, passing the three gray vans that had parked on the curb. The former occupants of those cars stood on the sidewalk and on the snow-trampled yard, staring up at a pair of men dressed in urban camouflage and holding P90s. Dew had told the four men in Squad One to lose the Racal suits and take positions at the entrances, two at the front door, two at the back. Pissed-off local cops always looked like genuine bad-asses, but Dew's boys looked like they'd kill a man just as casually as they'd squeeze out a fart.

The six Ann Arbor locals were ticked because they couldn't enter the house. They'd been told jack shit. All they knew was that there were definite fatalities on their turf, and some government guy wouldn't let them do their job. Five cars had responded already; the three parked in front plus one at each end of Cherry Street, rerouting all traffic.

A blue Ford slipped slowly past the east roadblock and pulled up to the house. A thick-chested man wearing a brown polyester sport jacket got out and stomped toward

Dew. Maybe fifty, maybe fifty-five. This guy didn't look like a happy camper, either. He had a jaw so pronounced and rounded that he could have passed as a cartoon character.

'Are you Agent Dew Phillips?'

Dew nodded.

'I'm Detective Bob Zimmer, Ann Arbor Police.'

Drew shook Zimmer's hand.

'Where's the chief, Bob?'

'He's out of town at a terrorism training conference,' Zimmer said. 'I'm in charge.'

'A terrorist-training conference? Damn, talk about your irony.'

'Look, Phillips,' Zimmer said, 'I don't know what the fuck is going on here, and I'm having a donkey shit of a day. I just got called to a house that had a gas explosion—mother and son are dead. On the way there, I get calls from the chief, then the mayor, telling me some feds are running the show, that some government asshole named Dew Phillips is in charge.'

'The mayor called me an asshole?' Dew said. 'The governor I can understand, but the mayor? I'm hurt.'

Zimmer blinked a few times. 'Are you making a joke?'

'Just a little one.'

'Now's *not* the time, mister,' Zimmer said. "Then I get to this lady's house, there's four of those feds in chemical suits, saying they have to wait for the fire to die down so they can go through it. Then I get a call from the mother-fucking attorney general of the fucking United States of fucking America, and *then* I hear you've locked down another house and won't let my men in.'

'That's a lot of phone time,' Dew said. 'I hope you didn't use up your minutes.'

Zimmer's eyes narrowed. 'You best quit your joking, Phillips.'

Dew smiled. 'Gallows humor, forgive me. If I don't laugh, I'll cry, or something like that. So you've made some calls, you've talked to some people, and you understand that I have authority here, right?'

Zimmer nodded. 'Yeah, but tell me what's happening in this house. We've heard multiple fatalities. College kids. What the fuck happened here?'

'You don't need to know that.'

The detective took a step forward until he was almost nose to nose with Dew. The sudden move took Dew by surprise, but he stood his ground.

'Fuck *you*, Phillips,' Zimmer whispered, quiet enough that he wouldn't be heard by the local cops standing only fifteen feet away. 'I don't care *who* called me. The chief, he's a nice guy and would cooperate, do whatever you tell him to do, but me? I'm stupid and I like to pick fights I can't win.'

'That saying must look great on your Christmas cards,' Dew said. 'How about this one: my name is Bob Zimmer and I dream of getting fired?'

Zimmer just smiled.

'I'm old, I own my house, and I invested wisely. You have me fired and I get to go fishing every damn day. This may be a shock to you, on account of my obvious cosmopolitan nature, but I don't exactly get a daily how-ya-do call from the attorney general. I wanna know the danger level to my boys, and to this town, and I want to know *now*.'

As if anything else could go wrong, here it was. A man Dew couldn't bully. The guy wanted to protect his men first, worry about his career second. Dew knew he didn't have to say jack to Zimmer, *shouldn't* say jack to Zimmer, but they already had two cases in Ann Arbor: if this was the place the shit would hit the fan, Dew wanted allies who knew the terrain.

Dew took a half step back to end the face-to-face stalemate. 'It's bad, Bob. Real bad. You've got six dead kids in that house.'

Zimmer's lip curled up in a snarl. He also kept his voice low, a quid pro quo that instantly showed he'd keep most of the information to himself. 'Six? If this is another little joke, now's the time to say *gotcha*.'

Dew shook his head. 'Six. Four by gunshot, possibly tortured first. One other tortured for sure, probably killed with a hammer to the head.'

'Jesus H. Christ. That's five. The sixth?'

'The gunman, did himself,' Dew said, then felt a surge of inspiration. 'But we don't know if he acted alone.'

'Are you telling me there's someone else out here? That why your men were at the other house?'

'We don't know for sure. As soon as we get more information on that, we'll let you know.'

'And why?' Zimmer said. 'Why are the feds involved?'

'The dead gunman inside may have connections to a terrorist cell. We think he was building a bomb. Maybe the other kids in the house found out, maybe they were part of it.'

'And what did this terrorist cell want with a soccer mom and her son?'

'We don't know,' Dew said.

'You've got to give me more than that.'

'No, Bob, I sure as fuck don't. I've already stuck my neck out giving you this much. So stop pushing me.'

Zimmer looked away, then nodded. 'Okay. So what do you need from us?'

'We need another hour. Then the scene is all yours. There will be another car here shortly, an agent and two science types to make sure there's no biocontaminants inside the house.'

'Biocontaminants? Like anthrax and shit?'

Dew shook his head. 'We don't know. We're setting up a temp biohazard lab at the University Hospital. We're taking at least one of the bodies there. Once the eggheads are done with their sweep, you can ID the kids and call the parents.'

The muscles in Zimmer's massive jaw twitched. 'We'll provide whatever support you need. And if you find the motherfucker who's responsible for this . . . well, we'd be just plain happy to take care of him.'

43

THE POISON PILL (PART TWO)

The Triangle on the collarbone no longer functioned. The fork had done too much damage, and the seedling simply shut down. When it died, it stopped making the chemical that maintained the crusty cap atop the reader-balls. The deadly catalyst inside each ball kept eating at the cap—but now there was nothing to replace the material that dissolved away.

One by one the reader-balls burst, spilling the catalyst into the Triangle's body.

The catalyst caused two reactions: first, it dissolved cellulose; second, it caused apoptosis.

Apoptosis means that the cells of the body self-destruct. Normally this is a good thing. Billions of cells 'choose' to self-destruct every day, because they are damaged, infected or their usefulness is at an end. The process can also be triggered by forces outside the cell, such as the immune system. Every cell in the body carries this self-destruct code.

The catalyst turned on that code in every cell it touched.

When those cells dissolved and released their cytoplasm into the surrounding area, they passed on this self-destruct signal.

The result? Liquefaction. It started slowly, a few cells here and there, but each dead cell compromised the cells around it, creating an exponential increase that within forty-eight hours would dissolve an entire human body.

Fortunately for the host, the remaining Triangles kept producing the chemical that not only replenished their individual reader-ball caps, it also counteracted most of the apoptosis chain reaction in his body. Unfortunately for the host, however, the concentration of the catalyst in his collarbone was too strong to be stopped.

There, the cellulose slowly dissolved, the cells slowly destroyed themselves, and the liquefaction began.

And so did the rotting . . .

44

IMPRESSIONISM

'Come on, Doctor,' Clarence Otto said, his voice tinny in her Racal suit's headphones. 'Suck it up. Now isn't the time for you to go weak on me.'

Margaret made it out of the living room, but only with the help of Agent Clarence Otto's strong arm. He also wore a Racal, the plastics *zip-zipping* against each other as he helped her walk. She'd seen plenty of dead bodies, but the three bloated college kids in the living room, tied to those chairs, their faces swollen, bluish-green skin—all of it was getting to be too much. And right after that little boy—that infested, crazy, sad little boy—burning himself alive. The only 'good' news was that Dew's men had been able to cover that one up. Just a gas leak, nothing to see here except for two dead bodies, move along, please.

Amos had taken the little girl to the temp biohazard lab at the University Hospital. Margaret could only imagine the child's fear—they were trying to reach the father, but no luck yet. Amos would interview her and get what information they could, but at the end of the day she was just a little girl who didn't even understand that her mother had been dead for two days.

Margaret clumsily shuffled through six photos, pictures of faces blown up from college ID shots. Six smiling faces, faces that would never smile again. One of the photos made her pause. The others had a posed smile, but this one showed a genuine laugh. It was a rarity, an excellent ID picture that captured someone's real personality. The name on the bottom read 'Kiet Nguyen.'

The killer.

A tap on her shoulder. She turned to look at Dew Phillips. Once again he wasn't wearing a suit—the sole unprotected person in a house full of Racal-covered soldiers and agents.

'I've already got pictures of all this shit,' Dew said. 'Come on upstairs. I figure you'll want to see this.'

Otto and Margaret walked up the creaking stairs and followed Dew into a bedroom. Inside, a Racal-wearing photographer took endless shots of a body tied to the chair. This one wasn't as bloated as the others, clearly a more recent kill. But the missing hands, the missing feet, the hammer sticking out of the skull, the pitted black skeleton lying on the floor . . .

When would this end? *Would* it end at all?

'I'm not talking about that,' Dew said, pointing to the skeleton. 'I'm talking about *those*.' He jerked his thumb to the other side of the room, to the wall.

Sketches and paintings covered the wall. She turned quickly, taking in the whole room in a new light—paintings, sketches, everywhere. This was the room of an artist. She turned back to the far wall. Three canvas paintings dominated the wall, all two feet by three feet.

The first, a close-up of that pyramid thing from the back of an American one-dollar bill. The highly detailed painting showed the circle, all done in shades of green. Someone had tacked a dollar bill to the wall, backside facing, obviously for comparison. Two things immediately stood out—the first was the glowing eye atop the pyramid.

There wasn't one triangular eye, but three, lined up corner to corner, so that the three glowing eyes made for one larger triangle. Their bases made yet another triangle of negative space. The other change was the Latin phrase in the banner below the pyramid. What should have read *Novus ordo seclorum,* or 'new order of the ages,' instead read *E unum pluribus.* The classic motto of the Founding Fathers: 'From many, one.'

The second painting looked more rushed, not as detailed. Black paint on the white canvas. Two stylized trees, maybe oaks or maples, reaching their branches toward each other. Between them on the ground, a single blue triangle.

The third painting, right in the center of the wall— that one stunned her.

Bodies twisted together. Well, no, not all bodies, some body *parts.* Here, a hand severed at the elbow, there, a thigh torn free from both hip and knee, strands of ragged flesh dripping half-coagulated blood streamers toward the ground. Horrid, twisted bodies, bound together with coils of razor wire that sliced bloody notches in tan skin. Triangles adorned all the bodies and the body parts, blue-black, more like textured tattoos than something that was part of the skin, or under the skin. A few faces looked out— some dead, some living and screaming. A strand of razor wire pulled tightly against the open mouth of a man, his eyes scrunched tight in agony.

The bodies acted like some kind of building material, creating an arch made of agony, fear and death. The arch rose up and gently curved to the right, off the canvas. Margaret found herself looking beyond the canvas, her mind subconsciously trying to fill in the curve's path. In the background of the scene, she made out the descending leg of another arch—multiple arches, at least two, but there might be many more outside the frame's reference.

She suddenly realized that two of the faces—and, judging by the skin tone, many of the body parts—were Kiet Nguyen himself.

'This is your self-portrait,' Margaret said. 'This is what you did with your time, before you killed all those kids.'

'That's Nguyen?' Otto asked. 'You're sure?'

Margaret handed him the photo.

'Sonofabitch,' Otto said as he looked from the painting to the photo and back again. 'Damn, Doctor, you've got sharp eyes. Okay, so if that's Nguyen, who are the other people?'

Margaret nodded inside her Racal suit. She was getting used to Otto's ability to ask the obvious question, make the simple connection that she and Amos sometimes didn't see.

'Oh my God,' Margaret said. She pointed to one of the faces, high up on the arch. This one was upside down, connected to a white man's body whose head and shoulders were on the canvas but whose feet extended beyond the frame.

'Is that Martin Brewbaker?'

At the sound of the name, Dew hurried over. He leaned close to the canvas.

'Goddamn,' Dew said. 'That *is* the little psycho. How the fuck did Nguyen know that guy?'

Margaret shook her head. 'I don't think he did, Dew.'

'Of *course* he did,' Dew spat. 'I'm looking at Brewbaker's face right there. The kid painted it, and that's that.'

'Is that Gary Leeland?' Otto said, pointing again to the canvas.

Margaret and Dew both leaned close.

'Holy shit,' they said in stereo.

Margaret waved the photographer over. 'I need shots of this, the whole thing, and get all the detail. Use a new disk, I'm taking it with me.'

She turned to leave, then stopped. Something about that dollar-pyramid bothered her. She turned back and walked toward it, until she was only a foot from the painting. Something about the Latin phrase.

Nguyen had painted the phrase, *E unum pluribus*. But that wasn't right. In Latin, 'From many, one,' was *E pluribus unum*.

Switch the phrase around, to *E unum pluribus,* and what did you have?

From one, many.

45

THE LIVING-ROOM FLOOR

He didn't know who sang the song, but he knew the words.

'Somebody knockin' at the duh-or, somebody ringin' the bell. Somebody knockin' at the duh-or, somebody ringin' the bell.'

Perry found himself in a dark hallway, the lilting melody filling the air with not only sound, but also a warning. The place seemed alive, pulsating, throbbing with a shadowy warmth; it seemed more like a throat than a hallway. At the hall's end stood a single door made of a spongy, rotten green wood covered with a vile, mucal slime. The door thumped in time with his own heartbeat. It was a living thing. Or maybe had been living once.

Or maybe . . . maybe it was waiting for its chance to live.

He knew it was a dream, but it still scared him shitless. In a life where waking hours are draped in the costume of horrid nightmare, where reality has suddenly become questionable, it's easy to be scared by dreams.

Perry walked toward the door. Something unspeakable lay behind it, something wet, something hot, something waiting for a chance to rage, to murder, to dominate. He reached for the handle, and the handle reached for him; it was a long, thick, black tentacle, wrapping around his arm, pulling him into the spongy green wood. Perry fought, but for all his might he was yanked forward like a child by an angry father.

The door didn't open—it sucked him in, joyous in a sudden meal of body and mind. The green wood engulfed him, the dank rot caressed him. Perry tried to scream, but the oozing tentacle forced its way into his mouth, cutting off all sound, cutting off his air. The door enveloped him, held him motionless. Mindless terror pulled at him, dragging his sanity under . . .

When he awoke, the fork remained stuck in his shoulder. The sweatshirt had tried to pull back to its natural position, catching on the fork and pushing it at an angle; the end of the utensil rested against his cheekbone. The wound didn't hurt because it was completely numb. He didn't know how long he'd been out.

He grimaced as he grabbed the fork with his right hand and gently removed it from his trapezius—it made a wet, sucking sound as it came out. Thick trickles of blood coursed down his collarbone and curled under his armpit. The front of his sweatshirt had changed from white to bright red with thin streaks of the dark purple. The stab wound alone wouldn't have been that bad, but twisting the fork had ripped open a large chunk of flesh. He gently fingered the wound, trying to ascertain the damage without setting off the pain button. His fingers also hit the corpse of the Triangle, which was no longer firm, but soft and pliable.

The hooks of this one were undoubtedly still stuck in his body, maybe wrapped around his collarbone, maybe wrapped around a rib or even his sternum. If that was the case, ripping it out might cause one of the hooks to puncture a lung, or even his heart. That wasn't an option. But it was *dead*, over which he felt an indescribably sick satisfaction. The fact that he would have to carry a corpse around embedded in his shoulder, however, tugged at the back of his mind, tweaking at the last vestiges of normality clinging to his tortured soul.

He carefully stood up and hopped to the bathroom. His ruined leg didn't hurt as much now, but it still throbbed complaint. Too bad he couldn't ride this game out on the bench, let one of the second-stringers come in and fill in his position.

Play through the pain.

Rub some dirt on it and get back in there.

Sacrifice your body.

Lines of dried brown blood patterned the linoleum floor. Chunks of orangish skin still floated in the tub, although the water level had dropped. He could tell the original depth by the tub ring left from tiny scab flecks.

Blood trickled from his shoulder. He grabbed the bottle of hydrogen peroxide from the cabinet behind the bathroom mirror. The bottle was almost empty, just enough left to clean the wound. Setting it down on the counter, he tried to pull off his sweatshirt, but a shooting pain in his left shoulder stopped him. He slowly raised the arm—it was sore and painful, but it still worked, thank God.

He clumsily peeled off the blood-wet sweatshirt using just his right arm, then dropped it on the floor and kicked it into the corner where he didn't have to look at it.

Perry wanted a shower, but he didn't want to clean the tub, and he was too grossed out by the floating scabs to stand in the ankle-deep water. He'd have to make do.

He grabbed a clean washcloth out from under the sink—he wasn't about to use anything that had touched the scabs or the Starting Five. Only now it wasn't the Starting Five anymore, was it? Perry smiled with the small victory. Now they were four. The Four Horsemen.

The Four Horsemen of the Apocalypse.

His smile vanished. The new name didn't exactly make him feel any better.

His head pulsed like a dying star. He wet the white washcloth and tried to wipe the smeared blood off his chest, ribs, shoulder and out from under his armpit. He dabbed at the wound itself; the washcloth quickly turned a sick shade of pink.

The wound didn't look all that bad. The Triangle, however, looked awful. Its 'face' was ripped open along with the skin that had covered it. At first it was hard to tell the difference between his flesh and the flesh of the dead Triangle, but after looking closely he could see that the thing's tissue was paler than his own, a gray-pink fading to white. It sure didn't look healthy. But then again Perry figured that if *he'd* been stabbed to death with a fork, *he* wouldn't look that great either.

He poured peroxide over the wound. Most of it ran quickly down his chest to soak into his pants and underwear. It was chilly. He didn't care. He dabbed at the fizzing wound with the washcloth.

He had only three Band-Aids—that would be just enough to cover the wound. He pinched together the ripped skin over the Triangle's dead head, then used the Band-Aids like sutures to pin everything down. The white absorbent patches on the tan strips instantly turned pink. It was just superficial blood now; it would clot up in only a minute or two.

The smell of Band-Aids briefly lifted his spirits. That smell carried a childhood association, the feeling that you were done hurting. When he was a kid, he'd get cut or scraped, he'd bleed and his mom would put a Band-Aid on it. Whether it was the Band-Aid or the TLC, the pain would be greatly reduced and he'd be back to playtime in nothing flat—unless, of course, his father wanted to teach him a lesson about crying.

Signs of weakness were not allowed in the Dawsey household. Perry couldn't count the number of beatings prefaced by his father's angry declaration, 'I'll give you something to cry about!'

Despite the pain, the Band-Aids did provide a little positive energy. The plastic scent filled his nostrils, and he couldn't help but relax a bit.

As he grew calm, he realized that it was quiet. Not just in the empty apartment, but in his head. There was no fuzzy noise, no lumpy sound, not even a little bit of static. There was nothing. He didn't bother to kid himself that they were all dead—he could still *feel* them. He felt a low buzz at the back of his skull. They weren't dead, but it felt different. Maybe they were . . . asleep.

If they were asleep, could he call someone? The cops? Maybe the FBI? The little bastards were deathly afraid of people in uniform—what kind of uniform, Perry didn't know. If they were out, he could try *something*.

He had to try.

'Hello?' Perry whispered, testing the waters. 'Fellas? Are you there?'

Nothing.

His mind raced like a windup toy that bounced off wall after wall, moving around quickly but with nowhere to go. He had to think. His cell phone was the obvious choice; it wasn't like he could get in his car and drive away from the danger.

But who to call? Just how many people knew about these Triangles?

Call . . . who? The FBI? The CIA? There was obviously

an airtight lid on leaks to the media regarding this situation, or he'd have heard about it long ago. He hopped quietly to the kitchen table and grabbed his cell phone. He hopped back to the couch and pulled the phone book out from under the end table. He started to flip to government agencies in the Yellow Pages, then inspiration hit him.

He quickly turned to the 'red' pages, the alphabetical listing of all the businesses in the area. He flipped to the *T*'s. There they were. There were two entries.

Triangle Fence Co. in Ypsilanti and Triangle Mobile Home Sales in Ann Arbor. Who the fuck would name a business 'Triangle'? What sense did that make? There had to be a connection. One or both of these had to be government fronts. *That* made sense—it made *perfect* sense! People in Perry's predicament were, sooner or later, going to pick up the phone and try to find help. And wouldn't everybody get the hunch to see if anything was named 'Triangle' in the phone book? And the government had to be ready to jump on the situation, so they probably had an office in every decent-size town in the country— or at least in the area of the invasion. So people would call, and then the Triangle Fence boys would come out in their Triangle Fence shirts with 'Bob' and 'Lou' stitched over the Triangle Fence Co. patch on their left breast (for effect, so none of the locals would think anything of it, because all repair/installation guys have their name on their shirt). They would come in to the house and quietly take Perry out to the van and drive him somewhere with Men in White Lab Coats, who would quickly and painlessly take the Triangles out of Perry's body. Sure, he'd be sworn to secrecy and all, but that was a small price to pay. This was a chance. This was *hope*. If nothing else, it was an opportunity to make sure that these little fuckers got what they deserved.

He opened his cell phone and dialed.

A woman's pleasant voice answered, 'Triangle Fence Company.'

Perry's words were a whisper, yet each syllable sounded cacophonously loud in the quiet apartment. 'Um, yes. I need help with . . . with . . .'

He grasped for words—should he come out and ask? What should he say? Was the secretary in on it? Was his phone bugged?

'Help with what, sir?' the pleasant voice asked.

Perry quickly and quietly folded the phone, hanging up without so much as a click. Just how was he supposed to ask? Was there a code word? His phone could be bugged. If he asked for help, would the Triangles know somehow? Would they punish him?

Stop it! How could they have bugged my phone? They don't even have arms. *And they're not testing me, they can't be— they're going to kill me anyway. They wouldn't be testing my loyalty or anything when I've already killed three of them. That's not logical. Think, man, tune them out . . . think!*

Perry breathed with slow control. A choking feeling of anxiety circled his consciousness—he might have only moments left in his big chance. And if the phone was bugged, it meant that someone knew of his condition and wasn't doing anything about it, which meant that any call he made was a waste of time anyway. He had to calm down and act now if he had any chance for survival. Time was running out.

He opened the phone again, this time dialing Triangle Mobile Home Sales. It only made sense—of course it would be the mobile-home place. They could drive out in an RV, you could hop in for a test drive and off you went. None of your neighbors would be the wiser, not even a little bit suspicious. It all made sense now.

'Triangle Mobile Home Sales,' a gruff male voice answered. This was more like it.

'Yes,' Perry said quietly, cupping the phone to his chin with his free hand. 'I was wondering if you could help me.'

'Well, that depends on what you need help with,' the gravelly voice responded, a tinge of lighthearted humor hanging in the words. 'What can we do ya for?'

Depends on what you need help with, the man had said. Now why would he say that? This had to be the right one. Had to be.

'I had seven to start with, but I got three,' Perry said in a rush. 'I think the others are still growing. I don't know how much longer I have.'

'Excuse me? Seven what?'

'Seven Triangles,' Perry said, unable to keep the grin off his face.

'Triangles?'

'Yes! That's right!' Perry fidgeted in his seat, as if his body couldn't contain the renewed energy coursing through his veins. 'You've got to help me. Tell me it's not too late for me!'

'Mister, I'm afraid I don't know what the hell you're talking about. Help you with what?'

'The Triangles, man!' Perry didn't hear his voice rising in volume. 'Stop playing games. I don't know your fucking code or keyword or whatever, I'm not James Bond, okay? All I know is that these things are growing in me and I can't stop them. Fuck your password shit, just put some people in one of those mobile homes and get them over here!'

Perry's blood went cold as he heard low-volume buzzing in his brain. It was softer than he'd ever felt before, but it was there.

The Triangles were waking up.

'Mister, I don't have time for these games. I don't appreciate—'

'I'm *not* fucking around here!' Perry's voice rang thick with desperate frustration. 'Goddamn it! I'm out of time I'm out of time! You've got to—'

who　are　you　talking　to

Perry's heart lurched in his chest. Adrenaline shot through his body. He reactively flung the cell phone across the room, where it landed softly on the carpet.

Panic clutched him as if he were a rabbit frozen in the headlights of an onrushing semi.

who　are　you　talking　to

'No one! I . . . was just talking to myself, that's all.'

why　are　you　talking　to　yourself

'No reason, okay? Just drop it.' Perry hopped up and moved to the bathroom; suddenly he needed to piss very badly. He felt the high-pitched buzz in his head, loud and intense.

They were searching, and it was stronger than before.

He stopped at the bathroom door, mentally grasping for a way to avoid what he knew had to be coming—the mindscream. He *had* to get that out of his thoughts. A song. Think of a song. Something intense . . . something from Rage Against the Machine. 'Bombtrack.'

Perry's brow furrowed as he focused his concentration on the song. (*"Burn, burn, yes ya gonna burn'* were the only words he could remember.) Perry thought it as 'loudly' as he could, not allowing anything else to enter his brain. (*"Burn, burn, yes ya gonna burn!"*) He let the words of Rage's singer, Zack de la Rocha, rip through his mind as if he were at a concert, drunk out of his gourd, swarming with thousands of other people in a violent mosh pit.

w h y   d i d   y o u   kill

Perry was concentrating so hard he almost didn't register the question.

w h y   w h y   w h y w h y   why

He couldn't believe it. They wanted to know *why* he'd killed the three Triangles. Fury welled up inside him, pushing aside his concentration, drowning his fear, crushing his panic. They had the audacity to ask *why*?

w h y   w h y   W h y   whywhywhywhy

'Because he was in me! What other fucking reason do I need? He was inside my body and I wanted him out. I want you all out!'

h e   w a s n ' t   h u r t i n g   y o u
n e i t h e r   a r e   we

'Not hurting me? I can barely walk, my shoulder is fucked up and my house is covered with blood. My blood!'

o u r   b l o o d   t o o   y o u   d i d
i t   t o   yourself

'Fuck you, you little cocksuckers! I didn't do it to myself! I have to get you guys out of me before you eat me up from the inside! I may look like the amazing walking incubator to you, but it's not going to happen!'

c a l m   d o w n   r e l a x   c a l m   d o w n
relax

'Relax? Sure, I'll relax, when the rest of you fucks are dead!' Somewhere in his weary mind, he realized that his rage had boiled over, slipped beyond his control. He wanted to hit something, anything, hit something and break it into a million pieces. 'If I have to cut myself

into chunks to get every last one of you, I'll do it and
I'll laugh—you hear me? I'll laugh my ass off the whole
time!'

calm down someone

coming calm down

'No one's coming, you bastards!' He shook with unbridled, primitive fury. He made little hops to keep his
balance.

someone is here calm

down calm down

Three knocks on the door ended the debate.

46

HOWDY, NEIGHBOR (PART TWO)

Perry stared at the door, not sure he'd actually heard it, hoping he hadn't.

Then came three more knocks.

c o l u m b o   C o l u m b o
c o l u m b o   columbo

'Shut up!' Perry hissed through clenched teeth, the stress wiring his jaws tight. 'It's not Columbo.'

'Hey in there!' the voice called in. A male voice. He recognized the distinctively deep baritone of Al Turner, who lived in the apartment directly above Perry's. 'Would you stop your screaming? You're driving me nuts.'

Al Turner was Mr. Blue Collar. One of those guys who, despite having passed the thirty-year mark, still measured his manhood by how much alcohol he could consume on a night out with the boys. A car mechanic, or something like that.

'Don't bother ignoring me, I know you're there!' Three more knocks. He was pissed. Perry heard the anger in his voice. 'Are you okay? What's going on in there?'

'Nothing,' Perry called back through the closed, locked and chained door. 'I'm sorry, I was having an argument on the phone.' Perry felt relief with that top-of-the-head lie. That would work. That made sense. That was logical.

Al yelled back through the door, 'Yeah? I've heard nothing but yelling from down here, and it's starting to get on my nerves, you know?'

Perry had been screaming his head off for one reason or another in his battles against the Triangles and

k i l l   him

he'd never thought about how much noise he was making. Al was

k i l l   him

probably at wits' end from all the commotion.

'Sorry Al,' Perry said. 'I'll keep it down, I promise. Woman problems, you know?'

'You can open the door, man. I don't have a gun or anything.' Al's voice sounded calmer.

'I'm buck naked, Al, just got out of the shower. Thanks for stopping by, I'll keep

k i l l   him

it down.'

Perry heard footsteps shuffle down the hallway. That had been as rude as can be, Perry knew, but he wasn't about to open the door and let Al see the Blood-O-Rama inside the apartment.

k i l l   him

They'd said 'kill him' again and again. Perry hadn't heard them the first few times . . . or maybe he hadn't *wanted* to hear them.

Perry whispered, 'Why the hell would I kill him?'

h e   k n o w s ,
h e ' s   a   t h r e a t ,
k i l l   h i m   k i l l   him

'He is not a threat!' Perry heard his voice rise again before he caught himself in midsentence, making 'threat' come out several decibels lower than the rest of his words. 'He's my neighbor, he lives upstairs.'

High-pitch.

Fuzzy noise.

Perry assumed they were accessing the term *upstairs,* or perhaps the building's layout. He was growing adept at knowing what they searched for; their retrieval process seemed to make images flash into his mind as well, bits and pieces of what they wanted.

he lives right above us fucker
he knows kill him he knows
kill him—

'Shut up,' Perry said calmly, quietly, but with as much authority as he could muster. He might be as good as dead, but he wasn't going to take Al with him. 'You can just fuck off, how's that? I'm not going to kill him. Forget it and stop asking. It's not going to happen. The only one I'm thinking of killing is myself and you four along with me. So shut up.'

The lumpy sound came again, low and long. Perry laughed inwardly. It was like they were lovers; the Triangles searched for the right words to avoid an argument.

don't kill us or kill yourself
fucker don't we're trying to
stop Columbo

Trying to stop Columbo.

Trying to stop the Soldiers.

Had the right people at Triangle Mobile Home Sales gotten the message? Maybe he should have called 911 a long time ago—maybe they could have gotten the things out when it still mattered, because it was too late now.

Perry felt tired and drained. It really *was* like an

argument with a lover. Whenever he had a knock-down, drag-out fight with a girlfriend, anger and other emotions flew around his head like dead leaves in an October storm. Such arguments exhausted him. He didn't need to sleep after sex—he needed to sleep after fighting. This felt exactly the same. It was only about 6:30 P.M., but it was time to turn in.

He entered the bedroom but didn't want to sleep there; the sheets remained spotted and streaked with blood. He was in there only long enough to grab a clean gray long-sleeved Detroit Lions T-shirt. Then he hopped to the bathroom, pounded four Tylenol and headed to the couch. He let himself fall into the inviting cushions.

He was out within seconds.

47

MARGARET SETS UP SHOP

Margaret called the shots. They commandeered a med/surg floor at the University of Michigan Medical Center. *Med/surg* is fancy-pants hospital slang for *medical/surgical*. Without Murray's approval she'd ordered not just one, but two portable BSL-4 labs installed in the wing. That SARS was a nasty sucker, couldn't be too careful, right? The hospital administration put up a fight, demanding to know the risks, the health status of the community and a bunch of other nicey-nice shit that Margaret simply did *not* have time to deal with.

She had an executive order. She had the deputy director of the CIA in her back pocket. These people were going to give her what she wanted, and that was that.

They had to be ready. Two cases in Ann Arbor, and they'd been so damn close to catching a live one. If they got another chance, she might get her shot to see just what the hell these triangles were.

Agent Otto came through the door, carrying a five-foot-long cardboard tube.

Margaret's pulse jumped up a notch—she wasn't sure if it was from seeing Otto, the portfolio, or both.

'Did you get the printout, Clarence?'

He flashed his wide, easy smile. 'No problem, Doc. I think I made some Kinko's employees happy. I'm guessing it's not every day they get sworn to secrecy at midnight and use their large color printer for national security.'

She helped him pull the rolled-up printouts from the tube, and they started taping the final artistic works of Kiet Nguyen up on the wall.

48

PROGRAMMING

Perry would never know how close he came to getting real help. The NarusInsight STA 7800, the machine that scanned all the calls, picked up the word *triangle* from his call to Triangle Mobile Home Sales but did not find any of the context words that would alert the CIA's watcher. Had Perry changed a few words, possibly even just one word, if he'd said, 'I had seven to start with, but I *killed* three,' instead of, 'I had seven to start with, but I *got* three,' help would have already been on the way.

But Perry didn't use the right words. The system didn't forward the call to the watcher. Still alone in his fight for survival, Perry slept.

He slept like the dead.

The Triangles did not.

The subconscious mind is a powerful device. Repeating things over and over to yourself, visualizing a success again and again, virtually programs your brain to go out and make those images a reality. The opposite also holds true—if you're convinced you're a loser, that you always seem to lose your job, that you can't save money, that you can't lose weight, you tell yourself *these* things over and over, and guess what? They come true as well. The subconscious mind takes the things it hears over and over and makes them reality. The subconscious mind doesn't know the difference between success and failure. The subconscious mind doesn't know the difference between what helps you and what hurts you.

The subconscious mind doesn't know the difference between good and evil.

All night long, Triangles repeated the phrase in Perry's head. More than a hundred times. Definitely thousands, perhaps tens of thousands or even a hundred thousand. Over and over.

k i l l   him
k i l l   him
k i l l   him

It was a short phrase, and they didn't even really have to 'say' it—all they had to do was send it to his auditory nerve, a high-speed data dump into Perry's programmable subconscious.

There were others close by, others of their kind. Sometimes they heard voices, like their own, but not coming from within the host's body. Some hosts were far away. One was very, very close.

They knew nothing of where they came from or what they were, but the stronger they became, the more they knew *why* they were here.

They were here to *build*.

And soon the Triangles would join with those of the nearby host, become one group, one tribe, then move to join even more of their kind. The glorious construction would begin. But first they had to keep the host alive, keep him out of danger, keep him away from the Soldiers.

k i l l   him
k i l l   him
k i l l   him

Mental and physical exhaustion held Perry in a deep, deep sleep. He was stone-cold out for just under fourteen hours. The Triangles incessantly repeated the phrase until the Tylenol kicked in, they caught a solid buzz, and drifted off with visions of the glorious construction that would soon become a reality.

49

REACH OUT AND TOUCH SOMEONE

Bill Miller stared at the TV. *Columbo* was on the *Sunday-Morning Mystery Movie,* but he wasn't really watching. His fingers drummed against the remote control.

What the hell was Perry doing? Didn't answer his phone. Didn't answer instant messages. Didn't answer his door. Bill hadn't gone this long without talking to Perry since they'd first roomed together in college. Something was wrong. Really wrong, like 'Oh, *fuck,* my parachute won't open' wrong.

Bill had called a dozen times so far, leaving a message every time but never getting a response. He'd watched his IM client, seeing if Perry would log on: nothing. He'd even left a friggin' note, like some psycho girl.

Perry was obviously home, and he wanted to be left alone. But man, this was Sunday. Fucking *football Sunday.* Their tradition dated back almost a decade, through tertiary friends that came and went, through seven girlfriends (five on Bill's side, two on Perry's— the only game that Bill had a chance of winning against the super-athlete).

Well screw this. Perry didn't get to hide in that tiny apartment, not when football Sunday was on. Bill needed to see him, needed to know everything was all right. Perry was capable of such violent outbursts—one incident might put him in jail. Bill had to reach him, just to make sure his friend wasn't about to fuck up his life yet again. Bill picked up the phone and called his best friend one more time.

50

COOKING UP A STORM

'Somebody knockin' at the duh-or, somebody ringin' the bell.'

He recognized the voice. Paul McCartney. Must be some Beatles tune, from when they were all whacked out on drugs and spouting that Peace and Love shit.

It was that fucking door again. Still rotting and spongy soft, although this time Perry wasn't walking down the dark hall. He was standing still, yet the door kept getting closer.

The door was coming for him.

A hundred tiny tentacles jutted from the door's bottom like the arms of a black anemone, wiggling, pulling, always moving forward. The door came toward him, slowly but steadily, the spongy green wood hungry for a meal.

Perry turned and ran, but at the other end of the hall stood another green door, this one also moving closer, this one also hungry.

Nowhere to go. One door or the other . . . or both. No matter what he did, what waited behind those doors would take him. In the dream, Perry started to scream . . .

Perry awoke, his eyelids flickering against the early morning light that sifted harshly through his window. He'd fallen asleep sitting up, head resting on the back of the couch. The position had made his neck stiff and tight. He rubbed at it with his good arm, trying to loosen up the muscles. He scraped his tongue against the roof of his mouth in an automatic effort to relieve the pasty feeling that comes from bad sleep. It wouldn't go away until he could get some water.

His cell phone rang loudly. Barely awake, he answered it before he could think of the consequences.

'Hello?'

hello hello sonofabitch

'Perry! You're home! Where the hell have you been, man?'

'I've been here . . .' Perry blinked his eyes against the rude sunlight. He slowly pushed his lethargic body upright. His voice still carried the grogginess of the morning, the sound of words that came out automatically without the guidance of an attentive brain. 'Been in my apartment.'

we know we've been here too

'You've been gone for days!' The voice on the other end rang with anxiety and excitement. 'We thought you'd skipped town or something. You've been home all this time?'

It was almost like a split personality, a sprint between intelligence and stupidity. Half of his mind raced in a dead panic (*the pain is coming!*), rushing to wrest control from the other half, the I-just-woke-up-and-I'm-damn-stupid half that was currently talking on the phone, oblivious to the disastrous situation rapidly surging to the boiling-over point.

'Perry, you there?'

Perry gave his head a little shake, still trying to clear the cobwebs. 'Who is this?'

who is who,
what are you talking about

'It's Bill, stupid. You know, Bill? Your best friend? Maybe you've heard of me?'

The intelligent, panicked part of Perry's mind slammed into control with the force of a missile hitting a passenger jet. He flung the phone away as if it were a tarantula. It landed on the floor only a few feet from him.

'Hello?' The word came faint, thin and tinny from the receiver.

w h o   i s   h e r e ,
w h o   a r e   y o u   t a l k i n g   t o ,
w h o   i s   here

Bill's voice sounded impossibly distant and small. Like an abused dog cowering at the sound of its master's angry call, Perry flinched with each word that trickled from the phone.

'Hello? Perry?'

He reached down and flipped the phone shut.

w h o   i s   t h e r e ,   w h o   i s
t h e r e ,   w h o   w h o   w h o   i s
i t   columbo

Perry's breath still came in shallow, quiet bursts. Like a kid caught doing something very wrong, his mind raced for an excuse, a lie, anything that would keep him out of trouble.

w h o   i s   t h e r e ,   w h o   i s
t h e r e ,   w h o   i s   there

'No one is here,' Perry said quietly.

c o l u m b o   i s   here
i s n t   he

'No!' Perry fought back panic, tried to keep his voice low—he didn't want another visit from Big Al upstairs. 'No one is here. It was just the telephone. It's nothing to worry about.' High-pitched noise ripped through his thoughts as the Triangles rooted around in his brain. Perry sat very, very still, wondering if a blast of angry shouting would hammer the inside of his head.

Low-pitched noise followed as the Four Horsemen added new words and phrases to their growing vocabulary.

t e l e p h o n e   s o   y o u   c a n
t a l k   t o   o n e s   w h o   a r e n ' t
h e r e   right

Perry worked his way through the Triangle sentence. They put *right* at the end of the sentence. They were asking a question.

'Yes, that's right, so we can talk to ones that aren't here.' He remained frozen on the couch like a hunted rabbit, waiting for the pain to sear through his head, a weed whacker trimming up his brain.

w e   d o   t h a t   w i t h o u t
t e l e p h o n e s   t a l k   t o   Triangles

'Are you talking to some of them now?' Perry carefully led the conversation away from the telephone call, still wary of the mindscreaming although he sensed no anxious emotions from the Triangles. It seemed that they understood the concept of a phone and realized that no one was in the room. There was a bit of high-pitched fuzzy noise before the Horsemen's response.

c a l l i n g   o n e   u p   n o w ,
w e   a r e   t a l k i n g   t o   them

'Are they nearby?' High-pitch sounded in his head.

h o w   f a r   i s   nearby

'You're familiar with the concept of distance?' He felt them looking up the word *distance*. Unbidden, images flashed through his mind—maps, a hundred-yard dash, third-grade story problems.

y e s . h o w f a r i s n e a r b y .
s h o w u s

He'd have to start them out on inches and feet. 'Nearby' was a relative concept and he wasn't sure how he'd explain it. He hopped toward the junk drawer to get a ruler. As he moved, the faint wisps of a foul smell drifted across his nose, and then it was gone. He sniffed again but caught no further traces of the scent. He brushed aside a roll of duct tape and pulled the ruler from the drawer.

He steeled himself. What he was about to do—educate them—made it even more real, even more hopeless. It was like admitting that they were just as normal as the Detroit Lions on Thanksgiving Day or Saturday-morning cartoons.

He slid up the sleeve on his left arm.

There sat the Triangle, bright blue under his skin. But the eye slits were still closed.

s h o w u s .

'I can't. His . . . his eyes aren't open yet.'

s o m e c a n s e e .
n o t a l l . n o t yet.

'So which one of you can see? My back? My . . . my balls?'

n o , y o u r a s s , s h o w u s

'No.'

s h o w u s

'No fucking way.'

S H O W U S

The low-level mindscream hit him, causing more fear than pain. What he had to do sickened him, but he had no choice.

He dropped his pants and bent over, gripping the counter edge for support. He held the ruler behind him at ass level, parallel to his butt cheeks, directly in front of the Triangle buried in his posterior.

'Do you see this?' Perry felt embarrassed, like a teenager who's pantsed in front of the girls, or someone caught masturbating. He felt his face flush red. He was standing there in his kitchen, pants about his knees, bent over like some silkyboy waiting for a bull fag to take it to him. He'd certainly rather have some three-hundred-pound convict sticking it up his ass than deal with the situation he had now. Even AIDS would be better than going out this way.

y e s   w h a t   i s   i t

He felt loud, high-pitch noise. Excitement rolled into his thoughts, an overflow emotion from the Triangles. He'd had all the Triangles covered up from the first moment they could see. The Triangle on his shoulder had enjoyed only a few moments of vision before Perry fucked up its whole day. Aside from an eyeful of fork, this ass-eye view was really the first thing they'd ever seen.

'It's called a ruler. It measures distances.' Perry closed his eyes and laid his head down on the counter. It felt cool against his warm face. 'See the lines and the numbers?'

He felt them accessing the new words.

y e s   l i n e s   a n d   n u m b e r s   yes

Their excitement level soared, leaking into his own mind. Perry fought it down. Anger crept into his thoughts—he wasn't going to let their emotions overtake him.

'Okay. The big lines represent inches. That's a unit of measurement. The numbers count how many inches there are. There's twelve inches on this ruler, twelve inches is called a "foot," which is a larger unit of measurement. Understand?' The fuzzy noise in his head was a speedy blur, then it was gone.

y e s .

t w e l v e   i n c h e s   i n   a   foot

'Okay. Now, there're the twelve inches in a foot, and
if you have three feet—'

t h r e e   f e e t   i s   a   yard

They were at it again, checking his brain like the Perry
Public Library. It was a redefinition of being used, and

o n e   h u n d r e d   y a r d s   i n   a
f o o t b a l l   field

there was nothing Perry could do about it. Nothing. His
anger continued to grow, his temper slowly mushrooming
like a nuclear pile approaching critical mass. Perry shut
his eyes tight and tried to

5 , 2 8 0   f e e t   i n   a   m i l e

control the emotions, but there were too many: excitement,
frustration, humiliation from being bent over the counter
with his ass exposed like some prison bitch waiting to be
taken, and rage at having his brain and memories fingered
through like a *Compton's Encyclopedia*.

His father's voice came to him, unbidden. This time it
sounded real and vibrant, not a memory but something
angry and new. *Look at yourself, son. Bent over like some
nancy-boy, you're a goddamned disgrace. I oughta teach you
some manhood, boy. You gonna let them treat you like that?
You gonna let them? Huh, boy? You gonna let them PUSH YOU
AROUND LIKE THAT?*

A narrow-eyed snarl slipped across Perry's face. He
reached his left hand over to the stove and cranked the
front right burner's knob to 'high.'

He stood and pulled up his pants. Their disappointment
overflowed into him, as pure and as powerful as the excitement had been.

l e t   u s   s e e .   l e t   u s   see

'You wanna see? See the fucking shit stains in my underwear.'

l e t   u s   s e e   l e t   u s   s e e   t h e   ruler

'Shut the fuck up, you've seen enough.' Part of Perry hoped they'd continue. He wanted to hurt them, teach them some manners. Another part of him (the part that had been all of him until a week ago, the part that was fading fast) struggled to bring his temper under control. He was split right down the middle, and he didn't give a ratfuck which part came out on top.

l e t   u s   s e e   S e e   SEE

Perry flinched as the Triangle volume started to rise. A mindscream fast approached. The part of Perry that hoped for a peaceful resolution shrank away to nothingness.

In that moment, he was his father's son once again.

'You want to see?'

Pain was coming, Perry knew. Truckloads of it. A clearance sale on agony.

'You got to learn not to talk to me that way. Tell you what, I'll show you how I cook your dinner.' Perry hopped up onto the counter.

He sat with his ass on the countertop, legs dangling over the edge, right ass cheek almost touching the edge of the electric stove, back resting against the cupboards that held his mismatched plates. He watched the burner slowly change from black to a soft, glowing orange. An orphaned, dried-out grain of rice sat

l e t   u s   see

on the burner. Perry watched closely. The grain was at first white, then slowly turned black.

It began to burn, sending a thin

l e t   u s   s e e   now

tendril of smoke toward the ceiling. The little stream thickened as the metal continued to heat, smoke rising in a tiny column then dissipating into

let, us see, .
we're warning you

nothingness. It was so black against the hot metal. There was the briefest flicker of an orange flame, and then nothing. The smoke quickly petered out, leaving a small black husk on the glowing burner.

warning you warning
you see See SEE

'You want to see?' Perry rolled onto his left cheek and hooked his right thumb under his waistband. They'd 'warned' him. Nobody 'warns' a Dawsey of anything. It was Perry's house, after all, and anyone under his roof was damn well going to live by his rules.

yes we want to see
now Now NOW, and
we're not going to
tell you again

Perry slid over so his right cheek hovered directly above the burner. He instantly felt the rising, searing heat. He pulled his pants down, exposing the right cheek to the burner only inches away. Blistering heat cascaded over his naked skin.

'Do you see now, fuckers?' He felt the overflow excitement again, coursing through his body, intense and stronger than ever.

what is it? is it dinner?
are we going to eat?
what is it?

'You don't know what it is?' Perry heard the malice in his own voice, the hatred and the anger that had once again taken over his body and thrown reason and common sense out some mental twentieth-story window to splatter on the concrete sidewalk below. He heard his father's voice within his own.

'Well, if you don't know what it is, maybe you'd better take a closer look!'

Perry slammed his right cheek down on the burner and immediately heard the answering sizzle. The scorching pain stabbed into his body, but it was *his* pain, and he welcomed it with the wide-eyed smile of a madman. His nervous system railed against the searing heat as his flesh bubbled and blistered and blackened.

NO NO NO NO NO
NO NO NO

The stench of his own burning flesh filled the room. The unbearable agony ripped through his every fiber. Later on he'd congratulate himself on his incredible willpower—he managed to keep his ass pressed firmly against the burner for almost four seconds, fighting against his body's primal directive to *get away* from the pain—

NO NO NO NO NO
NO NO

The mindscream hammered into his head and broke his superhuman concentration. Perry leaped off the stove and landed on his bad leg, which promptly gave way. He fell in a heap on the bloodstained linoleum floor.

NO NO NO NO NO
NO NO

He didn't have time to regret his actions; he didn't even have time to tell himself how stupid it was. He felt the scorching pain on his ass and the strong smell of cooked human flesh (and was there another smell in there?) and the jackhammer screaming that ripped into his mind and stirred his brains like a swizzle stick.

NO NO NO NO NO
NO NO NO

Despite the pain that had him whimpering like a little girl, despite tears streaming down his face to mix with the dried blood on the linoleum floor, despite feeling every injury flare back to agonizing life, he knew he'd killed another one. He held that satisfaction tight to his soul as he passed out.

Margaret, Amos and Clarence Otto stared at the photo-mural. Clarence had had the painting blown up to three times the original size, so that Nguyen's nightmarish vision took up an entire wall.

They'd all caught a few hours of sleep from around 2:00 A.M. to 5:00 A.M., then it was back to work. After two hours of staring at the mural, staring and *thinking,* Margaret still felt groggy despite five cups of nasty hospital coffee. Amos, as usual, looked none the worse for wear. Neither did Otto. Margaret hated them both.

Amos stood right in front of the photomural, his nose just inches from the wall. 'How did Nguyen know these people?' he asked.

Margaret stared and thought hard about the question. 'I don't think he knew these people at all,' she finally said.

Amos looked at her and crossed his arms. 'What, you're saying that the kid was a psychic or something?'

Margaret shook her head slowly, but kept her eyes fixed on the painting photo. 'No, I don't think so. Not psychic, but something *like* psychic. Something beyond the science we know.'

Where she could identify and match, she had taped the life-size pictures of the infestation victims' faces next to their life-size spot on the painting.

Blaine Tanarive.

Charlotte Wilson.

Gary Leeland.

Judy Washington.

Martin Brewbaker.

Kiet Nguyen.

There was an indefinable horror in seeing the real faces taped next to Nguyen's ghastly, painted renditions. Horror, yes, but that horror paled in comparison to the math.

Those six faces, she knew.

There were eleven other faces that she did not.

So there were more. At least eleven more. And who knew how many beyond that? The thing made of those bodies seemed to expand far beyond the frame. How many other faces would be on the rest of the . . . the . . . what was it? An arch? No, there were multiple arches.

The *construct*.

Why was she focusing on that? Why did she feel the need to name it? Was it significant?

Margaret slowly walked backward, taking in the painting. Her eyes traced the arch, trying to imagine where the other end of it would logically fall.

The construct would be huge. The two arches alone would be at least twenty-feet high.

Arches. Made out of human parts.

'Clarence,' Margaret said quietly, 'get me Dew on the phone. *Now*.'

INTERNET

Perry woke all at once, sitting straight up with eyes wide open. His sleeping mind had been searching his thoughts, not unlike the way the Triangles searched his gray-matter database, looking for an answer to the problem at hand. While sleeping, his brain had found a keyword to clutch, a distant beacon of hope in a dark flatland of despair.

That word was *Internet.*

How stupid he'd been to call on the phone, rummaging through the Yellow Pages trying to find Triangle this or Triangle that. How could the Soldiers make themselves known in the Ann Arbor Yellow Pages? America was a big fucking place. And who was to say that this Triangle infection epidemic was limited to the United States? It was probably global. And if you wanted to communicate with people all over the world, you needed a global medium. Not television, not radio, not phones, not newspapers— if you wanted to keep something quiet but let people know you were out there, there was only one answer, the only true global medium: the Internet.

He moved to rub the sleep from his eyes and suddenly had to bite back a scream as he rolled onto his scorched ass. He couldn't see the window in the living room, but the brightness of the apartment told him he hadn't been asleep long. If he ever got out of this alive, he'd buy himself a brand-new bed. Something he couldn't afford. Something so comfortable he'd never want to get out of it again. Something that was better than sleeping on linoleum floors.

The Four Horsemen were still out; he could feel them sleeping. Except . . . they weren't the Four Horsemen anymore, were they? Perry managed a malicious smile even though every inch of his body seemed to voice complaint. They weren't four anymore, he was sure of it. They were three. What would he call them? As if there could have ever been any doubt.

The Three Stooges were all that remained. That made the score Perry Dawsey 4, Fucking Triangles 3. Perry wouldn't quit until he got the shutout.

He fumbled his way to his feet (correction, 'foot") and hobbled to his Macintosh. Less than sixty seconds after he awoke, the Mac chimed its startup tone and began the boot process. Startup programs came to life, including his email and instant-message clients.

Why hadn't he thought of it before? He was on the Internet every damned day, for crying out loud. That's where the answer lay, that's what it was all about. He started up Firefox and went right to Google. He didn't think it mattered what search engine he used; the government would make sure that the Triangles' home page was easily found by those who knew what to look for.

His email client finished loading and immediately chirped at him. Sixty-four emails. He chanced a quick peek at the in-box.

From:	Subject:
Bill Miller	Where the hell are you?
Bill Miller	Dude, get back to me! It's not about the Cincinnati bowtie.

Branston Gumong	Hey dude top brands available for u
Peter Hurt	All top medications at top price
Pussy GalOR-e	Hot wet teen snatch, just 4 U!
Bill Miller	If I was that kid, I would breast-feed until I was 17 or 18
Mister T. Minga	You are huge cock for your woman?
Ithaca Tang Shen	Director of the Contracts Award and Review Department
A friend	Nigeria fortune waiting to be made
Bill Miller	Dine at just one American pink taco stand!
Bill Miller	A pond would be good for you (these are good movie lines, dammit, Stop ignoring me)

'Jesus, Billy, get a life.'

It went on and on. A quick count showed sixteen messages from Bill. Sure, Perry hadn't been to work, but wasn't that a little . . . stalkerish? Why was Bill trying so hard?

He's trying to contact you because he's your friend, dumbass. But what if there was more to this? What if Bill was . . . was *supposed* to be keeping an eye on him?

You're getting crazy paranoid, Perry old boy, knock that shit off and focus.

He had to concentrate on the web search. That's where the answer lay—it *had* to.

He typed in 'Triangles.'

He would have never thought there would be so much stuff. The entries were numerous: tons of Wikipedia shit, math up the ass, sites focusing on the 'Triangle Area' in North Carolina, and of course several on the Bermuda Triangle. Perry breezed through them, giving them little more than a cursory once-over.

He typed in 'triangles' and 'infected.'

Finally he found it. Fifteen pages into the search. To a normal person, it wouldn't have looked like anything out of the ordinary. But to Perry, the letters on the screen glowed with hope.

Triangles - You are not alone

We are here to help you. This page has all the information on dealing with your condition and making you better.

www.tomorrowresearch.com - 5k - Cached - Similar pages

Not alone.

Not alone!

His hands shook with excitement; he finally knew—really *knew*—that someone could help him. People knew about the parasites slinking their tails through his body.

He clicked on the entry. Perry stared with wide eyes, his pulse hammering both in his head and his wounded shoulder, his breath pinched tight in his chest.

Big letters at the top of the page read 'You are not alone.' The layout was stark and simple, not enough graphics to interest the casual browser should he stumble onto it. To Perry, however, the page was a godsend. Right under 'You are not alone' was a Triangle—it was the image embedded in his own skin, a stylistic rendering of the horror that sent tendrils throughout his body, and yet it was something he'd seen all his life. It was the pyramid from the back of a one-dollar bill, its eye glowing green at the top. This pyramid, however, showed three glowing eyes at the top, not just one.

Perry choked back tears—only someone who'd seen the blue critters under the skin would realize, *could* realize, the meaning of that three-eyed pyramid.

Underneath the Triangle was a short message. The words called to his desperate soul as if they were the writings of God.

YOU ARE NOT ALONE
If you have found this page, then you know what we're all about. We're here to help you. We know what's happening to you, and we can save you, but you have to act quickly. Your condition gets worse by the second. Click **here** to fill out the form with your address, and we will send doctors to you immediately. Be patient, be calm, we're here to help you. Do not panic, as it will only make things worse. Do not tell anyone else about your condition, not even your doctors—there are people out there that want to harm you. Stay where you are, fill out the form, and wait. Everything will be fine. Do not tell anyone about the Triangles. If you think you can't wait, dial 206-222-2898.

Perry almost wanted to get up and dance around the room. He'd found the way out. He'd hit the 'eject' button before the damaged fighter crashed into a mountain. He'd gotten the call from the governor just before they'd thrown the switch. He'd rushed out of the burning building—beautiful costar over his shoulder—just before the gas mains caught and the credits rolled over a mushroom cloud of fire and death. All he had to do was wait. He wrote down the number; he'd call as soon as he finished with the computer.

The form asked for his name, then his street address. He flew through it, backing up only to fill in a few typos made as his hasty fingers danced frantically across the keyboard.

It asked for his phone number; he typed it in.

He stopped for a brief second at the next question, wanting to finish and click 'send,' but the oddity of the query gave him pause.

Who have you told about your condition? List their full names and addresses, please.

Now why the fuck would they want to know that? Who cared? It didn't matter—he hadn't told anyone. He typed in 'none.'

Describe your current condition. Be as detailed as possible on what THEY look like.

He didn't have time for this shit. He needed help now. He clicked 'send,' completing the form. It didn't matter— they had enough information and he couldn't put it off anymore. They'd be here soon. All he had to do was wait. Wait for the cavalry.

His computer beeped. An instant-message window appeared.

From StickyFingazWhitey.

Bill Miller's handle.

StickyFingazWhitey: Good god, man! You're finally online!!!!! R U OK?

Perry stared at the screen. He was suddenly petrified, afraid to move. First the emails, then the call, and now this.

StickyFingazWhitey: I know you're there, fat boy. Talk to a brotha.

Bill was one of them. One of *them*. He'd IM'ed as soon as Perry had sent in the form. That wasn't coincidence.

Of course it is. You've been offline for days. He IM'ed you almost as soon as you came back on, that's all.

It couldn't be Bill; he'd known Bill for years. But if someone wanted to experiment on Perry, to *watch* Perry, who better to do that than his best friend? All they had to do was 'turn' Bill. That was the term, *turn,* what they do to make double agents.

StickyFingazWhitey: Stop jerkin' der Gherkin' and answer me. Seriously. Getting pissed. Don't make me smack you around, bitch.

IMs weren't enough for Bill. Perry's VOIP connection started to ring—Bill was trying to initiate an Internet phone call over the computer. The computer's digital ringing sounded far too loud in the quiet apartment.

w h a t   i s   t h a t   s o u n d   what

Perry jumped with surprise; the Triangles had been so utterly quiet he'd forgotten about them. He sucked in three shallow breaths, clenched and unclenched his fists. Did they know he'd just contacted the Soldiers? If they did . . . they would mindscream him any second now. Were they searching his brain?

n e w   n o i s e s .
w h a t   a r e   t h e   n e w   n o i s e s
w e   a r e   hearing

Perry grabbed the Mac with both hands and threw it against the wall as hard as he could. Plastic and glass smashed, with a bright flash of electricity. The pieces fell to the floor, leaving a scored burn mark on the wall, a fuzzy black snake marking the computer's sudden death.

w h a t ' s   g o i n g   ON
t e l l   US

'Nothing! Nothing is going on. I don't hear anything.'
He had to play it cool, relaxed, chillsville. He couldn't
let on that the Triangles' hours were numbered. He had
to keep them in the dark. It was only a matter of time
before this game was over, and if Perry wanted to win,
he had to play it cool. Just like Fonzie, honeybunny . . .
play it cool.

n e w   n o i s e s ,
w h a t   a r e   t h e   n e w   n o i s e s   w e   a r e   hearing

'Noises? I didn't hear anything. I'm sure it's nothing
to worry about.'

n o   o n e   i s   h e r e   n o   c o l u m b o s
anyone

'Nope, just relax, man, just chill.' Perry felt the Triangles'
oddly black emotions flowing through him. He tried to
nail down the vibe; anxiety, perhaps. His own emotions—
excitement, hope, fear, rage—stirred them up like a bunch
of hyperactive kids dropped in the midst of the Hershey's
chocolate factory.

i s   s o m e t h i n g   W r o n g
w h o   i s   t h e r e   who

Perry took a very deep breath and let it out slowly,
telling himself over and over again to relax. He repeated
the process ten times, feeling calm spread over his body.
Discipline, as Dear Old Dad would say. *Without discipline
you're no better than some two-bit cooze, crying over this and
crying over that.*

Perry knew he had to calm down, to chill out the Three
Stooges.

'It's okay, fellas.' Perry's voice exuded control. 'There's

no one here. Just relax. We're all going to go to sleep now, just chill.'

Perry closed his eyes. Relaxation swept over him like a warm wind. This was not the time for weakness—if he'd ever had a moment of self-control in his life, now was the time to exercise it. *You gotta have discipline, boy. Without discipline, people are going to walk all over you, and nobody but nobody walks all over a Dawsey.*

He laid his head on the back of the couch. This was a game, that's all, just like football, although this time the stakes were a bit higher than a Big Ten title. It was a game, and he was *winning*. A smile touched his face, only for a second, as sleep came and he drifted away.

53

MARGARET TALKS TO DEW

Agent Otto handed Margaret his cell phone. The weight surprised her—the cell phone was larger than any she'd seen in years.

'Hello, Dew,' she said.

'I assume you're calling because you have information for me, Doc,' he said. 'I'm trying to run an op here.' Even through the cell phone, she could hear his annoyance. She didn't have time for his attitude.

'We need satellite coverage,' Margaret said. 'Can you get that?'

'Why do we need it?'

'You know what, Phillips? Answer the fucking question, okay? Can you or can you not get satellite coverage?'

There was a pause. 'You might want to talk to me with a little more respect there, Doc.'

'Screw your respect. Answer the damn question or I hang up and go right to Murray. Can you, or can you not, get dedicated satellite coverage for the Ann Arbor area?'

'This isn't the movies, Doc,' Dew said. 'We can't just dial in an address and see a full-color picture of Mister and Misses Jones doing it doggy-style. It will take some time, but we can get the coverage. Now, if you're done with the potty mouth, you want to tell me why?'

Margaret held the phone with her right hand. With her left she rubbed her knuckles against her hair, so hard it hurt. None of this made any sense, none of this was *science*, but she knew what had to be done—she couldn't explain why, yet it had to be done anyway.

'The paintings of Nguyen,' she said. 'They had all the known victims, then eleven other people.'

'So?'

'So there are victims we haven't found yet.'

'You know we're working on that,' Dew said. 'We have scans of the faces, all-points out on them, over the whole state and into Ohio and Indiana. We're trying to track them down. Why is a satellite going to help with that?'

Margaret winced as her knuckles dug too deep. She forced herself to put her hand at her side.

'They're building something,' Margaret said. 'I think the victims are supposed to build something, something big.'

'What? What are they supposed to build?'

'Something in the woods, maybe. I think there are trees involved. Deep woods, even.'

'So then what shall I tell the satellite to look for?'

Margaret sighed. 'I don't know. Something with arches. Maybe twenty feet high.'

'And how long is this thing?'

'Dew, I just don't know.'

'Margaret,' Dew said. He spoke slowly, as if explaining something to a child. 'Changing a satellite's tracking is a big deal. We have to drop scheduled coverage from an area to redirect. Plus, we have to get squints assigned to look at the pictures, try and find what you're looking for—and since you don't really *know* what it is you're looking for, and we're covering a huge area, it's a practically impossible job. Now, with all that in mind, is this just a hunch of yours, or do you have something *real* for me?'

Margaret thought about it. She had nothing solid, nothing to go on other than the painting of an insane, murdering artist.

'It's a hunch,' she said. 'But I *feel* it, Dew.'

Even through the rough connection, she heard Dew's heavy sigh. 'Fine, fuck it. What have we got to lose? So this will take four or five hours. I'm telling them to look for something unusual, with arches, twenty feet high, length unknown. Yeah?'

'Yeah,' Margaret said. 'Yeah, that's right.'

'It will be done. And if you change your mind and want the satellite to look for unicorns or Santa's sleigh, just let me know.' With that, Dew hung up.

54

SPAM?

Murray Longworth's desk intercom buzzed softly. He pressed the 'talk' button.

'What is it, Victor?'

'Sir, I thought you'd want to know that something came in over the web.'

Murray felt his pulse quicken. 'When?'

'Less than an hour ago, sir.'

'Where is the client?'

'Ann Arbor, Michigan, sir.'

'Bring me the info immediately.'

Victor entered the office with a sealed folder. The computer boys were under strict orders to print any web info that came through, then delete all traces of the data from the system. Murray didn't like using the Internet, but he agreed with Montoya that it was one way to possibly reach victims without raising the press's attention. Apparently the hunch had paid off.

Victor left the room, and Murray broke the seal.

Ann Arbor, Michigan. Perry Dawsey. Dew was already there, had already had a run-in with one of the infected freaks, as had Otto and Margaret. It was a slam-dunk home run. Margaret's work had put Dew close. Dawsey listed no contacts—that was good. That made things easier.

Apartment complex—that wasn't good. No description of Dawsey's condition.

Dew was *already there*. So was Margaret, and she had an analysis facility ready and waiting. Finally, it was the break that Murray needed.

55

THE TRUTH

The voice tickled his thoughts, teased his muddled mind.

Where are they?

It was the voice of the Triangles: mechanical, and yet still alive.

Are you there?
Another is missing.

The voice of the Triangles, and yet it was different. Somehow almost . . . feminine. Not a woman's voice, but a woman's concern, a woman's depth of feeling.

Why don't they answer?
Where are they?

His eyes fluttered sleepily. The voice was something important, something he knew he needed to think about. The pain hung on his body like a weighted suit. Every inch seemed to throb and pulse in a muted symphony of complaint.

They won't make it.
they won't make it.
he is too strong.

Perry blinked again, clawing his way to consciousness. Triangles, but not his. Were these the ones his own infectors had mentioned when they said that strange phrase: *we do that without telephones talk to Triangles.*

He felt the Three Stooges stirring. The female voice faded away.

Perry wasn't ready to get up. He lay on the couch, weight on his left side, wondering if he should just spend the rest of his life there, on his good side, not bothering to get up and suffer any more pain or wonder what fabulous secret the Stooges might deal out next.

His ass still burned; it felt as if he were still sitting on the stove. A truly nasty smell filled the air. So this is what burning human flesh smells like? Wonderful. There was another smell, something more pungent, more . . . *dead*-smelling. But it wafted in and out and couldn't compete with the all-encompassing smell of Perry's Home-Cooked Rump Roast.

Why do you fight us?

And there they were. No mistaking that voice. Male, arrogant, bossy. His own beloved Triangles.

'Who was that other voice?' Perry asked, ignoring their question. 'There's someone else infected, isn't there? Who is it? Does he live in the apartments?'

We won't tell you.
Why do you keep killing us?
We're the only ones who can
save you now.

'What the hell are you talking about? Save me? I know I'm as good as dead.'

No,
it's the others who want to
kill you, not us. Not us,
Perry. We would never hurt you.

The Triangles weren't trying to kill him? Bullshit. They were going to burrow out his insides and wear him like a coat, or take over his mind and dance him around the street like a fucking human Muppet.

Someone is coming.
Is it Columbo?

Perry heard nothing. Was their hearing better than his? How strong were they now?

'You hear someone out in the hall? Is it the neighbor who was here before?'

No. Footsteps are
lighter, it's Columbo
kill Columbo.

'It's not Columbo!'

Perry painfully picked himself up off the couch, using the table to help him stand. Every movement brought fresh waves of pain.

'Why the hell do the police scare you so bad?'

Because they are coming
to get us.
Men are looking for us,
to kill us.
Why don't you understand?

'Take it easy. Don't get excited and start screaming in my head again, okay?' Perry breathed slowly. He tried to project his calmness, hoping that if the Triangles could overflow emotion into him, he could do the same in reverse. 'Why do you think they're coming to get you now?'

Don't you get it?
If they kill you,
they kill us.

It hit him like a bullet between the eyes.

Perry's analytical process stopped dead-still as the truth

suddenly rocked home. The truth that had been there from the start, and all he'd had to do was ask.

The Soldiers weren't coming to save him.

They were coming to kill him.

To keep the Triangle larvae from hatching. It made perfect sense, although part of his mind still fought against it. If the Soldiers wanted to kill him, then there was truly no way out, no escape, no chance.

He talked in barely a whisper. 'Do you mean . . . do you mean that the Soldiers are coming to kill *me*?'

Yes yes stupid! Yes coming to kill YOU!

He was fucked. He was completely and utterly fucked. The Triangles were killing him from the inside. Soldiers wanted to gun him down and stop the Triangles from becoming whatever it was they became. He had no idea who the Soldiers were, where they were, what they looked like. They could be anybody. Anybody. And he'd sent an invitation through the Internet, painted a fucking bull's-eye on his own forehead.

His father's voice filtered into his head, a once-faint memory now strong and vital. *It's you against the world, boy, you just remember that. The world is a harsh place, where only the strong survive. If you ain't strong, people will use you up and throw you away. You've gotta show the world who's boss, boy, show them with strength. That's why I'm so tough on you—that and because you're one stupid cornholing bastard and you piss me off every chance you get. Someday boy, you'll thank me. Someday you'll understand.*

For the first time in his life, Perry *did* understand. He'd spent a decade trying to escape his father's legacy of violence and abuse and anger, but now he knew that was a mistake.

'You were right, Daddy,' Perry whispered. 'You was always right.'

Fuck them all. He was a Dawsey, goddamn it, and he'd sure as hell start acting like one.

Columbo is here.

As the last of his sanity slipped away, Perry heard a knock at his door.

His eyes narrowed to predatory slits.

His father's voice: *You gonna let 'em push you around like that, boy?*

'No sir, Daddy,' Perry whispered. 'I sure as hell ain't.'

56

COMPANY

Bill Miller knocked on Perry's door again.

Enough was enough. Perry was home. Period. He'd logged on to his instant messenger not more than thirty minutes earlier, and signed off as soon as Bill sent him a message. Bill had immediately hopped into his car, and now he was here, outside Perry's door.

Perry could have signed on from anywhere in the world, of course, but his Ford was still under the carport awning, a foot of clean snow behind it—it hadn't moved for at least a couple of days.

Bill knocked again. Nothing.

Was Perry sick? Had he lost his temper, done something *really* bad, something he couldn't face? The guy was so sensitive about his violent streak, even a loud argument might fill him so full of guilt he couldn't face the day. Sick, guilty, whatever, Bill had to get to the bottom of this—his friend needed help, and that was that.

He gave it one more triple-knock.

'Perry, buddy, it's Bill.'

No answer.

'Perry, everyone's worried sick. You don't have to answer, but if you're there let me know you're okay.'

No answer. He fished in the pocket of his leather coat for a piece of paper to leave a note. The hair on the back of his neck suddenly stood on end, caused by the peculiarly strong feeling that he was being watched. He looked up at the peephole, hand frozen in his pocket.

He heard the door's chain lock slowly scrape aside, followed by the click of a deadbolt sliding back into its housing.

The door opened slowly. Perry's hulking form came into view. Bill heard himself breathe in sharply, a comical sound of surprise. Perry looked like a Bruce Willis stand-in from one of the *Die Hard* movies. His long-sleeved white T-shirt was spotted with blood, blood that looked black where it had dried in patches spreading down from the left shoulder. He stood on one leg, holding the door for balance; the other leg hung loosely beneath him, not touching the floor, like a hunting dog on point. The hanging leg had another T-shirt wrapped around its calf. Bill had no idea of that one's original color—it was now a deep, crusty burgundy, like clothes that had been dropped in the mud, taken off at the back door, and left to dry in the sun. Perry had a bruised bump on his head the size of a golf ball. An old scruff of bright red beard glowed electrically against his pale white skin.

No, not like Bruce Willis . . . like Arnold Schwarzenegger. Perry's muscles rippled with every movement, especially on his neck, which looked like steel cables wrapped tightly with veins, then with skin. Perry hadn't looked this defined, this big—this *threatening*—in years, not since they'd been sophomores in college. Bill realized, suddenly, that by hanging out with him every day, he'd lost touch with the fact that Perry Dawsey was a giant of a man.

Despite the haggard appearance, Perry's eyes were his most attention-demanding feature. Not because of the fact that the skin around them was black-and-blue, either from a shot to the face or some serious lack of sleep, but from the look *in* the eyes. The spaced-out psycho look, like when Jack Nicholson axed his way through the door in *The Shining*.

Bill had always been the type to trust his instincts. At this moment his instincts yanked at him to leave, to get the fuck out of there *right now*, fight-or-flight response kicking in with a 100 percent majority vote for flight. But Perry was obviously in trouble—something was very, very wrong.

Postal was the word that flashed through Bill's brain. *Perry has gone postal.*

They both stood for a few seconds without speaking. Bill broke the interlude. 'Perry, are you okay?'

There was no fucking question. As soon as Perry opened the door and saw Bill standing there in his black leather jacket with his neatly trimmed hair and immaculate appearance, Perry knew for certain that he was one of the Soldiers. Bill had been watching him all along. He might even be the one who put the Triangle seeds on him—who can tell with these crazy government fucks? When had they recruited Bill? After college? *During* college? How far back did this conspiracy go? Maybe that's why Bill had volunteered as a roommate so long ago. *That* made sense. *That* was logical.

Bill had come to check on the experiment. He'd probably freaked when Perry stopped going to work. When Perry filled out the online form, they sent Bill to look in on him. Why else would he be here *right now*? Bill was a fucking narc, waiting to sell Perry out to the Soldiers. Well, the backstabbing, traitorous snitch wasn't going to be telling his government butt buddies anything.

Not now.

Not later.

Not ever.

'I'm fine,' Perry said. 'Come on in.'

He took a small hop back into the apartment, making room for Bill to enter. Strange odors filtered out the open door. Bill's instincts clamored louder, swelling in volume and intensity, beseeching him to turn tail and run, baby, run.

'Well . . . uh, I have to be getting back to work, no bout-a-doubt-it,' Bill said. 'I just came out to see if you were okay, buddy. You don't look so good—are you sure you feel all right?'

Did Perry have any idea how bad he looked? Was he on drugs, maybe strung out on heroin or something? Bill couldn't stop looking at his eyes, the way they burned with intensity and simmering emotions. Bill had seen that look many times during the past ten years—it was the look that came over Perry's face just before he punched someone, the look just before the snap of the ball. That look was *predatory,* and it meant serious trouble.

But in those ten years, that look had never been fixed on Bill—until now.

Time to go.

Bill looked scared. He obviously hadn't counted on Perry figuring out *The Plan.* Nobody thought Good Ol' Perry was smart enough to figure out *The Plan.* They'd under-estimated him. Bill had underestimated him. And now that Bill knew the depth of his soon-to-be-fatal mistake, there was nothing he could do. Nothing except run.

But Scary Perry Dawsey was way ahead of the game.

* * *

Bill concentrated on speaking in a calm, neutral voice. 'Perry, you're freaking me out, and you look like you're about to get violent.' He slowly backed away from the door. 'I'm going to leave now. You're going to go into your apartment and calm down. You relax and I'll be back in a bit.'

'Wait!' Perry's word was a plea, pregnant with need, although he kept his voice almost as low and calm as Bill's placating tone. 'You gotta help me . . . I . . .' Perry swayed a little bit, his one good leg sagging under him. 'I . . . just can't . . .'

Perry collapsed, falling into the hall like a sack of rotten meat and bones.

Bill instinctively reached out to help his friend. Perry knew that he would. People just couldn't help such things. Especially the Government People, because the government is here to help you, right? But for Bill, it was too late. Too late to react, too—

—late Bill realized the trick. He tried to jump back, even before he saw the knife, but he was too close. He tried to jump back, to get—

—away, but Perry wasn't going to let that happen. As soon as Perry hit the floor, the rush of adrenaline blocked out all feelings of pain from his abused body. He rolled over his left shoulder and swung wide with the six-inch steak knife clutched unforgivingly in his right hand. The blade struck Bill's right inside thigh, sliding noiselessly through jeans, through skin, through quadriceps. It finally thudded to a stop at the femur, the tip embedding in the bone and snapping free. Perry watched Bill's eyes go—

—wide with shock, fear and pain. Bill stared down at the knife, at the blade sunk deep into his thigh. The blood didn't come until Perry wrenched the blade back for a second strike. Blood squirted out in a deep red stream, splattering on the hallway's off-white walls and landing on the burnt-orange acrylic carpet that had been ugly even when it was new.

Perry rolled up to his knees, head tilted forward, eyes flashing, lips curled in a demonic grin of anger and predation. He thrust the blade upward with the power of a knockout uppercut.

Bill tried to jump clear, but his wounded leg wouldn't hold his weight. He fell weakly backward, the knife's upward arc whizzing through the air, its jagged tip just barely missing his face. He landed on his back, blood still gushing from his leg.

Perry lurched forward, snarling, spittle flying from his sneering lips. He was a monster, a growling, six-foot-five vision from hell. He brought the blade down in an overhand thrust. Bill reactively brought his hands up, palms out, to protect himself from the slashing knife. Perry's strength drove the ragged, broken knife point clear through Bill's upturned right palm. Jagged metal tore through cartilage, tendons and scraped across metacarpals until the knife's wooden handle slammed into the palm, leaving five inches of the bloody blade jutting forth from the back of Bill's hand.

Bill's eyes reactively closed as hot blood splattered on his face. He never saw Perry's left hand ball up into a gnarled fist. The fist blasted into Bill's nose with a muffled crunch. A second blow hammered home, spraying fine droplets of blood onto his face and hair.

* * *

Bill's traitorous body fell limp.

Perry hopped off him immediately, grabbed his wrist and hop-dragged him into the apartment. Bill weighed maybe a buck-fifty; dragging him was effortless, even with a bum leg. Perry shut and locked the door.

He's not dead kill him killhimkillhim

'We're not going to kill him until I get some answers,' Perry said, his breath ragged from excitement and exertion. Blood, steady and red, pulsed from the cut in Bill's thigh, giving his jeans a rapidly spreading dark purple patch.

killhimkillhimkillhim

'Shut up! I'm not going to kill him. We're doing this my way.' Bill had to have some answers, and Perry was going to hear every last one of them.

The pure, narcotic effect of sheer hatred surprised him. Bill was the enemy. Perry wanted to kill the enemy. Bill was one of the Soldiers, sent to experiment, then observe, then exterminate. *Yes indeedee doodee, exterminate, but that's not going to happen, Billy Boy.*

Bill let out a moan. He rolled slightly on the floor. He coughed and spit out a large clot of blood. Snarling, Perry jerked him to his feet and pushed him backward across the living room. Bill fell heavily into the couch.

Perry's voice was a low rumble, a menacing drawl that hadn't escaped his lips in years. 'You want to get up when I hit you, boy? You gotta learn to stay down unless you're ready for some more punishment.'

He grabbed Bill's wounded right hand, which spurted blood in all directions thanks to the knife still embedded in the palm. Perry wrapped his hand around the knife handle and drove it into the wall just above the couch. The jagged tip punched into the plaster, pinning Bill's hand.

'You like that, snitch? You like that, spy? Then let's get you a second helping.'

Perry hopped into the kitchen and grabbed another knife from the butcher's block. He didn't even glance at the Chicken Scissors. Moving almost as fast as if he had two legs, he then hopped into the bedroom and grabbed a wrinkled, dirty sock from the floor.

Bill's head lolled from side to side as he struggled for consciousness, blood pouring from his leg, his hand, his nose. 'Please,' he murmured, his voice barely a whisper of escaping pain. 'Please . . . stop.'

Perry grabbed Bill's good hand. 'You talkin' to me, boy? You speak when you're spoken to. You got to learn better than that!' Perry shoved the sock into Bill's mouth, forcing the dirty fabric in so far that Bill gagged.

With a primitive grunt of aggression, Perry slammed Bill's good hand against the wall, palm out. He reared back with the fresh knife, then drove the blade through Bill's exposed palm.

Bill roared in pain, clarity of mind returning in full at a rather unfortunate moment. The dirty sock muffled his cries of agony.

Bill tried to pull free, which made the blades cut deeper still into his ravaged hands. His body simply didn't have the strength. He slumped back into the couch, a portrait of defeat—his bleeding hands stretching out on either side of his limply hanging head.

'Neighbors,' Perry said in a hiss, his eyes darting first to the window and then to the door. 'Nosy goddamned neighbors might be in on it.'

He hopped to the door and stared out the peephole. Even through the distorted view he could see blood on the hallway's walls and carpeting. Someone would notice it—he didn't have much time. Time enough, however, to get some answers from the informant nailed to the wall.

Kill him kill him.
Kill him!

Perry stared at Bill. His friend, Bill Miller. His . . . friend.

'My God, what have I done? What's happening to me?'

He is Columbo,
he is the Soldiers.

'He can't be.'

He's here, isn't he?
Why would he be here
now if he wasn't
Columbo? Killllllllll
himmmmmmm

They were right. The emails, the calls, that convenient instant message, showing up at his door. Bill knew what was going on. He knew *everything*. How callous, how heartless could this bastard be? He had feigned friendship while watching the Triangles grow and fester and swell and chew Perry up from the inside as if he were a fucking goddamned caterpillar. Bill had watched all along.

But he could only watch at work.

What about the rest of the time? What about all the time Perry spent at home, in the apartment, particularly in the last few days? How were they watching him then? Bugs? Hidden cameras? Watching his instant-message and email traffic? Maybe behind a light, maybe inside the TV. *Maybe inside the damned TV!*

And if they'd watched him all that time, then they were watching him now.

They were watching him carve up Billy the Betrayer.

They wouldn't just let that happen. They were coming, coming to rescue Billy. Perry took Bill's head in his hands and stared into glassy eyes.

'They'll be too late, Billy Boy,' Perry said quietly. 'You hear me? They'll be too fucking late to bail your ass out of this one.'

Bill screamed, but the sock muffled the noise.

'You'd best knock that shit off, boy,' Perry said, still staring into Bill's terrified eyes, eyes that revealed searing pain and pure, raw terror. 'Quit your cryin', boy, or I'll give you something to cry about.'

Bill screamed louder, trying to pull back from the bull-necked horror before his eyes.

Perry snarled as he grabbed Bill's broken nose and shook it viciously from side to side. Bill's body shuddered with fresh agony. He thrashed like a man in the electric chair, muscles contorting so violently that one knife-pierced hand pulled free from the plaster.

The blade still jutted from the back of his hand. Perry grabbed both Bill's blood-slick wrist and the knife handle, then slammed the blade back into the wall. This time he felt a distinct and sudden resistance as the blade dug deep into a wall stud.

Old Billy Boy wasn't going to pull that one free anytime soon, no siree, bub, not anytime soon.

Bill fought down the pain, his mind freaked beyond the point of clear thought. Somehow he found the inner power to stop screaming, stop struggling, despite this seemingly endless torture from a man whom only minutes before he'd known as his dearest friend.

Perry leaned in, so close that Bill felt the heat from his

breath. Perry held his fingers less than a half inch from Bill's nose, thumb and forefinger ready to grab again at a moment's notice, ready to inflict more of that brain-shearing agony.

'Like I said, boy, stop your crying or I'll kill you right fucking now.'

Bill stared up through tears that refused to be blinked away. The friend-turned-psycho leaned over him, perched on one leg. Bill's fresh blood had smeared all over Perry's shirt, wetting the brown-black stains.

The sock filled his mouth with a sickly dry-cotton feel. It tasted much as Bill imagined a dirty old sock should: moldy and suffocating. Warm blood continued to pour from his nose, down his face and onto his chest. Blood from his punctured hands rolled down his arms to collect in wet pools at his armpits, soaking outward in an expanding tacky-hot pit stain.

How had this happened? He'd come to check on his best friend and now he was crucified to the wall, staring up at the bloody, giant, wild-eyed, snarling, psychotic nightmare that was Perry Dawsey in name only.

'Okay,' Perry said in a whisper. 'Now I'm going to take the sock out of your mouth. And when I do, I'm going to ask you some questions. Whether you live or die is up to you—the second you scream, I'm going to pull that knife out of your hand and shove it through your eye and stir your brain like Skippy peanut butter. It's going to hurt. It's going to hurt a lot. And I don't give a fuck, but I think you already know that. Do you know I don't give a fuck, Billy Boy?'

Bill nodded in agreement. Perry's voice had grown calm, cold and relaxed, but his eyes hadn't changed. Bill's chest felt packed with coppery terror. Fear filled his mind, leaving no room for thoughts of escape. Perry was in charge. Bill would do whatever he said. Whatever it took to stay alive.

Oh Jesus, don't let me die here. Please don't let this happen, oh dear God, please!

'Good,' Perry said. 'That's good, Bill. I'm sure you've been trained well and warned about the consequences of this mission, so I won't feel a bit of remorse. If your voice rises above conversational levels, you're not going to be having a whole lot of fun. Do you understand what will happen if your voice rises above conversational levels, Bill?'

Bill nodded again.

Perry dropped to the couch, resting a knee on either side of Bill's thighs. Bill saw him grimace a bit, but then that fleeting expression vanished, the psychotic stare back in place. Suddenly Perry looked away, his eyes losing focus. He seemed to be staring at the wall, or perhaps some point *beyond* the wall. His head cocked to the right ever so slightly.

He looks like a dog listening to one of those ultrasonic whistles.

'Look, I'm telling you he'll talk,' Perry said. 'We don't need to kill him!'

Oh Christ oh Jesus oh my Lord he's completely insane and I'm going to die here, I'm going to die just like that.

Perry spoke angrily to his unseen companion. 'Fuck off! This is my show now. You just shut up and let me think.'

Bill felt his spirit sag down, weighted with doom. There was no hope.

Apparently the voice stopped. Perry's stare returned, a piercing fixation that drilled into Bill's eyes, which were wide, white and wet. Bill felt weakness slip over him, slowly pulling him into unconsciousness.

This time he didn't fight it.

57

DEW ON THE MOVE

Dew pinched the uncomfortable, thick cellular between his shoulder and ear, steered with one hand, and with the other punched an address into the Buick's dashboard GPS computer.

'How long since the client sent the form, Murray?'

'About twenty minutes.'

'Have we contacted him yet?'

'There's no answer at the number he gave us,' Murray said. 'We've sent a return email, but no response there yet, either.'

'Send Margaret and her rapid-response teams for me. I have to find this apartment complex. Tell the squads to get to Dawsey's apartment complex, but *do not enter.* Tell them to wait for my call. Leave my three teams at Nguyen's place to make sure the media doesn't get in until they finish scrubbing the place of any triangle references.'

Dew broke the connection and put the cellular away. He almost rear-ended an old woman driving a Civic. He leaned on the horn, trying to get her out of the way. It was Sunday, college on semester break, but there were still college kids crossing the street, slow and calm like they owned the world, like they were immortal. Right about now Dew would be more than happy to put that immortality up against the front bumper of the Buick.

He swung into the wrong lane and passed the Civic. The GPS said he was fifteen minutes away, but with traffic it would probably take just over twenty to reach Dawsey's.

58

BEST FRIENDS FOREVER (BFF)

Perry knew he didn't have much time—either the Soldiers were on their way, or Bill the Betrayer would soon bleed to death. The wet puddle on the couch grew steadily, as if Bill were pissing blood. Perry knew that if he timed it right, he could get the information and the Soldiers could save his friend. Correction. His *so-called* friend.

Bill's eyes glazed over again, and his head sagged forward.

'Oh no you don't, you little informant,' Perry said. He slapped hard with his left hand. Bill's head shot back so fast his temple bounced off the wall. The slap sounded red, warm and satisfying.

You don't know what suffering is, Billy Boy. But I'm going to do my best to give you a little taste of what I've gone through.

Bill's scared-rabbit look returned to his blood-smeared face. How could the Soldiers use some weak-ass like this? It was probably a trick—yes, a trick. Bill was trying to lure him into overconfidence.

'That shit isn't going to trick me, Billy Boy, *no bout-a-doubt-it.*' He was smarter than these fuckers. They didn't know what they'd started by fucking with a Dawsey, because a Dawsey doesn't take shit, no sir, no how.

Perry reached out and pulled the sock from Bill's mouth.

Bill breathed deeply, but other than that didn't make a sound.

Perry licked his lips. He tasted blood. He didn't know if it was his or Bill's. Eager for the final answer, he leaned in close and asked his vital question.

'Who the fuck do you work for, and what are the Triangles going to turn into?'

Perry's face was only inches from Bill's. The dark circles around Perry's eyes made it look as if he hadn't slept in days. The whites were so bloodshot that they took on a pinkish hue. Bright red stubble stuck out offensively. There were open sores on his lips; it looked like he'd bitten through them not very long ago.

But that question—triangle?

'Perry, wha . . . what are you *talking* about?' Bill knew it was the wrong thing to say, but he couldn't think of another answer. Perry's eyes swelled with anger, adding to the already psychotic stare.

'Don't screw with me, Bill.' His quiet voice carried the threat of death. 'You and your little Jedi mind tricks can just fuck off. I'm not buying what you're selling, junior. Now, I'll ask you again, what are the Triangles becoming?'

Bill's breath came in short, ragged gasps. What was this madness? What did Perry want to hear?

Bill tried to fight back tears of frustration and panic. Pain ripped through his body in a nonstop cacophony of raw nerves and cutting metal edges. It was so hard to think!

He struggled for words, struggled to make sense of it all. 'I don't know what you're talking about, Perry. It's me! It's Bill, for God's sake! Why do you want to do this to me?'

A smile crept across Perry's face. He reached out for one of the knives that had Bill's hands impaled on the wall. Bill's body went rigid with white-hot tension.

'Getting a little loud in here, don't you think, Billy Boy?'

'I'm sorry,' Bill said quickly, his hushed whisper filled with fear and pleading. 'I'm sorry, it won't happen again.'

'Goddamned right it won't, Billy old sport. If it does happen again, you'll be dead before you can apologize. Your warnings are gone. You're in Double Jeopardy now, where the points can really add up, so I'll ask you just one more time: what are the Triangles becoming?'

Bill's mind spun wildly for an answer, anything that would keep him alive even a little bit longer. He had to come up with some bullshit and fast, but it was so hard to think, impossible to concentrate. Perry was going to *kill* him.

'I . . . I don't know, they didn't tell me that.'

'Like hell they didn't,' Perry said, never losing his predatory stare. 'You've got one more chance, Billy, and then I'm going to carve you up.'

Bill scrambled for an answer, but he couldn't make his mind focus past the pain, past the psychotic situation, past death that stared him in the face. What had Perry called him? The 'informant?' Informant for what? For whom? What raving paranoid vision did Perry see through those bloodshot eyes?

'Perry, I swear, they didn't tell me!' He watched the rage flare up in Perry's eyes. Bill kept talking, his voice a nasal, pleading, pitiful cry. 'It's not my fault they don't tell me anything! They just told me to keep an eye on you, let them know what you were doing.'

That reply seemed to strike a chord. Perry's look changed, as if Bill's words answered some important question, but he still looked far from placated.

Bill continued, clutching to one faint glimmer of hope. 'It's not my job to know what the hell they turn into.'

Perry nodded as if he accepted the story. 'Okay, maybe you know and maybe you don't,' he said. 'Just tell me who you're working for.'

'I think you know that already,' Bill said quickly. He held his breath, waiting for a violent reaction. The salty tang of blood mingled in his mouth with the tangible taste of fear. The flicker of hope glowed a bit brighter as Perry nodded and smiled.

Dizziness swept over Bill. The room seemed to spin. He couldn't keep this up. 'Perry, you're out of control. You're paranoid . . . you're hallucinating . . .'

A shiver rippled through Bill's body. The apartment suddenly felt so cold, so icy cold. Black spots formed in front of his eyes, and another dizzy spell threw the room into crazy, unpredictable motion.

The ratfucker was passing out again. Perry bitch-slapped him three times, three vicious lefts, each harder than the last. It felt so good to lash out like that. You can't let people faint on you, not when you need information. All this pussy-ass narc needed was a little Dawsey-style discipline. You've *got* to have discipline.

Bill blinked a few times, but his eyes were once again clear and lucid. Perry had hit so hard that his hand stung from the slaps. The right side of Bill's face started to swell almost immediately, growing red and plump like a Ball Park frank.

k i l l h i m k i l l h i m k i l l him

'Shut the fuck up!' Perry screamed at the top of his lungs. He'd had just about enough of the Triangles, oh yes sir he had. They were in his house, after all, *his house,* and a Dawsey was always the master of his castle. He knew if he didn't take control, if he didn't *take charge,* he'd go crazy. He just couldn't stand it anymore, couldn't stand that voice in his head every fucking minute of every fucking day. 'You shut your little mouths or I swear as soon as I'm done with the informant here I'll turn the Three Stooges into the Dynamic Duo, no matter what it does to me!'

There was an ultrabrief burst of high-pitch as the Triangles accessed *Dynamic Duo,* then nothing.

He felt something inside him change, as suddenly and definitely as the switch thrown on an electric chair. The power structure had just traded hands—he knew it, and the Triangles knew it. He wasn't afraid of them anymore.

It's my house, Perry thought. A confident smile parted his bleeding, cracked lips. *It's my house, and you're all going to live by my rules.*

Bill's arms grew heavy, weak, yet he couldn't relax, couldn't let them drop and pull against the blades stuck through his palms. Only by keeping his hands very, very still could he maintain the pain at just below a screaming level. The tension of facing that agony and the fear he felt anticipating Perry's next move had his muscles taut with stress, tiring them quickly.

Perry started blinking rapidly. He shook his head, violently, like a dog shaking off after a swim. Then he looked right at Bill, his bloodshot eyes suddenly wide with terror.

'Bill, help me,' Perry said. The affected accent was gone. It was his friend again, not the creature that was torturing him to death.

'Perry . . .' Bill fought for the words. He had to act now. 'Perry, you have to . . . call . . .'

He wasn't sure how long he had before his strength gave out and his hands fell, the weight pulling down against the knives in grinding torture. For some odd reason, that thought rang worse than the concept of a knife through the eye—how much longer till his arms would give out? He already felt the burn, his deltoids and biceps simmering with fatigue. He didn't have much time, not much time . . . hard to believe he was going to die like this.

'Call . . . the police.'

The word seemed to rebound inside Perry's head. He'd been free, free of their control, for just a few seconds. He could have kept them at bay, too, would have, but Bill had to go and prove them right.

Call the police, Bill had said. The mothafuckin' po-lice.

We told you.

Could they sound smug? They sounded smug. Without conscious thought, Perry let go of his friendship for Bill Miller.

Enough fucking around. He had to get the info and get it now.

'When are they coming for me, Billy?'

Bill said nothing. Perry grabbed a handful of shirt and roughly shook Bill to emphasize his words. 'When are they coming to get me?'

Bill's eyes showed clear and fearful for only a moment, then went glassy again for the last time. His head nodded down limply. He didn't move.

Perry hit him until his own palms bled. It didn't make any difference—Bill wasn't coming out of it this time. Perry felt at Bill's neck, not knowing how to check for a pulse. Perry checked his own neck, found the jugular, which beat strong and true. He probed the same spot on Bill's neck and felt nothing.

Kill him, you have got to kill him, please do it now.

'You got your wish. He's dead.'

The informant's eyes remained open, fixed in a perpetual, empty, half-lidded stare. Perry stood on his good leg and looked at the corpse.

Bill was dead. A traitor's death, and well deserved—he'd been one of them.

No bout-a-doubt it.

59

THE CALL

Al Turner fumed. Not only was that damn freak-of-nature kid raising holy hell again, but Al's hemorrhoids were worse than ever. He'd used what seemed like a gallon of Preparation H, but he might as well have been smearing mayonnaise on his asshole for all the good it did.

'My name is Al Turner,' he said into the phone. 'I already called once. I'm in apartment B-303. He lives right downstairs, and he's been screaming his head off for days. I've had it.'

'Sir, a car is on the way. You're willing to file a formal complaint?'

'Absolutely. I've been down there and asked him to shut up and I'm not dealing with it. He's nuts. I think you better tell your people to be careful, though—he's a huge guy. I mean pro-wrestling huge.'

'Thank you, sir. The officers will be there as soon as possible. Please stay away from the apartment. The officers will handle it.'

'No problem. I'm not going down there. That guy is a freaking fruitcake.'

60

STEPPIN' OUT

We want to see.

Perry stood quietly.

'So whose eyes are working now?'

All of us can see.

He'd be damned if he'd let his balls see anything. That was just too fucking *much*. He slid his T-shirt sleeve up past his elbow, giving the Triangle on his forearm a full view of Bill Miller's corpse.

Yes, he's dead, you are right.

Perry pulled down the shirt and turned to stare vacantly at his former friend. The situation hit home, coming to rest in his mind with a heavy, cold-iron weight. Bill's blank eyes stared at the floor. The trickle of blood easing out of his nose had slowed to a stop. Blood covered the couch and carpet as if Bill had just come out of the shower, fully dressed with his clothes soaking wet, and sat down to watch *CSI*. Except he hadn't just sat down. Perry had put him there. Bill's hands had steak knives jammed through the palms, nailing them to the wall. Blood streaked the wallpaper, sticky, gooey and red.

Oh Jesus, what the hell is happening to me?

He'd killed Bill. Tricked him, stabbed him, dragged him into the apartment like a trapdoor spider snatching a hapless insect back into a lightless, hopeless den, nailed him to the wall and tortured him before letting him bleed to death. Bleed to death while Perry shouted questions in his face. It was a shitty way to go.

He'd just murdered his best friend. He should have been swamped with guilt, overwhelmed with it, yet surprisingly he felt nothing but a cold, icy satisfaction. Only the strong survive, and that little informant hadn't been strong enough to cut the mustard.

'We've got to get the hell out of here.'

The high-pitch searching sound echoed in his head.

We need to go to Wahjamega.

It was a strange comment, but nothing the Triangles did seemed to surprise him anymore.

'What the hell is a Wahjamega?' Perry asked quietly.

Not a what, a where.
Wahjamega.
In a place called Michigan.
Do you know where it is?

'Michigan? Sure. You're in it. I'll have to look up Wahjamega. Let me MapQuest it.'

Perry turned toward where his Mac used to sit before he remembered he'd smashed it to bits.

'Uh, I think I have a regular map.'

We need to go there.
There are people who can help us.

He felt their excitement, pure and unbridled. Images flashed in his head: a dirt road he'd never seen before, black movement in a dense forest, a pair of sprawling oaks, tree limbs vibrating in tune to the throbbing forest floor—and a brief flash of the green door from his dreams. Another image: a pattern, a set of lines that looked like a

Japanese kanji character. The symbol was nothing from his memory, it was *theirs,* and it held power.

Can we see? Show us.

He hopped to the junk drawer. In the back was a much-abused Michigan road map. Most of the Upper Peninsula was obscured by a huge ink stain in the rough shape of a kidney bean, but it didn't mar the map's southern area. He found Wahjamega in the 'thumb' area that was Michigan's hand shape. He folded the map a few times, leaving Wahjamega visible, then found a pen (one that didn't leak) and circled the town. Perry scrawled, *This is the place.* The phrase, and the circled town, seemed to call to him, and he wondered why he had written the words.

He turned his arm so that the Triangle could see the map.

There was a pause, then a brief flicker of the searching sound, and then overflow emotion exploded in his body.

Yes that's it!
That's it!
We must go to Wahjamega!

Their joy felt exquisite, all-encompassing, a drug that instantly roared through his veins and pulsated in his brain. The strange symbol again filled his world.

A pattern of lines and angles. The image seemed to swell before his eyes, glow with power like some mystical talisman. Everything else faded away, the world turned to black, leaving only the symbol floating before him, powerful and undeniable. This was Triangle overflow, he knew, but he couldn't stop it. He didn't *want* it to stop. The symbol was their purpose, their meaning for existence. They wanted it more than they wanted food or even survival.

They have to build this, and I have to help them, help them build . . . it's so beautiful . . .

Perry shook his head, fought his way out of the narcotic trance. His breath came in short gasps. The fear again, but different this time, different because he'd actually *wanted* to *help* them. They'd been in his thoughts before, but never so bad as that.

He realized he was holding a knife in his left hand. The map lay on the counter, drops of blood blocking towns like the craters of some nuclear bomb run. He saw that the knife tip was bloody before he felt the pain. Like a ventriloquist's dummy, he slowly turned his head to examine the underside of his right forearm.

In that short trance, he'd carved the symbol into his skin. Three inches long, it shimmered in wet red lines. The deep scratches oozed a little blood that trickled down in thin rivulets, rolling past either side of his thick biceps. He hadn't felt a thing. He stared at his handiwork:

The Triangles wanted to go to Wahjamega, *needed* to go the way a junkie needs another fix. Wanted to go to

Wahjamega and build something this symbol represented, whatever the hell that was. If they wanted something that badly, it couldn't be good for him. But he didn't have anywhere else to go. The Soldiers were coming, and at this point one direction seemed as good as the next. The important thing was to get the flying fuck out of the apartment.

Putting his exhaustion up on a mental shelf, he hopped to the bedroom. That strange smell hit him again. A nasty smell, a rotting smell. This time it didn't waft away on some invisible air current, but lingered. He ignored it—he had more important things to worry about.

He hauled a duffel bag out of the bedroom closet, then thought better of it and grabbed his backpack. Nothing big, just the nylon one he'd used to haul books around campus a million years ago. He imagined that hopping with a weighted duffel bag hanging from one arm might prove difficult.

As he put the backpack on his bed, he saw that it glistened with spots of wet blood. It took him a few seconds to register that the sticky red smear had come from his hands.

He was still covered in blood, both Bill's and his own.

Time was a factor; he knew that far too well. After all, there was a man crucified to his living-room wall. A dead guy with friends and coworkers who wore snappy little uniforms and who would love nothing more than to put several bullets into Perry's diseased body, but he couldn't go outside covered in blood and gore.

He quickly hopped to the bathroom and stripped his clothes. They were soiled with blood, both wet and flaky-dry. Perry felt the burst of overflow excitement as the Triangles in his back, his arm and in . . . in . . . in *other places* . . . looked upon the world together for the first time.

There wasn't time for a full-out shower; a naked sink-washing would have to suffice. Besides, he didn't even want to look in the tub and see the floating remnants of the scabs that heralded the start of this waking nightmare.

The last clean washcloth quickly turned pink as he scrubbed the blood from his body. Flakes of dry blood fell into the running water. He turned off the sink, let the washcloth fall to the floor, grabbed a towel and started drying off.

It was at that moment he noticed his shoulder.

Or rather he noticed the mold.

The mold was under the Band-Aids, green gossamer tufts peeking out past plastic edges. The fine little hairs looked like the last downy strands growing on an old man's head before baldness finally takes hold.

That's where the strange smell had been coming from: his shoulder. The musty, rotten scent filled the bathroom. The Band-Aids remained firmly affixed to his wound, but under the strip he saw something else, something black and wet and horrible.

The Band-Aids had to come off. He had to see what was in there. Perry used his fingernails to pull a small corner of Band-Aid off his skin, enough for him to get a good thumb-and-forefinger grip, then slowly tore it off.

The flap of skin peeled back; a gummy ribbon of stagnant black goo ran down his chest, hot at first, and ice cold by the time it had reached his stomach. The smell that had only hinted at its power during the past day was now released, a satanic genie billowing out of a bottle; it filled the bathroom like a cloud of death.

The dead stench instantly made Perry's stomach turn inside out—he spewed bile into the sink, where some of it mingled with the running water from the tap and headed down the drain. Perry stared at the wound, not even bothering to wipe the vomit from his mouth and chin.

There was more of the viscous muck packed in the wound, like black currant jelly at the bottom of a half-empty jar. The dead Triangle had rotted. Horror stole his breath and made his heart hammer a triple-time beat of desperation.

The consistency resembled a rotten pumpkin a month after Halloween—pasty, runny and decomposing. Green tufts of the same gossamer mold spotted both the wound and the dead Triangle. Shiny black rot clung to the mold filaments.

The most disturbing part of the image in the mirror? He wasn't sure if all the rot came from the dead Triangle's fork-punctured corpse. Some of the green mold looked as if it grew right out of his skin, like a creeping, crawling messenger of demise.

The sink's running hot water slowly clouded the mirror. In a daze, Perry wiped the steam clear—and found himself face-to-face with his father.

Jacob Dawsey looked haggard and gray. He had sunken eyes and thin, smiling lips that revealed his big teeth. He looked as he had in the hours before Captain Cancer finally stole him away.

Perry blinked, then fiercely rubbed his eyes, but when he opened them his father still stared back. Somewhere in his brain, Perry knew he was hallucinating, but it didn't make the experience any less real.

His father spoke.

'You always were a quitter, boy,' Jacob Dawsey said, his voice the same thick growl that always preceded a beating. 'You get a little boo-boo and now you want to give up? You make me sick.'

Perry felt hot tears well in his eyes. He blinked them back—hallucination or no, he wouldn't cry in front of his father.

'Go away, Daddy. You're dead.'

'Dead and still more of a man than you'll ever be, boy. Look at you—you want to give up, let 'em win, let 'em put you down.'

Perry felt anger surge. 'What the hell am I supposed to do? They're *inside* me, Daddy! They're eatin' me up from the inside!'

Jacob Dawsey grinned, his thin, emaciated face showing the teeth of a skeleton. 'You gonna let 'em do that to you, boy? You gonna let 'em win? Stop acting like a woman and do something about it.' The steam steadily clouded the mirror, slowly obscuring Jacob Dawsey's face. 'You hear me, boy? You *hear me*? You do somethin' about it!'

The mirror clouded over. Perry wiped at it, but now only his own face stared back. Daddy was right. Daddy had always been right; Perry had been a fool to try and escape what he was. In a violent world, only the strong survive.

Perry took a slow, deep breath, and prepared his mind for what he had to do.

Time to get his game-face on.

61

THE CALL (PART TWO)

Officer Ed McKinley turned left onto Washtenaw Avenue and headed east toward Ypsilanti. Traffic slowed all around the Ann Arbor police cruiser, just a touch, even for people who traveled at the speed limit. In the passenger seat, Officer Brian Vanderpine stared out the window, far more alert and attentive than usual.

'Eight dead,' Brian said. 'Man, that's a lot.'

'That's the tenth time you've said that, Brian,' Ed said. 'How about you give it a rest?'

'I just can't get over this. Shit like this doesn't happen in Ann Arbor.'

'Well it does now,' Ed said. 'I'm not surprised, really. We've got foreigners from all over the damn planet going to school here. And every last one of them thinks America is evil.'

'Yeah, we're evil, but they sure are happy to come here and get an education from us.'

Ed snorted. 'Yeah. I guess the schools aren't evil, just everything else about our culture. Funny how that works out so well for them.'

'I would love to find the bastard responsible for all this,' Brian said. 'You think the feds know what they're doing?'

Ed shrugged. 'I dunno. Something fishy is going on,

that's for sure. They show up exactly when this shit goes down. Not before. We get no warning, just a body count.'

The radio squawked: 'Car seventeen, come back.'

Brian grabbed the handset and thumbed the 'talk' button. 'Car seventeen here, go ahead.'

'How far are you from the Windywood apartment complex?'

'We're heading east on Washtenaw at Baldwin,' Brian answered. 'Only a couple of minutes away from Windywood. What's up?'

'Disturbing the peace. Complaint is from an Al Turner who lives in apartment B-303. Says the guy below him is screaming and has been for days. The screamer is listed as Perry Dawsey, apartment B-203.

Brian turned to look at Ed, a quizzical look on his face. 'Perry Dawsey. Why does that name sound familiar?'

'I wonder if that's the same kid that played linebacker for U of M a few years ago.'

Brian again thumbed the 'talk' button. 'Roger, Dispatch, we'll check it out.'

'Be advised,' the dispatcher said. 'Complainant says Dawsey is very large and potentially dangerous.'

'Roger that. Car seventeen out.' Brian hung up the handset.

Ed frowned. 'Very large and potentially dangerous? That sure sounds like the Perry Dawsey I saw play.'

Brian squinted against the bright winter sun. He remembered watching U of M's 'Scary' Perry Dawsey. 'Very large and dangerous' certainly fit the bill. It was just a disturbing-the-peace, but he didn't like the sound of this call, not one bit.

62

PLAY THROUGH THE PAIN

In through the nose, out through the mouth. One last, deep breath.

Focus.

Play through the pain.

Perry reached up with his right hand and sank his fingers deep into the wound. He didn't bother trying to control his screams of pain, he just hooked the fingers and scooped. Fingernails scraping hard against his open flesh, he yanked the Triangle's squishy black corpse out of his body. The tail offered only minute resistance before it broke off, weakened by rot that had turned the body into little more than paste. Perry tossed the handful of gore into the sink, where it landed in the trails of puke and steaming water.

He scooped twice more, screaming anew each time, grabbing everything he could out of the wound. Blood again poured down his chest, running down his crotch, down his inner thighs to form small puddles on the floor.

Pain filled his mind, rusty barbed wire wrapped tightly around his soft brain, but he knew he had to stop the bleeding. Stop it fast. He stared at the wound—it was now a fist-size hole, and quite a bit beyond the abilities of simple Band-Aids.

He scooped up the bloody washcloth from the floor

and hopped into the kitchen. He pressed the cloth to the wound, jamming it painfully into the hole, trying to stem the flow of blood. The duct tape was in the junk drawer, silver and big and ever so sticky. He had to let go of the wound so he could use both hands to tear off big strips of tape, which he stuck to the edge of the counter.

He again crammed the washcloth deep into the gaping, bleeding wound. He lashed a piece of tape on top of the cloth, then stuck it firmly to his back and chest. Repeating the process five more times, he had a duct-tape starburst with arms spreading out from the wound, over his shoulder, over his chest, down his chest and under his arm. Wasn't exactly the Mayo Clinic, but, as Daddy used to say, good enough for who it's for.

Bill's friends would be here any minute.

It was time to go.

He used a handful of paper towels to wipe the blood off his body as he hopped for the bedroom. He jammed clothes into the backpack. Two pairs of jeans, three T-shirts, a sweatshirt and all the clean underwear and socks he could find.

With one leg rendered nearly useless and his left shoulder screaming with pain every time he moved, he pulled on his jeans. Each second was an eternity of anxiety; he expected the door to crash inward, smashed open by one of those heavy door rammers you see on *Cops* when the police break into yet another slime pit of a house. The door rammer (on which some clever soul would stencil the witty words *knock-knock*) would be followed by goons in biowarfare suits, every inch of their bodies covered so they wouldn't come into contact with the Triangles. They'd be toting big-ass guns, and they'd have itchy trigger fingers.

He threw on a black Oakland Raiders sweatshirt and

struggled with socks and hiking boots, his ravaged leg making even this simple task difficult.

Perry wanted a weapon, anything he could get his hands on, something to let him go down fighting, go down like a Dawsey. In the kitchen, he tossed the whole knife rack, Chicken Scissors and all, into his backpack. He grabbed his keys and coat. He didn't even give a second glance at Bill, who still stared blankly at the carpet.

Bill, rudely enough, didn't bother to get up and see him out.

Perry left the apartment, his eyes scanning up and down the hall, looking for Soldiers. He saw no one. He realized he'd left the map inside, but he didn't need it—if he made it out of Ann Arbor alive, he knew exactly where he was going. He started to move down the hall, which was still bloody from his battle with Bill, when the Triangles spoke again.

And their words stunned him. It was the worst thing he'd heard yet.

A   h a t c h i n g   i S   coming.

63

HOWDY, NEIGHBOR (PART THREE)

A   h a t c h i n g   i s   coming!

Perry's mouth went dry. His face flushed with hot blood, he felt his very soul shrivel and blacken like an ant burned by a magnifying glass. Hatching. It was coming. He'd been right, it was like the caterpillar and the wasps—he'd served his purpose, and now it was time for their gruesome exit.

His big body began to shiver uncontrollably.

'You're hatching?'

N o t   u s ,

s o m e o n e   e l s e   i s   n e a r b y   nearby.

He felt a minor wave of relief combined with a trace of hope—not the hope that he had been saved, but the feeling that there was someone else, someone in the same predicament, someone *like* him who could *understand*.

Perry hopped toward the stairs that led to the outside door. He didn't notice his foot hit the blood-soaked carpet; subsequent hops left a string of footprints with wet red traces that echoed his boot's tread pattern.

It felt good to be dressed again. He'd felt scummy all covered in blood, in clothes that should have been incinerated rather than washed. He was dressed and getting out of the apartment that had held him prisoner for days.

His shoulder throbbed loudly where he'd scooped out the rotting Triangle. The jostling backpack straps pulled against the washcloth and the wound, but the duct tape held firm. It was going to be a bitch removing that 'bandage.' Maybe he'd be dead by then, and he wouldn't have to worry about it.

We're hungry.
Feed us feed us.

Perry ignored their words, concentrating instead on managing the stairs. He leaned heavily against the sturdy metal rail, cautiously taking one step at a time. It was amazing how much easier things were when you had two feet.

Feed us now.
Feed us now a hatching is coming.
A hatching!

'Just shut up. I don't have any food.'

He made it to the ground floor without incident. After days in the cramped apartment, it would be nice to be back outside again, no matter what the weather—it could be the burning pits of hell past that door, and he'd hop out whistling 'Singin' in the Rain.'

A wave of overflow panic hit him, a blindside tackle that had his adrenaline level soaring before he realized the fear wasn't his own.

'What is it? What's happening?'

Columbo is coming!
Columbo is coming!

The Soldiers. Perry hopped out the door into the winter wind and blinding sun. The temperature was only a smidgen above zero, but it was a beautiful day. He made it to his car and put the key in the lock when his eyes caught the lines and colors of a familiar vehicle; his mind exploded with warning.

About fifty yards away, an Ann Arbor police cruiser

pulled into the apartment's entryway and headed in his direction.

Perry hopped around the front of his car, which was tucked neatly under the carport's metal overhang. He wedged himself between the front bumper and the overhang, hiding from view.

The cruiser slowed and pulled up against the sidewalk directly in front of the main door to Perry's building. Perry's instincts screamed at him—the enemy was only fifteen feet away.

Two cops stepped out of the car, but didn't look in his direction. They popped their batons into their belts, then walked toward the building with that relaxed, confident cop attitude.

They entered his building, the dented metal door slowly swinging shut behind them. They were too late to save their little informant. They'd find the body within seconds, then they'd come looking for Perry, shooting all the way.

Brian Vanderpine was first up the stairs. His feet thudded on the steps, which suffered the full brunt of his 215 pounds. Ed McKinley followed without a sound; Ed was always lighter on his feet, despite the fact that he outweighed Brian by ten pounds.

They didn't need to say anything going up the stairs to the second floor. It was just a noise complaint, no big deal, but given the day's events every call had them on edge. Brian hoped Dawsey lived alone; he didn't really want to deal with a domestic dispute.

They were called to this apartment complex at least twice a week. Most of the time people didn't realize how thin the apartment walls were, and how noise carried. Usually the appearance of uniformed cops at the door embarrassed the hell out of them, and they shut up quite nicely.

Brian and Ed climbed the first half flight of six stairs and turned to head up the next six when Brian stopped so suddenly that Ed bumped into him. Brian was looking down. Ed automatically looked at the same spot.

Traces of red marked large footprints on the stairs.

Brian knelt next to one of the footprints. He gently touched the print—his fingers came away with dabs of red. He rolled it around his fingertips for a second, then looked up at Ed.

'It's blood,' Brian said. He'd known that it was blood even before he examined it; he knew the smell.

Brian stood. They both pulled their guns, then moved quietly up the steps, careful not to step on other red footprints. As they came up to the second floor, they saw the blood on the wall and the bright red puddles in the carpet. It was a lot of blood, probably from a severe wound.

Large blood streaks led right under the door to Apartment B-203. Someone who was bleeding badly had crawled—or been dragged—into that apartment.

They took positions on either side of the door, pulses rocketing, backs to the wall, guns pointed to the floor. Brian's mind worked feverishly. This blood was fresh, and there was enough to indicate the victim might even be bleeding to death. He had no doubt that the wound was caused by some kind of weapon. And if the victim was still in that apartment, he or she might be trapped in there with the assailant.

Adrenaline surged through Brian's system. He reached down with his right hand and knocked hard on the door.

'Police! Open up!'

No one answered. The hallway remained deathly quiet.

Brian knocked again, hitting the door harder. 'Police! Open this door!' Still no answer.

He spun out to stand in front of the door. Giving a quick look to Ed, who nodded agreement and readiness, Brian put all of his 215 pounds into a push-kick aimed just below the door's handle. The wood crunched, but the door held fast. He kicked it again, harder this time. The lock's bolt ripped from the wall with a splintering of wood. The door slammed open.

It suddenly occurred to Perry that his car was useless. The cops would be out of the apartment in seconds. They knew who he was; they would be looking for his car. Probably wouldn't make it fifty miles, but he also wouldn't make it far on foot.

The hatching is coming soon.

The hatching. Some poor bastard was at the end of the Triangle rope. What would it look like? How bad would the pain be?

The trip to Wahjamega would have to wait. He'd be lucky if he made it out of the parking lot, let alone all the way to Wahjamega. There was only one place he could go. Someone was close, someone who was also infected. That person would understand Perry's condition, understand what he had done with Bill, hide him from the cops who would be swarming all over this place in minutes.

'Can we watch the hatching?'

Yes, we should watch.
Yes, watch and
see, see.

'Where is it? Tell me where to go, quickly.'

c o m e   t h i s   way.

Perry froze. The other voice, the female voice. It was faint, but clear.

T u r n   around.

He put his hands over his ears, his face a childlike expression of pure fear. It was all too much, *too damn much,* but he couldn't panic now, not when the cops would be rushing out the apartment door in a matter of moments. He turned and found himself facing Building G.

h u r r y   h u r r y .   t h i s   w a y
t o   safety.

He didn't understand, didn't want to. All he wanted to do was get away from the cops. Perry launched himself forward at a dead run-hop, sprinting on the verge of losing his balance. He fell twice, hitting the snow-covered black-top, landing facedown both times before scrambling madly to his feet.

It took him fifteen seconds to reach Building G.

Brian Vanderpine and Ed McKinley would both remember every moment with total clarity. In their combined twenty-five years of police work (Brian's fourteen and Ed's eleven), they had never seen anything like the crazy shit in Apartment B-203.

The door slammed open. Despite Brian's desire to point the gun into the apartment, he kept it trained at the floor. Nothing moved. Brian stepped inside. He immediately saw the body on the couch, bloody hands nailed to the wall with steak knives in some horrible parody of the crucifixion.

Brian would check the body, of course, but he already

knew that the man was dead. He tore his gaze from the corpse—the perp might still be in the apartment. There was blood *everywhere*.

The smell hit him like a fist: the odor of sweat, of blood, of something horribly rotten and *wrong* in a way he couldn't immediately define.

Brian pointed his gun straight down the short hall that led to the bathroom and bedroom. He was suddenly grateful for the dozens of calls he'd made to this complex, calls that had made him familiar with these apartments, all of which had the same layout.

Ed swung around to the right, pointing his gun into the tiny excuse for a kitchen. 'Holy shit. Brian, look at this.'

Brian took a quick peek. Dried blood covered the kitchen floor, so much that in most places the white linoleum looked a dull shade of reddish-brown. Even the dining table was covered with dried blood.

Brian moved down the hall, Ed only a few steps behind him. The tiny hall closet hung open and empty except for one long coat, a gaudy Hawaiian shirt, and a large University of Michigan varsity jacket. That left only the bedroom and the bathroom.

That smell, that *wrong* smell, was stronger as they reached the closed bedroom door. Brian stood half-covered by the hall corner and waved Ed to check the bathroom, which was open. Ed was in and out in three seconds, shaking his head to signify it was empty. He mouthed the words *more blood*.

Brian knelt in front of the bedroom door. Ed stood behind him, a step back. They avoided standing close enough for one shotgun blast to take out both of them. Feeling his heart hammering in his chest and throat, Brian turned the handle and pushed the door open. Nothing. They quickly checked the closet and under the bed.

Ed spoke. 'Check the wounded man, Brian, I'm calling this in.' As Ed grabbed his handset and started talking to the dispatcher, Brian ran to the body. No pulse; the body was still warm. The man had just died, probably within the last hour.

The victim sat on the couch, head hanging down, arms outstretched, a steak knife pinning each hand to the wall. Blood covered the area, soaking the victim's leg and leaving huge red stains on the worn couch cushions. The victim's nose was a disaster, broken and ravaged. The face: swollen, cut, completely black-and-blue. Blood had spilled down the man's face and soaked his shirt.

Brian mentally pieced together the story, feeling his anger rise at the attack's savagery. The perp had attacked this victim in the hall, cut him (either with one of these knives or another weapon), then dragged him into the apartment and knifed him to the wall. The blows to the face either came in the hall or after his hands had been pinned.

Shit like this wasn't supposed to happen in Ann Arbor. Fuck, this shit wasn't supposed to happen *anywhere*.

Violence in a domestic dispute was almost always followed up with remorse. Many times the assailant would call the cops after he or she had done something to hurt a loved one. That wasn't the case here. Whoever had done this hadn't felt a damn shred of remorse—people who felt remorse didn't leave messages written on the wall in the blood of the dead victim.

It was the worst butchering Brian had ever seen, and it would remain the Number One Smash Hit throughout his career. Although he'd never forget a single horrible detail, it was the writing on the wall that forever symbolized the savage slaying.

Numerous bloody palm and fingerprints showed that the murderer had used his hands to smear a message above the victim's hanging head. A single word written in bloody three-foot-high letters that left still-wet snail trails of red running down the wall:

Discipline.

HOT PROSPECT

Margaret kicked open the swinging men's-room door. She leaned in and shouted urgently. 'Amos! Let's go, man! We've got another one!'

A toilet flushed. Amos lurched out of a stall, stumbling as he fought to pull up his pants. Margaret turned and sprinted down the hallway. Amos ran to keep up.

She skidded to a halt in front of the elevator. Clarence Otto held the doors open. She and Amos entered, the doors shut and Otto hit the button for the parking garage.

'How far is it from here?' Margaret asked.

Clarence pulled out a map and gave it a quick study. 'About ten minutes, give or take,' he said.

Margaret grabbed Clarence's strong arm, her face electric with urgency. 'What's the victim's condition? What are his symptoms?'

'I don't know that, ma'am. Dew is en route, backed up by two rapid-response teams in full biosuits. I believe it's an apartment complex.'

Margaret let go of his arm and tried to compose herself. 'Do you think we'll get this one alive?'

'I think so, ma'am,' Clarence said. 'Dew should already be there. The victim filled out a computer form. Instructions on that say to stay put and wait for help. I can't imagine anything going wrong at this point.'

THE GREAT ESCAPE

Perry shut the outside door behind him, took a quick look up the empty hallway, then glanced back through the window just in time to see one of the cops sprint out of Building B and jump into the police cruiser. The car's red and blue bubble lights flashed.

Perry grinned sadistically. 'Fuck you, coppers,' he whispered. 'You'll never take me alive.'

Maybe they hadn't known what to expect when they pulled up. They probably thought Bill would have Perry all hog-tied and ready for delivery. They'd underestimated Perry. He was sure they wouldn't do it again.

He turned and looked down the hallway of Building G. He felt something, something strange. A kind of buttery warmth in his chest, perhaps an oily feeling deep inside. It was unlike anything he'd ever felt before. Perry realized he'd felt that feeling coming on as he'd sprinted for Building G, but once inside, it grew stronger.

The hatching is coming, the hatching is coming.

The Triangles' rambling reminded Perry that his escape was only temporary. More cars were surely on the way. It was only a matter of time before the cops spotted him. He'd be shot down, of course, killed while 'trying to escape' whether he hopped his little ass off or lay down on the ground in front of twenty witnesses. It wouldn't matter; the Soldiers would either buy the witnesses' silence or make them disappear as well. He had to get inside—he had to find the other Triangle victim.

'Which way do we go, fellas?' They had been the ones, after all, who'd shown him the truth about the Soldiers, about Billy the Informant. They had been the ones to tell him that men in uniforms would come, and they were right. They had been the ones to warn him in time to escape the cops.

Go to the third floor.

Damn they learned fast. There was now almost no delay between their hearing a new concept, like directions, and their mastery of the terminology.

He hopped up the stairs. With each step the oily feeling in his chest grew a little bit stronger. By the time Perry reached the third floor, he felt the strange sensation in every fiber of his being.

He moved down the hall until his Triangles stopped him.

This is it.

Apartment G-304.

On the door was a little branch wreath, painted in soft pastels, with little wooden ducks holding a pink *Welcome* sign. Country art. Perry hated country art. He knocked. There was no answer. He knocked again, louder and faster.

Again no answer.

Perry leaned in so his mouth almost touched the door's edge. He spoke quietly, but loud enough to be heard on the other side. 'I'm not leaving. I know what you're going through. I know about the Triangles.'

The door opened a crack, snapping taut the chain lock. Perry heard a stereo softly playing Whitney Houston's version of 'I'm Every Woman.' A chubby face peered through, a face that might have been attractive had the woman had any sleep in the past four or five days. She looked angry, harried and scared all at the same time.

As soon as he saw the face, the oily sensation damn near overwhelmed him. Now he knew what it was—he somehow *sensed* the presence of another host. Before she even said a word, Perry knew she was infected.

'Who are you?' she asked.

He couldn't miss the tinge of hope in her voice, hope that this man had come to save her.

Perry spoke in a calm voice. 'I live in this complex. My name is Perry. Let me in so we can talk about what we're going to do.'

Through the crack of the door he could only see two inches of her face, but it was enough to show she wasn't convinced.

'Are you from the government? From . . . *CSI?*' Fear hung from her words. Perry felt his patience running thin.

'Look, lady, I'm in the same fucking boat you are— I've got the Triangles too, okay? Don't you feel it? Now open the door before someone sees us and calls the Soldiers.'

The last word struck home. Her eyes opened up wide as she took in a quick hiss of breath, and held it. She blinked twice, trying to decide if she should believe, then shut the door. Perry heard the chain slide free. The door opened, and she looked at him expectantly, hopefully.

Perry hopped in quickly, shoved her out of the way, then slammed the door shut and locked it (chain and deadbolt and even the shitty lock on the knob, thank you very much). He turned around with a light hop—and found himself staring at a huge butcher knife poised only a few inches from his chest.

He put his hands up lightly, at shoulder level, and leaned away from the blade until his back hit the door.

A mixture of emotions etched her brown eyes, anger and fear predominant above all else. If he said one wrong word he'd find that knife buried in his chest. She was a tall woman, about five-foot-seven, but fat pushed her weight to around 170 pounds. She wore a yellow house-coat with a green and blue flower pattern. It hung on her, like a hand-me-down four sizes too big. The Triangle Diet Plan had done wonders for her as well—she must have been at least 225 before she was infected. Fuzzy gray bunny slippers adorned her feet. Her blond hair, pulled back into a messy ponytail, looked out of place against her middle-aged face, a face that radiated fear and hopelessness.

He was much bigger than she was, but he wasn't taking any chances. One thing he'd learned on the playground early in life was that fat people were strong people. They didn't look it, but carrying all that extra weight made for powerful muscles that could be surprisingly quick at things like punching or grabbing—or stabbing.

'Jesus, lady, put the knife down.'

'How do I know you're not with the government? Let's see some ID.' Her voice quavered, as did the knife's point.

'Come on,' Perry said, his temper steadily creeping higher. 'If I was from the government, do you think they'd send me out with government ID? Use your head! Tell you what—let me roll up my sleeve, okay? I'll show you.'

He slowly dropped his backpack to the floor, wishing he'd left the top open so he could quickly grab his own kitchen cutlery. But if he tried for it, she might panic and stab him.

Perry pushed up his sleeve.

The wave of overflow excitement hit him like a severe drug rush.

That's her that's her.
She's going to hatch soon,
that's her.

'Oh my God.' Her voice was a hoarse whisper. 'Oh my God, you've got them, too.' The knife fell to the carpet.

Perry closed the distance with one short hop. He caught her with a big overhand left that slammed her cheekbone. Her head snapped down and back. She cried out a little as she fell to the floor. She lay sobbing and motionless on the pale yellow carpet.

Stop it now stop it
now Now NOW!

Perry winced at the pain from the mild mindscream. He had figured that would happen, but at least he'd gotten in a good lick first. You had to show women who was in charge, after all.

'Bitch, if you ever pull a knife on me again I'll carve your fat ass up.' The woman sobbed with pain, terror and frustration.

Perry knelt next to her. 'Do you understand me?'

She said nothing, her face hidden in her arms, fat shaking like a Jell-O mold.

Perry gently stroked her hair. She cringed at his touch. 'I'll only ask you one more time,' he said. 'If you don't answer, I'll put my boot in your ribs, you fat fuck.'

She looked up suddenly, tears streaming down her face. 'Yes!' she screamed. 'Yes, I understand you!'

She was yelling. It was as if she wanted to piss him off, was *trying* to piss him off. Women. Give 'em an inch and they take a mile. Her tear-streaked face reminded him of a glazed doughnut. No room in life for tears, woman, no room at all.

He continued to stroke her hair, but his voice took on an icy-cold quality. 'One more thing. If you raise your voice above conversational levels again, you're dead. And I mean there's no question about it. Cross the line with me again and I'll fuck you with that butcher knife of yours. Do you understand?'

She just stared at him with a pathetic look of disbelief and utter helplessness. Perry held no sympathy for her. She was weak, after all, and in a violent world only the strong survive.

Perry's voice bubbled with anger. He talked slowly, each word clearly defined. 'Do. You. Under. Stand.'

'Yes,' she whispered. 'I understand. Please don't hit me again.'

She looked so pitiful—blood trickling from her cheek, fear in her eyes, her face lined with tears. She looked like an abused woman.

Like his mother looked, after his father had finished with a 'lesson.'

Perry shook his head hard. What the hell was happening to him? What was he becoming? That answer was simple— he was becoming what he *had* to become to live. Only the strong survive. He stared at the woman, fighting to push his guilt down somewhere deep, somewhere he didn't have to deal with it. The Perry that had controlled his aggression for ten years . . . there was no more room for that person.

He wiped the tears from her face with a gentle touch.

'Now get your fat ass off the floor and make some food. Feed us, we're hungry.'

He felt excitement well up fresh and strong. The Triangles knew food was on the way; it made them happy. Very happy. The emotion was powerful, so powerful that Perry couldn't help but feel a little of their happiness himself.

66

OVERTIME

Dew stared out the Buick's window, watching the flurry of police activity outside, the big cellular phone pressed to his ear. By the looks of things, he'd arrived maybe ten minutes too late. *So close.* The missed opportunity made him boil inside.

'It's a really, really big SNAFU, Murray,' Dew said. 'Fucking locals are everywhere, and more on the way.' He could almost see Murray's face turning red.

'Did the rapid-response teams go in?' Murray asked. 'Why don't they just take over?'

'They didn't go in at all,' Drew said. 'They called me first and I waved them off. You think it's a bad situation now, try bringing in eight P90-toting goons wearing biosuits and watch the press jizz all over themselves.'

'Oh for God's sake,' Murray said, his voice tired and ragged. 'The press is already there?'

'Yeah. The local cops were first on the scene. Press picked it up on a scanner, maybe. We didn't have a chance at information control. The cops are keeping the media at a distance, but there's no way we can go in without being seen by at least three network news teams.'

The radio and TV stations had already been buzzing with news of Kiet Nguyen's murder spree and subsequent suicide. News didn't get any bigger than that, unless, of course, the cops mounted a manhunt for a former University of Michigan linebacker who'd left a mutilated corpse in his apartment. With those two murder stories flying, coverage of a gas explosion that had killed a mother and son had disappeared completely.

'Remember, the Dawsey kid was a major celebrity in this town,' Dew said. 'Bunch of fucking liberals here in the media, they're giddy to see a football player live up to billing as a creature of violence. This isn't D.C., Murray, this is Ann Arbor, Michigan. This is a long-haired, pot-smoking little college town. A fugitive killer football player is their story of the decade, and the *guv-ment* trying to cover it up is icing on their hippie cake.'

'Dew, considering the situation, do you see any way we can bring Dawsey in alive?'

'That's your call, L.T.,' Dew said. 'You have to appreciate just how many cops are looking for him. There's a dead body in his apartment—they're not just going to stop looking just because I tell them we're on the case. They want Dawsey, and they want him bad. If he's in any kind of advanced state of infection, the cops might see his growths. If they capture him, expect *someone* to get a camera on him and a boatload of reporters fighting to know why he killed a man. If he's arrested, and we can't get to him right away, the triangles might make national news before the night is out. If the reporters see triangles, that SARS bullshit won't cut it. Cops take Dawsey alive it blows this whole thing wide open.'

'What do you suggest?'

'I recommend we take him out ASAP,' Dew said. 'And we get the local cops in on the action. They're just looking for an excuse to pull the trigger. Maybe we connect Dawsey to Nguyen. I'll tell them Dawsey probably has an explosive vest, or a biowarfare agent, whatever. I'll make sure there are clear orders to shoot Dawsey on sight, but to stay away from his body until our crews can remove him.'

'Margaret needs a living victim.'

'So we get the next one,' Dew said. 'If you want to keep this secret, I told you what we need to do.'

Dew waited through a long pause. L.T. had a hell of a decision to make.

'No,' Murray said finally. 'She needs that kid alive. It's more important than secrecy. Whatever it takes, bring him in alive.'

'That's not going to be easy,' Dew said. 'The locals are really on edge.'

'Then we connect Dawsey to Nguyen. I'll take care of it from our end. We'll inform the local cops, you just validate the story.'

'What story?'

'That Dawsey has knowledge of a terrorist bomb, that he absolutely must be taken alive no matter what the cost. Bring him in alive, Top.'

Murray hung up. Dew ground his teeth. Murray's plan would work, and Dew knew it. The cops would do whatever it took to get Dawsey alive.

Dew alternated his time between looking out the window at the army of police and looking at digital photos of Dawsey that Murray's people had transferred to the big cell phone. One was Dawsey's most recent driver's-license photo. Another was a close-up from Nguyen's painting of the human arch—where the other faces writhed in terror and agony, Perry's scrunched in raw rage. Additional photos came from the kid's college football days.

Dew focused on one such picture, a typical preseason publicity shot from Dawsey's sophomore year.

'You are a big fucker, ain't you, kid?'

In the posed picture, late-summer sun blared down on his maize and blue uniform. Most times these shots showed a kid's best smile, but this one was different. Dawsey smiled, sure, but there was something else, something around the eyes that bespoke a savage intensity. It was almost as if Dawsey's very being vibrated aggression, as if he couldn't handle putting on the pads and *not* hitting something.

Maybe it was the pic, maybe it was the fact that he'd seen the kid play on TV. Dawsey had been a rare one, a veritable beast who dominated the game every time he set foot on the field. Kid played meaner than a bull with a cattle prod up his ass and a rat trap snapped on his nuts. It was a damn shame, really, the knee injury that ended Dawsey's career. Dew remembered seeing that on TV, too. Dew had watched men blown in half by land mines, men impaled with giant splinters from trees hit by artillery fire, men decapitated and twitching, rotten and bloated, yet there was something about watching the super-slow-mo replay of that kid's knee bending ninety degrees the wrong way that had made Dew's stomach almost rebel.

He stared hard at the picture, memorizing every detail of Dawsey's face. Big boy, sure, big and strong and mean and dangerous, sure, but that's why man invented guns. Fuck Murray's orders—being an All-American didn't make you Superman, and a bullet in the head would bring 'Scary' Perry Dawsey down just as it would anyone else.

Someone had to pay for Malcolm's death. Dawsey was as good a target as any.

67

THE COUCH DANCE

Perry sat on a pale yellow couch that looked brand-new, sinking back into the apartment's welcome shadows. He always found it strange to be in another Windywood apartment. With an identical floor plan but different furniture and decorations, it was as if his apartment had been taken over and redecorated with watercolor seascapes, matching curtains, lace doilies and enough country-art knickknacks to gag a camel.

He munched on a chicken sandwich, cautiously peeking between the slats of the venetian blinds. He'd lucked out with Fatty Patty's apartment; from her window he could see the flurry of activity in front of his building. Seven cop cars—five local and two from the state police—threw a visual cacophony of red and blue lights against the pitch-black night.

Observing the scene, he saw the reasons for his narrow escape. Fatty Patty had been watching out this window, and from this third-story perch she had seen the police cruiser a long way off. Her Triangles warned Perry, got him out of harm's way. It only made sense, really; they were protecting their own. Keeping Perry alive was vital— he was a walking incubator, after all, and if he died the Three Stooges probably died with him.

The cop cars' flashing lights created a disco effect on

the falling snow. It was well past midnight and there wasn't a star in the sky. If he was going to move, it would have to be later that night when the starless darkness covered everything and the soft snow swallowed every little sound with an insatiable hunger.

But he wasn't going anywhere until he saw Fatty Patty pop. He *had* to know how it happened. She sat on a yellow chair that matched the yellow couch, nibbling on a sandwich of her own. She cried silently, fat jiggling in time with the tiny sobs. She held a thrice-folded paper towel to a fresh cut on her forehead. Perry had told her not to cry out loud. She hadn't listened. He'd cut her; the noise had stopped. Like Daddy always said, sometimes you just had to show women who was in charge.

He noticed she'd used masking tape to hang a Michigan road map on the back of the front door. She'd scrawled a red line on U.S. 23 moving north away from Ann Arbor. The line turned west at 83, then followed a series of small roads until it hit the town of Wahjamega. Around the town she'd drawn several red circles and written the words *This is the place.*

Near Wahjamega, in neat ruler lines, she had drawn a symbol in red ink:

Perry looked at the design he'd cut into his right arm. The scabs were still fresh. Sure, his was a bit messy, but then again it's a tad harder to make straight lines with a kitchen knife, right? What did that symbol mean to the Triangles? Did the meaning even matter? No, it didn't—*nothing* really mattered anymore.

'They told you to go to Wahjamega, too, eh?' Perry asked. She nodded quietly. 'Do you have a car?' She nodded again, and he smiled. It would be easy; all he had to do was wait for the cops to clear out, then he and Fatty Patty could drive to Wahjamega. As for what waited there, he really didn't want to know, but he was going anyway.

This was his second chicken sandwich (with Miracle Whip, mind you, and with a side of Fritos, it really hit the spot). He'd already polished off lasagna leftovers, some chocolate cake, a can of Hormel chili, and a pair of Twinkies. His hunger was long gone, but the Triangles constantly urged him to eat. And eat he did.

Munching away on the sandwich, he felt surprisingly content. He wasn't sure how much of that enjoyment was his and how much was overflow from the Triangles; the things beamed with near-orgasmic pleasure at the steady flow of nutrients. The line between what *they* felt and what *he* felt was beginning to get a little fuzzy, like the way he now truly *wanted* to go to Wahjamega.

Have to watch out for that, Perry old boy. Can't fall into their little trap. Got to keep your own thoughts or you're as good as dead.

He decided to kill another Triangle as soon as he finished the sandwich. That would redefine their relationship. Nothing like a little self-mutilating demarcation to set things straight.

In front of his building, the Columbos scrambled

around like little ants. Perry reveled in his third-floor view. The drama below unfolded like a soundless, long-distance version of *Cops*.

The police had knocked on Fatty Patty's door. She'd given an award-winning performance. No, she hadn't heard anything. No, she hadn't seen a huge man wandering around the building. She was afraid of Perry, but thanks to her Triangles she was scared *shitless* of the cops. So she chose the lesser of two extreme evils.

He stared out the window, careful to stay in the shadows, and wondered if they knew he was watching. But that didn't make sense: if they knew where he was, they'd come after him.

Unless they were *already* watching him.

Perry's eyes narrowed. He flicked his gaze about the apartment. Could there be a secret camera in here somewhere? A bug? Were they listening to him? They'd been watching him in his apartment, of that he had no bout-a-doubt-it, so maybe they were set up to monitor Fatty Patty as well. If that was the case, his great escape was nothing more than jumping out of the fire and back into the frying pan.

And, come to think of it, how did he know for sure that she even had the Triangles at all? Maybe she didn't have any. Maybe this was a setup. Maybe she had some machine that told his Triangles that this was a safe haven. Maybe she was just there to keep an eye on him. Maybe they were combing through his apartment 'gathering data' while they knew damn fucking well that he sat up here with Fatty Patty, chewing away on a chicken sandwich and Fritos.

Perry's gaze nailed her to the yellow chair. She had that expression gazelles wear after being brought down by a lion, before the bite to the jugular, before the final coup de grâce. He set his plate down on the coffee table.

'Where are they?' Perry asked quietly.

'Wha . . . what?' New tears filled her eyes and rolled down her fat cheeks. Did she still think this was a game? He picked up his butcher knife and patted the flat of the ten-inch blade against his palm—each time the blade slapped lightly against his skin, she winced as if hit by a tiny electric shock.

'Don't fuck with me,' Perry whispered, smiling all the while, not because he liked this or because he was trying to scare her, but because he was in *control*. 'Where are they? Show me.'

Her chubby face changed as the words fell into place like the clicking tumblers of a lock.

'You mean my Triangles, right?' She rushed the words out with an incredibly servile tone. He felt a powerful stab of homesickness—the eagerness to placate, the desperate desire to avoid a beating; it reminded him of his mother.

His mother talking to his father.

'You know damn well that's what I'm talking about.'

'I'm not playing games, I swear.' She was terrified, he could see that as plain as day. Despite her tangible fear, she kept her voice low and controlled. That was good.

She stood up and pulled off her huge nightshirt. She did it quickly and without noise, but the expression on her reddening face revealed humiliation. Her tits hung pendulously—huge, round mountains with massive aureoles and nipples the size of a dime. She was still fat, yet her stretch-marked skin seemed far too big for her body. Perry revised his earlier estimate of 225 pounds— before the Triangles, Fatty Patty must have weighed 260 if she'd weighed an ounce.

She had the Triangles, all right, three on her stomach. Tears streamed down her face and leaped from her quivering chin to fall in bright sparkles on her tits. She turned to the left without being asked. He saw the Triangle on her left hip, its black eyes staring coldly back at him, blinking every few seconds.

It was a much deeper shade of blue than his. Something black and solid like thin rope stretched out from under each of the Triangle's sides, snaking under her flesh with one spreading farther around her hip.

Her skin didn't look healthy at all. Pus-oozing blisters marked the Triangles' edges. Above the Triangles' body, her skin showed signs of stretching, as if the creature had grown too large for the pliable tissue to contain. When he looked at his own Triangles, their eyes held a glassy, unfocused stare. The one on her hip was different. It stared back at him malevolently, the triple-blinking eyes conveying the universal emotion of hatred as clearly as the beam of a high-powered flashlight through a snowy winter night.

'Fork you, buddy,' Perry said quietly. When he made his move on Fatty Patty, he'd kill that one first.

'Lose the pants and spin,' Perry said. She didn't hesitate; she dropped the pajama bottoms and stepped out of them. She wasn't wearing panties. She spun slowly, revealing a Triangle on each ass cheek and one on the back of her right thigh. They all stared at him with an unmistakable hatred. He wondered what they were saying about him, what messages they were sending into her head.

It struck him as odd how healthy all her Triangles looked. The pus-oozing sores were her own, of course. It had never occurred to him that someone might not fight, that someone might just let it happen. The concept was pathetic, but apparently she'd done just that.

Daddy was right. Everything Daddy had ever said, it seemed, was right. Perry wondered in amazement how he could have ever thought different.

'You weak-ass bitch,' Perry said. 'You didn't try and do anything, did you? You just let them grow?'

She stood in front of him, naked, trembling with fear and humiliation, her hands unconsciously covering her pubic region.

'What was I supposed to do? Cut them out of me?'

Perry didn't answer. He set the knife on the coffee table, his stare a clear warning against any sudden movements. He pulled off his shirt. The duct tape had turned black around the edges, a little line of stickum nicely framing the silver straps that held the blood-soaked washcloth in place. He picked up the knife and slid the blade under the duct tape. The tape parted with only a small ripping noise. The knife danced as he repeated the process, severing each strip. The washcloth, thick with coagulated blood and the jellylike black goo, fell to the floor.

The smell hit both of them instantly—an invisible demon that climbed into their noses and down their throats, pulling at the contents of their guts. Her hands went to her mouth as Perry laughed. He breathed deeply of the noxious, rotting odor of death.

'I love the smell of Napalm in the morning,' Perry said. 'It smells like *victory*!'

Thin jets of vomit spewed from between her fingers, spraying across the room and landing on the couch as well as the end table and the carpet. The reek seemed to billow out of his shoulder like mustard gas.

Perry hoped it was just the remnants of the Triangle tail rotting into a putrid black ooze that produced the smell, not pieces and parts of himself. But in his heart he knew that was a pipe dream. Was the one on his ass rotting, too? The frayed, fibrous, unbreakable noose around his soul grew tighter and tighter—he couldn't leave them in, and he couldn't take them out.

Fatty Patty lay on the floor, convulsing and retching, making quite a stink of her own. He ignored her, instead staring out the window. Third story. It wasn't like twenty stories or anything definitely fatal, but it was nothing to sneeze at. Especially if you landed on your head. He tried to remember if there were bushes below. He'd heard stories about men surviving ten-story falls because they'd landed in some shrubbery. He hoped there were no bushes.

He moved closer to the window. It was dark outside; the light from the kitchen turned the window into a weak mirror. He could see himself through the venetian blind's slats. One good running start would take him clear through, carry him to the sidewalk below in a shower of jagged glass. Perry reached for the blind's cord and pulled down.

The slats lifted, and his wide-eyed reflection stared back at him from only two inches away. The mirror image made his brain ground to a halt—his eyes, they were still blue, but the irises weren't round.

They were triangular.

A half breath slid into his lungs, then his throat locked up. Bright blue, triangular eyes . . . what the fuck, what the *fuck*?

Perry closed his eyes tight. He was hallucinating, that was all. He rubbed hard with his fists, then opened his eyes again. The breath slid out of him, slowly, then back in, deeply. His irises were round again. No, not *again,* they had been round all the time; it had just been another hallucination, that's all. He blinked rapidly, feeling a semblance of control ease into his chest, then he shut his eyes again and gave them one more hard rub. He knew what he had to do. Time to jump, time to get this shit over with. He shook his head to clear it, then looked out the window—

—and found himself staring at a full-body reflection of his father. The skeleton-skinny man stared back, his gaunt face cracked by a smiling, angry expression. Perry remembered the look well; it was the look Daddy always wore just before the beatings began.

'What are you doing, boy?'

Perry blinked, shook his head, and looked again. His father was still there.

'Daddy?'

'I ain't your daddy, boy, and you ain't my son. No son of mine thinks of giving up. You giving up, boy?'

Perry searched for an answer but found none. Daddy was dead. This was a hallucination.

'Just because I'm dead doesn't mean you can't embarrass me, you little shit,' the reflection said. 'Did your daddy give up when Captain Cancer came calling?'

'No, sir,' Perry said. The ingrained response to his father's question came quickly, automatically.

'Goddamned right he didn't. I fought that sonofabitch to the bitter end. And do you know why, boy?'

Perry nodded. He knew the answer, and he drew strength from it. 'Because you're a Dawsey, Daddy.'

'Because I'm a Dawsey. I fought till I was nothing more than the walking bag of bones you see here. I *fought,* you little cocksucker. I was *tough.* I taught you how to be tough, son, I taught you well. What are you, boy?'

Perry's face hardened. The hopelessness vanished, replaced by angry determination. He might die, but he'd go out like a man.

'I'm a Dawsey,' Perry said.

In the window, the weak reflection of Daddy smiled his toothy smile.

Perry let go of the cord; the venetian blinds *zipped* closed, once again obscuring his reflection.

He turned and looked down at Fatty Patty, who was still coughing and gagging, rolling her naked roundness in her own vomit. Triangles looked up at him from her ass cheeks. He felt no pity for her, only disgust at her weakness. How could anyone be so pathetic as to just sit back and let this happen without even *trying* to fight?

'It's a violent world, princess,' Perry said. 'Only the strong survive.'

If she couldn't be bothered to fight for herself, Perry sure as hell wasn't going to do anything to save her. Besides, he wanted to watch the hatching. You can't win, after all, if you don't know your enemy.

She convulsed for the next five minutes, her jerky contortions flipping her onto her back. Perry wondered what might be wrong with her; the smell was overpowering, sure, but it couldn't make someone go into an epileptic seizure, could it? What was her problem?

The question seemed to answer itself. The Triangles on her stomach began to twitch and jitter under her flabby skin, as if she suffered muscle spasms. But he saw instantly that the twitching wasn't from her muscles.

The Triangles were moving on their own.

68

THE HATCHING

Perry sat on the couch, transfixed by Fatty Patty's ordeal. They are hatching! Hatching! Hatching!

The Triangles twitched under her skin, slowly picking up speed, jittering faster and faster. Her convulsions stopped suddenly; she rolled onto her back, fingers sticking into the air, locked like skeletal claws. Her face wrinkled in a wide-eyed blast of panic and a teeth-baring, breathless scream. It was a look of such utter, unbearable agony that Perry couldn't suppress a shudder.

And he was next.

He felt sick, as if a gnarled hand squeezed and twisted his intestines. It was a physical reaction to a mind pulled in opposite directions. On one side he felt hopelessness, far worse than anything he'd known since this ordeal began. He watched this fat woman writhe with terror, watched her face contort and scrunch as she tried to scream but couldn't find the air to do so. Her body shuddered in agony, making her flesh jiggle endlessly.

Despite this horror show, which held the promise of a painful death for him as well, he felt an impossible level of euphoria, a feeling that this was the beginning of something great and something wonderful. Joy and ecstasy ripped through his mind, better than any drug, vastly superior to sex—this was clearly an overflow emotion, but it was so strong, so clear, so vivid and so pure he was no longer able to separate it from his own. At that moment, the Triangle feelings saturated his very being.

He thought of killing her, slicing her throat with the butcher knife, ending her misery. But he couldn't bring himself to stand up, to reach for the blade, because he had to know what would happen. Besides—she was dying anyway, and wasn't a birth always a happy occasion?

A wave of fresh pain washed across her body, making her jerk like an electric-chair victim. She rolled a little from side to side, but mostly stayed on her back, that wide-eyed death stare fixed on some interesting detail of the stucco ceiling. Perry watched, surprised and disgusted, as she suddenly pissed all over the floor.

The Triangles picked up speed; they seemed to pulse as they sought to break free. Their large heads pushed out against her pliant, stretching skin, then sank back for another try. With each thrust, Perry saw the Triangles' outlines, saw that their bodies had grown to a shallow pyramid shape.

It reminded Perry of the good old days of Jiffy Pop on the kitchen stove, the swelling volume of popcorn slowly expanding the tinfoil covering. The Triangles weren't going to stop—they were clearly intent on popping out of her skin like a champagne cork, celebrating their new life in the new world.

Blisters burst one by one, coating her skin with thick, yellowish pus. Blood trickled from the edges of the Triangles, shooting out in thin jets each time they thrust outward.

They are hatching.
Is it beautiful? Let us see!
They are hatching. Hatching!

Perry ignored his own Triangles, his attention locked on those of Fatty Patty. Her Triangles thrust out farther, her skin started to tear. They pushed their way out like little turkey timers at Thanksgiving, the red pop-up button telling everyone when the big bird was done and it was time to eat. The three on her stomach were the worst to watch—they had started by only pushing up a quarter of an inch or so, a minor throbbing, a pulsating blister in her gut. Each throbbed up at a slightly different rate, now picking up steam, pushing out almost six inches in a quick jump, stretching the skin on her stomach like little triangular penises becoming erect and flaccid, erect and flaccid, erect and flaccid, spurting blood-threads in every direction.

He couldn't see the ones trapped underneath her wide ass, but he imagined they struggled, pinned by the weight of her body.

There were noises. Not just the pathetic little whines escaping the weak-willed woman, but faint clicking noises as well. They grew a bit louder every few seconds and seemed to coincide with the Triangles' outward thrusts. With each click he felt his happiness and euphoria spike upward like a heartbeat pulse on an EKG machine.

The one on her hip, the one that had stared so malevolently, so insolently, was the first to break free. It ripped out of her, not with a tearing sound but rather with a loud *splurt* followed by a *splat* as it hit the far wall, right where Perry's *Sports Illustrated* cover would have hung had they been in his apartment. The hateful creature stuck, wriggling and weak, temporarily trapped in its own slime.

It bore little resemblance to the Triangles that remained locked inside his own body. It still had the unmistakable Triangle head and the black eyes, but there any similarity ended. It looked no more like the larva lurking under his own skin than a butterfly looks like a caterpillar.

The black things he'd seen snaking under her skin were tentacles of some sort, more than a foot long, and thick. They looked very strong and solid. The Triangle shape had grown into a shallow three-inch-high pyramid, each side of which held one black eye. The eyes no longer stared up—now they looked *out,* so that if the thing walked on those tentacles, it would be able to see in all directions.

The creature's wriggling freed it from the wall. It fell to the carpet, where it struggled to right itself.

Perry's emotions flickered back and forth from fear and disgust to elation and indescribable joy, like a strobe light on a dance floor, leaving each alternating emotion a freeze-frame picture in his mind's eye. This shit could drive a guy crazy. Somewhere an emotion of his own called to him to get up and kill this thing, but he remained fixed on the couch, too overwhelmed to move.

The newly hatched Triangle attempted to stand on floppy tentacle legs. It looked very wrong and odd, because the legs had no rigidity. They weren't at all like an insect's skinny, multijointed legs or an animal's muscular limbs, but something new and different. With a shake and a continuing wobble, the creature rose up on the tentacles; once up, the pyramid point stood about a foot off the ground.

They will grow,
they will grow.

The tail that had anchored itself in Fatty Patty's body

dangled limply from the center of the Triangle, a weak limp-dick appearance, dripping blood and pale slime. It hung down to the floor, where the last inch or two lay unmoving on the carpet. The newly hatched creature stood there on unsure legs, its clicking noises loud and distinctive.

Fatty Patty let out a small scream as the three Triangles on her stomach broke loose almost simultaneously. They sprang out like vicious jack-in-the-boxes, streaming trails of blood and pus as they came down in different parts of the room.

One flew through the air and landed on the couch to Perry's left, as if it had just stopped by to watch the Lions game on a frosty fall Sunday afternoon. He got a much better look at this one. Its pus- and blood-covered skin was no longer blue but a pockmarked, translucent black. He could see strange, alien organs inside, something fluttering spastically that must have served as a heart, and some other colored bits of flesh, the purpose of which he wouldn't dare venture a guess. The end of the tail had landed on his leg—it moved a little, leaving a slime trail on Perry's jeans. The tail's end was ragged and torn, slowly leaking purple blood. That must be why they thrust so hard to escape her; they had to separate from the tail, most of which was left behind in Fatty Patty, an umbilical cord and safety cable they no longer needed now that they were free of her incubatory body.

The Triangle struggled to lift itself up, but one tentacle-leg slipped between the couch cushions. Perry gazed down at it with the strobe light of emotions still flashing at MTV-video speed. He felt a primitive urge to smash it, while simultaneously he felt compelled to gently lift the newborn from the couch, hold it adoringly, and set it on the floor to walk for the first time, beaming down at it with the proud smile of a new parent.

Turn her over,
turn her over.

The command yanked Perry from his maddening emotional conflict. 'What did you say?'

Turn her over.
They are hatching.

They wanted him to roll her over so the Triangles on each ass cheek could hatch properly. He looked at Patty's shuddering body, now covered with blood, pus, vomit and purple slime.

She had ceased all movement. Her eyes were glazed and fixed open, her eyebrows raised, and her face frozen in a sneer of terror. She looked almost dead. Caterpillar dead. All hosts probably died—it made much more sense than having the ex-host in a position to kill weak hatchlings. What had finally done her in? Some toxin? Screaming mental overload?

That thought crystallized Perry's emotions into two camps, polarized his hatred of the Triangles and the overflow euphoria at the hatching. He pushed back the happiness, the joy—those emotions weren't his, and he didn't want them in his head anymore.

Turn her OVER.
Turn her OVER NOW.

The mindscream slammed his attention back to the dead Fatty Patty, and suddenly he knew how they had killed her. He recognized the look on her face and the whimpering noises she made, realized why she'd just lain there as the things ripped free from her body, why she didn't put up a fight. It was because an all-out mindscream had paralyzed her.

They'd screamed so loud, it killed her.

Perry jumped off the couch and knelt next to her body, His knees slipped a little in the thin film of puke/blood/pus/purple that coated the carpet. He moved quickly; he didn't want another mindscream, one that night be bad enough to make his brains drip out his ears like a McDonald's Gray-Matter Shake.

Turn her over, they are hatching. They are hatching!

Perry put his hands on her shoulder and pushed, only to find that instead of rolling over she just slid across the muck. She was dead weight, pardon the pun.

Repetitive clicking noises filled the room. Some came fast, some slow; all had different pitches and volumes. He could *feel* his Triangles growing impatient; another mind-scream was rapidly approaching, the crack of the master's whip on the slave who can't perform. The power had changed hands once again.

He put his bad knee on her left shoulder and reached across her dead body. He grabbed high up on her right arm. He pulled back on the arm, slowly turning her. She *flumped* onto her stomach, her tits squishing out like half-inflated inner tubes.

Free from the weight, the Triangles on her ass wasted no time. They thrust only a few times before ripping free in a great gout of blood, an orgasmic finish to their necrophilic sex/birth. One flew out at an angle, hitting the kitchen table before falling to the floor. The other sailed upward in a steep arc, flying toward the lampshade. Like a LeBron James jumper swishing through the hoop, the Triangle slid through the lampshade's open top. It hit the illuminated bulb, first with a sudden sizzle, then a loud *crack* as the tiny body exploded. Black goo splattered against the inside of the lampshade, a wet silhouette as it slowly dripped toward the floor.

Thanks for saving me the trouble, Perry thought.

A wave of anger and depression crashed over him, overflow emotions again, fighting for mental space with his own feelings of villainous satisfaction at the newborn Triangle's untimely death.

What happened?
Where did he go?
Why doesn't he answer?

His Triangles still couldn't see, he remembered, because he remained fully dressed. They only *sensed* that the newborn was gone. He felt their random anger coursing through his body—he had to choose his words carefully.

He slid up his sweatshirt sleeve and held it up to the lamp.

'He hatched right onto a lightbulb. It was an accident.' In his voice he heard that servile tone, the tone of Fatty Patty trying to placate him, the tone of his mother trying to avoid a beating. 'It fried him on the spot.'

His answer appeared to satisfy the Triangles. They said no more. The steady clicking slowed considerably. The baby Triangles were crouched down on their tentacles, resting their pyramid bodies against the carpet. Their eyes closed, they stopped moving—they appeared to be asleep. Only an occasional click escaped their still bodies.

The strange aroma of burned Triangle flesh filled the room, slightly overpowering the odors of Perry's own rotting shoulder, the vomit and the smells of birthing that floated in the still apartment air. He felt his own Triangles fall asleep—their constant mental buzzing slowly fading away into near nothingness, like a barely audible car radio tuned to AM static.

He was alone, left to gaze upon the facedown, dead Fatty Patty. He knew he didn't have much time. In addition to the three Triangles in his own body, he had five hatchlings to deal with, creatures that he knew nothing about. How long would they sleep? What would they do when they awoke?

Apart from the questions that raged through his mind, he knew one thing for certain—he wasn't going to end up like the weakling lying on the living-room floor, giant fist-size holes left in her corpse. If he had to die, it wouldn't be like a victim, waiting nicely for the Three Stooges to rip out of his rotting body.

If he was going out, it would be on his feet, fighting every step of the way—like a Dawsey. His shoulder throbbed, his back itched and his mind spun feverishly, thinking of a way to kill them all.

69

FLASHBACK

On Dew's twenty-second birthday, he'd been getting piss-faced drunk at a small bar in Saigon with his three closest friends, all members of his platoon. The bar had white walls, Christmas lights across the ceiling and plenty of working girls. Hell of a party that turned out to be. Dew had stumbled to the bathroom to take a piss, and in midstream heard a bone-thumping explosion followed by a scream or two. He wasn't *quite* sobered up by the blast, but what he saw when he came out of the bathroom obliterated his buzz completely.

The white walls were streaked with chunks of bone, bits of hair and bright-red trails slowly dripping down the wall like living Rorschach blots. The blood and bits belonged to his buddies and the seven-year-old suicide girl who'd entered the bar wearing the latest fashion in homemade explosive backpacks.

That incident, that hated memory, was the first thing to enter his mind when he walked into Perry Dawsey's apartment. So much blood—on the walls, on the floor, on the furniture. The kitchen floor looked like a pattern of brown and red rather than the original white. There was even blood on the kitchen table, some of which had slowly spilled over the edge and dried in a thin, brittle-brown stalactite. The apartment crawled with Ann Arbor cops, state troopers and men from the Washtenaw County coroner's office.

'It's really something, huh?'

Dew looked at Matt Mitchell, the local coroner who'd escorted him to the crime scene. Mitchell had a crooked smile and a glass eye that never seemed to look the right way. His face held a small smirk, almost an expectant look, as if he were waiting to see if the gore would make Dew blow chow.

Dew nodded toward the body. 'You got an ID on the couch-potato Jesus over there?'

'Couch-potato Jesus?' Mitchell looked at the body, smiled, then looked back to Dew. 'Hey, that's pretty frickin' funny.'

'Thanks,' Dew said. 'I've got a million of 'em.'

Mitchell flipped through a small notepad. 'The victim is William Miller, a coworker of Dawsey's and apparently a friend—they went to college together.'

'Isn't this an awful lot of blood to come from one victim?'

Mitchell gave Dew another quizzical look, but this time it held a bit of surprised respect. 'That's pretty observant, Agent Phillips. Not many people would have noticed that. You seen stuff this intense before?'

'Oh, maybe once or twice.'

'We're still typing all the spills. There's more in the bathroom and even some in the bedroom. I'll tell you right now it's not all from the victim. You hit that nail right on the head.'

Mitchell walked into the kitchen, being careful not to disturb the cluster of evidence for technicians gathering samples from the floor and the table. 'I think there's another victim we haven't seen yet,' he said.

'Another victim? You mean Dawsey had another victim and he took the body with him?'

Mitchell gave the apartment a sweeping gesture. 'How else could you explain all this?'

'Ever think it might have come from Dawsey himself?'

Mitchell laughed. 'Yeah, right, from the perp himself. I'd like to see someone lose this much blood and keep on kicking.'

'Find anything else?'

Mitchell nodded and pointed to the kitchen counter. An evidence bag held a wrongly folded map. 'Maybe something, maybe nothing. That map was on the kitchen counter. There were some tacky, bloody fingerprints, not dry yet, so he was looking at it not very long ago. He'd circled Wahjamega.'

'That a town?' Dew asked as he picked up the evidence bag holding the map. The bloody fingerprints were still wet enough to smear the plastic. The words *This is the place* were scrawled on the map in handwriting so bad it was barely legible.

'Yeah,' Mitchell said. 'About, oh, ninety minutes or so from here.'

'You notify Wahjamega police to be on the lookout?'

'They don't have any—town is too small—but we let the Tuscola County Sheriff's department know, yeah. Hell, every cop in the state is on the lookout anyway.'

Dew nodded approvingly. Maybe something, maybe nothing, as Mitchell had said. Dew leaned more toward the 'something' side—it didn't take a genius to figure out Dawsey hadn't circled Wahjamega on a whim. The map didn't show much in the way of civilization around the town. In fact, it looked like there might be a shitload of trees.

Trees.

Deep woods, even.

As soon as he got out of this apartment, he'd have Murray's boys focus the satellite coverage on Wahjamega instead of Ann Arbor.

The brown-polyester-wearing Bob Zimmer wove through the crowded apartment, dodging the photographer and another cop before stopping in front of Dew and Mitchell.

'This just gets better and better, Phillips,' Zimmer said. 'I just talked to the governor. Again. FBI says Dawsey and the Vietnamese kid were working together—they found a bunch of emails. Homeland Security raised the alert level to fucking red, to "severe." Dawsey has knowledge of a bomb.'

Dew nodded. 'I told you someone else might be involved in those murders. We figure it was Dawsey.'

'To think there's a cell right here in our midst,' Zimmer said. 'And why didn't someone bother to pick up a fucking phone and let us know there's terrorists in town?' His eyes showed doubt, as if his bullshit meter was going off, but they also showed he'd follow through. Bullshit or no bullshit, Bob Zimmer wasn't taking any chances with the safety of his men or his town.

'Nguyen was what we call a sleeper, Bob,' Dew said. 'He's just another foreign college student. He stays quiet until he's needed, then boom. Only we don't think he's operating under directions, we think he just snapped. Somewhere along the line, he or his buddies recruited Dawsey.'

'Why the hell would a white-collar American fall in with terrorists?' Mitchell asked.

'We don't know yet,' Dew said. 'Maybe he was bitter at "the man" because he worked some shit computer job and didn't pull in millions in the NFL. It doesn't fucking matter. Dawsey might know about a bomb—we don't know where it is, we don't know what it is. We have to get to him and fast.'

Zimmer stared at Dew. 'I'll tell you right now, I don't like this,' he said. 'We've got nine people dead, at least one killer is on the loose, and there's a goddamn bomb out there somewhere. I can't help but think we could have prevented this if you'd let us know you were watching this Vietnamese kid.'

'We had to see who would contact him, who would supply him,' Dew said. 'It was a sting, Bob, but it went bust. The key thing to remember is we don't want anyone else getting killed. And if you want to save lives, just make sure your men know exactly what they're dealing with. Now, if you'll excuse me, I have to go make some calls.' Dew walked out of the blood-splattered apartment, leaving Bob Zimmer to grind his teeth in frustration.

70

DEAR OLD DAD

His shoulder pulsed with a deep, steady, low-frequency throb. His ass echoed the beat. This internal-rotting thing was getting serious.

He had no idea how close his own Triangles were to hatching. The areas where he still had them—middle of his back just below the shoulder blades, left forearm, his left testicle—had stopped itching or hurting. A brief glimmer of hope flashed in his head that they might be dead, that they had just passed on in their sleep like some beloved grandpa. But that was bullshit.

He'd rather have the itching back than what he felt right now. The spots felt numb. Completely numb. Something in his mind flashed 'localized anesthetic.' He wondered if they were doing so much damage that the pain would have incapacitated him, shut him down, so they had to block the pain, letting him continue normally, letting him pursue those all-important duties of *eating,* of *avoiding the Soldiers.*

He shuddered, remembering the black tentacles snaking underneath Fatty Patty's skin minutes before the hatching. She hadn't looked as if she were in pain or any discomfort at all. Perhaps she'd felt this same numbness. Perhaps she'd been numb for days. The real problem was he had no concept of the timetable.

When his slumbering Triangles awoke, how long before they started screaming in his head? How long before their final death-song?

He didn't have the luxury of waiting. He had to assume that when they awoke, he'd lose his last chance to purge them from his body. On top of that, the Columbos were outside, and it would only be a matter of time before they figured out where he was. Dawn was about to break. They'd see him when he made a run for it. They probably had bugs in every apartment anyway, listening, doing their Big Brother gig. Spy satellites could be searching for him right now, X-ray vision peering through the walls and ceiling, seeking him out.

'I don't know if you can hear me, Daddy, but I know you're right,' Perry said. 'Time to shit or get off the pot. Time to show them who's the strong one—time to show them all.'

71

CHEAP BUZZ

Her bathroom layout was identical to his, but there the similarity ended. Hers was decorated in seashell colors, everything matching perfectly, from the pale yellow towels to the porcelain clamshell soap dish. Every surface sparkled.

It wasn't until Perry swallowed six Tylenol from a bottle he found in the immaculate medicine cabinet that it clicked. The pills slid down his throat, and it all fell into place.

At times the Triangles had acted weird, showing emotions instead of talking in their monotone robotic voice. Not just when they were mindscreaming incoherently, but when they were talking to him in a singsong voice, a lilting mental speech that sounded almost silly compared to their normal businesslike vocal patterns.

They acted like that right after he took Tylenol. And *silly* wasn't the right word for it—the right word was *stoned*. Stoned out of their collective little gourds. Something in the Tylenol got them higher than a kite. He'd accidentally discovered a weapon to wield in the final battle.

Perry smiled.

'Put on a good buzz, boys,' he said, then swallowed back six more Tylenol. 'You're going to need it where you're going.'

The Tylenol-buzz was the final piece in his puzzle to

outsmart them all: the Triangles, the hatchlings, the Columbos . . . everybody. Perry would show them who was King Crap. No bout-a-doubt-it.

He had a *plan*, kiddies, a big-brained plan that would expose the stupidity of his conspiring enemies.

Be a hot time in the old town tonight. Don't fuck with a Dawsey.

He quietly hopped back into the living room. The hatchlings were still asleep, their slumbering clicks punctuating the silence of the apartment.

Perry hummed a tune, the words rolling through his mind.

Burn, burn, yes ya gonna burn.

72

TOP

Dew's vision felt fuzzy. He pulled off his leather gloves and rubbed his eyes. The cold clung to his clammy fingers. His breath streaming out in billowing cones, Dew put the gloves back on and refocused his attention on the apartment complex's snow-covered roads.

The cops hadn't found a damn thing during the night—the giant-size All-American psychopath was still running around like a rolling land mine waiting to bump into something and explode. Not a word from Wahjamega, either. Murray had dispatched several agents to the town. There were extra state police patrolling the area, the local police force was alerted to the danger, and NSA signal-intelligence agents scanned almost every line of communication in and out of the town. That, and the fact that Perry's face was plastered on every TV screen in the Great Lakes area, made it unlikely he'd slipped into Wahjamega unnoticed. The public was alert and looking; at least in the Great Lakes region, the hunt for Perry Dawsey had already taken on the mythical proportions of the O.J. Simpson chase. Another murdering football player on the lam.

The murder was about seven hours old—if Dawsey had fled, he could already be in Indiana, Chicago, Fort Wayne or on the Ohio Turnpike heading for the East

Coast, but Dew knew that Dawsey hadn't gotten far. Let the public think what they want, let them get the man's description and keep a sharp eye out. Dawsey might surprise them all, you never knew, and if Dawsey *was* heading somewhere, it was better that Joe Public knew enough to steer clear.

Dawsey's Ford remained safely under the carport's snow-covered metal awning. No cars had been reported stolen in Ann Arbor for two days—no motorcycles, mopeds or even a freaking ten-speed, for that matter.

So Dawsey probably hadn't driven anywhere, and on top of that it looked as if something was wrong with his right leg. Brian Vanderpine, the Ann Arbor cop who'd discovered the murder scene, was the first to notice Dawsey's bloody footprints in the apartment hallway. Despite the fact that blood was splattered all over the hall, Vanderpine only found prints made by a left foot. They hadn't found any marks that might have been left by a crutch, so Vanderpine ventured the hypothesis that Dawsey was hopping.

So now you had a man—a huge man—without a car or any means of transportation, committing what amounted to a spontaneous murder, leaving in a hurry, probably without the time to plan anything or the forethought to call a cab (they'd checked, and no taxi had picked up a fare anywhere near the area that day), and he was hopping all the way. That was the key—people would remember if they saw someone hopping, and no one had reported any such person despite the ubiquitous news coverage.

All of these elements led Dew to one conclusion: Dawsey probably hadn't left the apartment complex at all. Most everybody figured he was long gone, but they based their decisions on fabricated info saying Dawsey had terrorist connections that could help him fade into the woodwork.

The army of cops had checked inside every apartment in Building B, so he wasn't there, but how far could he have gone? There were seventeen buildings in the complex, with twelve apartments in each building, four apartments each on three floors. An army of cops had knocked on every door in the entire complex, asking if anyone had seen or heard anything strange. No one had. But not all the apartments were occupied. Some people were at work, some were just gone. There hadn't been time for a background check on every apartment owner to find out if each one was supposed to be home or not. No signs of forced entry—Dawsey hadn't broken in anywhere.

But that didn't mean Dawsey wasn't *in* one of those apartments. Maybe with a hostage. Maybe forcing someone to say that everything was fine.

Dew stuck with his instincts. If Dawsey had blood on his feet, he might also have it elsewhere on his person. The obvious bloody footprints had led out to Dawsey's car, but each print held less and less blood, and at the car the last of it appeared to have worn off his boot. A man wounded, hopping, moving fast . . . he might fall, and if he did, that hypothetical additional blood might leave a mark in the snow.

So Dew had walked a circle around Building B. He'd found nothing, so he'd walked around again, staring at the ground the whole time. He walked back to Dawsey's car; disturbed snow in front of the hood indicated that someone, probably Dawsey, had stood there not too long before.

All the footprints in front of the car were from a left

foot. You had to look very closely to see that detail, but once he saw it, he couldn't *un*see it. Dawsey, crippled leg and all, had stood right there. Hell, he'd probably watched Vanderpine enter his apartment building.

Dew squatted in front of the car. His cold knees throbbed at the effort.

The CIA's lead agent has arthritis, he mused. *There's something you don't see in the movies.*

Crouched in front of the beat-up, rust-speckled Ford, Dew looked at the door to Building B. He felt an unexpected surge of adrenaline—Dawsey had been in this same spot. Dawsey *had* watched the two cops enter the building, watched the door shut behind them, and then he . . . he did what?

Dew looked around his position, trying to see the terrain through the eyes of an infected man. On his left was Washtenaw Avenue, the main road that shuttled traffic between upscale Ann Arbor and low-rent Ypsilanti. It was full of ever-present thirty-five-mile-per-hour traffic. If he'd gone that way, *someone* would have noticed the hopping man.

Dawsey wouldn't have wanted that. Too much noise, too many people. Dew looked to his right, down the apartment complex's road. There were more apartments. A shitload more apartments. Almost no traffic, curtains and shades all drawn against the winter cold, nobody looking, nobody walking. *That's* what Dawsey wanted. It was quiet, it looked full of hiding places—bushes, shrubs. The cop army had searched all of those hiding places and found nothing, not even a footprint or snow knocked off a bush branch.

But it was the dead of winter—why hide in a snow-covered bush when you could hide in a nice warm apartment? That's what Dawsey had seen. He had just committed a brutal murder, then watched two cops enter his building. Dew reminded himself of the raging paranoia exhibited by all the victims. Dawsey had watched the cops go in, known they were coming for him, known they'd find the body. He'd wanted to find a hiding place and find one fast.

Dew came out from the hiding spot, grunting as he stood, his knees complaining against the unkind treatment. He walked toward Building G. Despite the fact that his pulse raced like a high-octane engine, he moved with deliberate slowness, examining the ground with a renewed focus.

73

BURN, BURN, YES YA GONNA BURN

The one on his back was going to be the toughest. Perry had explored Fatty Patty's cabinets and found a cigarette lighter, two bottles of wine, three bottles of Bacardi 151, and half a fifth of Jack Daniel's. He'd already knocked back a whole bottle of wine; a buzz rolled thickly through his head. It wasn't a Wild Turkey buzz, but he'd chugged the entire bottle, so the real kick was probably still brewing in his gut.

Three left: his back, his left forearm, and his balls.

For what he was about to try, he wanted to be very, very drunk.

There was no clever way to remove the Triangles, and the risk seemed greater than ever. The Triangle on his forearm might be close to the artery. The one on his back was right over his backbone—its barbed tail could be wrapped around his vertebrae. Pulling that one out might injure or even sever his spinal cord. The one on his nuts, the one he'd managed to not think about for days . . . well, he'd just have to get a lot drunker first.

He wasn't certain he could pull any of them out, but he could kill them where they grew. They'd rot, sure, but if his plan worked, he would dial 911 and head straight for an emergency room. Let the doctors figure it out. The Soldiers wanted to whack him and stop the Triangles from hatching; maybe if there were no more Triangles, the Soldiers wouldn't kill him. Maybe maybe maybe. They might kill him anyway, but they might keep him alive so they could interrogate him. Even if they took him prisoner so they could probe his mind with their secret machines and TVs that could read thoughts, he'd still be *alive*.

And, most important of all, he would have *killed* those *motherfucking* Triangles. Then, even if the Soldiers brought him down, no one could ever doubt that he died like a Dawsey.

He wasn't going out as a human incubator. He wouldn't let them win. A painful fever seemed to grip his muscles. His joints ached with the dull kick of a bass drum. The rot. The rot from his shoulder, his ass, spreading to other parts. He could fight the Triangles, maybe, but how could he fight black bile rot flowing through his blood?

The gig was up. Time to shit or get off the pot.

The sleeping hatchlings filled the apartment with clicks and pops. A Garth Brooks song filtered faintly through the floor from the apartment below. In his own mind, all was quiet, not a peep from his own Triangles.

Perry stuffed the lighter into his front pocket, grabbed the liquor bottles and his butcher's block that held his knives *and* his Chicken Scissors. He hopped clumsily for the bathroom.

Burn, burn, yes ya gonna burn.

74

THE FED

Dew knelt, staring at the spot in the snow. He thought he'd imagined it at first, the frenzied creation of a tired mind and tired eyes. As he stooped down to look closer, he knew it was real.

A tiny, dark pink streak on the pavement's thin snow. It was small, only about a half inch long and less than an eighth of an inch wide. Wisps of fine powder almost covered the mark.

Dawsey had fallen, right here. Dew looked back to Dawsey's car; if you drew a straight line from the rusty Ford through the blood spot, that line pointed directly to the door of Building G.

Dew stood and moved toward the door, pulse racing, adrenaline pumping. He kept his eyes fixed on the ground, looking for another blood spot, just to be sure.

His sleepiness vanished, possibly from the thrill of the hunt, or more likely from a well-honed instinct for self-preservation.

It was party time.

The first real action since Martin Brewbaker, the infected psycho who'd killed his partner. Brewbaker hadn't been a big man, nor had he been an athlete, but he'd proved something Dew had known since he'd been eighteen—being a killer isn't about being strong or fast or well trained, it's about being the first to pull the trigger, it's about attacking before the other guy is ready, it's about the willingness to go for the throat right off the bat. The growths had made Martin Brewbaker that kind of man. Dawsey had those same growths, but Dawsey *was* a big man, he *was* an athlete, and he was violent and vicious even before he was ever infected.

Dew felt a flash of déjà vu, the sense that he was again entering Martin Brewbaker's house, walking down the hall just before the crazy fuck lit the place on fire and buried a hatchet in Malcolm's guts. The old Sinatra tune rang in his head.

I've got you . . . under my skin.

75

BACARDI 151

Perry shut the bathroom door behind him and spread his goodies out on the sink counter.

Bottle of Jack Daniel's: check.

Two bottles of Bacardi 151: check.

Butcher's block with knives and Chicken Scissors: check.

Lighter: check.

Towels: check.

Fatigue clutched at his body. He started the tub and flipped the lever on the stopper, allowing the basin to fill up with cold water.

He stripped down, taking off everything but his socks and his underwear. He grabbed the longest towel he could find, twisted it into a rope, then poured some Bacardi on it. It soaked into the terry cloth, filling the small bathroom with the strong smell of rum. He flipped the long towel over his back, feeling the cold, wet, rum-soaked spot send chills up his spine. He positioned that cold spot right over the Triangle. One end of the towel went over his left shoulder, the other under his right arm. He tied the ends together, making the towel hang like a bandito's bullet strap.

Sí, señor. El Scary Perry is a baaad man.

He soaked the end of a smaller hand towel with Bacardi,

then laid it on the toilet. With the preparation finished, he took four long, uninterrupted swallows of Jack Daniel's.

Perry sat on the tub, the cold porcelain sending another wave of chills through his body. He held the knife and the lighter with his left hand. In his right he held the rum-soaked towel.

It was time.

Burn, burn, yes ya gonna burn.

Perry flicked the lighter. He watched the tiny orange flame shift and turn.

Yes, ya gonna burn.

76

CLOSING IN

Dew stood just inside the front door to Building G. He shivered slightly, but not from the winter's cold. Like every other building in the sprawling complex, Building G had twelve apartments, four each on three floors.

Perry Dawsey, the one-legged killer, was in one of those apartments.

Dew pulled his notebook from a jacket pocket. He quietly flipped through the pages, eyes looking down at the book one second, flicking back to look up the stairs and down the hall the next. He half expected to see the hulking nutcase tearing down the hall or the stairs, hopping madly, ready to do an encore presentation of the Bill Miller Crucifixion.

Dew reviewed the notes he'd collected from the cops. Building G had been checked by a pair of state troopers. There had been no answer at apartments 104 and 202. Dew put the pad back into his coat pocket, hand brushing against the .45 just to make sure it was there. If his hunch was right, he had a chance to kill Dawsey and do it with no press, no interference from the local cops.

Going in alone was dangerous, probably stupid. But Dawsey probably had a hostage right now. If the rapid-response teams closed too quickly and Dawsey saw them, he might drag that hostage out into the open where the cops could intervene. That would complicate things.

Dew pulled out the big cellular and dialed. It rang only once—they were waiting for his call.

'Otto here.'

'Get the squads in position,' Dew whispered. 'I'm in Building G. Do not—I repeat, *do not*—approach until I say so. I'll stay on the line. If the connection is cut off, move in immediately, understand?'

'Yes sir. Margaret and Amos are with me. They're ready.'

Dew pulled his .45. Adrenaline surged through his veins. His pulse raced so fast he wondered if a heart attack would take him down before Dawsey could.

77

CONJECTURES

Racal suits were not built with comfort in mind. Margaret Montoya sat in the back of gray van number two, along with Amos and Clarence Otto. Both men also wore the bulky suits. All they had to do was put on the helmets, pressurize and they were ready to battle with whatever bacterium, virus or airborne poison Perry Dawsey might spew forth.

Only Margaret knew it wasn't a bacterium, and it wasn't a virus. It was something different altogether. Something . . . *new*. She still couldn't put her finger on it, and it was damn near driving her mad.

'So this couldn't be natural,' Margaret said. 'We'd have seen it somewhere.'

Amos sighed and rubbed his eyes. 'Margaret, we've had this conversation already. Several times.'

He sounded exasperated, and she couldn't blame him—scientific curiosity or no, her mouth had run nonstop for hours. There was an answer here, if she could only get a handle on it, somehow talk it out.

'We don't know it hasn't been seen before,' Amos said. 'Just because it hasn't been recorded, that doesn't mean it's not known somewhere in the world.'

'Maybe that holds true with a regular disease, something that makes people sick. One sickness is much like the next.

But this is different. These are triangles under people's skin—there would have been *something*. A myth, a legend, *something.*'

'You obviously don't think it's natural,' Otto said. 'So you agree with Murray? That it's a weapon?'

'I don't know about a weapon, but it's not natural. Someone made this.'

'And leaped *decades* ahead of any known level of biotech,' Amos said patiently. 'This isn't cobbling together a virus. This is creating a brand-new species, genetic engineering at a level that people haven't even theorized yet. The meshing of new organic systems to human systems is perfect, seamless. That would take years of experimentation.'

'But what if it's not designed to build those systems, the nerves and the veins?'

'Of course it's designed to do it,' Amos said. 'It built them, right?'

Margaret felt a spike of excitement, a brief flicker of insight. There was something here, something she couldn't put her finger on.

'Yes, it built the nerves and vein siphons, but we don't know if it was designed to build *those* specifically.'

Otto shook his head. 'I just don't follow.'

'Blueprints,' Margaret said. 'What if the initial seed, or spore, or whatever, is designed to read blueprints, like the instructions built into our DNA?'

Amos stared at her with a mixture of two expressions— one said, *I hadn't thought of that,* and the other said, *you're taking the fuck-nut bus to Looneyville.*

'Go on,' Amos said.

'What if this thing *reads* an organism? Figures out how to tap into it, grow with it?'

'Then it doesn't need people,' Otto said. 'Why wouldn't we have seen this in animals?'

'We don't know it hasn't infected animals,' Margaret said. 'But maybe there's something else going on here, more than pure biology. Maybe it needs . . . intelligence.'

Amos shook his head. 'Needs intelligence for what? This is all conjecture, and besides the fact that you are obviously one crazy bitch, who would make an organism like that?'

The pieces started to fall into place for Margaret. 'It's *not* an organism,' she said. 'I think it's a kind of machine.'

Amos closed his eyes, shook his head and rubbed the bridge of his nose all at the same time. 'When they commit you, Margaret, can I have your office?'

'I'm serious, Amos. Think about it. What if you had to travel great distances, so great that no living organism could survive the trip?'

'So you're talking even longer than a plane trip to Hawaii with my mother-in-law.'

'Yes, much longer.'

Otto leaned forward. 'Are you talking *space travel*?'

Margaret shrugged. 'Maybe. Maybe you can't send a living creature across space for as long as it takes to get from Point A to Point B. But you can send a machine. An unliving machine that consumes no resources, and has no biological process that could wear out over time. It's just *dead*.'

'Right up until it turns on,' Amos said. 'Or hatches or whatever.'

'The perfect infantry,' Otto said. 'An army that doesn't need to be fed or trained. You just mass-produce them, ship them out and when they land they build themselves and gather intel from their local host.'

Amos and Margaret stared at Otto.

'Okay,' Amos said. 'For the sake of a crazy science bitch and a gung- ho junior spy that's watched too many movies, let's say you've got this "weapon." What good does that do you? You send these things across the universe, stopping on Vulcan for a couple of brews, of course. But why?'

'Two reasons,' Otto said. 'The first is recon. Gather intel on the environment, the people, the opposition. Maybe that's why it's not in animals, because . . .' His voice trailed off. He couldn't finish the thought.

'Because if it can read DNA, maybe it can read memories,' Margaret finished. 'It needs the cultural context to know the threats, to know what can stop it.'

Agent Clarence Otto beamed at her. He nodded slowly. That smile of his was almost enough to take her away from this insanity, and she found herself smiling back.

'Why don't you two just fuck and get it over with already?' Amos said. 'If we can lose the flirting for a moment, I'm still not convinced. Your ideas don't really make sense. In Margaret's fantasy land, these things are here because Alf can't make the trip himself. So why are their little machines gathering intel?'

'Intel is the first reason,' Otto said. 'The second is to use that intel to create a beachhead. Establish control of a defensible area so you safely receive reinforcements.'

The van fell quiet for a few moments. A sense of dread filled the air. Finally, Amos spoke, fear ringing clear through his sarcastic tone.

'Otto, if you don't mind, I like you better when I think you're just a dumb-ass CIA agent,' he said. 'How about you leave the science to us and have a nice cup of shut the fuck up?'

Otto nodded, then sat back.

They quietly waited.

78

A NICE HOT BATH

Perry raised the tiny flame to the rum-soaked hand towel. It caught instantly, bursting into flame with a loud *whoof,* singeing his hand. He whipped the flaming towel behind him like a horse flicking its tail to ward off a swarm of flies. The flames slapped against the bandolier towel's wet spot.

It, too, ignited instantly, scorching the thin flesh above the Triangle. The flames caught Perry's hair, which disintegrated in a scalp-searing *whoosh.* The smell of rum, burned flesh and singed hair filled the bathroom.

Scalding pain raged against his back as flames scampered up the towel. He started to stand, his instincts screaming to MOVE, to RUN, to STOP, DROP and ROLL. His skin bubbled and blistered—he let out a small scream but forced himself to sit back down on the tub. He switched the knife from his left hand to his right.

Letting loose a roar mixed of equal parts pain, fury and defiance, Perry stabbed the blade into his left forearm, right through one of the Triangle's closed eyes. He knew it went all the way through, because he felt the blade tip dig into his own flesh on the other side. Blood and purple gushed onto his hand, almost making him lose his grip on the knife. With a primitive growl and a sick smile of insane satisfaction, he punched the knife tip in again and again, like a pointed pick into a bowl of ice.

His back continued to burn.

Face contorted with pain, he fell backward into the tub.

There was a quick *hiss* as he landed in the cold water. The fire ceased, but the burning sensation continued. A wave of joy washed over him even as he writhed in agony.

'How do you like that? How the *fuck* do you *Howdy Doody like that?*'

His ravaged arm filled the tub with diluted blood, making the water look like cherry Kool-Aid.

Not done yet, kids, Perry thought. *No bout-a-doubt-it, got one more round to go.*

With his right hand, he squeezed down on his left forearm. He thrashed in the shallow red water, his face twisting into a gnarled mask of agony.

79
APARTMENT 104

Dew ignored his aching knees and crouched in front of the door to Apartment G-104. His thick fingers worked lock-picking tools with the delicate grace of a ballerina pirouetting across the stage.

The lock clicked with a tiny sound, and Dew silently turned the deadbolt back. He stood, pulled his .45, and took a deep breath.

They're gonna pay, Malcolm.

He opened the door and slid into an empty living room, devoid of any furniture. He did a fast check to make sure there was nothing in any of the rooms—they were empty as well. He ran out the door into the hall, headed for the next apartment.

80

THE CHICKEN SCISSORS

Perry lurched out of the tub, bloody water sloshing all over the floor. He grabbed a clean towel, looped it into a granny knot, then bit back the screams as he pulled it tight against his mangled forearm.

He was in serious pain, but he could handle it. Why? Because he had *discipline,* that's why. His arm bled like a proverbial stuck pig. The towel quickly soaked through with bright red—he didn't know if he'd hit an artery and he didn't care, because he'd punched through all three of the Triangle's eyes. A thin, greasy black tentacle hung from the cut, blood coursing down it to piddle on the floor.

It didn't matter. He'd be in an ambulance inside of five minutes.

He grabbed the towel's ends, took a deep breath, and pulled the terry-cloth tourniquet even tighter. A fresh wave of pain erupted from his arm, but he bit back the scream.

The Triangles awoke.

No, not Triangles, *Triangle*.

The one on his back was dead, burned to a crispy-crisp, and the one on his arm was sliced in half. Only one remained.

Which meant there really was only one thing left to do.

No bout-a-doubt-it.

s t o p   S T O . p   S t o P
F u c K E j e r   F u e k I r r
a Shwhoeld

The voice in his head sounded weak, thin, frail. He couldn't understand many of the words.

'Shouldn't have fucked with a Dawsey, big dog. You understand that now, don't you?' He shuffled slowly forward, resting against the sink counter.

h a s t a r t y   f u c k e r t
f u c k e r t   S t o p e   S T O P E
H e l p   hELP

'There's no help for you,' Perry said. 'Now you know what it's like.' The butcher's block sat on the sink counter. It called to him.

The bathroom door rattled violently. Tentacles slid under the door and squirmed like lunatic black snakes. In jagged disbelief that cut through his hazy vision, Perry watched the doorknob turn.

He launched himself against the door just as it began to open, his right shoulder slamming it closed. He locked the door and took a step back, eyes wide with shock as the black, ropy tentacles continued to worm their way under the door.

He heard the clicks and pops of the hatchlings, but he heard more—he heard their womanly voice in his head, not as strong as the confused pleas of his own Triangle, but strong enough, and desperate, angry. The voices were separate now. They all sounded the same, but were individual instead of the group they had been while still inside Fatty Patty's body.

So many words crushed together. It was like trying to

focus in on one snowflake during a blizzard, but he picked out bits and pieces.

Stop!

Don't do it!

Sinner!

You'll burn in hell!

Don't kill him don't kill him!

The tentacles pushed and pulled at the door, rattling it, trying to force it open, but they didn't have enough strength. Perry watched in horror as they slithered in, pulled at the door, slid back under—too many to count, moving too fast to track.

He turned back to the sink. He ignored their pleading voices. They couldn't get in, and he had unfinished business. He looked at the butcher's block.

Looked at the Chicken Scissors.

He shook his head, he couldn't do it. The doctors could cut it out, the doctors could *fix* it!

The sink's top was at waist level; he reached into his wet underwear to lift his scrotum and rest it on the counter, but when he touched it, his hand instinctively flinched as if he'd just unknowingly grabbed a rattlesnake.

It hadn't felt right. It hadn't been soft and pliant; it had been hard, crusty, swollen, with solid bumps that didn't belong.

stttop Stop STopej
you cag't Do NO NOG
NO NO

The Triangle's voice wavered badly. Perry didn't know if it was the Tylenol coursing through his body, the fact that it was the only Triangle left, or a little bit of both. It didn't matter. He reached into his underwear again, ready for the horrid, stomach-churning feeling this time, and lifted his scrotum up to rest on the edge of the sink.

It was the most horrible thing he'd ever seen.

Tears instantly poured down his cheeks. Not the tears of pain that had sneaked out of his eyes once or twice during his self-mutilation sessions, but tears of frustration, tears of a man who's lost everything.

There wasn't a doctor in the world who could help him now.

He hadn't looked at this Triangle since the day he'd pulled that tiny white thing from his thigh. He hadn't examined his balls since then. Not even once. Had he looked, had he *seen*, he might not have fought at all.

The Triangle was huge. It was almost black under the skin of his scrotum. The center of the pyramid head pointed up as if his balls rested under a fleshy pup tent. Most of his pubic hair had fallen off, leaving his skin bald and unprotected. His left testicle was hidden somewhere under the Triangle. His right testicle was barely visible, the end of it pushing against the inside of his scrotum, stretching the skin. His dick jutted out at an odd angle—the Triangle had grown right underneath its base. There was little room left for the tissue that connected the penis to his body. It looked as if it were on the verge of falling off, severed at the bottom by the edges of the ever-growing Triangle.

But that wasn't the worst of it.

The tentacles had grown under his skin, just as they had in Fatty Patty, right out the sides of the Triangle. One tentacle reached up and over his right testicle. Another spread from his scrotum down into his inner thigh, a cord-like infection pulsing huge and misshapen.

The last tentacle? The last one was the worst of them all.

The last tentacle reached right up the side of his penis, distending the skin, a thick, black vein that wrapped around and around, that reached almost to the end, as if it were pointing at the head of Perry's dick. Pointing and mocking.

His naked body shivered with fear and dread. Dread because he knew he couldn't do it, he couldn't cut off his own dick and balls. The little fuckers had won they had won they had won fuck them all to hell *fuck you all to hell!* Perry leaned forward, his unit still on the sink, and yanked one of the steak knives from the butcher's block. He laid his arm down on the sink, palm up, and placed the point of the knife at his wrist just below the hand. He'd heard somewhere that you have to slice down the *length* of your wrist, not crosswise, to do it right.

His father's voice: 'What are you doing, boy?'

Perry's tears fell into the sink. Sobs racked his body. He looked up into the mirror, and once again instead of his own ravaged reflection he saw the tight-skinned face of his skeletal father. Jacob Dawsey's eyes glowed bloodred, his lips so taut they didn't move when he spoke—he was nothing more than skin and bones, his muscles long since consumed by Captain Cancer.

'I'm sorry, Daddy,' Perry said through choked sobs. 'I can't do it. I'm gonna end it right here.'

'You can still win, son. You can still beat them all.'

'Daddy, I can't. I just can't!'

'You gotta do it, boy!' Daddy's voice took on the harshest of tones. 'You've come this far—you can't stop now. A man's gotta do what a *man's gotta do!*'

Perry hung his head. He couldn't do it, and he couldn't look at his father's face. He pressed the blade against his wrist. A drop of blood formed around the knife point. Two quick slashes and he'd be done.

Sorry, Daddy, but it's got to end here.

He took one last look at his misshapen, monstrous genitals, blinked back the tears and gathered his strength to . . .

He wasn't sure he saw it at first.

It happened a second time, and he knew he hadn't imagined it.

His genitals *jiggled*.

h a t c h u i n g   t i m e d d f

for   hatfhueing   timy

f o r t   hatchfring

No.

No sir, no how, no way. If he killed himself right now, the Triangle would still hatch out of his body and join the others, do whatever hatchlings do, dance around the dead bodies of the silly humans, play gin rummy, watch *The Brady Bunch* or whatever else they did he didn't know and he just didn't give a fuck.

Perry screamed at his genitals. 'Fuck you! Fuck you *fuck you fuckyou!* It's *not* going to happen, do you understand?'

The Triangle in his scrotum jiggled and twitched. He watched in horror and absolute rage as it started to bounce outward, pushing both to break free of the skin and to break the tail, the umbilical cord that had kept it alive all this time.

Perry grabbed the Chicken Scissors.

He cut his underwear twice, one snip on either hip, and the wet cloth fell to the floor.

He pulled his body away from the sink, just a little, so that there was a space between his hips and the counter, just enough of a space for the Chicken Scissors to slide, one impossibly thick blade resting atop his scrotum, one impossibly thick blade below.

h a t C h i n g Her' we We
CoME Heert Wer Comesfg

If Perry Dawsey had any scraps of sanity left, they slipped away, snapping like a bungee cord pulled past its limit, both ends recoiling back from the break at wind-whistling speeds.

'At least the voices will stop.'

The first sound was the metallic scraping of the Chicken Scissors.

The second sound was a scream.

APARTMENT 202

No one had answered at Apartment 202, and Dew was halfway through picking the lock when he heard the horrible scream. It was a man's scream, and one that sent a wave of fear dancing at the base of Dew's spine. There was something in that scream, something beyond pain or fear.

Dew jumped up, his knees popping loudly in the still hallway. The back staircase was closest. He sprinted up the steps, pulling out the cellular as he ran.

'Otto, get them in here!'

YA GONNA BURN . . .

Perry stumbled out of the bathroom, bleeding, coughing, crying, dripping snot and spit and blood everywhere. He was so far gone he didn't see the hatchlings scatter about the room, hopping out of his way as fast as their uncoordinated little bodies would carry them. They filled his head with nonsense words and abstract phrases.

Juggling an armful of stuff, Perry whipped the first bottle against the wall just inside the door; it shattered, spreading Bacardi 151 all over the wall and floor.

He saw one of the hatchlings dash toward him. He grabbed the bloody Chicken Scissors. The hatchling leaped for his leg, wrapped its tentacles around his calf. He felt a stabbing, cutting pain, but it was distant, like the sound of a shout from a mile away. He arced down with the Chicken Scissors and punctured the hatchling's body.

A five-part scream ripped through his head, a woman's scream that poured from each of the hatchlings.

'Why can I still hear them?' Perry mumbled, his voice bordering on suffused hysteria. 'I got them all . . . *why can I still hear them, goddamn it!*'

He lifted the scissors, taking a moment to stare at the jittering, wriggling hatchling impaled on the bloody blades. He flicked his wrist, flinging the hatchling across the room.

It fell on the floor, broken, twitching, staining the carpet with purple goo.

Perry looked up and growled a primitive challenge, but the rest of the hatchlings stayed away. He moved to the door, stepping over Fatty Patty's body. He noticed that her lower legs and hands were gone, gnawed to bloody stumps. The hatchlings popped up and down in a sickening dance, chirping, clicking, filling his head with disjointed threats.

You're going to pay
You bastard.
You'll get yours.
And very soon.

Perry ignored them and hopped to the entryway. He juggled his armload of goodies as he unlocked the three locks, then opened the door. He smashed his last bottle on the door frame. Rum soaked the carpet.

You're a bad man.
We'll be coming for you.
We're going to get you.

He looked back at the hatchlings, who stared at him with utter spite, black eyes gleaming with absolute hatred.

Perry said nothing, his mind incapable of articulating words. A thin string of drool hung from his lip, swinging in time with his uncoordinated movements. He dropped the Chicken Scissors to the floor.

In his arms he held two more things. One of the things was the lighter. He flicked his Bic.

Perry Dawsey stared at the room with eyes much older than his twenty-six years. He bent and touched the flame to the rum-soaked floor.

Flames shot up instantly, a warm blue at first, but quickly turning yellowish-orange as the carpet caught fire.

He dropped the lighter. Now he held only one thing. The flames grew, crawling up the door frame, reaching for the ceiling.

Perry looked back at the hatchlings one last time. They ran around the apartment like some satanic version of the Keystone Kops, bouncing off walls, furniture and one another in a blind terror—the fire quickly spread back from the door frame into the apartment proper, and there was no place for them to avoid the flames.

'Yes you gonna *burn*,' Perry said quietly.

He turned to leave, but the map caught his eye. Fire tickled the paper's bottom corner.

Perry reached out and tore the map from the door. He left the apartment, went to his right and started hopping as the flames spread out into the hallway behind him.

APARTMENT 304

Dew came up the stairs just as the flames lashed out into the hallway, five feet high and growing fast. The place was going up like a dry Christmas tree. He stopped, looking for a target. On the other side of the hungry flames, he saw a huge naked man clutching something in each hand.

Through the distorted, waving heat haze, Dew saw that the man stood on one leg. The other hung limply, the foot a few inches off the floor. The man turned and hopped away, his bulk already obscured by the raging flames.

Dew started firing, emptying the seven-round magazine in less than three seconds. The lethal .45-caliber bullets disappeared into the fire—Dew didn't know if he'd hit Dawsey or not.

And there was only one way to find out.

He popped a fresh mag into the Colt .45, hesitated for only a moment, then sprinted toward the raging fire.

HIPPITY HOPPITY

With a coordination born from complete lack of regard for safety, Perry leaped to the next landing, clearing six steps in one hop. When he landed, blood splattered from his crotch. Momentum slammed him into the wall, but he didn't fall; instead he turned and cleared the next six steps with one powerful thrust. When he hit the second-floor landing, the towel fell off his arm, leaving him completely naked save for his socks.

Anyone watching would have thought it was impossible, that he was sure to break his neck. But he kept hopping, not knowing that Dew Phillips was only a few steps behind.

The outside door burst open, swinging wildly on its hinges, slamming so hard the handle gouged a chunk from the brick wall. Perry, wide-eyed and screaming, hopped out into the snow, the cold hitting his naked body like the fist of Old Man Winter.

He hopped fast, remembering somewhere, somehow, that he was supposed to get a car, go to Wahjamega and finish this crazy odyssey. He also wanted to get to a hospital, because some stupid motherfucker had just shot him in the left shoulder. That had almost knocked him over, but he'd been hit harder many times.

Oh, but he needed a hospital for a few other things, too, eh, Daddy-O? A hospital to stitch up an arm that gushed bright, steaming blood onto the road's packed snow, a hospital to piece together whatever was sliced in his calf so he could walk with two legs again, a hospital to treat the huge burn blisters on his back and head and ass, a hospital to pull that bullet out of the back of his left shoulder, a hospital to suck the rotting black goo out of his shoulder and ass.

And, above all, a hospital to sew his dick back on.

85

ONE SHOT, ONE KILL

The front door to Building G hadn't quite closed when Dew Phillips smashed it open again. He raced out onto the snowy pavement, trailing smoke and flames behind him. He rolled once, twice, a third time, then stood, the flames defeated, his jacket a smoldering ruin of acrid polyester.

He was in that place again, that murderous place, the spot in his mind where he sent his feelings and emotions and morals when there was killing to be done. He wasn't Dew Phillips anymore; he was Top, the death machine that had taken more lives than he could count.

Dew dropped into a shooter's crouch and brought up the .45 with the stone-still grip of a brain surgeon. He saw everything: the snow-covered dead branches of the winter trees, each iced needle on the frosted pines and shrubs, every car, every hubcap, every license plate, every slushy footprint. Police dotted the lot like dark blue alligators sunning on a riverbank. A trio of gray vans raced in: one from his right, one from his left and one on the far side of the hopping, blood-streaming freak.

Dawsey hopped across the parking lot, a sprint for freedom when there was no place to run. He seemed to notice the police cars, and he slowed. Dawsey stopped, then turned. With the desperate optimism of a madman, he hopped toward Dew.

Dew sighted in on a face contorted with fury, pain, confusion and hate. The massive man raged forward, huge and horrible, every muscle fiber twitching and visible even from a distance. He hopped on his blood-glazed right leg, covering amazing distances with each thrust. His left leg hung at an angle, limp and along for the ride. Third-degree burns covered his right arm. He had no hair left, only crusty black marks and blisters that perched lecherously on his skull. A long streak of black goo decorated his chest, goo that appeared to ooze from a softball-size purple sore on his right collarbone.

Blood streaked down both legs, pouring from where a penis should have been.

Nightmarish above all this were the face and the eyes, eyes that stared straight out with both the cold, intense look of the predator and the wild, panic-stricken flight of prey. A mouth that couldn't decide between a snarl or a scream, a mouth that hung open, lips curled up to show teeth that gleamed a Colgate white in the afternoon sun.

Dew saw all this in less than two seconds. A brief instant where details stood out like raised letters on a brass nameplate.

That look. That expression. Just like Brewbaker. Just like the man who'd killed Mal.

One .45-caliber slug and Dawsey's head would evaporate in a cloud of blood and brains. Somebody had to pay for Mal's death, and this crazy fucker would fit the bill just fine.

Dew aimed for that psychotic smile.

His finger tightened on the trigger.

Dawsey kept coming.

One shot, *one shot . . . goddamn it, Mal, I miss you.*

But Dew had his orders.

He dropped his aim and pulled the trigger.

The bullet smacked into Dawsey's right shoulder and spun him around like a rag doll. He almost made a full spin before he crashed to the ground, his steaming blood melting into the dirty driveway snow. The map fluttered to the ground.

Dew lowered his weapon and started to move forward, then stopped short. He stared, disbelieving, as Dawsey scrambled back up to stand on his one good leg. His expression hadn't changed, not one lick, no surprise or agony visible among the tumult of emotions that rippled across his face. Huge muscles twitching, a grin of wide-eyed madness chiseled on his face, hopping on one powerful leg, Dawsey lunged toward Dew.

Dew raised the .45. There was one place he could shoot that the kid wouldn't get up.

'You sure are one tough bastard,' Dew said quietly, then pulled the trigger.

The round smashed into Perry's knee, the same knee that had ended his football career. The once-broken patella disintegrated into a bouquet of splintered bone. The bullet ripped through cartilage before it bounced off the femur and exited through the back of his leg along with a misty cloud of blood.

Perry crumbled. He fell face-first onto the snow-covered pavement and slid to a halt only a few feet from Dew. This time he didn't get up. He stared at Dew, breathing heavily, the insane death-grin plastered on his face.

And his penis was still clutched in his fist.

Dew gently stamped out the flaming map, then picked it up. Keeping the barrel trained on Dawsey's grinning face, Dew looked at the map. It was burned through in places, but the red line running from Ann Arbor to Wahjamega was still clearly visible. Also in red, a strange, Japanese-looking symbol.

Dew looked at Dawsey—the same symbol, scabbed over and bleeding in places, was carved into his arm.

Dew held the map so Perry could see it.

'What's here?' Dew demanded. 'What the fuck do you want with that pissant town? What's this symbol mean?'

'Someone's knockin' at the door,' Perry said in a singsong voice. 'Somebody's ringing the bell.'

86

FREE RIDE

Three gray vans closed in on Dew and Perry, sliding to a halt on the packed snow. Like ants rushing from a mound, biosuit-covered soldiers poured out. The police in the area moved toward the vans, but kept their distance from the bizarrely dressed men carrying the squat, lethal FN P90s.

Margaret and Clarence were the first to reach Dawsey and Dew. Clarence pulled his Glock sidearm and tried to cover the damaged man, but Margaret dashed in and knelt next to his charred body, her knee dipping into the steaming pool of spreading blood. She tore her eyes away from the severed penis clutched in his hand.

He was still breathing, although for how long that would last she couldn't say. She'd never seen a human being so messed up yet still alive. She didn't see any triangles on him, but with all the blood and the third-degree burns it was hard to tell. Yet he was alive, and that, at least, was something she could work with.

She almost jumped when he spoke.

'Somebody's ringin' the bell,' Dawsey said. 'I gotta go to Wahjamega. Do me a favor, open the door, and let 'em in.'

Margaret swallowed hard. She could barely believe her eyes—this ravaged man, whose blood was turning the slush as red as a Slurpee, talked through a smile of sheer madness.

'Open up that fucking green door, you fucking bitch!' Dawsey's thick hand shot out fast-fast and grabbed her Racal suit, pulling her down until his lips mashed against her visor, spreading blood and spit on the clear plastic. His wide, insane eyes were just an inch from hers.

'Somebody's *knocking at that fucking door!*'

Clarence smashed the butt of his Glock against Dawsey's cheek, opening up yet one more wound. Dawsey flinched but kept snarling, his eyes burning with the fury of pure insanity.

'Hit him again!' Dew screamed.

Clarence whacked Dawsey twice more in rapid succession. The big man's grip relaxed, and he fell back to the ground, eyes half-lidded, the smile still on his face.

'You okay, Doc?' Clarence asked.

Margaret fought to regain her composure, her breath coming in irregular gasps. For a second she'd been sure Dawsey would rip right through the suit and tear her throat out. He was so fast, and so damn strong.

'I'm fine,' she said. She stood and waved over two soldiers who waited with a stretcher.

She could only imagine what that poor man had gone through. What kinds of thoughts could make a human being self-inflict that kind of damage? Margaret wondered if he'd provide any answers.

She couldn't know what terrors awaited in the months to come. For Perry Dawsey, the infection was over. For the rest of the world, it was only the beginning.

87

THE JUMPER

It had all happened so fast that wisps of smoke still curled from the freshly fired .45. Dew had done his job yet again, but he didn't feel any better. He was no closer to discovering the parties responsible for this horror, for killing his partner. Dew said nothing, kept a grip on his weapon, watched Clarence Otto direct the rapid-response team as they set up a small perimeter around Dawsey.

A third-floor window shattered outward. Dew looked up, saw the flame tongues billowing out, greasy black smoke roiling toward the sky. But he saw something else, something burning, something falling. A brief flailing comet, whipping, ropelike extensions making it resemble a flaming medusa's head.

The thing hit hard against the snow-covered pavement, flames seeming to splash outward before they roared upward again. He stared, disbelieving, the back of his mind already making a connection that his conscious thoughts refused to allow. The flaming thing stood, or at least tried to stand, burning, boneless legs supported a body all but obscured by jumping flames. There was a small screech, a pitiful thing, the sound a weak woman makes when she feels severe pain.

A thin trail of fluid shot from the thing to land in a steaming, boiling black streak on the dirty snow. The creature shuddered once more, then *popped,* flaming pieces scattering across the parking lot. The pieces burned brightly like wreckage from a crashed airliner.

Suddenly Margaret was at his side, her protective helmet gone, her black hair hanging about the biosuit, an ashen look of dread on her face.

'Now it makes sense,' she said quietly. 'Oh my God now it all makes *sense.* Dawsey, the others—they're just *hosts* for these *things.*'

Dew let his mind make that connection, let himself accept the unimaginable. This was no time to start doubting the obvious, no matter how fucked up the obvious might be, and he still had a job to do. The sound of approaching men tore his attention from the dwindling bits of flame. Cops were coming on the run, local boys, state troopers, at least a dozen, with more probably a few steps behind.

Dew turned to Otto and the biosuited agents. All of them stood with guns at the ready, casting snap-glances all around the parking lot, looking to see if there were more of the nightmarish creatures.

Dew barked orders in his booming sergeant's voice. 'Get Dawsey in the van! Squad Three, police those pieces and do it now! Move move move!' The soldiers scurried to obey Dew's commands. He turned to face the cops, who closed on the burning building. He stepped forward, thinking of what bullshit to say, thinking of a way to explain the creature, but the cops rushed right past the burning pieces and through Building G's main door.

Bob Zimmer sprinted up to Dew, his eyes on the flames shooting from the broken third-floor window.

'Did you get him?' Zimmer asked.

'Yeah,' Dew said. 'I got him. He's dead.' The cops hadn't

seen the falling creature. Or if they had, they hadn't made sense of it; perhaps they were too far away. Or perhaps, his conscience nagged him, perhaps they were too worried about the *people* in the burning building to care about something peculiar but obviously not human falling from the third-floor window.

'Are there still people in there?'

'Probably,' Dew said. 'I didn't get anybody out before Dawsey ran.'

Zimmer didn't nod, didn't acknowledge Dew's comment. He stepped toward the building, directing other cops inside, shouting orders to the first cops emerging from the building escorting confused and scared residents.

The biosuited soldiers were already dousing the pieces and scooping up what bits they could. Dew watched the last of them hop into the vans. Everyone was loaded up except for Clarence Otto and Margaret Montoya. She stared at the building, a blank look on her face. Otto stood by her side, waiting for Dew's next command.

Dew pointed his finger south, in the direction of the hospital. Otto put his arm around Margaret's shoulder and quickly guided her to the van that held Dawsey. Dew closed the doors behind them. The vans quietly pulled away, avoiding the confused rush of policemen, then sped out of the parking lot.

Somewhere in the distance, Dew heard the faint approach of sirens: ambulances, the fire department. He looked up at the third floor one last time—the window was all but obscured by the raging fire, flames shooting up at least twenty feet into the sky. There wouldn't be anything left in that apartment.

Amid the shouting chaos, Dew calmly walked to his Buick. He shut himself inside the Buick and stared at

Dawsey's singed map, at the strange symbol so neatly drawn there. The symbol matched the one carved into Dawsey's arm. The words *This is the place* neatly written in blue ink. It wasn't the same hand that had scrawled *This is the place* on the map in Dawsey's apartment. This writing was clean, measured.

The writing of a woman.

'Fuck me,' Dew whispered. Dawsey hadn't run randomly at all—there had been another infected victim in that apartment, a victim that was likely still in the apartment and burning to a crisp. She'd sheltered Dawsey; they were working together.

It was very possible they knew each other before the infection. They lived in the same complex, after all. But if they *hadn't* known each other before contracting the triangles, then that meant victims could somehow identify each other, help each other.

And, more important, if they hadn't known each other, it was possible they had independently decided that Wahjamega was the place to be. And if that was the case, then the only possible conclusion was that they wanted to go there because of the infection.

Or, possibly, the *infection* wanted to go there.

Margaret's words replayed in his head: *They're building something,* she'd said.

Dew thought back to the burning creature that had fallen from the third-story window, then scrambled for his big cellular.

Murray answered on the first ring. 'Did you get him?'

'We got him,' Dew said. 'Alive, exactly the way you wanted him. The stakes just went up. Listen and listen good, L.T. I need men in Wahjamega, Michigan, and I need them now. And none of those ATF or CIA commando wannabes. Make it marines or Green Berets or fucking Navy SEALs, but get me men, at least a platoon and then a division, as fast as they can get there. Full combat gear. Fire support, too. Artillery, tanks, the whole works. And choppers, lots of choppers.'

'Dew, what the fuck is going on?'

'And that satellite, is it redirected to Wahjamega yet?'

'Yes,' Murray said. 'It already made a pass. The squints are looking at the images now.'

'I'm going to take a picture of a symbol and send it to you as soon as I hang up. This symbol, that's what the squints are looking for, got it?'

'Yeah, I got it.'

'And I want a surveillance van punched into that satellite, and I want it there in thirty minutes. And a chopper *better* pick me up in the next *fifteen minutes*. I don't care if we have to commandeer the fucking Channel Seven Eye in the Sky, you get me transport *ASAP*.'

'Dew,' Murray said quietly, 'I can't get you all that so fast, and you know it.'

'You get it!' Dew screamed into the cellular. 'You get it right fucking now! You can't *believe* the shit I just saw.'

PARTY TIME

It was the third time he'd seen that symbol, only this time it wasn't scrawled on a map or carved into human skin.

This time it was from a satellite image.

Four hours after he'd shot Perry Dawsey, Dew Phillips stood next to a Humvee, his booted feet on a dirt road that was frozen solid. A map and several satellite pictures were spread out on the vehicle's hood. Rocks had been placed on the pictures to hold them in place against the stiff, icy breeze that cut through the winter woods.

Trees rose up on either side of Bruisee Road, trees thick with undergrowth, crumbling logs and brambles. Bare branches formed a skeletal canopy over the road, making the dark night even darker. The occasionally strong gust of wind knocked chunks of wet snow from the branches, dropping them on the assemblage below: two Humvees, an unmarked black communications van and sixty armed soldiers.

Around Dew stood the squad and platoon leaders of Bravo Company from the 1-187th Infantry Battalion. The battalion was also known as the 'Leader Rakkasans,' an element from the Third Brigade of the 101st Airborne Division out of Fort Campbell, Kentucky. The Rakkasans were the current Division Ready Force, or DRF, a battalion that stood ready to deploy anywhere in the world within thirty-six hours, regardless of location. The fact that the deployment location happened to be about 620 miles from Fort Campbell, and not thousands of miles across an ocean, made them that much faster.

A pair of C-130 Hercules transport planes from the 118th Airlift Wing had taken off from Nashville less than two hours after Dew's panicked call to Murray Longworth. Those C-130s landed at Campbell Army Air Field thirty minutes after takeoff. Thirty minutes after that, loaded with the first contingent of the 1-187th, the C-130s took off for Caro Municipal Airport, an active airport not quite two miles from where Dew now stood.

Back at the tiny airport, more C-130s were landing. It would take fifteen or so sorties and several more hours to bring in the entire battalion task force. But Dew wasn't waiting for the full battalion. With four sorties complete, he had 128 soldiers and four Humvees—that was the force available, and those were the men he was taking in.

Most of those men wore serious expressions, some tainted with a hint of fear. A few still thought this was a surprise drill. These were highly trained soldiers, Dew knew, but all the training in the world don't mean jack squat if you'd never been in the shit. All the squad leaders, at least, had seen serious action—he could tell that by their calm, hard-eyed expressions — but most of the men carried the nasty aura of combat newbies.

Their leader was the battalion commander, Lieutenant Colonel Charles Ogden. Normally a captain commanded the first company in, but the urgency, the unknown enemy, and the fact that they were operating on American soil demanded Ogden's direct attention. A gaunt man in his forties, Ogden was so skinny the fatigues almost hung on him. He looked more like a prisoner of war than a soldier, but he moved quickly, he spoke with authority, and his demeanor was anything but weak. His skinniness was also deceiving: he could go toe-to-toe with any of the young bucks in his unit, and they all knew it. Dew could sense that Ogden had seen action, and plenty of it. He was grateful to have a seasoned combat veteran in charge.

'So why here?' Ogden asked. 'What's so special about this place?'

'You got me,' Dew said. 'All we know is that there were cases in Detroit, Ann Arbor and Toledo. Wahjamega is easy travel distance from all of those. And there's a lot of farmland and forest around here, huge tracts of space for them to hide in. We think they're gathering, either the human hosts or possibly as hatchlings, maybe both.'

On the helicopter ride from Ann Arbor, Dew had talked to Murray and filled him in on what little they knew about the hatchlings. Murray initially demanded that Dew keep the info from the ground troops, as they 'didn't have clearance,' but Dew fought and quickly won that argument—he wasn't leading men into battle who didn't know if they might be shooting American civilians or some inhuman monstrosity. Which of the two was worse, Dew couldn't really say.

'What's the story on our air support, Lieutenant?' Dew asked.

Ogden checked his watch. 'We have three AH-64 Apache attack helicopters, ETA is twenty minutes. A company of the 1-130th Army National Guard out of Morrisville was doing live-fire exercises in Camp Grayling, about a hundred and twenty miles northwest of here.'

'Armament?'

'Each bird has eight AGM-114 Hellfire missiles with HEAT warheads,' Ogden said.

Dew nodded. Twenty-four antitank missiles would make a really big bang. Plus, each Apache had a thirty-millimeter chain gun that could take out an armored personnel carrier from four kilometers away. All in all, that provided exceptional air support for this mission.

He had ground forces. He had air support en route. The Michigan State Police were throwing a cordon over the area, evacuating residents and keeping everyone else out.

Ogden picked up a satellite photo. It showed the warm colors of an infrared shot. Most of the photo consisted of the blues and greens typical of a nighttime forest, but in the middle was a bright cluster of reds with a strange pattern the squints had outlined in white.

The squints had also marked what measurements they knew: *width approx 135 feet, length approx 180 feet, height unknown.* Dew looked at those measurements and thought of Nguyen's painting—would it be made out of people parts? Was the painting symbolic or literal?

Ogden tapped the photo. 'And that's what we're going after?'

Dew nodded.

'So what is it?' Ogden asked.

Dew shrugged and tapped another photo, showing a different angle of the strange construct. 'We don't know. We think it might be some kind of doorway. The victim was raving about a "doorway" in Wahjamega, and we found this.'

'Are you fucking kidding me?' Ogden asked in his ever-calm voice. 'A doorway? Like a portal or something? Are we talking *Star Trek* shit here, Dew?'

Dew shrugged. 'Don't ask me. All I know is that if you'd seen what I'd seen, you'd know why we're here. You have a problem with that?'

'No, sir,' Ogden said. 'A mission is a mission.' He carefully examined the picture. 'Those four crossbeams, whatever they are, run directly east-west. Is that significant?'

'How the hell should I know?' Dew asked. 'All I know is we've got to blow it up.'

Ogden leaned closer to the picture. 'No telling how tall it is. You got a normal shot?'

Dew produced a detailed picture of the same area, the resolution so fine it revealed individual branches of the bigger trees. The strange design was visible, but barely, its green and black shading blending into the natural ground colors. This one had been taken by aerial recon, not even an hour earlier. Intel guys had highlighted the construct. The area around it was a patch of exposed forest floor surrounded by the whiteness of the winter woods. Five yellow circles marked vehicles spread across the map—three cars, a pickup and an RV.

'That construct, or whatever it is, melted the snow,'

Ogden said. 'It's hot all right. Damn thing blends in so much it almost looks camouflaged. What are those marked vehicles?'

'Abandoned cars,' Dew said. 'Local police found them, nobody home. We think that the triangle hosts drove them here, ditched them, then walked to the construct.'

'What about all these little red dots on the infra-red shot?'

'Those are the hostiles,' Dew said. He produced a sheaf of papers. Each held a composite artist's rendering based on Dew's brief glimpse of the burning creature that fell from the third-story window. He didn't know it yet, but the picture was a passable representation of the hatchlings. He passed the sheets out to the squad leaders.

'The red dots are individual heat signatures, either human hosts or something that looks like these critters.'

A soldier saw the sketch and laughed out loud. Dew fixed him with a death stare; his voice took on a new and dominant tone. He'd commanded boys just like these, and seen them die by the truckloads.

'You think this is funny?' Dew said. 'These things are responsible for the death of at least fifteen people, and if you don't get your shit straight, *you'll* probably be dead within the hour.'

The soldier fell silent. The only sound came from wind hissing through the barren branches.

Ogden pushed the satellite photos out of the way and smoothed the map. 'If I may suggest, sir, we should break into a primary assault group of eight squads, which will attack from the west, and two containment groups of two squads each, one north and one southeast of the target.'

Ogden tapped three spots on the map. 'Here, here and here. The woods are too thick to get the vehicles in, so it's all on foot. We have enough men in place for containment groups one and two. Containment group three is at the airport. They will move out shortly and can be in position in fifteen minutes. Artillery will be guns-up in thirty minutes.

'The Apaches will be here before the infantry sets up the full perimeter, so they'll stay on-station about a mile out. Once artillery is ready, we send in recon to take a shitload of pictures, then paint the target with a laser and have the Apaches blow the living piss out of it. After that the west containment group moves in and we clean up.'

Dew stared at the map for a moment. Ogden had the west group moving in from a hill, giving them the high ground. If the hatchlings ran, they would probably follow the easiest path, a narrow valley that ran north to southeast—and that would take them directly into a killing zone of dug-in squads.

'That's an excellent plan. You tell your men to kill anything that moves.'

'What about the hosts that drove here?' Ogden asked. 'They're civilians.'

Dew looked hard at Ogden. 'Like I said, anything that moves.'

Dew turned to face the men again. 'You've all seen the picture. Whether you believe it or not doesn't matter. We don't know how dangerous these things are, so assume they are dangerous in the extreme.'

The looks on the soldiers' faces said it all. Half of them simply didn't believe they were about to go up against some movie monster; the other half did believe it, and those men had wide-eyed expressions of fear.

'Keep your lines tight,' Ogden said. 'Know where your man is on your right and left. Shoot anything in front of you. It doesn't matter if it looks like a critter or your Aunt Jenny, it's the enemy and you shoot it just like you would an enemy soldier. Now get your squads ready. We move out immediately.'

The grim-faced young men hurried away, leaving only Ogden and Dew.

'You know what's fucked up here, Dew?'

Dew nodded. 'Yeah. Just about every last bit of this thing.'

'Besides that, of course,' Ogden said. 'If this is some kind of a gateway, like they're going to bring troops in through that crazy thing or what have you, why the hell would they build it two miles from a landing strip?'

Dew grunted once. He'd been so thrilled at the easy access, that question hadn't crossed his mind.

'Maybe it's above their pay grade,' Dew said. 'The only thing that makes sense is they just didn't know. Whoever they had run recon on this, that party either just plain missed the airport or didn't know what it was.'

Ogden nodded. 'That's got to be it. Kind of weird, though—they are obviously high-tech as hell, and they screwed themselves with location, location, location. I don't know what these things are, but looks like we're kicking their ass on intel.'

Dew nodded. The satellite images gave him total command of the area, images he wouldn't have had if not for Margaret Montoya's hunch. Without her demands they would still be trying to bring a satellite online, and might not know the exact location of the construct for several hours—and Dew Phillips had a feeling that every second mattered.

The door to the black communications van flew open. A man ran out, a printout clutched in his fist. He slid on the frozen dirt road, regained his balance and slammed the printout down on the Humvee's hood.

'That thing just heated up in a hurry,' the squint said. 'Here's an updated infrared.'

The picture looked almost the same, except the squint hadn't outlined the strange symbol. He didn't have to. Its lines blurred into a smudgy mess of reds, yellows and oranges.

'It just turned on,' Dew said. 'Move your men out, Ogden, right now. Move containment squads one and two into position as planned. We're not waiting for the artillery or the third containment squad. We attack right now.'

Perry moaned softly in his sleep. A dozen electrodes taped to his head and chest measured his every movement. Heavy canvas straps pinned his wrists to the hospital bed. His arms flexed and twitched every few seconds, pulling at the straps. An electrical beep echoed his pulse. The hum of medical equipment hung in the room.

A man in a Racal suit stood on either side of him. Each held a Taser stunner, but neither had any firearms or knives—or anything sharp, for that matter. Couldn't be too careful. If Dawsey broke the straps, a feat that really wouldn't have surprised anyone staring at his huge musculature, they would stun him into submission with fifty thousand volts from the Tasers.

They'd stopped the bleeding, but he was still touch and go; the bullets in each shoulder had been removed; his burns, including most of his head, were packed in wet bandages; they'd pulled the Triangle carcasses from his arm and back; the visible rot had been scraped from his collarbone and his leg, but the damage continued to slowly spread—that one the doctors didn't know how to cure. His knee was slated for surgery the next day.

And his penis was packed in ice.

He moaned again. His eyes were squeezed tightly shut, his teeth bared in a wolflike predator's warning. He was dreaming a dream that was both familiar and worse than ever.

He was in the living-room hallway again. The doors were closing in on him. The doors were hot; his skin blistered and bubbled, growing first red, then charring black, smoking with a putrid stench. But he didn't cry out in pain. He wouldn't give them the satisfaction. Fuck 'em . . . fuck 'em all. He'd go out like a Dawsey. The cancerous doors closed in, marching on their tiny tentacles, and Perry slowly roasted to death.

'You beat 'em, boy.'

In the dream, Perry opened his eyes. Daddy was there. No longer skeletal, but sturdy and solid and as full of life as he'd been before Captain Cancer came a-courtin'.

'Daddy,' Perry said weakly. He tried to take a breath, but the broiling air scorched his lungs. Every fiber of his being hurt. When would the pain end?

'You did good, boy,' Jacob Dawsey said. 'You did real good. You showed them all. You beat 'em.'

The doors moved closer. Perry looked at his hands. The flesh seemed to sag, then melt into a flaming pudding. It fell from his bones and sizzled when it hit the ground. He refused to cry out. After you cut off your own cock and balls, all pain is relative.

The doors moved closer. Perry heard the creak of old wood and ancient iron, the low moan of hinges frozen shut with centuries of rust.

'It was hard, Daddy,' Perry croaked.

'Yes, it was hard. But you did what no one else could've done. I never told you this before, but I'm proud of you. I'm proud to call you my son.'

Perry closed his eyes as he felt the flesh of his body sag and start to fall away. The tunnel filled with an emerald-green light. He opened his eyes—Daddy was gone, and the doors were opening. There was something moving in there.

Perry looked inside . . . and started to scream.

They were almost here.

Dew and Charles Ogden lay flat on the snow-covered forest floor. It was cold as a bitch. Dew stared through night-vision binoculars, the green-tinted picture sending goose bumps racing under his heavy winter fatigues.

'I don't know what the fuck that thing is, but it can't be good,' he said. 'Got any more wise-ass cracks about *Star Trek*, Charlie?'

'Nope,' Ogden said. 'I'm good.'

'We getting any radiation readings?'

Ogden shook his head. 'No, at least not this far away. Geiger counters show nothing. Dew, what the hell is that thing?'

'I got an idea, like I told you before, but I hope to all that's holy I'm wrong.' He couldn't shake Dawsey's mad ravings about a 'door.'

Dew glanced behind him. Two soldiers worked compact digital cameras, sweeping the lenses across the nightmarish scene. There were two such cameramen with each platoon.

'You getting all this?' Dew asked.

'Yes, sir,' the men answered in unison, both their voices small and filled with awe.

The hatchlings were bustling around a pair of

monstrous oak trees that dripped with melted snow. The trees' dead branches formed a skeletal awning reaching out and over perhaps as many as fifty hatchlings of various sizes, some as small as the one he'd seen jump from the third-story apartment, some almost four feet tall with tentacle-legs as big around as baseball bats.

Jesus Christ. Fifty. And we thought we'd got them all. How many hosts to make fifty of these things? How many hosts went totally undetected until they hatched?

The hatchlings had built something strange. Something organic, maybe even alive. Thick, fibrous green strands— some the size of ropes, some the size of I-beams—ran in all directions, from the trunks to the ground to the branches and back again. There had to be thousands of them, like some monstrous three-dimensional spiderweb, or a modern artist's jungle gym. At the center of all these strands, between the towering, sprawling oaks, was the construct that had generated the colored pattern on the infrared picture.

Made from the same strange fibrous material, the construct had the primitive, ominous aura of a Stonehenge or an Aztec temple. The four crossing lines, the ones that ran east-west, were high arches, the apex of the smallest one near the construct's center reaching just over ten feet. The tallest arch, the one at the open end, rose a good twenty feet into the night sky. The four arches looked like a framework cone half buried in the frozen forest ground.

He didn't know what the freakish thing was made of, but at least it wasn't people.

The two parallel pieces of the tail—for lack of a better word—stretched back some thirty yards from the arches. They were each as thick as a log and had a line of thin, spiky growths running down their lengths.

The hatchlings crawled about the massive construct, clinging with their tentacle legs, a moving mass scampering across the strand-maze with the ease of darting wolf spiders. They splashed through the suddenly muddy forest floor—the heat from the construct had melted all the snow around the two oak trees.

Dew and Ogden were about fifty yards from the construct, staring straight into the cavern created by the arches.

'How far out are the Apaches?' Dew asked Ogden. Ogden waved to his radioman, who quietly moved over and handed Ogden a handset. Ogden whispered for a few seconds, then said, 'ETA two minutes.'

The seconds ticked by. Dew heard the faint approach of the Apaches' rotors. The hatchlings suddenly scattered from the skeletal green construct, some taking refuge in the sprawling oak trees, others staying on the ground.

'What's happening?' Ogden asked. 'Did they hear the choppers?'

'Maybe so. Let your men know it's go time. We might have to . . .' Dew's voice trailed off; the construct started to glow.

The fibrous arches illuminated the oak branches and the forest floor with a suffused white light. Faint at first, barely discernible, the glow quickly grew so bright that Dew couldn't look through the night-vision binoculars.

'Dew, what the *hell* is going on in there?'

Dew shook his head. 'I don't know, but I don't like it. Let's take two squads forward. We have to get a better look.'

Ogden softly called out orders. Dew rose to a crouch and quickly moved forward, ignoring his popping knees. The snow crunched and dry branches snapped underfoot.

He was painfully aware of how quiet the Airborne soldiers were in comparison, almost silent despite the noisy footing. Once upon a time, Dew would have moved through the woods without a sound—getting old was a bitch-and-a-half.

He stopped after advancing thirty yards. The cover of night was gone. The construct's glow lit up the two oaks as bright as day. Long shadows radiated away into the forest. The very ground itself seemed to vibrate with an ominous rhythm, a rapidly pulsing heartbeat of some monstrous evil. Dew felt a sense of trepidation, of *wrongness*, like he'd never known before.

This shit's going south in a damn hurry.

'Give me some normal binoculars,' Dew snapped. Someone handed him a pair that were, of course, army-green. He stared into the depths of the archway, where the light was brighter than anywhere else, so bright it hurt his eyes and he had to squint to see anything at all.

'Ogden, ETA on the Apaches?'

'Sixty seconds.'

A blast of anxiety ripped through Dew's body. He'd never felt fear like this, never felt *anything* like this. Even in the midst of the hand-to-hand fighting that had wiped out his platoon back in 'Nam, even when he'd been shot, he hadn't been this scared; he couldn't say why.

The construct grew still brighter. One of the soldiers suddenly dropped his M4 rifle and ran, screaming, back into the forest. Several of the others slowly stepped backward, fear wrapped up in their young faces.

'Hold your positions!' Ogden shouted. 'Next man to run gets shot in the back! Now get down!'

The bounce of long shadows betrayed the motion of the hatchlings sprinting toward the platoon. Their strange, pyramid bodies slid through the woods. Like swarming insects, they'd detected a threat and were rushing out to meet it, to protect the hive.

'Ogden, we've got company!'

'Squads Four and Five, hold this position!' Ogden shouted. 'All other squads move forward to support! Fire at will!' Gunfire erupted before he finished the last sentence.

Dew didn't move. The construct's glow didn't fade, but it *changed,* sliding from the blinding white to a deep emerald-green glow. Suddenly Dew realized he was looking not just *into* the arch, but *beyond* it—the field of green reached far off into the distance.

Stunned, he glanced up from the binoculars. The construct hadn't moved; neither had the woods behind it. He again peered through the binoculars. The field of green was *inside* the arch but stretched back for what must have been miles. But that was impossible, simply *impossible.*

M4 carbines and M249 machine guns roared all around him, but Dew remained steadfast. A man's scream filled the night as one of the hatchlings made it past the hail of bullets. Dew didn't flinch, or even notice, because he saw something in that field of green.

He saw movement.

Not the movement of a single hatchling, but movement so massive that it *was* the field of green. His eyes picked out individual creatures a fraction of a second at a time, like seeing a single ant in the midst of a swarming, angry hill. It was an *ocean* of creatures, reaching for the archway, pouring forward from some impossible distance.

'There must be millions of them,' Dew muttered, the horror creeping across his skin like a coat of millipedes.

A gun erupted only a few feet from his ear, shattering

his trancelike focus. A hatchling rolled almost to his feet, flopping and twitching. Ogden had shot it dead just as it leaped to attack. The surrounding gunfire slackened but was replaced by more screams—the hatchlings swarmed in.

'We're being overrun,' Ogden said calmly, his voice raised only enough to be heard over the shrieks and battle cries of his own men.

'Ogden, call a full strike now!' Dew roared. 'Tell the Apaches to fire everything they've got—*everything they've got!*'

Ogden grabbed the handset from the radioman. Dew drew his .45. A four-foot-high hatchling ripped through a patch of underbrush, its black eyes fixed with fury, its tentacles whipping forward as it closed for the attack.

Dew fired five times at point-blank range. The black, pyramid-shaped body shredded like soft plastic, spilling great gouts of viscous purple liquid on the snowy ground.

Sounds came from all directions: gunfire, pounding feet, branches breaking, howls of pain, desperate pleas for help, and the horrific clicking and chittering noises of the hatchlings. He turned to see a hatchling closing in on a fallen and bleeding soldier. Dew double-tapped, firing twice, dropping the hatchling. As Dew ejected his empty magazine and loaded another, the wounded soldier drew his knife and threw himself on the hatchling, driving the blade in again and again until purple streamers arced across the white snow.

Eyes scanning for the next target, Dew backed up to Ogden, trying to protect him long enough to call in the air strike.

'Leader Six to Pigeon One, Leader Six to Pigeon One,' Ogden said into the handset. 'Full strike, repeat, *full strike* on the main target. Hit it with everything you've got.'

As if on cue, the gunfire suddenly stopped. Dew looked for an enemy and found none standing. A few hatchlings twitched on the ground, but their struggles were soon ended by shots from the angry soldiers. Men lay bleeding and moaning on the forest floor; the skirmish was over.

Dew raised the binoculars just as he heard the rapid-fire roar of the Apaches launching their missiles. The sea of green had reached the archway. For one brief milli-second, Dew saw something he'd never forget, never be able to block out, for as long as he lived.

It was at least eight feet tall, an L-shaped, segmented red body covered in a strange green iridescent shell that must have been armor. Six thick, multijointed legs on the ground and four strong arms clutching what looked like a weapon. What might have been its head was covered with a helmet made from the same iridescent green mate-rial, a helmet that had no holes for eyes or mouth.

And there were *millions* right behind it, waiting to pour out.

It was the only look he got. The first creature stepped out of the arch—the impossible became a reality as the foot set down on the forest floor. Like watching in slow motion, Dew saw the clawed foot step on a twig.

The twig snapped.

Then the sky opened up.

Sixteen missiles smacked home in the span of three seconds. The roar of a dying god, a fireball so huge and violent it knocked small trees right out of the ground, roots and all. The concussion wave picked Dew up and threw him like a straw doll. Soldiers fell all around him. He hit the frozen ground hard but ignored the pain and rolled to his knees.

The fireball rose into the sky, lighting up the forest

with the glow of a late-evening sun. A chunk of arch rose majestically into the air, spinning wildly, one end trailing fire and sparks. Two of the arches were completely gone, one stood tall, and one was shattered but half standing, sticking out of the ground like a cracked and broken rib.

A fusillade of Apache chain-gun fire ripped through the site, each thirty-millimeter bullet kicking up a small geyser of mud. The broken arch, the one that looked like a rib, fell to the ground and shattered into a dozen pieces.

Dew stared desperately through the binoculars. Were they gone? Had the missiles hit in time? He cursed the smoke as he hunted for movement, the movement of a million creatures spreading out through the trees, attacking.

The whistling roar of another missile barrage filled the air. Dew looked up in time to see eight more glowing smoke trails streaking toward the archway like striking ethereal snakes. The missiles slammed home, sending up another roaring fireball. Dew threw himself facedown on the ground as clods of dirt, sticks, and maybe even green strands sailed overhead with lethal speed.

And then it was over.

The last fireball floated up into the sky like a miniature dying sun. In a zombielike daze, Dew stood and moved forward.

The green light had vanished. Someone had shut that door, and shut it with *authority*. Daddy was gone as well, this time for good; he somehow knew that for certain.

Perry's eyes fluttered open. For the first time in a week, his thoughts were his own. The pain was gone, but he knew that was because of drugs. Pain is the body's way of letting you know something's wrong; but he was more in tune with his body now, and he didn't need the pain to tell him he was in trouble.

The voices were gone, but the echoes of some fifty screams remained. The hive at Wahjamega had been wiped out. He felt their absence. Like a fever finally breaking, their destruction released him from the madness. Some of it, anyway.

He weakly turned his head enough to see the biosuit-clad men on either side of his bed. He was tied down, couldn't move his arms. The room was all white. Wires seemed to run off his body in every direction. A hospital. A *hospital*. He'd done it, he'd won.

A voice came over a loudspeaker.

'Mr. Dawsey, can you hear me?'

Perry nodded, slowly and dreamily.

'My name is Margaret Montoya,' the voice said. 'I'm in charge of your recovery.'

Perry smiled. Like anyone could 'recover' from what he'd been through.

'It's over, Mr. Dawsey,' Margaret said. 'You can rest now, it's all over.'

Perry laughed out loud. The drugs weren't all that, apparently, as the laugh brought a stab of pain from deep within his right shoulder.

'Over?' he said. 'No. Not over.'

It wasn't over, babycakes, not by a long shot. Not a fucking Howdy Doody chance of that. The Wahjamega nest was gone, but they weren't *all* gone.

Somehow he could still *sense* them. He could hear their calls, their signal to gather, to *build*. Far away and faint, but he could still sense it.

It was only beginning.

No bout-a-doubt it.

Blackened tree trunks burned in the aftermath, their branches ripped free by the force of the blast. The two proud oaks were devastated: one was completely aflame, its remaining branches a crown of fire reaching into the night sky; the other was split in two, white wood exposed to the winter cold.

Chunks of the green strands littered the ground, most burning fast with a sparking, bluish flame. A few soldiers appeared, walking slowly through the lifting smoke, their M4 rifles sweeping in continuous, cautious arcs. The moans of wounded men filtered through the air, mingling with the sound of crackling fires.

Fighting back the fear, Dew walked to the area where the archway had stood. There was no sign of the creatures, no sign of the green glow that had stretched outward into infinity.

Ogden approached him, moving through the smoke, his demeanor as calm as if he were strolling through his own backyard. He held the handset to his ear, the radioman following him like a lonely puppy.

'We count fifty-six hatchlings,' Ogden said. 'All dead. Some may have gotten through when we were overrun, but the rear guards didn't see any, so it looks like we got them all.'

'Fifty-six,' Dew mumbled.

'We lost eight men,' Ogden said. 'Six from the hatchling attack, two from shrapnel caused by the rocket strike. Another twelve wounded, maybe more.'

'Fifty-six,' Dew said again, his voice distant and strange.

'I'm going to check on the wounded. I'm ordering the Apaches back a half mile and calling in evac for the more seriously wounded.'

'Fine,' Dew said. 'That's fine.'

Ogden strode off, calling out orders in his calm, commanding voice, leaving Dew alone in the center of the obliterated archway.

Dew stared at the carnage, at the dwindling flames, and shook his head.

If there were that many here, how many more are out there? How many more hatchlings on the way, waiting to build another one of these doorways?

Dew didn't know the answer. For the first time, Malcolm's death seemed insignificant, a small loss in comparison to the massive threat looming on the horizon. He was exhausted. Too much action for an old fart.

And there would be no rest, not for a long time.

Not for him.

Not for anyone.

ACKNOWLEDGMENTS

For every good thing I've ever done, every last success, I can look back and see exactly where my parents taught me that behavior or instilled the motivation that made it possible. All the stupid crap I've pulled, well, somehow I managed to figure that out myself.

My father was my high school football coach. He watched his 120-pound son get the crap knocked out of him every day in practice by kids who were a lot bigger, a lot faster and a lot stronger. In a game of strength and speed, I was small *and* slow—physics was not my buddy. Because I was his son, he couldn't say anything or show any special treatment.

He never tried to paint a happy face on things. He'd just say, 'work hard and good things will come.' I believed him. I learned how to get up and come back for more, no matter how many times I got hit. I learned to love being a stubborn little bastard who no one could keep down.

The result of my father's influence is the novel you hold in your hands. I've made it into publication after fifteen years of writing failures and well over one hundred rejections. You have to *believe* in hard work and be a stubborn little bastard, you see, to keep getting up after that many hits. For that, I say 'thank you, Coach.'

My mother was a teacher who had to deal with a very,

very hyper little boy. When the doctors prescribed Ritalin, she told them to go screw (in that nice way mothers have of telling you to go screw so that it actually sounds like a good idea). She would not medicate me into submission. She constantly supported my imagination, from my stories and drawings to the countless weekends I spent geeking out with friends and immersed in role-playing games.

She took me to the bookstore every week and bought me whatever I wanted, sometimes four or five books at a time. She took me to the library, where we'd both check out an armful of novels. I consumed books like they were Pez. No reading lists, no 'Honey, put down that silly science fiction'; as long as my nose was in a book, she didn't care what it was. She cultivated a love for words and for stories that will never go away. My mother is the catalyst for the creativity and energy you find within these pages. Class, say 'thank you, Mrs. Sigler.'

Thanks also go to Jeremy 'Xenophanes' Ellis, who made the hard science in this book accessible, entertaining and accurate.

To Major Thomas Austin, U.S. Army Corps of Engineers, and Sergeant Donald Woolridge, U.S. Army, who took the time to make sure my military facts accurately reflected the brave men and women who are the very reason I have a country to love in the first place.

To Julian Pavia and all those crazy kids at Crown Publishing for getting behind this, working their tails off and believing in the power of the Junkies.

To Byrd Leavell for taking things to the next stage.

To all of my friends in the podcasting and blogging community. You are too numerous to mention here, and if I leave someone out, the link-bait would prove most abusive.

And, most important of all, to my wife, Jody, for putting up with a very, *very* hyperactive husband and being the first victim to suffer through the rough draft of this book. You have given up far too much while I pursued this obsession, and I can't thank you enough.